WALK EGYPT

by VINNIE WILLIAMS

✢✢✢✢✢✢✢✢✢✢✢✢✢✢✢✢✢✢✢✢✢✢✢

WALK EGYPT

19 60

THE VIKING PRESS
New York

FOR MY FATHER AND MOTHER

Joseph and Vivian Ahlsweh

WALK EGYPT

PART

I

One

THE WOMAN's name was Toy, and it suited her no more than silk on Sunday or the cotton she wore the rest of the week. Silk and cotton are amenable fabrics, easy to the hand and accepting a bit of lace or ruffle. The woman was like linen, strong and reticent and keeping her character through all things.

When she was born, and the midwife folded the flannel back from the crumpled tiny face, her mother said wonderingly, "She's so teeny, like a little old play dolly."

Her father laughed excitedly. He had been drinking, but not much, just enough to put a ridge on his nose and red on his chin. "What you going to name her? We sure can't call her Harl." His name was Harl, and they had been certain sure she would be a boy. They had not considered girls' names.

Her mother kept looking at her. She said again softly, "She's so teeny. Look at them little fingernails, can't hardly see them. And her hair—" It was like mullen fuzz. "Why, there was more hair on that dolly I got when I was a young'un, Mary Husband her name was."

"Now that's a fool name for a doll."

"No, it wasn't. I'd just took to reading, and I was studying about Jesus. The story kept saying Mary's husband, Joseph, all the way through, and I just figured Husband was her last name. I'd never heard of husbands before, just misters."

"Then you got me." But he was impatient. He wanted to get back to the other men, who were crowded around in front of the little house. They were going on a coon hunt. A big bull coon had been seen up on Atkins' Ridge, eating the new corn and challeng-

3

ing charity. They would take guns and dogs and hunt him down. "Well, what you going to name her?"

"Maybe Dolly, only Annie Goforth just named hers Dolly, and when they take to playing together, they'd get mixed up." She thought and said triumphantly, "I'll name her Toy, that's what, 'cause she's going to be my little play-pretty, ain't you, sugarpie?" And she breathed gently on the small damp cheek.

Toy and Dolly, Pet and Li'l'bit were common names through the Georgia hills. Once a writer-man had come through looking for a story. He had gone here and there, collecting words like "booger," "piddling," "sashay," and "jook," expressions like "give the preacher a pounding" and "crazy as Puddletown in Piddle Valley near Tolpuddle." By and by he had been diverted by the names. He was curious about names that had no notch to fit them in, names that came neither from story-book nor Bible, names like Toy and Dolly.

An old man explained with gentle courtesy, "Why, you see, gals in these parts marry kind of young. They've left Pretend, but ain't got to Real yet."

Dolly's mother was fifteen when she was born; Toy's mother was fourteen.

Long years later Toy thought of changing her name. She would call herself Ruth, who gleaned in alien fields, or Martha, who did the work of the world. Not that she was sorry for herself. That was licking an empty plate. Still, if a name suited a dog, say it.

Dolly was lucky. She had been born looking like a Christmas doll. She had brown curly hair, a round body, and red lips that chirked up in a smile. The first day in school the teacher had called the roll. "Dolly Goforth?"—and though she was new to the valley, she had looked right at Dolly. But when she called, "Toy Crawford," she looked at Avis Lankford, who had curly yellow hair and eyes as hard blue as taws. She was palpably astonished when Toy raised her hand, but tried to hide it by adding quickly, "My goodness, you seem to be the only one wants to learn to read," for Toy had taken a front seat while the others had fought for the back ones, hating to put on shoes and shed summer. She added, "Those were pretty flowers you brought, Toy. What are they called?"

Several of the children had brought fruit, late peaches or early apples, and flowers, mostly roses or zinnias. The teacher had accepted them with thanks but without comment. Toy's throat closed in agonized shyness.

Avis Lankford called, "They ain't nothing but old bobwhite peas." She was furious because the teacher had said nothing about her roses. "They're just old field trash."

The other children giggled, partly from the excitement of the first day at school, partly because giggles are as endemic at seven as tears are at fourteen.

The teacher said firmly, "They're lovely," but the hurt was done. Toy felt her soul shrink in upon itself.

She had always loved bobwhite peas. They were lost among the brighter fall flowers, maypop and yarrow, bitterweed and goldenrod, but to her mind they were the most beautiful of all. They were small and pink and orchid-like on their long stems, with delicate violet freckles. But it had been a mistake to bring them to school. It had been a mistake to take a front seat—she heard the hisses of "Teacher's pet!" It seemed as if she never did anything right, never looked right, a girl who was a head taller than anyone else her age and so thin it took two of her to make a shadow, a girl in a dress too short, with ragged light hair and greenish eyes.

She tucked her head into her shoulder.

Dolly chided later, "Sugar, why you pay any mind to what folks say?"

"I can't help it."

"Now, you could if you would."

Words did not help. She continued to tuck her head into her shoulder and into her books. She had longed to start school—she had scratched off the days on a bit of stick until it began—and now books were a door opening where so many others closed. For the first time she learned the stretch of the world. She opened her geography, and, why, Plum Gap was a fly speck, Georgia a cherry seed, and the United States—

She measured purple distances with a thumb and forefinger. Why, she could tie a thread about the United States and fly it like a June bug. She could run a rabbit around the world on a summer afternoon.

Yet, Aunt Baptist said, the shoulder-blade of a rabbit contained her world. The midwife pulled one from a dinnerplate.

"This is your house." She pointed to the socket. "Deep or shallow tells if you'll be rich or poor. This one's deep. You'll have your share of this world's goods." Her finger moved on to a little hole. "Cradle. You going to have you one young'un, maybe two —there's a nick here—though looks like the second will be stillborn or early dead." Her finger tapped opaque white spots. "Sickness. The biggest is death, the pale horse 'thout a tail and a mane made of little finger bones."

This was the bone of her life. Years later she would laugh to think how she had trembled before the bone. For a bone has no character without the flesh surrounding it. A bone is numb, but flesh blows hot and cold; and it is the measure of a man how he bears his flesh.

It is the measure of man how far he reaches beyond his flesh.

Two

A N APRIL morning in 1929 when she was thirteen years old, Toy was hanging clothes. She put Harl Junior's blue shirt next to Tessie's yellow dress, her own green-striped skirt by her father's brown pants. She threw the towels and pillow cases over the boxwood. The bucket was empty.

A rind of water remained. She debated whether the Confederate rose or the tomato seedlings needed it more and settled on the rose. She was finished, she did not have an excuse in the world to stay outside. Still she lingered, reluctant to return to the house and her mother's querulous voice and swollen body.

She leaned on the fence and looked across the pasture. Maude, the mouse-chinned, trace-galled mule, rolled in the new grass like a colt. In the sky two marsh hawks gripped claws and rolled over and over in a joyous loop-the-loop.

Spring was running up the mountains, and she longed to be out and racing it through the white drifts of serviceberry. She would flee up the slope of Atkins' Ridge, and spring would keep pace in the thin new leaves of the trees, dogwood and catawba, spruce and balsam. She would outrun spring and drop breathless, high up and far away, on Ellie Bald, where no trees had grown since time began. But when she looked around, she would see that she had not outrun spring after all, for everywhere would be violets and cinquefoil and fiddlehead ferns.

Lying in the grass, she would consider Ellie Bald. Folks said it was not the only bald in the mountains, that there were half a dozen more, some a quarter of an acre wide, one a thousand acres. No one knew why the trees stopped at an invisible line, and oatgrass and sedge took over. A Cherokee legend said that once the Ulagu, a great hornet, lived on one of the mountains and foraged forth to eat children, but the Indians banded together and killed the hornet. The Great Spirit was so pleased that he decreed that henceforth various mountaintops would be bare of trees, the better to serve as lookouts against further Ulagus.

A teacher had told them, "I think there was a huge infestation of gall wasps that laid eggs in the tips of tree twigs and killed them. Hence the Indian legends. All legends have a basis in events, the great flood of Noah, the king who burned his hands and could not feel the burns—he had leprosy—even the loaves and the fishes."

Toy had been shocked. Everyone in the hills read the red-letter Bible—Two-Seeds-in-the-Spirit Baptists. She had had some miserable nights believing that the teacher was the Devil and waiting to snatch her soul to the coal pits. However, the teacher was fired, and everyone's soul was safe again.

The girl dug her chin into her lapped wrists, a toe stroking the mossy bottom rail of the fence. There was something of the squirrel in the sharpness of her face and movements. She went in starts and skitters. Her father joked, "Toy's got grace in her soul, but not her shoe."

She moved in skitters, because she was always divided against herself. One part of her said, "Be a woman. You've got it to do"; and the other part said, "No, run off and play by the river." She never knew until she started which part she would follow.

"Toy—Toy!"

The voice doused her thoughts like winter water. She could not run away to the river, or even down to Aunt Baptist's, for her mother was in bed and calling, and her father had been gone two days, no one knew where.

She took the bucket and walked around the house to the side porch and up the steps into the kitchen. She set the bucket down on the deal table and went to her mother's room on begrudgeful feet.

Rose Crawford hoisted herself on her pillows, a dough-faced black-haired woman, hand laid across her belly in the ancient protective way of women with child.

"It took you long enough to git those clothes out."

Toy studied the floor. It was of heart pine laid on oak beams. The walls of the house were fieldstone chunked with dobbin, a rarity here where most houses were built from green pine. John Crawford, her great-grandfather, had built it in 1870, the year his son, Ard, was born. He had built it remembering the stone cottages of his native sheep downs in Wales. The windows were no more than slits; the four rooms were separated by wooden partitions head-high. The side porch-and-kitchen was a wooden tail tacked on after-times.

"You ice-hearted as your daddy. You know I'm down and need every bit of help I can get, but you go off and piddle around. . . ."

The walls had never been painted, but time and touch had colored them honey-brown. Toy loved to run her hand along the sleek, warm wood. She did so now, hardly thinking. The furniture was white ash and mostly hand-turned, the benches and chairs and beds in her, Tessie's, and Harl Junior's room. The living-room furniture was oak from Sears Roebuck, yellow enough to glare away time. Her mother wanted a suite for her bedroom, but still after fourteen years of marriage she slept on a hand-turned cord bed.

Harl had promised to get her store furniture. Over and over he had promised. First, though, he was obliged to build a "club-house" across the pond.

"Why, sugar, a year from now you gonna be tiptoeing through dollar bills instead of tulips, like the song says. Time I get through renting it for dances and all-night fishing and hunting parties . . ."

A turkey wing-bone tacked over the front door to take off troubles did not do so. The Fellowship Class of the Baptist church, renting the clubhouse for an all-night sing, had a bolt of lightning fly down the chimney and burn a path up the aisle. A group of Atlanta fishermen nearly suffocated when the chimney, stopped up by swallows and bats, drove smoke back upon them.

"They was cork-high and bottle-deep," Aunt Baptist said, "or they'da smelled it."

Excuses made no difference. No one wanted to risk renting the clubhouse. If neither God nor the Devil loved the place, the people of Gristle wouldn't take the chance. So it stood, sagging lower from year to year, a cap of pine needles slanted drunkenly across its porch roof.

Harl said cheerfully, "Well, now, you can't lose cutting timber. There's this feller's got a woodpecker mill and a contract to cut cedar on Teaspoon Hill. Says if he had money for new saws, he'd make me a half-partner."

When the cedar was gone, the fellow was gone too. A pile of sawdust was the only earnest that he left.

It went like that. Three times the rope on Rose Crawford's bed was replaced, and each time it tightened on her soul. When she married she had been an easy, happy girl. Now she was only tongue and tears.

"The night you was born, he took off on a coonshine," she moaned. "And when Tessie come he was gone on a fox-hunt. . . ."

Toy stopped listening; it was a tale told weekly. The words were there, but she had lost the meaning long ago. She hung along the doorjamb, her gaze on the floor, and wished she were away and gone. The house had a damp and musty smell, though spring stirred around the windows. There was a faint plumlike fragrance of serviceberry. The bees would be riding the blooms on Atkins' Ridge and filling their leg-bags. Serviceberries made the best honey, better than apple blossoms.

". . . he don't care none," her mother's tale ran on. "But he's pure got to be to the mill today to grind, for Yellow Tom is sick and can't make out to do it. You belong to sweep the yard—if a spark gits in that pine straw, we'll go up like light wood—and the corn's to be chopped, but if your daddy don't git to the mill in another hour-two— Well, you gonna have to go find him."

Toy's gaze flashed up from the floor. Go find her father . . . Get out of this house, get up on Atkins' Ridge. Go down to Goforth's store—

"No, you don't, missy. I ain't giving you leave to roam and ramble. Oh, I can read your mind. You just like your daddy. You got a light foot, ready to light out from work. Now you listen to what I'm saying. My voice ain't wind over your hand."

Rose Crawford levered herself up on the bed to put pith into her words. "Now first you go to Goforth's store and ask them apple-whittlers have they seen him. They ain't, you go on over to Tuck Tate's . . ."

Toy listened while her eyes sought the grist mill. It was barely visible through the trees that lined Mumbling Creek, just a corner of red brick and a bit of shingled roof. In the winter, the branches stripped bare, it was plain to see, straddling the creek as square and sturdy as the day her great-granddad had built it.

John Crawford had been Welsh and a minister, which is one and the same thing, for every Welshman has a sermon in his soul. He had left the mines of Pontypridd when he was twenty, the blue of the coal dust in his cheeks, and walked to Cardiff, where he shipped on a freighter to Boston. There he jumped ship and began walking south along the shelf of the Appalachians.

It was late summer, the purple-loosestrife days, the tall-corn and county-fair days, and he spoke of them in later years with an old wonder in his voice: the balloon ascent and the Indian he had seen, the blue crabs and persimmons he ate, and always the singing—the little parks with their bandstands, the Irish saloons, the Negroes rolling the resin on the Charleston docks, the singing of a country careless of itself and careless of others.

It was in Charleston that he grew sick for the sight of mountains and valleys and turned west toward the sag of the Blue Ridge. He came to Plum Gap and saw a girl picking blackberries. She had yellow hair and wore a brown dress, and she warned him not to drink water that ran under hollow stones. "It's lonesome water. You do, and you'll never get going again." He drank it. It tasted of heart leaf, and a month later they were married. He never left Plum Gap, nor wanted to, and his gravestone read, "He died in God, and God lived in him."

Folks wondered, "Now how did such as John Crawford get him a son like Ard?"

Ard was short for Arduous, which was how John Crawford thought men should earn their bread, by arduous labor. "God promised man only bread and water," he was fond of preaching.

" 'In the sweat of thy face shalt thou eat bread.' " But folks said Ard leaned too heavy on the word, especially when it came to taking toll at the mill.

Millers took one toll in those days, eight pounds of meal from the fifty-six in a bushel of corn, but Ard Crawford took one and a half tolls if you watched him, two if you blinked your eyes. Everyone knew it, and no one could do anything, so they salved themselves by saying that the Lord would take the last toll. Ard Crawford never let this fret him. When he lay dying, Yellow Tom came to him and said, "Mr. Ard, a poor man done come. He got seven children, a woman with a wen, and a blind mule. You gon toll him?" Ard Crawford raised his head and whispered feebly, "Keep him poor. Toll again."

Harl Crawford, Toy's father, had a nickname. It was Hug-Me-Tight. It came from his childhood. There had been a rhyming game popular with children. Someone would shout, "Adam and Eve and Hug-Me-Tight went over the river to spend the night. Adam and Eve fell in. Who was left?" And always it was Harl Crawford who shouted the answer first, "Hug-Me-Tight," and submitted joyfully to the ensuing squeezes. He loved to be loved, he would do anything for love, and the second word on his tongue was "Yes." The first was "Sure."

People said, "Well, some play the fiddle and some play the fool." Harl Crawford did both, and each time Rose bore him a child he played the promise box. He would go to the mill every day, and plant her a pear tree. He would take her to Atlanta. He would build a beehive.

Words were the easiest thing he did. People liked him as they would a dog who licked itself around in front of a woman; they were fond and embarrassed. But Toy loved him. She loved him because he was all she had. Her mother, Tessie, and Harl Junior did not count.

Her mother said, "Well, don't just stand there with your feet all over the floor. Get on!"

She fled to the room she shared with Tessie and Harl Junior, and took a dry dress off a peg. When she returned to the kitchen, Joe, the redbone hound, ambled up to her. He never begged, but he put himself in the way of food.

"You sorry old rag-sucker."

The dog dropped his brown leather ears. He was a pecan-cracker and crayfish-catcher, and, failing these, a rag-chewer. Now when Toy scraped cornbread, grits, and egg yolk into a pan for him, he drooled. He was licking the corners clean before she left the room.

Tessie and Harl Junior came hurrahing around the house. Tessie was in front, dress standing out from her spine, and Harl Junior was after her with a root pistol, and a cook-pot on his head, handle turned backward.

He yelled, "Bang, bang! You're dead," and complained as Tessie kept running, "That ain't fair. You belong to fall."

Tessie said calmly, "You ain't hit me yet," and started across to the grove of oak trees.

Toy called to her. "Tessie, I'm going hunting Pa. Now you and Harl stay round the yard, hear? Don't go running off to the branch." Unconsciously she assumed her mother's voice.

Tessie swerved back. She was twelve, with light red hair and blue eyes, teasing to look at. Already men's eyes turned to her twice.

"Let me go too, Toy?"

Toy shook her head firmly. "No, Ma might need you."

"Me," Harl Junior begged. "Take me, Toy." He was a thin child of ten with light, tenuous hair and bruises under his eyes. People said he would not make old bones.

"You neither."

She knew he would cry, and he did, easy tears. He threw out an accusing arm. "I hurt myself." He showed a scratch. "It hurts!" The last word was a howl.

Toy said unfeelingly, "It'll be well 'fore you're wedded twice."

Tessie yelled after her, "You're mean! If I was mean as you, I'da hung myself when a 'tater vine would do." She grabbed up

a chunk of clay and ran and threw it after Toy. It fell short and
broke apart in small damp clods.

Toy did not bother to look back. She gained the pasture and
began to run, turf springy under her feet. She edged past Maude,
and the mule's ears flickered. Yellow Tom said that the Devil rode
a jumping mule, and its name was Maybe. Maude was Maybe's
sister. Maybe she'd work, and maybe she'd bite; maybe she would
chase you, and maybe she wouldn't. Today she decided she
wouldn't. She rolled over again, the spring fret in her, and Toy
crawled through the farther rails.

Wind wimpled her hair. The morning was acrid with the smell
of mule and cotton poison, damp from dew and the creek beyond
the trees. Toy slid down the bank, mullen like flannel under her
feet, and hesitated on the mill road. Should she see if her father
had returned to the mill?

As she hesitated, a car started up behind the trees. A minute
later an old truck came into sight on the yellow road. It stopped
and Lovick Jones, the postmaster, stuck his head out. He was a
clown-shaped little man, anger coming hard to his face.

"Toy, where's that daddy of yourn anyways?"

She came and leaned against the running board. "I don't know,
Mr. Lov. Ma sent me out to look for him."

"I swear, I've about trotted my heels off looking for him. I
come last week, and I come this, but I ain't going to come again.
You tell him so."

Toy grabbed the door, alarmed. "Please, Mr. Lov, don't take
your business off. Pa will turn up—"

"He don't watch out, he'll turn up done in— Aw, now, I didn't
mean nothing by that." He hurried to make amends. "Sure,
honey, he'll turn up. You tell him old Lov will be back."

She watched the truck rattle off, fear heavy in her. Mr. Lov
was just talking, but truth was in his talk. Pa had no more idea of
trouble than a robin around Hell.

She began running.

Gristle was a mile and a half off. The road doglegged along the bottom of Atkins' Ridge, following the course of the creek. The sides were pleached with long-lingering smilax and white bindweed. Warblers pursued caterpillars in every tree and bush, for it was the third week in April, and birds were pouring over the mountains. Raccoon-marked yellowthroats, cheeky firetails, and little parulas hung from every twig. A month earlier it had been robins.

Aunt Baptist had told her, "I had me a robin pie last night. They et all my pink camellia buds, but they taste brown right on."

Toy hopped a puddle and wished that she could go visit the big midwife. She never got enough of her talk. It circled the valley and came back home all in the same breath. Best of all she loved to hear Aunt Baptist talk about herbs. She liked to go with her when she gathered them.

"This here is ginseng"—a wrinkled, spindle-shaped root. "Chinese men think it makes 'em hornier. You can't hardly find it no more. Guess they gonna have to depend on their natural juices." Cherry bark: "Folks use this in cough syrup, and sassafras bark in perfume. You know they can't make perfume without whale vomit? Wish I'd been on the beach when Jonah got washed up."

Most of all Aunt Baptist liked to toll out the names of plants. "Adam's-flannel, Aaron's-rod, Noah's-ark, Jacob's-ladder, apple of Sodom. You notice that none of them is named out of the New Testament, the Book of Love? They named out of the Book of Wrath."

Once she asked timidly, "Aunt Baptist, you—you a Christian?"

"Why, you know the Devil is a Christian. So maybe I ain't."

Aunt Baptist's talk was obliged. It might be scandalous, but you were obliged to listen.

She reached the fork in the road. The right prong dipped down to Gristle, the left climbed to a little hill above the creek and Aunt Baptist's house. Five or ten minutes would neither help nor hurry Pa, even if she could find him. She traced an indecisive circle with her toe.

A hen-hawk quartered the sky. Her thoughts followed it. It was curious how birds of prey told what they were by their pattern of flight. The hawk soared with elbows a-kink like the boogy-bird it was to chickens and rats. The vulture's wings lay flat, the tips upturned in pious disclaimer. And the eagle made a giant cross against the clouds, X marks the spot.

The hawk cried out. Sound echoed it on the road. A truck was approaching from Gristle. Toy could hear it before she saw it, old and weighed down with baskets of corn. It stopped, and a big fair-haired man leaned an elbow out of the window.

"Hello, Toy. Your daddy to the mill?"

Wick Bloodworth was one of the few men during the last year or so who did not make her feel queersome. Aunt Baptist told her once, "Well, Wick sees beyond his eyes. He sees with his sympathy."

Toy felt a lift and a release, turning to him. "No, sir. I was just looking for him. Ma says likely he's to Goforth's."

"Well, Flonnie promised me Indian pudding tonight if I got fresh meal." He smiled, eyes a quickening blue. "She don't make it often, so I figured I'd best take her up."

People did not understand how a fine, hard-working someone like Wick Bloodworth ever married Flonnie Ansley, slugabed, flocks unfed. Yet he acted as if he had gotten the prize from the top of the Christmas tree.

Toy smiled faintly, repeated, "Ma says likely Pa's to Goforth's."

"Get in." He opened the door. "I'll take you a piece."

She climbed in, and he backed around. She leaned against the scuffed leather of the upholstery, noticing that the floorboards of the truck were swept clean. Most farm cars were filthy with sand and shavings and little tin mule and bull tokens from chewing tobacco. She thought of the apple-whittlers at Goforth's and shivered.

Wick asked, "Booger get you?"

She shook her head. "No. Things is—just crowding in, I reckon."

"They'll do that. Flonnie says the same thing. She says, 'Times I think of all I got to do—and I just stand in the middle of the floor and turn round and round.' "

His voice was tender, and Toy, listening, thought how fine it was for a man to speak so about a woman, taking a fault and turning it into a favor. Most men scoffed, "Now women was made from a crooked bone—and what can you expect from a crooked bone?"

The road took a final dip; they were at the head of Main Street. Wick looked at her. "You want off here?"

"Along abouts."

He drove a block and stopped before Goforth's. He stretched an arm across her breast to open the door.

"Now hope you find your daddy. Tell him I got grist."

Then he drove off and left her to face the apple-whittlers at Goforth's.

Three

GRISTLE was a county seat, with a population of 518. Once the population had numbered over ten thousand, but that was back in 1829 at the height of Georgia's gold rush.

Prior to that Gristle was a quiet town. It had been carved out of Cherokee lands in 1819, and the population was farmers and fur trappers until gold was discovered on Mumbling Creek. Suddenly the hills were cluttered with the shacks of pre-Forty-

Niners, sutlers and gamblers and women who smoked and curled their little back hairs. When the gold ran out, so did the seekers. They moved to Licklog, later Dahlonega, or took the Oregon Trail. What remained was a hard core of farmers and small businessmen. The three biggest buildings in Gristle were the cotton gin, the Mimosa Hotel, and the courthouse. The courthouse was two stories high and built of homemade brick overlaid with a plaster tempered by years to pale gold. It had a motto carved over the front door, "Justice Lives Here," only the "v" was blotted out with ivy.

The Baptist church was next door to the courthouse and fourth in size. Its bell rang High God, Low God, No God but My God. Yet Gristle's soul lay somewhere between church and courthouse, between Heaven and Hell. It lay in Goforth's store.

Goforth's was a brown barnlike building, steps and stone area set with Nehi bottle caps, little disks of purple, red, green, brown, and yellow. John Goforth supplied his customers with empty cans for spit-cups, a bowl of althea twigs for use in snuff-dipping, and Trot—soda crackers and peanuts parched together on the wood stove (and making for active use of the outhouse).

The store carried work shirts and women's shoes, tobacco and plows, salt and coffee, needles and neat's-foot oil. The responsibility had graved lines in John Goforth's forehead. He had a round gray head with a thin hooked nose, and he wore glasses. With the close-clapped set of his body, he looked like an owl possessed by mistake of pants.

He was a great teller of tales, mostly apocryphal, and willing to seek out his audience. Today they were clustered on the long porch, drawn forth by April like earthworms by the sun, a half-dozen men in overalls and old felt hats, chairs canted back, heels hooked over the rungs.

The storekeeper was supervising a Negro packing ice into the small stilted icehouse by the store.

". . . so Preacher say, 'John, I don't have that last nickel on my bill,' and I says, 'That's all right, I'll take it out in preaching.'

He says, 'Now you know I got no nickel sermons,' and I says, 'Well, Preacher, I'll go twice.' "

A boy, his britches buttoned with a thorn, sniggered and cuffed a hand across his mouth. The canted men chuckled. Two old men with a checkerboard between their knees looked up, and one frowned.

"Now, John, you always throwing off on preachers. Folks going to think you an atheist."

"Why, Henry, you know I'm in the front pew every Sunday."

A man with ragged hair and broken brogans interrupted. "Now I'd as leave be an atheist as one of them Pope-lovers. You hear what Al Smith done? Gone over to Wall Street now he got beat."

"Thought you voted for him, Bill."

"I done so." He leaned over and spat between two fingers. "I wouldn't vote the Republican ticket if it was headed by Jesus Christ."

John Goforth said slyly, "You sure was between the Devil and the deep last election, wasn't you, Bill?"

"Wasn't the onliest one."

The second checker-player hooted. "You my meat, boy." He jumped several squares. Victory made him expansive. "Now I'll tell you boys why I wouldn't vote for one nor the other. Wouldn't vote Smith, 'cause Rome'd be washing their feet in the White House. Wouldn't vote Hoover, 'cause during the war he told folks to make biscuits out of half flour and half corn meal. I said, 'If I can't get me a real biscuit, I don't want one.' "

John Goforth said, "Now getting down to natural facts—"

Toy drew a breath to plump up her courage and crossed the road. The storekeeper interrupted himself.

"Well, hello, Toy. You come to see Dolly? She's round back."

"No, sir." Toy kept her eyes on his face and tried not to feel the silence that washed her from head to foot. She knew the names and faces of the men on the porch, but she no longer knew their eyes. "I'm—I'm looking for my daddy."

"Why, honey, I ain't seen him, not since day before yesterday."
He turned. "Any you fellers seen Harl?"

Coke Williams' lips moved. "I did." He was a tall man with a
still, pale face, evil-minded as a monkey, and at home in every
dark corner of the county. "He come by my house last night,
baited for widow, blue tie and yellow shirt."

Someone guffawed, but it was quickly smothered. Someone
hummed, "I'm a tomcat's kitten—"

John Goforth spoke quickly. "Reckon not, hon. Likely your
daddy's visiting. I mean—I hear tell there's a funeral over to
Rezin and you know how your daddy loves a funeral."

Toy edged a heel back. The storekeeper held her with a gesture. "Can't Yellow Tom do the grinding, honey?"

A man called from farther down the porch, "Nope, he's sick.
I went by his house last evening to get him to bring his mule,
come plow a garden patch for my old woman, but he was down
with his stomach."

"Reckon he is, then. Tom ain't like a lot of niggers, say sick
when they're just sorry."

The Negro packing ice worked stolidly, sweat sheening his
plum-colored face.

Coke Williams drawled, "You want to find your daddy, try the
old Fallon place, Bess Tripp. You'll find his pants, you don't find
him."

John Goforth wheeled indignantly. "Now quit that, Coke."
He told Toy, "Run on, sugar, play with Dolly. I'll send Lige here
to look for your daddy."

Toy went gratefully, glad to get away from the looks and the
voices.

John Goforth's house stood behind the store, rambling and
white with a tin roof and a dog-trot. Formosa azaleas were massed
around the front, pine trees let down curtains of wisteria on each
side. Behind were a chicken run, a smokehouse, and a fenced pasture. Two cows and a horse grazed among rills left by the
spring rains.

Dolly was balanced in a tire swung from an oak branch, bare heels controlling her sway, hands busy with two pig bladders. She bounced up when she saw Toy. "Hey, come get you one."

Toy accepted the balloon. "Where'd you get them?" It was too late for butchering; everyone butchered in the fall, at first frost.

"Couple I hung up in the attic around Christmas and forgot. Ma came across them this morning when she was setting out a squirrel trap."

Toy batted hers. It bounced against the mock-orange hedge, but the thick membrane was impervious to thorns. "You ought to save 'em for swimming."

Dolly shook her head. "I got more."

So she and Dolly played with the bladders, batting them to each other and up in the air until they got stuck in the trees and couldn't be pried loose even with fishing poles.

Dolly dropped her pole. "Aw, let the old things be. I know, let's play Anthony Over."

They separated to either side of Dolly's house, Dolly carrying a ball. Toy took the left side of the house, because it looked down the road into Gristle and up the cut-off to the old Fallon farm—it would always be called that no matter how often it was rented out. The Tripps lived there now, a couple from up Carolina way who had moved in last month.

Gristle knew the Tripps' name better than their faces, for they had come into town only twice to buy supplies; they seemed to be their own best company. They looked like brother and sister rather than man and wife, both big and black-eyed, the hair springing coarsely from their foreheads like goats' horns. They moved impatiently, and violence lay in the very boss of their cheeks. Tales drifted back of the fury with which Bess Tripp cleaned house, flinging buckets of boiling potash water on the walls where other women would have flung dippers, how Jack Tripp blew up a stump full of snakes and filled the air with rattle-buttons enough for the Devil's coat.

Lovick Jones had said, "I've seen folks like them before. If they like you, they'll do anything for you. But if they say they'll kill you, why, they will."

Toy shivered. She hoped Pa wouldn't get mixed up with such as that.

Dolly yelled from beyond the house, "Here it comes." The red ball trickled over the roof and bounced down a few feet from Toy. She ran and caught it and threw it back.

She was half turned from her throw, and that was how she saw Lige heavy-hoof it down the cut-off from the Fallon place. His face was lavender, his breath hasseled like a sick dog's.

Toy started to run and did not know why, except it was about Pa. She knew it was about Pa. Azaleas crashed in her path, but she went through regardless, never hearing Dolly's "Here it comes," the plop of a ball.

Whittlings had slid from lap to floor. The men on the porch closed Lige in as if they would squeeze his story out physically.

". . . when I were coming back," Lige's voice was babbling, guttural with terror, "Lawd God, yon it was, foots poking out bushes. I looks, and it were him, it were Mr. Harl!"

John Goforth cried, "My God!" And on a down-note, "My God."

Coke Williams' lips were drawn back. "He's been asking for it, and by God, he got it. You reckon it was the big feller?"

"Couldn't be no one else. We all knowed how Harl was, no harm to him—" John Goforth saw Toy. Quickly he pushed out of the circle. "Honey, you go on home."

"No." Her voice came squeezed past her lips. "Where's Pa? What's happened to Pa?"

"Nothing, honey. Now it's all right. We'll take care of everything. You go on home—"

She turned and ran up the cut-off, never hearing the yells after her or men's feet in pursuit. The road was wagon-wide, two orange ruts cut through trees and bushes. She saw small individual

things clearly, the yellow pollen scum on the puddles, a mule
shoe rusty and discarded, the sun striking gold from a mica stone.

She saw the foot, because she sought it. She might have passed
by as Lige had done at first, half hidden as it was in the bushes by
the road.

It was a foot, but it was in a woman's shoe, a black pump with
a buckle, and she stopped, not believing it, and her hands went
out and pulled the bushes.

Her father lay in the weeds. He wore a woman's frilly blue
shirtwaist and a brown skirt, and you could beg him and pull at
him—"Get up, Pa"—but still he would lie in the flatness which
was death.

Four

TIME would leach away the pain, but not the picture. Toy
would remember the picture, her father dressed in a
woman's clothes, lying among bushes, leaves clotted at the back
of his head. She would remember other things, too, her mother
screaming, "Nononono," and throwing herself back and forth on
the pillows, eyes closed and face purple. "He was my dependency!" As if Harl Crawford had ever been anyone's dependency
but the wind's.

She would remember a burial, the minister intoning, "Harl
Crawford has fallen asleep in the clasp of the Georgia violets"—
and someone sniggering behind her. "I bet that sure is a disappointment to ole Harl."

Before and after the funeral they all came, of course. They
came in pairs, and they came in groups, and not a one but
brought something. The dish covered with the napkin was the
excuse borne by curiosity, for they came not only to give but

to get. They gave hams, pies, jellies, and potato salad, but they got something tastier in return, grief, and not theirs.

The food was soon eaten up. It looked a lot on the kitchen table, but it was little on the spoon with two children whose appetites had been sharpened by excitement and a mother who declared, "I got to eat to keep my strength up. The young'uns got no one but me, and dear Lord know what will happen to the poor creatures if I got took down." She said this from the bed, where she held court among pillows, a thin blanket smoothed over her prominence.

The few men who came said, "Now remember, Miss Rose, any little chore I can do for you—" and all the women said, "Now you got to be brave, honey. Any little thing I can do—" They said this every day for a week, then every other day for another week. The third week they said nothing at all, for no one came. The shooting of Harl Crawford had been replaced in their interest by other things: the load of bootleg liquor wrecked near Flowing Wells Church, and how the congregation poured out and sopped it clean; the five-dollar gold piece old Elias Bowes had had melted and made into gold teeth; the new pointer pup Coke Williams had bought and was trying to break of chicken-chasing with a block and chain.

Rose Crawford could not believe it when two days and then three passed without anyone's coming to listen to her tell how strong she had to be. Previously she had gotten up and made a pretense of work, cooked one or two meals and dabbed around the yard with a dogwood broom. But when the fourth and fifth days passed without anyone's coming and declaring, "Rose, you ought to take better care of yourself, 'specially now," she went back to bed and asked God to kill her.

"I don't want to live in no world where folks got hearts like stone," she moaned. "Nor bring a young'un into it. Take me, Lord. Kill me!"

The first time Toy heard her, she ran and hid behind the barn. The second time she ran across the pasture toward the mill.

Shadows stretched violet under the laurel shrubs, red under the sassafras, long and gray under the sycamore and oak, for shadows take their color from what is over them, as people do. Toy's shadow was no color and every color. It wavered with her across the field where the mule relished chickweed with a long lip, and slid with her between the fence rails, disappearing when she ran into the cool near-dusk of the mill. Floured cobwebs tried to hold her at the doorway, but she pushed through them. The mill was still, stones and wheel. The only sound in the silence was the rustling of mice and insects, the low burbling of water.

Toy climbed the ladder to the loft and dropped down on a heap of old sacks.

There were windows in the loft, but they were blind with dust except for the few that were broken and stuffed with rags. After a while Toy removed a piece of old shirt and looked down on the race and wheel.

The mill had not changed since the day the itinerant Quaker millwright had laid it out. He had built mills all up and down the Georgia fall-line, he told Great-Granddad John; "But I have never saw a place that begged for a mill like yonder. Thee has a strong-flowing pond on the right and a natural creek. The mill can be set between—an overshot wheel would be best because of the gully. Now thee would be a fool not to build one."

So he had laid it out, cutting every interior board from a pattern as a dressmaker cuts a dress. The brick front rested on level earth, the back straddled the gully on tall fieldstone stilts. The millwheel, eighteen feet high with cups fourteen inches deep, hung on the back. The trough, or headrace, led the water from the pond to the top of the wheel, from where it spilled away down the gully into Mumbling Creek. Wheel and trough were built of cypress, as was the floodgate that released the water into the race. Mill box and joists were made of heart pine, the forty-eight-inch-wide stones were granite.

Someone moved below in the mill. Toy sat up. There was a thud as the wooden beam that lifted the floodgate was thrown.

Beside her, water began to roar down the race, jumping and spar-
kling in the sun. The millwheel lurched and turned. Below her
the stones started; they shook the mill.

Yellow Tom came up the stairway. He did not see her until he
reached the top, and then he nearly tumbled back.

"Godamercy, child, you like to scare the breath out me, setting
there so quiet. What's you doing?"

She did not answer. He waited a moment, then nodded his
head just as if she had.

"Well, reckon that's good as anything. I'd do it myself, I has
the time. But I ain't."

He came on up the ladder and checked the elevator that
brought grain from below and dropped it into the hopper. The
hopper was a wooden funnel that trickled corn onto the stones.
The harsh grinding took on a muted note. He did not appear to
pay any further attention to the girl, but he was watching her out
of the corner of his eye.

Yellow Tom had come to the valley fifty years ago from somewhere in Florida, a yellow-faced runaway boy with lash marks
from neck to knobby knees. Time had erased the marks and added
measure to the man, for he would turn his hand to any work from
scraping chitlins to liming outhouses. He was a streak of lean
cured by age to a tough resilience, and folks called him "a good
nigger." His eyes were blue and hid their thoughts behind turtle lids.

Now he began humming, high and fluting, as he turned on the
fan which blew the chaff away. "What makes Satan hate me so?
He gots me once, and let me go. . . ."

After a while, Toy asked, "Whose corn?"

"Mr. Wick's."

"Reckon he'll get his Indian pudding."

Wick and Flonnie had been the first to come when news about
her father got around. Flonnie had offered to take Tessie and
Harl Junior for a couple of days, and Wick had offered to build

the coffin, since Tuck Tate, who generally made them, was over at Cardiff mule-trading.

Rose Crawford had screamed and tossed around on the bed when "coffin" was mentioned, and Flonnie and Annie Goforth tried to hold her down, pleading, "Now, Rose, you got to get hold of yourself. You got to think of the baby."

Toy had run outside—it was the first of her running off—and pretended to feed the chickens, but she scarcely heeded if the least got most, as she usually did. She heard John Goforth and Wick walk out on the front porch, and the storekeeper tell how the sheriff caught Jack Tripp.

". . . hunting him all over creation, and you know where the scaper was? In his own house, by God. Sheriff went down to ask Bess Tripp had she seen him, and he come to the door and slung Harl's pants and shirt down on the ground. 'Arrest them,' he yells, 'don't arrest me.' "

There was the scrape of a match, a drift of cigar smoke.

Wick said tentatively, "That's how come Harl had on women's clothes?"

"Uh-huh, got caught in the bedroom with his pants in the parlor. He jumped into the first thing to hand, but Jack Tripp jumped last."

"He in jail?"

"Yes. But I don't reckon he'll stay."

Nor did he. Two days later the sheriff turned him loose until court in September—explaining reasonably, "He ain't going nowheres. He's got a crop in the ground." And Jack Tripp strode to freedom, declaring, "He had it coming to him. I'd do it again, by God."

Toy could not believe it. She could not believe that God must wait to punish a killer; he should strike him down dead now—"An eye for an eye." Then she remembered, "The mills of the gods grind slowly . . ." Jack Tripp would be dust come September, and she would blow him off her palm. . . .

Yellow Tom said, "How come you up here anyways?—not that you is disfurnishing me."

She replied, "I'm waiting."

She could not have said what she meant by that. Was she waiting for Ma to stop crying and carrying on, for the summer to be by and gone so September could come? Was she waiting for Jack Tripp to die, so Pa could live again without laughter around his name?

Yellow Tom said, "Waiting is toting an empty sack. Life don't stand around in heaps waiting on you to pick it up. Life is a moving thing, you gots to catch it."

She said, "I'm waiting on them to kill that Jack Tripp."

"You gots you a long wait till September, then maybe they won't."

She sat up, staring at him. "What you mean, maybe they won't? They will—they got to! He killed my daddy."

"If folks rode Got-to, we'd a-been in Heaven day before yesterday. Now we don't talk 'bout killing no more. It makes my ole mouth feel like I been licking a brass pot—"

She interrupted fiercely, jumping up. "It don't make me feel like that! Only time I can taste my rations is when I think about September and that bastard's blood running down his heels!"

"I don't want to hear no more! You jes thinking 'bout yourself, you ain't studying on Tessie and Junior, what they gon do this summer while you waiting for blood."

She said defensively, "I was too thinking of them. I figured—I figured—" She broke off.

"You figured nothing; now I gon tell you. You gon puts in a garden, corn and sass and cow-chop. I gon to come tomorrow morning, and we gon make us a garden."

Five

THE *Gristle Monthly* announced the calendar for the fall term of circuit court in the September second issue, three days before court was to convene. The sixth item down read: "State of Georgia *vs.* John Tripp. Manslaughter."

Toy read it, pressing a fingernail so hard against the last word that the paper tore in a tiny triangle.

She said bitterly, "They don't figure Pa's killing is important enough to put first. They got it after chicken-stealing."

She did not know what she had expected from the paper, but she had thought that a man's death would leave a bigger hole in newsprint than this: "State of Georgia *vs.* John Tripp. Manslaughter."

She burst out, "Why, they don't even say Pa's name."

Aunt Baptist told her, "It's the way newspapers do such."

She cast the paper away violently. "Then they no better than wasps' nests, full of meanness and buzzing."

"Now I know how you feel, but you got to get over it. You got to quit being so hard-headed. For a hard head carries a soft behind."

The big midwife had been a present help the summer long. Her thick boots had tramped the mill road weekly. Her heavy hands had taken hold of things. Yet putting and taking were not understanding.

Now she added, "Toy, you got to quit counting on the trial fixing everything."

"I got to count on something."

She did not know why people could not see. She did not know why Aunt Baptist did not understand. She had to count on something or everything was wasted—the endless summer when she had been a mother to her own mother and Tessie and Harl too, the work she had done that only a mule and a man belonged to do.

Yellow Tom had come and plowed a garden for her. He laid out ruler-straight furrows and helped her put in what she needed: corn, for meal is the keystone of life; cow-chop, pumpkins and gourds that rambled along the fence with the briars; yams to hill for winter; sorghum cane for syrup when first frost came; tomatoes, beans, collards, and turnips.

He said, "Now you gots you a start."

She had a start on something else too, though she did not know it; she had a start on being the prop of the family. She had thought of her mother as being the prop until the day the wood ran out.

It was soon after the garden had been put in. She did all the housework, washing and cleaning, but with an eye out for her mother's directions. Mainly she wished that her mother would make Tessie and Harl Junior help. Tessie, especially, wouldn't turn her hand no matter how Toy asked and threatened. The redheaded girl would stick her tongue out. "I ain't got to do it; you ain't Ma."

One morning she went to get wood for the breakfast fire. There was a bare armful left, and clothes to be boiled later.

She got breakfast, and went in to her mother, who was sitting listlessly in a chair, looking down the road. An old dress was drawn around Rose Crawford's body, her feet were bare, and her black hair looked like a winter bird's nest, dry and falling to pieces.

Toy said, "Ma, we're 'most out of wood."

Rose Crawford did not look around. She said querulously, "You'd think Flonnie Bloodworth would come see me. She ain't been in a week. Nor Ruby Williams—after all I done for her."

"We could take the sled, go up the ridge and get some."

Her mother's voice brightened. "Though Annie Goforth said as how she might drop by." She heaved herself up. "Reckon I'll walk a piece down the road. Might meet her." Her voice trailed away as she waddled out of the house.

A trembling little bubble moved up and down in Toy's chest; it was a bubble that wanted to laugh and cry, both at once. She turned away and got out the wood sled. She went up on Atkins' Ridge and chopped branches and brought it back loaded. It took her an hour, and by then the sun was high and hot, the wash pot stifling. She boiled clothes while up in the woods Tessie's and Harl Junior's voices rose light and laughing. The bubble in her chest went away, and a stone came in its place.

She got supper, cornbread and greens and fried sidemeat. She fixed a plate for her mother, who had napped away the afternoon, and then sat down with her own. By and by Tessie and Harl Junior ran in, their faces streaked with play and sweat.

Tessie yelled, "Where's my dinner?"

Harl complained, "I'm hungry."

Toy kept eating and did not answer. Tessie stopped by the table, scowling.

"You didn't set our plates out."

Toy said, "I ain't Ma."

Harl had wandered over to the stove. Now he let out a wail. "There ain't nothing left to eat."

Toy said, "I didn't have to fix you nothing. I ain't Ma."

Tessie said, "Ma," and then on an ascending shriek, "Ma!"— and ran into the bedroom. Toy could hear her voice. "Ma, Toy ain't fixed us a bit of supper!"

The bed springs creaked. "She ain't?" Her mother waddled to the door, listlessly brushing hair from her eyes. "Toy, why ain't you fixed the young'uns nothing?"

Toy kept her gaze on her plate. "They want me to cook for them, all they got to do is haul the wood." Her gaze flashed up. She burst out, "They're up in them trees the whole enduring day." She wanted to cry, but she kept her eyes fiercely on her mother's face.

Rose Crawford hesitated. Her gaze went from the two younger

children to her older daughter's face, slid away uncertainly. She said weakly, "Now, Tessie, you and Harl help Toy some, you hear?"

She edged back into the bedroom; the door closed.

The two children stared from the door to Toy. Tessie said doubtfully, "You can't make us"—but it was a question.

Toy said, "I can't, but your belly can."

It was dusk-dark and a pint of tears later before the two had gathered enough wood for a fire; and when Toy said, "Now you going to help me around here," they nodded, chastened by hunger and shock.

It was easier with the two children helping, but they could not be depended on. They brought wood willingly enough; it gave them an excuse to woods-roam. They gathered eggs, so they could chase the chickens; and they picked huckleberries and blackberries, but it was summer style, one for the lard bucket, two for the mouth. The main bulk of work, especially the garden, fell on Toy.

The garden had started up in May, but the flare of the thin new leaves above the sandy soil seemed to signal all the garden devils, weeds and insects and drought. The weeds were a torment; thirst made them bloom, chopping made them flourish. They were the chosen seed.

They were bad, and the insects were worse, but the drought was a near disaster. The summer was a soul-searer. The world seemed to curl at its edges and turn yellow. Small fires broke out spontaneously in the dry woods. Yams were woody and without taste. The creek bed cracked, its rocks showing like bones; the garden panted. Toy had to carry water from the well each evening, cedar bucket on bucket, and watch the earth receive it with scarcely a trace. Later she carried water from the pond, when the well grew dangerously low. The pond was always full, for it was fed by seven springs.

The first ear of corn was a miracle, the first panful of beans a triumph.

She told her mother joyously, "It looks like the garden's going to make."

Rose Crawford said sorrowfully, "I'da helped you if I could, but seems like I can't hold out to do nothing." She pressed both palms to her swollen stomach.

Rose Crawford could not work, but she could wander, and that summer her feet fanned the hills. She was down to Goforth's store and up to Flonnie Bloodworth's. She was over the ridge to Coke Williams' and down the road to Lovick Jones's. She would sit in some kitchen, hands clasping herself, and say sadly, "I'm so proud for you, got you a nice home and a good man. I tell you, Annie" —or Adella or Flonnie—"you don't know how the Lord is blessing you right this very minute. Look at me, hardly salt enough for bread, them poor young'uns to raise all by myself . . ."

John Goforth said disgustedly to his wife, "She got the young-'uns to raise, why don't she stay to home and do it?"

"God makes the oak, but he makes the willow too. Rose can't help it that she's got no pith."

"Now you can tell she's a willow all right, all that weeping."

Imperceptibly, during the summer, Toy and her mother switched roles. Girl became mother, and mother became child, but the full import of this did not strike Toy immediately.

Suddenly the garden engulfed her. It surged overnight from panfuls of beans to hamperfuls. The gourds ran away from their vines, the rabbits she caught in her box traps tasted of sassafras but had bean curds in their stomachs, the bluejays' bills dripped red from tomatoes. They had a regular flyway between their nests along the creek and the garden.

Aunt Baptist said briskly, "If you don't get that stuff off the bushes, it'll be ruined."

So she canned. It was garden to hamper to kettle and around again. Aunt Baptist and Annie Goforth helped her a time or two, but after that she did it alone. Rose Crawford cut a panful of green tomatoes for pickle—she was inordinately fond of sweets and sours—and then her foot found the doorsill.

Yams must be dug and hilled, the vines put aside for the mule, the nubs for the hogs; Yellow Tom had traded her two shoats for her father's Sunday suit. The gourds must be kicked free for cow-chop or hung to dry for marten nests. Martens kept hawks away from the chicken yard, and now every egg was needed, down to the pecan-sized latter one. The sorghum cane was gold-green, and only waited for the first frost to sweeten it.

The last week in August three men came to the mill and wanted corn ground. Yellow Tom said, "It's starting. You gon have to decide pretty soon now."

Toy was with him the morning the three came, Ammi Watts and two men from across the ridge. She always tried to be at the mill Thursday mornings, the one day they stayed open in summer, for she felt her presence was due Tom. He did not need her help, for during the hot weather grinding fell away to nothing but dibs and dabs. Now, with cold weather around the corner, men wanted something heavier behind their belts than soda biscuits. They wanted cornbread heavy with grease and cracklings, and the mill must be run every day.

Toy watched the meal flow from the stones into the bin. She listened to the water burble behind the mill and heard it tread-milling the wheel-cups.

"I couldn't run no mill."

"Womenfolks runs mills. Miz Hunt over to Clary runs one, gits her toll like any Jack-the-Bob. Now, Miss Toy, you knows when the rush is on my hands gon be full. I can holds out to husk, I can holds out to shuck, and I can holds out to grind. But I can't holds out my ole hand and say, 'Toll.' "

Toy burst out, "I can't neither. The nos dreen right out of me!"

Take Ammi Watts, for instance. When they had finished grinding his corn, he had sidled up to her. "Now, honey, you ain't gonna toll me, are you? You know all them young'uns I got, I can't hardly make ends meet as 'tis." His voice dropped. He leaned forward, rank tobacco breath in her face. "You toll John

Goforth or one of them rich fellers twice, make up for me. They won't know no different."

She had shaken her head, confused and upset. "I can't do that." Her mouth tried to say, "I got to have the toll, too"—but a picture of the Watts children came to her, ricketty-jointed and ragged, sand-lappers for sure. She had let him off without taking toll.

Yellow Tom had looked grave. "You lets him off, Miss Toy, them others gon expect it too. Big dog wants what the little dog gits."

Now she said, "You seen how I done with Ammi Watts. If I run the mill, I'd be—" She stopped. She had started to say, "as bad as Pa."

"Well, what's you gon do then?"

"Get someone to run it, I reckon."

There were men aplenty she could get, she thought, but they fell on two sides of the fence. Either they were like Ammi Watts, wouldn't work if it was tasting pie in a pie factory, or like Wick Bloodworth, hard workers who would take on the added job only to oblige her. She hated to ask the first, and she wouldn't ask the second.

The Negro said, "Well, you gots to decide soon. We gon be in a corn-rush week or two."

A few days later Aunt Baptist brought the newspaper with the court calendar.

Six

JUDGE KISH WHITEHEAD, who would preside over the trial, sat between the Bible and the American flag and in front of a parrot. The parrot was a misanthropic bird with a filmed eye and one claw perpetually upraised in protest. The judge carried it around on his circuit and during lulls in court would share sunflower seeds with it.

The parrot, grizzled by time, was still the more colorful of the two. He was green with pipings of red and blue on his cheeks. Judge Whitehead was round and pallid, a man who absorbed the arguments before his bench and reflected them back like a mirror.

The judge offered the parrot a seed. The bird accepted it, clinging to the bars of the cage, tail thrust through, squawking faintly. The judge said, "Hush, son."

Toy trembled. It was her first time in a courtroom, and she had not thought it would be like this, the rustle of sacks as people ate their lunches on the benches around her, the fan slowly revolving on the cracked ceiling, the lawyers conferring together in low voices, feet propped on chair seats.

She thought bitterly, Like dogs. Can't do nothing unless they lift their legs.

The bitterness had been accumulating slowly. Court had opened at nine o'clock, and it was now two. Lunch recess was over, but still the lawyers talked—Rob Tyson, who was county prosecutor, and Abe Greene, Jack Tripp's attorney. They had gone out to eat together, arm in arm. Toy's stomach tightened, remembering this.

She had expected court to be a holy thing, like church. She had thought of the judge as a sort of God sitting on high and shining wisdom out. She had thought of the lawyers as the dark and the bright angels, the bat wings of the first blackening the truth, the Jehovah's sword of the second cutting it free. She had thought that voices would roll out like trumpets.

The truth was this: nothing said by nothing-kind of men, the crack of fried-chicken bones, and the click of the parrot's beak sidling up and down the bars.

The words burst out of her throat, low and violent. "They're carrying on like it was a box supper."

Aunt Baptist said, "It's how folks is."

Toy knotted her fingers and wished she had not flared out so.

No one, not even Aunt Baptist, must find a spot on her surface to slip a fingernail under and prise up to see what lay underneath—bewilderment, anger, pain.

Suddenly her mother whimpered. Toy looked and thought, She's not helping none.

Rose Crawford was sitting on the front bench. Her face was gaumed over with sorrow, but it fooled no one. Delight was nearer the surface than the baby was to birth. Rose Crawford would have crawled to the trial over tacks and through torment.

Toy thought bitterly, Gleaming herself around!

Now her mother started and shrank back dramatically against her companion, a woman with a long lip to lay on sorrow. The woman patted her and glared at Jack Tripp, who had thumped his chair down on the floor. Toy's eyes had hardly left him since she entered the courtroom. There was a fascination about a man going to die and knowing it less than had the strong bull of Bashan that Moses sacrificed.

He looked like a bull, too, with his meaty shoulders, almost spindly legs, and small black-polled head. He had been canted back, talking over his shoulder to his wife, and Bess Tripp seemed as unaware of death as he. Her voice came to Toy, heavy and husky.

"We got to trade that ole mule 'less you file down them teeth. Critter's about to starve to death, can't eat grass, much less corn."

"Don't reckon they'll get filed, then. Critter's liable to take a chunk out of my arm I try." He slid an eye to her. "You file 'em."

Bess aimed a powerful swipe at him. "It's all right if I get bit, huh?"

He ducked, chuckling, chair thumping on the floor. His eyes swept the room boldly. He lifted a hand to someone, and Toy looked away. How could he carry on so? Dead and didn't know it.

Abe Greene looked up and frowned. He said a final word to Rob Tyson and came over. "Look, Jack—" He murmured in the other's ear. Jack Tripp pulled a solemn face, winked at his wife, and faced around.

Abe Greene called, "We're ready, your honor." A rustle of expectancy went over the room.

It had been a dull morning. The chicken-stealing case had been concluded, grand larceny involving the theft of a fighting cock named Goober valued at a hundred dollars. There was a petty point of law involved: Cock-fighting was illegal, so ostensibly no rooster was worth more than a dollar.

The lawyer for the prosecution had won a conviction by arguing solemnly, "Well, Judge, the reason this rooster is so valuable is that every hen he treads"—he paused dramatically—"lays an egg with a double yolk." The culprit had been remanded to the county jail, and the case of *State of Georgia* vs. *Jack Tripp, Manslaughter*, had been called.

There had just been time before lunch for the prosecution to call three witnesses; the sheriff, the doctor, and Elijah Clarke Johnson. The first two witnesses' testimony had been as expected, but the Negro's was different.

Abe Greene, the defense counsel, said, "Now, Elijah, you say you went to the Tripp house and knocked, and when no one answered, you came back, and that was when you saw the foot sticking out of the underbrush. Now how come you didn't see it when you were going? You've got good eyesight, haven't you?"

Elijah stuttered, "Y-yes, suh. Yes, suh. Gots good eyes. Mr. John Goforth tell you. Yes, suh."

"Well, why didn't you see the foot?"

Elijah squirmed in anguish, his eyes appealing to John Goforth, who stared back, uncomprehending. Finally he burst out. "Mr. John, honest t'God, didn't takes but a speck, just a little old pinch—"

"What did you take?"

Elijah's voice died in agony; his head sank on his breast. "Trot." He burst out, "I couldn't he'p it. I gots a piece up de road, and you gemmen knows Trot." His voice died again. "Reckon I done it de other side de road from where Mr. Harl was at."

The room bulged with mirth. Even the judge's mouth moved in a dim, uncomprehending smile. Toy sat taut, eyes fierce against the waves of laughter. They were laughing! Her father lying dead, and because some nigger had to step behind a bush—

Now the unimportant part of the trial was over. People sat up straighter, noses pointed with expectancy.

Rob Tyson got up. "Call as my first witness Rose Crawford."

Rose Crawford wore a dress on the bias with age and her condition, and her black hair was parted crookedly and caught over one eye with a red clip. She walked to the witness chair, trundling her body before her.

Rob Tyson bent toward her. "Now, Mrs. Crawford, don't you worry none. We're all friends here. I'm gonna ask you a couple questions and you answer like it was your daddy asking."

Rose began to nod and stopped. Her eyes were fixed on Abe Greene. The defense attorney had taken out a knife and a bit of wood.

He and Rob Tyson were both noted for tongues that could talk a preacher past Sunday, but there resemblance stopped. Rob Tyson was middle-aged and as fat as his hide could hold. He had a pone on his red neck, collops on his wrists and ankles, and dewlaps past his belt. The fat gave his voice a cave in which to gather resonance, and it emerged to huff and puff witnesses down.

Abe Greene was younger and loose-coupled. He had an enormous nose, black eyes dusted with weariness, and black hair that lay in thickets on his forehead and around his ears. His hands and arms were peculiarly hairless, however, and some folks said that was why he carved in court, to show off his slender white hands. Others swore he did it for a more practical reason. A hostile witness, glancing over to find Abe Greene wood-carving instead of listening, would find his tongue stumbling, disconcerted.

Rob Tyson, following Rose's glance, turned to the judge. "Your honor, will you instruct the defense attorney to give this proceeding the attention it warrants?"

Abe Greene lifted eyes and knife. "I'm listening, Judge," he said mildly.

Judge Whitehead sighed. "Mr. Greene, you will give the proceedings as full attention as you can. Go ahead, Mr. Tyson."

"Mrs. Crawford?"

The jury, arms folded across their chests and jaws shiny from shaves, listened.

The questions seemed aimless, and Toy heard them, puzzled. What had where her father and mother met ("A dance. They was playing 'Sourwood Mountain,' and he told me about this old fisher-coon he'd caught"), and how many children they had had ("Six, not counting this one. Three live, three dead under the willows on the hill. I mind the night little Jacky passed on—"), to do with her father's death?

"Now, Mrs. Crawford, we know all married folks have their little set-tos and you and Harl was no different. What did you all quarrel about mostly?"

"Him helping ever'body and not doing nothing for hisself. 'As ye have done it unto one of the least of these . . .' he was always saying, and he'd not toll a man with a sick wife or sorry young'uns, not even when we didn't have meal enough ourselves. Day he was due to put me in a garden, why, he'd have to visit the sick, or he would be off helping track down some varmint raiding traplines when he was due to grind, or over welcoming new neighbors, taking them a tat of this or that."

The room tightened. The questions were nudging close to the heart of the matter. Rob Tyson paused dramatically before asking his next question.

"He visit the Tripps when they moved in?"

"He sure did. Took them a pup. He said they'd need them a good coon hound, living up on the hill thataway." She added accusingly, "They still got it."

"What did he say when he got home?"

"He said the woman was six of a witch, and the man was half-dozen of a devil. He said she was gonna get in trouble, she didn't watch out!"

All eyes swiveled to Abe Greene. His knife was working delicately. He never looked up. Toy thought, It ain't nat'ral, and suddenly her breath came shallow, from the top of her lungs.

"Why did he say that?"

"He said she cut her eyes at him and Jack Tripp caught her and laid a fist along her jaw. She hit him back; then they really set to!"

Jack Tripp called, "A woman, a dog, and a pecan tree. The more you beat them, the better they be. Only mistake I made was not beating him, but how can you beat a feller brings you a pup?" His voice was righteous.

It was a fine point of etiquette. There were approving nods around the room. Rob Tyson stuck an angry lip out.

"No, you made you another mistake—a kind of permanent one." He went on quickly before the judge could rebuke him, "Now, Mrs. Crawford, what was the last thing Harl said to you that evening before he took off? First, where was he going?"

"He was going over to Tuck Tate's to help him with this sick horse. He'd been promising Tuck to look at it a day-two. I said, 'Now don't you get gone. You know tomorrow's grinding.' And he said, 'Sugar, you know I got six toes on my right foot. The extra one is to carry me home.' I said, 'Never mind your toes. Just look out where you set your heels.' And he said, 'They won't trip, if you know what I mean.' And he laughed and went off and that was the last I seen of him."

Silence lengthened; Rob Tyson let it. He wanted the words to seep into the jury's mind, the play on "trip" and "Tripp" to be absorbed by everyone. Toy saw eyes turn and harden on Jack Tripp, and the dark-faced man sit up abruptly, scowling.

"So your husband as much as said he wasn't going near the Tripps. Why you reckon he changed his mind?" Inwardly he was braced for objection: "The question calls for a supposition on the part of the witness!" Abe Greene continued to work. The wood was shaping up to a rooster.

Rose Crawford cried, " 'Cause she tempted him, that's why. He had to go past her house to get to Tuck's, and likely she come out and waved that black hair at him, tempting him like King David. He was weak, but he hadn't oughta been killed for that. It was her fault, her fault right on!"

Jack Tripp surged up from his seat. Abe Greene moved, though it was hardly a move. His white hand darted out and closed on the big farmer's blue sleeve. His face was languid as ever, but the fingers dug in peremptorily. Toy saw Jack Tripp sink back, lips tight, face ugly. Bess leaned forward and spat words into the lawyer's ear, eyes furious on Rose.

Rob Tyson let another interval pass so everyone might observe the byplay, then asked in hushed tones, "Mrs. Crawford, when you expecting the little one?"

"Day-two. The doctor said as how I shouldn't come here this morning, but I felt I had it to do." Her voice was righteous; she raised a hand from cupping her stomach and brushed back her hair.

"So you going to have four mouths to feed, and no help. Mrs. Crawford, how you been making out since your sole support was taken away, foully done in by the accused?"

Abe Greene said languidly, not looking up, "Object to foul," and rounded the rump of his rooster.

"Objection sustained." Judge Whitehead hauled himself up from watching the flies on the fan. "The attorney for the prosecution will refrain from inflammatory language."

Rob Tyson gazed contentedly at the jury. "I will rephrase the question. How you been making out since Harl—died?"

"I ain't been. I got no help but God, and looks like He's deserted me. I got it all to do myself, scratch up rations for the young'uns, chop and haul and wash, and the condition I'm in—"

The lawyer cut in smoothly, "Thank you, Mrs. Crawford. Your witness, Mr. Greene."

He sat down, satisfied that he had implanted his idea, that a poor husband is better than no husband to a woman with three children; and as she had no meal in her larder, the least the jury could do was grind up Jack Tripp's bones to make her bread.

Abe Greene untangled himself from his chair and slouched over to Rose, who eyed him as a hen would eye a hawk. His opening words were casual enough.

"Mrs. Crawford, I hear you've got a mighty nice garden."

Rose examined the question, then shoved her answer forth grudgingly. "I reckon."

"You've got tomatoes?"

"Yes."

"Mrs. Crawford, what's planted next to the tomatoes?"

Rose cried out, "Now, what kind of fool question is that? Next to my tomatoes? I don't know, and it don't matter. We're here about my poor dead husband that scum yonder killed."

"You don't know what's planted next to the tomatoes," Abe Greene repeated. "All right. Maybe you can tell me something about your mill. For instance, who's carried corn there this summer?"

"I don't remember. Anyways, what do it matter—"

"You don't remember, or you don't know?" The question came so smoothly that it slid past some people without snagging on their attention. Others began to sit up and take notice. Toy felt a premonitory tightening of her stomach muscles.

Abe Greene said languidly, "Well, Mrs. Crawford, how about this? How many quarts of tomatoes did you can last year?"

"None." She was confused. The sheer inconsequence of the questions drew her answers. "I never was much hand to can. I always just swap meal for what I want to the store."

A low murmur broke out at the rear of the courtroom, where

the women were congregated. Heads pressed together, lips
pursed. Only a sorry woman *bought* tomatoes. They had known
Rose Crawford did, but it was different hearing it, worse.

Abe Greene nodded understandingly. "Last question, Mrs.
Crawford. What does Mr. Goforth have next to buttons in his
store?"

Rose answered instantly, "Ribbon, that pretty slick kind."

Talk rose. "No wonder she don't know what grows in the garden. She lets that young'un . . . Same way with the mill. It
would shock her shoe, she set foot in it. . . . Same with Harl.
. . . Yeah, two of a piece. Wouldn't work, neither of them." The
final words came out strongly: "One I'm sorry for is that gal."

Toy felt the eyes. They eroded her. They left her nothing
that was she, herself, Toy. She was a husk nailed to a seat, and
she could not move, she could not run away.

Abe Greene said pleasantly, "That's all, Mrs. Crawford." He
sat down and picked up his wooden rooster.

Rob Tyson got up and drew from Rose that she had helped
can green-tomato pickle the previous month. This admission was
obviated, however, when Rose added righteously, "Toy made
me help. She made out she couldn't do it by herself, but she done
all the beans by herself—"

He said quickly, "Thank you, Mrs. Crawford. Tuck Tate to
the stand."

Tuck Tate was a big, bumbling man in overalls. He was cross-
eyed, and he smelled of his stockyard. The odor was as much a
part of him as the big feet squeezed up under his chair and the
dozen or so dogs that always accompanied him, running.

"Uh-huh, Harl was s'posed to help me with this horse, but he
didn't come. So I went down the road a piece looking for him.
Then I seen him."

Rob Tyson encouraged. "Go on, Tuck, where? Just tell the
court what you saw."

"Well, I seen Harl standing to the Tripps' gate, talking to Mrs.
Tripp."

"Did you hear anything they said?"

"Well, she asked him to help her move this barrel."

"A barrel, eh? Tuck, how big was Harl Crawford?"

A big hand moved and measured a spot halfway down a big chest. "Why, he come up to here."

"A little man," Rob Tyson translated carefully. "Didn't you think it strange that a big, strong woman like Bess Tripp would ask a little man like Harl to help her?"

"Well—I figured she had her reasons." His eyes tried to hide in each other at the snicker that rounded the room.

"What did you do then?"

"Went on home. Give the horse the medicine myself."

"You decided Harl wouldn't show up any more that night?"

The big man nodded his head seriously. "I figured time he got thu with Mrs. Tripp, he wouldn't be in no shape to hold down a horse."

The laughter blew past his ears like wind; it meant nothing to him. The only thing that was important was the lawyer's turning away, Abe Greene's shake of head releasing him from cross-examination and the stand.

Abe Greene uncoiled himself and stood. "I have only one witness."

This was the part of the trial everyone had been awaiting. The only question was, Would Abe Greene put Jack or Bess Tripp on the stand?

Abe Greene said, "Call John and Bess Tripp to the stand."

The flies echoed the hum of astonishment, they buzzed after scraps of food on lap and lip. Judge Whitehead roused from sunflower seeds and somnolence.

"Mr. Greene, you know well and good you can't call two witnesses at once—"

Abe Greene interpolated smoothly, "Your honor, Bess and John Tripp are one witness. They are man and wife, and does not the Bible say, 'A man shall cleave unto his wife and they shall be one flesh'?"

Rob Tyson bounced up, sputtering. "Your honor, you know this is some trick! You know—why, everybody knows—"

A man yelled from the back of the room, "Go on, Judge, let 'em both take the stand."

Abe Greene called, "Thank you, sir, but I made the request not out of frivolity but for a very practical reason. We are here after the truth, and it does not matter how we find it, does it, so long as we find it?" He added casually, "I'm willing to stipulate that my clients answer cross-examination separately."

"Well—" The Judge hesitated, plainly torn with curiosity. "Go on, then." He sucked in a saving lip. "But it is very irregular. I must warn you—"

"Thank you, Judge." Abe Greene turned. "Jack, Bess."

A second chair was brought up. Jack and Bess Tripp were sworn in and sat down. The man wore blue serge pants and a blue work shirt, and the woman a pink cotton dress with puffed sleeves. The clothes suited them no more than civilization.

Abe Greene said, "Now what are your names?"

The man's long upper lip curled back. "Jack Tripp, Bess Tripp. You know that good as me, Abe."

"It's just for the record." Abe Greene was unruffled. "Now, Mrs. Tripp, tell the court your name before you were married."

"Tripp."

There was a stir over the courtroom at the husky word.

"Explain that, please."

"Nothing to explain. We're cousins, come from Oconee County in Carolina up near Tamasee, place called Tripp Nation. Nothing but Tripps there."

"How long have you and Jack known each other?"

"Since we were squawling young'uns laying next to each other to a barn dance. When he yelled, they changed my diapers. That's how close we was."

The tightness in the courtroom loosened; there were snickers. Rob Tyson's lip came out like the spout of a pitcher.

Abe Greene drew a finger down his cheek. "You-all go to school together?" The question was addressed to the man.

"Sure did. The Calhoun Place school two miles from Tripp Nation. We had to cross the branch to git there. Times the water would be so high after the spring rains, we'd have to wait half a day for it to lower. Times we'd wade it and I'd carry Bess, or she'd carry me, one." He grinned.

Someone whispered behind Toy, half admiring. "Bet she could do it, too."

"Jack, tell the court how you got that scar on your neck."

The big man lowered his chin, scowling, but not before Toy caught a glimpse of a long, ragged cicatrix stretching from ear to collarbone.

"That ain't nothing. There was just this old wildcat—" He broke off. Plainly his mind had been prepared for the question, but not his mouth.

"What about the wildcat?"

"Well, we was cutting thu the woods one day, and Bess seen a crow's nest up a sycamore tree. Now nothing wouldn't do but she climb up and git her a baby crow, teach it to talk. She got the fancy from my brother, Rad—he was always catching hisself possums and coons and deer and such and teaching 'em tricks. So she started shinnying up this tree, and directly I heard her squawling. I look up, and by God, here's this mama catamount coming at her, nose down and hell for leather. She'd taken over that crow's nest for her babies—you know how cats do—and she wasn't about to let nobody git near 'em." He broke off.

"Go on."

"Well, I yells to Bess, 'Jump!' and she done so, but the cat jumps too, comes at Bess with teeth hot and tail afire. Bess turns to run, only she stumbles over this root—she always did have feet too big for her shoes—and goes down. Wasn't nothing for me to do but grab that old cat. She gimme this love-pat before I bashed her brains out against a tree."

Abe Greene said, "Jack, how old were you then?"

"Twelve."

It shook even Toy. Then she thought wildly, What's all this got to do—

"Now, Bess, tell us what happened when you got married. When were you married, by the way?"

"Why, we jumped the broom two years come Thanksgiving." She seemed to find this vastly amusing: a great laugh shook her body. She let her teeth sink into her words with the same gusto, Toy imagined, that they would sink into a berry pie. "Now that wedding was a sight, I mean. I reckon every Tripp in the county come, and twicet as many as wasn't. Ma cooked for two weeks ahead, cleaned up for three weeks after."

Rob Tyson broke in. He had surged to his feet, his face plum-colored. "Judge, I must protest. I don't see a reason in the world for this line of questioning—"

Abe Greene interpolated smoothly, "The same reason, Judge, as when my esteemed colleague questioned Mrs. Crawford about her courtship and marriage. I am trying to establish a background, so Mr. Crawford's death—the very tragic event for which my client is on trial—can be understood in its proper light."

Rob Tyson cried, "Proper? What's proper about shooting a man in the back?"

Judge Whitehead slammed his hand down on the desk. "Mr. Tyson, that will be enough of that. You know that remark was entirely improper. Jury will ignore it."

Rob Tyson sat down, trying to look chastened, but with a satisfied little tuck in the corner of his mouth. The jury was staring thoughtfully at Jack Tripp. Now he had shot a man in the back, hadn't he?

Abe Greene gave the other lawyer a long, considering look, then turned back to Bess. "Go on."

Bess was looking sullen, but her words came easily enough. "Well, we had us this wedding, and time we got thu getting hitched—why, half the men was likkered up and the rest was willing. That's what started the fight, a jug and a jealous bone."

"What fight?"

"This one between Jack and the O'Connor boys, all five of them, from Davie, who wasn't but thirteen years old, on up to Dwayne. They're fool Irishmen, and I told Ma and told her not to invite them, but she made out their feelings was gonna be hurt, they didn't get an invite. So I says, 'All right, you can invite them if you want, but I wouldn't risk a huckleberry to a persimmon but we don't see trouble 'fore the evening's out.' So they come, and first thing DeBreen O'Connor says to me is, 'You been sick, Bess, that old rag knotted round your head?' I had me on a white dress, Judge, and a veil come down from my great-granny. I says, 'Not as sick as that sister of yourn is gonna be getting married in a field dress and not but one kind of cake on the table.' And I says to Jack, 'Now I won't git this veil messed up if they kill you.' He says, 'I'll stay 'way from them if they stay 'way from me.' But it wasn't no time he turned up missing. I suspicioned where he was, and run for the oak grove down behind the outhouse. Sure 'nough, there was the fool, drinking corn and trading riddles with them O'Connors. Courting Hell 'fore he got to Heaven."

She paused for breath.

"Dell O'Connor says, 'Four stiff-standers, four down-hangers, two lookers, two crookers, and one dirty switch-about lags along behind.' Jack says, 'Hell, anybody knows that. It's a cow.' DeBreen says, 'Well, what's this? Riddle riddle to my rocket. What a pore man th'ows away, a rich man puts in his pocket.' Jack studies and says, 'It ain't nothing.' 'Yes, it is,' says DeBreen. 'It's snot. What us O'Connors th'ow away and you damn Tripps pick up. You just squatting on a mess of poor man's snot.' And Jack gives a yell and reaches out a fist, but them O'Connors jump him, all five, and drag him down, and Dwayne drags his pants down and gits his knife out."

She paused to reach for breath. Jack Tripp's eyes hid behind his brows and looked at memory.

"I run at them and yells, 'Quit that. Leave him be!' Dwayne looks over his shoulder, grinning, and says, 'Bess, what'll you give me for a whole man?' and I says, 'My dress and veil for that sister of yourn. I'll take them off now.' He says, 'Git 'em off,' and I says, 'Leave me go in there,' and he does. So I goes in the outhouse. Directly I come back, carrying them wadded like, and suddenly I th'ow them at Dwayne and yells, 'Take them!' I'd pure *plastered* them. You oughta seen them scutters jump. Same time I brung round this piece of light wood Pa kept in there to mash wasps and laid it along Dwayne's head. Wasn't nothing for Jack to clean up them other four."

"Now, Bess, tell us about the day Harl Crawford came to see you."

"Mr. Crawford?" Bess looked surprised, then aggrieved. Her round bottom lip poked out. "I swear," she said righteously, "every time I think of the way that little scutter done—and me only trying to be neighborly—"

"Start from the first."

"Well, the way it was, I had me this barrel of meal, and I'd been after Jack and after him to tote it from the porch to the kitchen—I mean, it's a chore going way out there ever' time you want to make you a pan of bread—but he never done it. So I just made up my mind to move it myself, only I had me this hurt arm. Give it a lick with the ax. But directly I seen Mr. Crawford come down the road, so I go out and ask can he help me, and he said he would. But time he come thu the kitchen, here he bangs against the shelf, upturns this pan of syrup all over hisself, me too. I said, 'You can't go nowheres like that; the flies will tow you off. Give 'em here, I'll rench them.' So I sets water on to hot, and time I turns round, he slides an arm round me.

"He says, 'You're a big woman, ain't you?' And I says, 'Let go. You ain't a big man.' He says, 'I'm bigger'n I look. I got a lot of love, and nowheres to put it.' I says, 'You got you a wife.'

And he says, 'I got me something says she's a wife, but she won't prove it.' He says, 'Come on.' But I says, 'No, I'm true-blue.' And right then here comes a whistle, and here comes Jack with a rifle in one hand and three rabbits hanging from his belt."

"Jack, what happened then?"

The big man growled, "What you reckon? I come in the house and here I seen these britches hung from a chair. I jumped for the bedroom. Only the scutter dived thu the window and took off into the woods, Bess's ole skirt flapping round his legs. I th'owed a shot at him, but he kept agoing—"

"You didn't know you hit him?"

"Not till next day. The sheriff come told me."

The lawyer asked a few more things, tucking ends in, then turned to Rob Tyson. "Your witness."

The other jumped up and yelled, "You always do that, shoot first and ask questions later on?"

"I sure do, if a feller's pants is in my parlor and he ain't in them!"

No one laughed. The drama was too intense. Toy no longer had any thoughts or feelings. A vast numbness possessed her.

The lawyer roared, "How many people you reckon would be alive today, everyone done like you?" The Tripps looked at him like baited bears and did not answer. "And how you explain there wasn't a speck of syrup on Harl Crawford's pants when the sheriff found them next day—and don't go making out you washed them! There was sandspurs all over the cuffs."

Abe Greene spoke up, his voice sharpening for the first time. "Objection. It hasn't been established that there were sand—"

Bess Tripp cried, "I washed them all right. I—I reckon I hung 'em to dry over the fence near some sandspurs. That's why—"

The lawyer sneered. "Your wash sure must be a sight. Now isn't it true that two-three times, front of other folks, you invited Harl to come visit you?"

"I was being neighborly—"

The lawyer continued to pound away, trying to make Bess

admit she had "lured" Harl, and Jack Tripp that he had beaten Bess several times for "making up" to other men. He went at them this way and that way like a dog trying to loosen a bear from a rock wall. The Tripps lowered their heads and held on. Sweat smeared them and the lawyer both when he finally resigned. "That's all."

The sun was burning a hole through the western pines, the evening train clattered over a distant trestle, and papers rattled as the lawyers got ready for their summations.

Rob Tyson rose and said Jack Tripp was too dangerous to leave run. Who else would haul off and kill for nothing "poor Harl Crawford, your friend and neighbor lo, these many years"? And the widow, what about her? Were she and her children to cry "Vengeance!" and no one to lend an ear? "Will wolves run free while lambs lie bleeding?"

Abe Greene got up and said would any red-blooded man have acted differently from Jack Tripp? Granted he should have asked questions first and shot later, how could you ask questions of a shirt-tail going out the window? "And all you hunters know that a running animal will draw a shot." If you looked at it one way, Harl Crawford had brought his end on himself.

Rob Tyson retorted that this was a lie.

The judge summed up. He made no effort to interpret the evidence. He dropped facts like lumps in the jury's lap. "If you believe this . . ." he said. "On the other hand, if you believe this . . ."

The jury looked from solid sin to limp virtue. They were out of the room for ten minutes. When they returned, the foreman rose.

"Not guilty."

The woman in front of Toy brushed chicken crumbs from her lap and got up. She said loudly, "Well, they showed some sense."

The man with her said, "Hush," and peeked over his shoulder at Toy, who had gotten up too, though she hardly knew that she had moved. She was an automaton controlled by the touch of Aunt Baptist's fingers on her arm, moving her back into life, into the world.

What was the world? Was it these shifting shadows with the shapes and faces of men and women she had once known and now knew that she had never known? Was it a vast courtroom where a fly's wings and a parrot's fleshy tongue and a man's soul weighed equally on some great, incomprehensible scale?

No, the world was a riddle, a worse one than "Riddle riddle to my rocket."

It was a worse riddle because it had no answer at all.

Seven

THE BABY was born the next morning. Toy was awakened by her mother's moaning. She thought at first that she was still asleep, the moans part of her dreams, nightmares full of vast squeaking bodies that pursued her over sand even as the sand dissolved beneath her feet. She came fully awake.

Annie Goforth was already sitting up on the pallet in the corner, drawing a shawl over her nightdress.

"I heard." She rose and bent over the woman on the bed. Rose Crawford was writhing in her sleep, teeth clenched, leaders rigid on her throat. "I reckoned it would come tonight, the trial and all. That's why I come. Well, best run for Aunt Baptist."

Toy picked up a dress. Dawn drew saw-teeth over her flesh, but she hardly shivered. Later warmth would come with light, but now things had a chill gray anonymity. Edges blurred and ran together, so did thoughts. Dew plopped intermittently on the roof, shaken from the trees by the wind, which went on to goose-hiss down the chimney. The fire stirred and muttered. Far off a rooster tried to rouse the sun, failed, and fell silent.

Toy heard the sounds and gave them names, but it made them no more familiar. Nothing was familiar any more, not the world, not the house, not even herself. Everything appeared to her as though seen through water. Known images were refracted, distorted. Sound was muffled. Words had a shape but not a meaning and hands reached out but could not touch her. She had thought of death and gone to bed drawing her feet up under her. But death was riding paler horses in other yards. So sleep had come at last, but with it came the dreams. The lost and the surrendered chased her, and the Halloween sheet she wore during the day and called Toy Crawford dissolved before these truer ghosts. She cried, and no one came.

Waking brought her from cries she could not utter to cries she would not utter. She put her shoes on, and all her movements were under water, slow and heavy.

Annie Goforth came from the other room, swirling a braid into a bun. "Now, I thought you'd gone."

The words came from someone else. "I'm going."

The world was healing along the horizon. It had been bruised purple-black, but now it was fading to green and orange. Soon it would be light, but night is not so easily cured, no more easily than man's thoughts are cured by man's words. It would come again, and the lost would parade around her bed.

Mist lay over the pasture. Yarrow gave off an aromatic odor under her heels. It mingled with the rank smell of the mule slumbering in her shed. A toad exploded in Toy's path as she slid under the farther bars, a huge wart-house with a missing toe.

It took her ten minutes to reach Aunt Baptist's. She opened the gate and went up on the porch, treading her way between screen frames where roots and berries dried. Her first knock roused no one but the grass finches who slept under the eaves. She knocked again, and footsteps came. A face pressed against the window.

Toy called, "It's me, Toy Crawford. Mother's took."

Aunt Baptist grunted something, and the steps went away. Toy leaned against the wall.

The house was creosoted red, the only house in Gristle painted so. It had been built by a frail man from the coast who thought mountain air filtered through creosote was healthy. A month after he moved in, he was bitten by a fox and died of rabies. The house stayed empty for six months until Aunt Baptist came. She declared, "I been married three times and widowed twice. I ain't afraid of a man living nor dead."

She had moved in, but she stayed out most of the time, yarbing in the hills and granny-wifing. Bay bushes and vetch matted the stake-and-rider fence. The cow's milk was sour spring and fall because of the bitterweed that bloomed unchecked in the pasture. Chinaberry, pine, and sweet gum dropped their trash on roof and yard. Apple of Sodom thrust up prickly leaves and hung orange fruit everywhere between the rows of turnips, yams, and catnip. Sodom berries dried on the screen frames on the porch. There was nothing better for making a woman "come 'round."

There were bundles of cherry bark, a peach basket full of yellowroot split and dried, and—Toy's nostrils pinched—a Mason jar of poison hemlock seed. It had a nasty mouselike smell.

The door opened. Aunt Baptist surged out, split oak basket swinging from a massive arm. "Let's go."

The sun was edging up, and the grass shouldered dew aside to measure its height against the sun. A robin and a locust chanted in a bush. The air had a moist vinegar taste like a sponge held to lips.

Aunt Baptist growled, "When your ma get took?"

Toy panted. "I reckon—maybe an hour-so back."

"Then we gonna be lucky if the young'un ain't already out and walking round the kitchen. Seventh babies come quick, or they don't come at all, one." Her step quickened. "Tessie, Harl around?"

"No'm." Toy took a running tuck in her steps. "They're to Mrs. Goforth's."

Aunt Baptist grunted, then came to a sudden halt on the path, pawing through her basket. She turned over scissors, knives, cord, pads of old sheeting, bottles of senna syrup, and ether, and came up with a cake of soap in her hand. It was big and yellow-harsh with lye.

"Now you can catch a young'un 'thout the rest of this stuff, but you got to have clean hands to do it with."

She went on, and Toy followed; and a moment later they heard the first of the screams.

They came in waves over the warm blue world. They reached a level ululation and broke suddenly, only to start again a few minutes later.

Aunt Baptist panted. "Something's wrong."

Annie Goforth appeared in the door of the house, waving a frantic hand. The big midwife sent her voice booming ahead.

"It come?"

"Trying—"

"Git out the way."

An arm like a flail brushed the slender woman aside. Toy followed Aunt Baptist in, hardly knowing where her feet were taking her. The kitchen held coolness, but the bedroom was full of wrung-out sweat, the air parched with pain. Was that her mother? Toy held to the doorjamb, unable to take her eyes from the flensed flesh. Rose Crawford lay flaccid, her face a swollen purple bruise, her gown ripped and bloody. Her legs, broken-veined and swollen, were tied firmly together at the ankles.

Aunt Baptist slung her basket from her and yelled, "Sweet Jesus on the waves, what you go do that for?"

Mrs. Goforth was wringing her hands. "I swear, I didn't know what to do. The water ain't come, and it was trying to git out the wrong way—"

"A dry birth ain't gonna kill her, but that'll kill her or the baby, one." Aunt Baptist whipped the rag free, spread the legs, and put out a hand. "Head's coming all right," she said grudgingly. "Well, ain't nothing to do but snake it out best we kin." She flung over her shoulder at Toy, "Get me water. Get me my soap."

Toy stumbled out to the pump. The screams had started again, and they tuned her every sense to quivering pitch. She saw the periwinkles massed around the pump, the Bremen chickens stumbling after bugs—Yellow Tom had smashed their toes so they couldn't run off—the dog, Joe, panting under the firethorn. She thought automatically, He ain't had nothing to eat in the longest. Then she saw the feathers and bloody scraps of feet and beak on the ground where Joe had caught and eaten a mockingbird. She grabbed the bucket and hurried back to the kitchen, water slapping her legs.

Aunt Baptist washed, splattering floor and wall, the soap puckering up her skin. She regarded the marks with satisfaction.

"It ain't good soap if it don't grit you. You got anything to eat around?"

"No." Toy was shamed at the admission.

"Well, give me a mouthful of coffee grounds, then. I can work on an empty belly if I have me a mouthful of grounds."

Crunching them powerfully between her teeth, the big woman went back into the bedroom and shut the door.

Toy moved around and began gathering a breakfast together. There wasn't much to do with, and no one could tell when Aunt Baptist might want to eat again—but it would be there when it was wanted. And the making filled her hands.

It could not fill her mind.

Her hands moved from coffee pot to grits kettle while her eyes went through the window to the mill, and her mind followed.

People passed along the road. They came with the backs of their trucks and wagons heaped with corn, and they went with sacks of meal. They came hunched forward over reins or steering wheel, and they returned leaning back fine and loose, the companionship at the mill slackening their minds and muscles.

They went, and scarcely one turned his head to look up the hill to the stone house, and none came and stood in the door and asked, "Can I help?" Joe, the hound, crouched under his bush, shivering at the muffled screams. The birds fluttered from low limbs for ones higher up. Even a stray cat gave pain the privilege of a turned head. Only man went by without a sign.

Her mother gave a single shriek. A cup of grease fell from Toy's hand and broke, lard running off into cracks in the floor. Aunt Baptist shouted, and she ran in. The big midwife thrust something into her hands.

"Take it. It's dead." She bent back over the woman on the bed.

Toy caught one glimpse of the bed—no, not a bed, a bloody field—and then she fled. She went into the kitchen with the damp, towel-wrapped bundle and put it on the table. It lay between a bottle of ketchup and a box of salt. On the box a small girl slanted an umbrella against the rain and grinned.

Toy thought, A shoe box'd do. For the bundle would have to be buried, of course, like a dead bird or cat.

Her hand went out and drew back the cloth. Her eyes prepared to measure. Hand and eye stopped.

It was mostly purple-red torso with matchstick arms and legs sprawled out. It looked like a skinned rabbit, but it had been a little girl—there was the soft female fold between the thighs. The skull was lightly fuzzed in black.

Toy's breath left off.

The face was her father's face.

No, babies don't look like anyone. How can they, casuals of conception? How can they look like anyone, ending the flight to birth, beginning the flight to death? Resemblance was in the eye of the beholder.

The baby looked like Pa.

And it came to Toy like a revelation: it was Pa lying dead,

Pa dead not once, but twice, the first time in a woman's skirt, the second time in a little girl's flesh, Pa dead twice, God's last joke.

Now she knew that God had nothing better to do than play jokes. God used man's tears as a salt for His savor, and He grew fat and happy and played jokes. Man thought God was a dolly he could take to bed to lull him to sleep. God was a dolly, yes, but when you held Him, He did not say, "Ma-Ma"; He said, "Me-Me."

A while later Yellow Tom came and stood in the doorway. He said nothing about the baby—what was there to say?

"Miss Toy, Mr. Watts say you don't toll him none."

She got up. "I'll come."

She went out the door. She stepped over the trash of mocking-bird feathers and crossed the pasture to the mill, Yellow Tom following.

Ammi Watts was standing by the bin, holding a sack under the last of the meal trickling from the stone. He jumped when he saw her and tried to grin, but it kept sliding away.

"Now I told Tom not to bother you. I told him to tell you much-obliged."

"I took much-obliged to the store last week, but they wouldn't give me a thing for it."

"W-what?"

She laid her hand on a sack. "Eight pounds you owe me."

He screamed automatically, "I'm a poor man!" He tried to stretch his mouth into the old cajolery. "Now, honey, you know your daddy never tolled me. He had a heart for poor folk."

She looked at him. Poor folks. Hands full of nothing, mouths of much-obliged.

She said, "My daddy's dead, you remember. I'm running the mill now."

PART
II

One

WHEN Toy was small, the mill had been her favorite play-place. Familiarity had not dimmed its wonder or dulled the song its wheel sang. She would go there and sit on the little landing halfway between floor and loft and hear it go around. The vibrations tickled the soles of her feet and her throat, and little songs would rise.

> The stone goes round,
> The corn falls down,
> Mice run by,
> And so do I.

Other times she slid down the bank west of the mill, clinging to alder and willow, and fitted her back into a hollow place in the turf. She would hang her feet over and let the waters of Mumbling Creek weave her toes and thoughts together. She thought how a mill was a cupboard with low shelves where every little animal could eat. Minnows swarmed around the pond dam, corn grains fell everywhere—some took root and grew, the miller's second toll—and so did Nehi bottles containing a last few trickles of sweetness; raccoons would race dogs for grape soda.

Toy would sit and watch the solemn pacing of a turtle, a mother quail towing a skein of babies into the thickets of Chickasaw plum, and a song would rise in her throat.

> The water is running, running, running;
> The turtle is sunning, sunning, sunning;
> Men are whistling, summer's thistling,
> And I—and I—

The day that she put her hand on Ammi Watts's sack, the songs stopped. The mill shook her feet but never again her fancy. She was a skin stretched around a hollow place. She gave back sound but not music, for music comes from behind the skin, the form that faith and hope and charity put on when they keep company with men.

Ammi Watts drove back to Gristle and told the story of his tolling around Goforth's store. Everyone snickered. They couldn't swallow spit before telling the tale around. "You heard how that Crawford gal done Ammi Watts?" Because the funniest thing in the world is a calf the first time he butts and waits for the milk to come down, and it doesn't.

But when they went to the mill with their own corn and found themselves facing the same hard measure, it was different.

First they tried to pet her with words. "I swear, a pretty gal like you oughtn't be messing around a dirty ole mill. See—you don't even know—your daddy didn't give level measures like that. He give heaping ones."

Her eyes never fell beneath the level of theirs. "He's the only miller done it."

Gum-grease didn't work, so they tried tongue-whip. "Now you listen to me, young'un, you got no more business running a mill than nothing. We gonna get a man—"

"Crawfords built this mill; Crawfords can burn it." For she had thought of that, too, and what she would do in such a case.

So they retired and warmed their hands over "Just wait," but it was short comfort, for Toy ran the mill better than her father had ever done—almost as well as her great-grandfather, that faraway John.

First she climbed up on the high-pitched roof and mended the cedar shingles. They had been shedding like leaves and letting rain in to mold the meal. She put out poison and scourged the rats and mice away. They ran for water and died in the weeds. Finally she got a dime notebook and kept account of who had meal ground and what trade she took for it. For inevitably there were those who could not pay in meal, but could pay in mending fences or making half a dozen willow-withe baskets for the mill or piecing a quilt.

Once, though, it seemed as if "Just wait" had become "Now see." One of the great millstones cracked. One day the roar changed to a moan, and when Toy went to look, she saw the heart of the stone broken from eye to iron band. Her father had set it carelessly off center, not much, not by more than half an inch, but half an inch was bad as a foot.

Near-despair seized her. It looked as if God was loading her back with stones. He wanted to build a prison to hem her in; He wanted to build her tombstone, and He was about to do it. She walked outside and sat down on a bench in the sun. After a while she got up and walked the three miles to Tuck Tate's stockyard.

The big cross-eyed mule-dealer was thrown into womanish confusion at her visit, even more by her request.

"G-Go 'ross the mountain and git you stones from Blankenship's mill? But it's been blowed down, blowed down and forgot five year or more."

"I know, but I heard somewheres that Old Lady Blankenship snaked out the stones and has them setting in her front yard."

"I remember now." The big man shook his head gloomily. "But she won't give 'em up. I hear tell she thinks her old feller entered into them stones. She calls them Jim."

"You hitch up your best team and take me over anyways, and I'll grind you a year free."

They set out before sun-up the next morning, two spans of mules pulling the heaviest oak-bottom wagon the dealer had and snorting breath on the chill air. It was a cold February day, glass skimming the reeds in the wayside ditches, sounds breaking sharply as brittle twigs.

Toy's feet were fire, her hands ice, when they got to Hart, the knot in the highway that called itself a town. Blankenship's mill lay beyond it. Traces of it poked up around the algae-

scummed millpond, bricks and mill gears and rods, frayed belt-
ing and a rusty Nehi sign.

Widow Blankenship lived across the road in a tall old weathered house with scallops of gingerbread on the eaves and iron
briars of climbing roses across the porch. The millstones lay on
either side of the front steps. The widow, a woman as small and
dried out as a peach pit, wore two aprons. She removed the
outer, dirty one before leading Toy down a dim wide hall into a
bed-sitting room. A stove glowing cherry red was the only
point of color or warmth. She listened while Toy stumbled
through the story of the cracked stone, and pursed her lips.

"Your daddy musta been mighty careless, setting a stone off
center. Now any miller worth a pinch of salt knows you got
to set the stone right first thing." She paused. "Why ain't your
daddy or mammy running the mill? What they thinking of,
sending a gal way off here?"

Toy said, "My daddy's dead. My ma's sick."

Sick was a better word than addled. The baby's birth and
death, coming on top of the jury trial, had done something to
Rose Crawford's brain; she had no more sense than last year's
bird nest. She seemed to have half forgotten, or only dimly remembered, the baby, the trial, even her husband's death.

One time she would say, "Now when your daddy comes
home . . ." but another time she would add with a little pleased
smile, "But your daddy ain't around no more for me to ask, is
he?"—and giggle like a child who has been told her dolly is
dead, because she knows it does not really matter if dolls die.

Forgetfulness made her both amenable and stubborn; it depended on how the wind blew. One time tell her, "Shell the peas,"
and she would do it; another time say, "Snap the beans," and she
would say haughtily, "I got other things to do," and roam away
to visit.

She was always visiting. First Gristle considered her half sorry,
half funny, and then after a while a nuisance. When they saw her
coming, people would say, "Here she comes. Bolt the door."

Locks did not bother her; she considered them something turned against other people, not her. She would circle the house, looking for an entrance, and if she found an unlatched screen she would slide in, giggling. If she did not, she would stand pressed against a lighted crack and mew for admittance.

The first two or three months Toy tried to keep track of her mother, but the mill would not let her. There was the grinding, and now there was the cracked stone.

She looked at Mrs. Blankenship and repeated, "Ma's sick."

Mrs. Blankenship's lips closed suddenly. "Crawford—you're *that* Crawford."

Toy felt something tighten in her. She was not going to get the stones, she thought bitterly; He had defeated her again.

The old woman brushed her apron. It was a proud white apron, not used to keeping company with any garment less pure.

" 'Behold, happy is the man whom God correcteth; therefore despise not thou the chastening of the Almighty.' " She fixed her eyes sternly on the girl. "You got to know that—you got to feel that to be saved. Now how you feel about how the Lord done you? You feel He made things hot for you?"

There was a red-letter Bible on a rhododendron-root table. There was a sampler above the oak sideboard: "Sweetly to My God I Cling."

Toy looked at the old Christian and closed her teeth. She said, "No. His will be done."

The old woman nodded, satisfied. "That's right. The Lord has a plan. You don't know it, and I don't know it, but it's written right there in the Lamb's book of life. It's right there in the twenty-first chapter of Revelation, the reward: 'And God shall wipe away all tears from their eyes, and there shall be no more death, neither sorrow, nor crying, neither shall there be any more pain.' "

Was that all of Heaven, Toy wondered—a place of "no mores," no more sorrow, sickness, or sin? A wad of cloud-cotton stuffed between your heel and Hell?

The old woman continued violently, "Now that's why I can't stand Job, questioning the will of the Lord the way he done. The Lord didn't do half enough to him just taking away his camels and his sons and giving him boils like He done; He ought to have struck him dead in his tracks. He questioned the Way of the Lord, and the Truth of the Lord, and the Multitude of the Years of the Lord."

She paused for breath and glared at Toy. Toy held her lips together. Some wisdom whispered to her to keep quiet.

The woman got up and hobbled to the mantelpiece. The stove flared up; the heat drew out the decades of odor ground into the pine boards—greasy greens and spareribs, mold and Negro help. She took down a conch shell and held it up.

"You know what this is? One of my boys brung it to me from Miami. He said it was a shell, but it ain't no shell. You know what this is?" She nodded her head solemnly. "It's the tooth of leviathan. Sometimes I set here and look at it and see him down there squatting on the ocean bed. 'Sharp stones are under him; he spreadeth sharp-pointed things upon the mire. He maketh the deep to boil like a pot.' " She ended practically. "He could swallow you and me in one gulp, he had to—like drawing Jordan into his mouth."

She came back and sat down, eying Toy. She said suddenly, "I never figured to part with them stones."

Toy went stiff with hope.

"My ole feller said they were the best ones he ever cut. They was new when the mill got blowed down, hardly been used."

Toy ventured, "They're furrowed out and dressed good. I seen that."

"Well, he liked him a good stone. Only I do kind of hate to let them go, they're so eye-catchy out there." She paused. "Now them stones is worth a heap of money."

"What'll you take for them—you wanted to sell?"

"What'll you give—and I'm just asking?"

Take did not see eye to eye with Give for fifteen minutes.

Finally they agreed; Toy would pay five dollars cash and five dollars within the next two months.

She went out to Tuck Tate, who was shifting back and forth beside the mules, alternately cuffing them and his hands to keep warm. They got two Negroes, gave them a quarter apiece, and, using logs and poles, levered the stones up onto the wagon. Each was forty-eight inches wide and weighed a ton; Toy held her breath when she and Tuck remounted the seat and the big man snapped the whip. The mules laid their bellies to the ground and "scratched" furiously, moving their feet rapidly and no more than an inch at a time. Slowly the wagon moved.

Tuck panted, turning out of the gate. "Don't know why you wanted all two. Ain't but one stone cracked."

Toy answered, "I got to look ahead."

She wondered what Gristle would say when she returned with two stones.

Gristle said, "She's chinchy and a cheat."

When news of the cracked stone had first got around, relief swept Gristle. Their anger against Toy had been in direct proportion to their guilt; they disliked her because they had done wrong by her. Now it was as if God had condoned their meanness. So relief was succeeded by righteousness. "By God, that'll teach her. Now if she show the right spirit—" If she crawled in the dirt, why, maybe they would help her get another stone.

Their teeth closed on bile when Tuck Tate's wagon rumbled down Main Street. For one stone said, "I don't need you," but two stones said, "Ever."

There was a lot of talk about building another mill, but it never got off the tongue and on the ground. The only thing that got off the tongue was a song to save their faces.

> The Miller called to his daughter Toy,
> "Toy, O Toy, I'm almost dead.
> If to you my will I make,
> Tell me the toll you mean to take."
> She said, "Daddy, you know my call—

> Out of a bushel, I'll take all,
> Take all the grain, sweat on the sack,
> And beat the old farmer if he comes back."

A song about someone is a terrible thing. It gives the singer pretensions above gossip; children remember the words of a song when they don't know the meaning.

The first time Toy heard the song, something rose in her and cried out, "It ain't me you're talking about." The second time she listened, she knew that this was something else added to her portion on this earth.

Two

THE fall when Toy was seventeen, the old mule, Maude, died. She stood motionless for three days with half-drooping ears, then walked over to her shed, lay down, and composed her hoofs.

It was the passing of the last shred of a happier time. Toy felt a latching in her throat. She looked at the shabby old carcass and thought, I bet you hated it, missing winter.

A mule could get fine and fat and woolly during the winter, for there were only scrap-ends of things to do. A mule could eat her corn and consider it a fine joke put over on the world that she was getting something for nothing, and Maude always had. She would roll the grains over her pendulous lips, her eyes squinched in glee. Catching her in the spring had been an enduring pain.

Just the same, her dying now wasn't as bad as if it had happened in the spring. There was only cane-grinding to do and some firewood to be hauled, and Toy could trade for that and any other small chores that came up. In the spring she would buy a fine new mule.

One morning the following March, as she cut across the pasture to the mill, she thought, It just as good be tomorrow. The spring rains had been falling light and early this year; the ground was becoming soft and workable. By the end of the month corn should be planted, and in early April the garden.

She thought, shifting the jar of cold tea she was carrying, A sugar mule, a white sugar mule, not a cotton one.

Cotton mules were small and light and often old, and most of the farmers hereabouts had them, for they were cheaper, cheaper to buy and cheaper to feed. A sugar mule, now, was a big fellow. He ate big, but he pulled big, and he would look big before the wagon. When she drove down Main Street, a white sugar mule trotting smartly in new traces, folks would see that Toy Crawford was taller than her shadow.

A yell arrested her as she started to climb over the fence. Tessie hung on the far pasture bars. "Chinchy—that's all you are!"

It was an argument continued from last night through breakfast this morning.

Toy called back, "Now I'm telling you for the last time, you ain't getting no seventy-five cents."

They needed the money for other things than shirtwaists, and that's what Tessie wanted, a new shirtwaist for the dance next week in Gristle.

She had broached it at supper, but even before the words left her lips, Toy knew something was coming; she had not complained once about how hard it was to cook for a brother who wouldn't eat, a mother who was never around to eat, and a sister who didn't care what she ate.

She burst out, eyes shining, "Toy, they got the prettiest cloth to Goforth's, blue with little white stars on it like—and it don't cost but thirty cents a yard. Seventy-five cents, and I could make me a blouse for the dance, use the other fifteen cents for—"

Toy started to demand, And how you figure we gonna eat, we don't save every cent for a mule? You figure God's gonna send quail from the sea like he done Moses? But she was too tired. She said flatly, "No," tried to retrieve some of the flatness. "You got two-three blouses—"

"They're about to fall to pieces. They're just ole mop rags! I got to have—"

It had gone on like that; it was still going on, and it would go on for the next two weeks, one way or another. Tessie wasn't like those people Isaiah told about whose strength was to sit still, not while she had legs and a tongue.

Toy closed her ears and her thoughts and went to the mill.

Spring had blown the plum thickets into white bloom and unfolded the tight-fisted skunk cabbage by the margin of the pond. The first grist flies had appeared and were quartering the corncobs heaped for burning. Yellow Tom was tapping away in the weeds at his tombstone.

Toy called—it was a ritual greeting—"Now I still say a grindstone is a fool thing to make into a tombstone."

The man rose, one long yellow paw half raised in greeting. "Well, it's good as nothing and better than a heap."

The stone was the cracked one discarded four years ago. Tom had smoothed the furrows with mallet and chisel and incised his name and what he thought was his birth date. The rest was blank.

"You ain't picked a verse yet?"

"Can't find one to fix my mind on."

Four years and a bad sickness had pulled him down, his head into his shoulders, his hands to his knees, and his blue eyes to the Bible. He spent more and more time sitting in the sun and turning through the Book with a big slow thumb, mumbling verses to carve or console.

Toy said, "Save yourself. Put RIP."

"Naw, I ain't gon cheat Jesus. Ise fixing to gives Him something to fill out His eye. It gon be the tale, but it gon be the truth."

"Well, it's your doings."

She went on down the bank of Mumbling Creek and dropped the jar of tea into the water, so it would stay cool. She stood for a few minutes, looking around and listening to the quiet before the business of the day.

Fool ideas niggers got, she thought, a grindstone for a tombstone. Though the way Tom explained it, it sounded reasonable. "Takes you one them wood tablets. Cow nudge it, down it come, and God gots to scratch round in the weeds, He want to raise your bones. Takes you one of them mon'ments. They ain't raised to the dead; they raised to the living, folks making out they the upper crust when they jes crumbs right on."

He had picked the place where he wanted to be buried, on the little bluff beside the mill, overlooking the race. "I don wants to be no setting-stop by the door. Why, the pants of folks' britches'd wear off my name before God seen it Judgment Day."

She climbed back up the bank and said, "I'm fixing to buy the mule tomorrow."

Tom dropped his chisel. "Naw, now. Where you gitting it?"

"Swap Tuesday over to Cardiff. John Goforth's taking me."

Yellow Tom shook his head. "Swap Tuesday. Un-nuh, there's a sight I loves to see."

"Why, come, you want."

"Naw, reckon I best stays here, gits on with this stone." He slanted an eye. "Proud you gitting out, though. 'T'ain't nat'-ral how you is, in a mad-jam all the time—"

"I like how I am."

"You gots mill, you gots money—"

"Thirty dollars." It was buried in a jar under the boiling pot in the yard.

"Uh-huh. What else you gots?" He answered her silence. "Nothing. Why, cat yonder gots more than you." The cat was spring-swollen with young. "Gots—"

She cut in fiercely, "You talking about men, quit. Adam drew

Eve from a rib, and men been trying to keep women under their thumbs ever since—"

"You been listening to Aunt Baptist. Them's Aunt Baptist's words wearing your spit."

She said breathlessly, "You set fire to the cobs. I told you before, the flies is about to tow us away." She hurried into the mill.

It was her refuge more than the farmhouse on the hill, more than the money in the jar. The walls were the adamant coat she put on, the stones were the voice she raised when men plumed themselves on the doorsill with "I, I, I . . . ."

She leaned against the gear that raised the sluicegate. The water boiled down the race, and the cups caught it. She picked up a sack of corn, carried it over to the sheller, and dumped it in. She threw the lever, and a deafening roar arose as gears meshed and iron teeth began to tear the grains from the cobs. The sheller, as well as the stones, was turned by the water wheel. She waited only to see if the pipe which blew the chaff off through a hole in the wall was clear—yesterday a rat had gotten in and fouled it up—before returning to the door.

Grinding was beginning to taper off. Still, there would be plenty of folks on the road today. There had been a good crop last summer, lots of rain to make big plump ears. One Saturday in November she had shucked five hundred bushels, ground seventy-five, and only stopped because Tom got sick.

Unconsciously she flexed her arms, standing in the doorway. They were lean and brown, veins standing out like whipcord. Four years had filled her out, and she walked firmly now, setting her feet down in a straight line. She was straight-lined all over, straight brown hair tucked behind her ears, high cheekbones, straight brows over light green eyes. Her lips were shaped more for truth than for poetry, and she wore a dress of an indeterminate print.

Yellow Tom shaded his eyes toward the road. "Here come somebody."

Lovick Jones's old sedan snorted into sight.

Toy was glad that the postmaster was the first. Not that she gave him any more satisfaction than anyone else, but he was easier to meet than most. First he had tried to be righteous like the rest; then he forgot what he was trying to be righteous about.

"Hi, Toy."

She said politely, "Hi. How you?"

"Never felt better nor had less." He choked a little at his wit, body shaking like a bowl of clabber. "You hear what the President said on the radio day-two ago?" It was a rhetorical question. He knew she had no radio, had indeed only heard one half a dozen times. "He said we gonna have a new deal. He said he was going to put wings on prosperity and call it the blue eagle."

Wick Bloodworth got out after him and said, "Well, he can do it if anyone can."

Flonnie had died last year. She had been buried in December beneath a blanket of holly, and her gravestone read:

> She had Rachel's face, Lydia's kind heart,
> Martha's care with Mary's better part.

Since then women had not let Wick alone. Some came with cooking ("Thought you'd appreciate this, Wick, you doing your own. I mean, no man can't cook the way a woman can") and some came with coquetry ("Wick, can you help me with this trace? I swear, it takes a man to do such things. I'm so weak. See these little ole thin fingers?") and some, widows, came with children "I swear, I don't know what I'd do without these, Wick. It's a terrible thing to be alone." Wick gave the first thanks, the second help, and the children pennies, and that was all.

The thing Toy could not understand was how he could keep on thinking the world was so fine. Flonnie was not his first loss.

One May evening, when he was eight years old, a tornado had bellowed out of the green-streaked, black-bulging west. It took twenty seconds to pass over the Bloodworth farm, but it took the house—only the cellar-hole and a few boards remained—

and Wick's family with it. Later his mother and youngest sister were found, but never his father or other sister.

He had become a kettle-cousin, living around from relative to relative, licking the kettle for his supper. By the time he was fourteen he was doing the work of two hired men and making split-oak baskets to sell, big farmer baskets for measuring grain, and egg and pie and picnic baskets, sewing baskets and clover-seed baskets, and little baskets for women to balance on their hips or across a mule's neck. When he was sixteen he bought himself a piece of land with the basket money. He carpentered, he tinkered with stoves and clocks and when he was twenty-five and had ten acres cleared, and a house built, he married Flonnie Ansley, shiftless, pretty Flonnie, against whom an old woman tried to warn him: "You know what you're getting."

His smile was like the sun. "I know I'm lucky."

When Flonnie died, he had paid dry-eyed and meticulous attention to every detail of her burial, and then vanished, leaving his neighbors to feed and water his livestock. Two weeks later he had returned and said, "The church needs a new roof." He had put one on and been under it every Sunday since.

Toy said blankly, remembering all these things, "You making out, Wick?"

"Fine as frog hair." He hauled out a basket of shelled corn, which he carried into the mill and dumped into the bin. There wasn't every man would do that. Some forgot she was a woman; some remembered she was Toy Crawford. The thought came to her, He's like a mountain oak. They took their shape from the storms they faced, and became strong and enduring. What shape was she? A water ash, light and the limbs writhing away from the elements?

He straightened and smiled. His fair hair was dusted with meal-powder. Streaks of it were down his dungarees where he had passed his palms.

He shouted above the sheller, "I'll bring in the rest."

She followed him to the door and watched while he unloaded

Lovick Jones's corn—she recognized the worn, shapeless baskets—while the postmaster stood in the weeds, funning Tom, who had gone back to his smoothing.

". . . looks like you coulda found a stone wasn't cracked. Crack ain't respectful to the Lord."

"Naw, Lord love a crack."

"How you make that out?"

"Well, my ma use to say, 'I can beats your rear, but I can't crack you; the Lord already done that.' "

The postmaster chortled and waddled back. "I swear, ain't niggers a sight?" He dropped on the bench by the door and wiped his head while Wick Bloodworth carried in the last hamper. "I got to set if I set on my thumb. I mean, it's a chore unloading that corn."

The sheller took on a hollow sound; Toy knew that it had chewed up the last ear. She took a stick and batted the belt loose from the gear, dodging the powerful back-whip. She leaned against the lever which released the stones and heard them begin grinding the grain trickling down from the hopper. She made a mark in her toll book and returned to the door.

Two men had driven up, Old Man Willing and his youngest son, a boy of about fifteen. Both were grist for Lovick Jones's tongue.

". . . ought to come hear John Goforth's radio. Right after the President talked, they played "The Star-Spangled Banner," and by God, you could hear all them people scraping to their feet like they was in the next room."

Old Man Willing wavered around on his blueberry-root cane. "No," he shrilled. "It ain't nat'ral, bowing down to no song like it was God."

"Now you don't bow down to 'The Star-Spangled Banner,' Grandpa. You stand up."

"Same thing. Nobody ought to stand up nor bow down to nothing but the Lord. Anything else is just idol worship!"

"Bet you'd stand up if it was the old Stars and Bars going by."

For Old Man Willing claimed that he was one of the guard who had defended the bridge and courthouse at Elba, Alabama. Folks believed him, too, for he always told how he had shot at six Yankees and missed. They figured that if he was lying, why, he would have at least killed them.

"No, I wouldn't now! I wouldn't stand up for no scrap of cloth nor song. That's why the South oughta won the war. Then 'Dixie' would be the national piece, and 'Dixie' will let a feller set down and eat when it's played."

Lovick Jones collapsed into titters and turned his attention to the son.

"Alvin, how you feel about the radio? Don' you want to grab holt a gal when you hear 'Springtime in the Rockies,' squeeze her some and call it dancing?"

The boy's ears stood out like distress flares. He choked. "Naw."

"Maybe not." The postmaster appeared to let his eye pass over the lanky frame before him. "You're tall enough, God knows—but reckon you just ain't long enough." He guffawed, Old Man Willing cackled, and even Wick Bloodworth smiled gently. It was part of the ritual called "making a man." The boy must suffer it along with pimples and night sweats.

Toy watched absently, her mind back at the farmhouse. Had Tessie given the mattresses an airing as she had told her? Had her mother found the new bottle of paregoric she had hidden on the smoke-shelf of the fireplace? Ma would drink off a bottle in an hour if you let her. Had Harl Junior quit beating the new puppy? The boy had grown up into a thin, serious youth and punished the dog for every fault. He would whip it and weep, "He's got to learn right." Looked like he would grow up to be a preacher or go to the chair, one.

Toy's upper lip flattened. Preachers—she had had a gracious sufficiency of them, in the family or not. She had thought that she had gotten shut of them three years ago. First Brother Ansley called.

He accused, "You ain't been to church lately."

She could not answer.

"Well, I'll be looking for you next week."

She would not answer.

He waited a second and said sharply, "You coming, ain't you?"

She said, "No," and added for his white hairs, "sir."

He was a tall old man with thick-veined hands, shabby clothes, and a weathered skin from circling the hills to bring the Word. Now, staring at her, he drew a Bible from his pocket and began to read.

" 'Asahel the brother of Joab, was one of the thirty; Elhanan the son of Dodo of Bethlehem, Shammah the Harodite, Elika the Harodite, Helez the Paltite, Ira the son of Ikkesh the Tekoite, Abiezer the Anethothite . . .' "

The words rolled out sonorously, the catalogue of King David's mighty men who came to him at Adullam. It did not matter where the Bible fell open; it did not matter what he was reading; it mattered only that he read. For here was the rhythm which is the very wellspring of religion, the surge and roll of drums in every line: "Come . . . behold . . . O ye" —words the very shape of drums and beating against eardrums, pounding out a hollow place in the mind so the Word might enter.

" 'And when they came to Nachon's threshing-floor, Uzzah put forth his hand to the ark of God, and took hold of it; for the oxen shook it. And the anger of the Lord was kindled against Uzzah; and God smote him there for his error; and there he died by the ark of God. . . .' "

The Word of the Lord and the Wrath of the Lord and the eternal Why of the Lord.

Brother Ansley closed the Book and demanded, "You notice what I done? I let the book fall open, and then I read where my eye come on, and them was the Lord's words to you this very minute. He's demanding, 'You putting yourself up higher than David who had mighty armies and feared Me? You figure you can set your will against me like Uzzah done? He knowed he wasn't supposed to touch the ark with nothing but the staves of acacia wood, but he done it, and you see what I done to him, struck him dead. I can do you the same way, I want to.' "

Toy said, "The oxen shook it—"

Brother Ansley thundered, "You speaking with the Devil's tongue now, trying to turn the Bible against me. Well, let me tell you, I can quote Hell out of you every day of the week, so don't you try nothing with me! Down on your knees like the sinner you are and beg God to forgive you! If'n you humble yourself and contrite yourself enough, maybe He'll think on it. Down on your knees!"

Toy had risen and was holding to the table, panting. She could feel her very body shake. Brother Ansley had dropped heavily to his knees, still talking, his eyes fixed off somewhere in ecstasy. "And when we get through, I'll pick up your Bible and do like I done just now, let it come open, and them's gonna be the Words—"

Harl Junior skittered into the room from outdoors and slid to a halt, gawking.

Brother Ansley shouted, "Boy, go get the Good Book. I'm gonna give you precious gifts!"

The child darted across the room and dragged a book from a shelf. He hurried back, pale and anticipatory, and begged breathlessly, "Mister, bring me a jack-the-box?" He held out the Sears-Roebuck catalogue.

It did not defeat Brother Ansley—nothing of this world could —but it broke the rhythm. He lashed out at Toy and the child, calling down fearful things on them for the sacrilege; and he prayed. But Toy stood like stone—hating him for the terror on the little boy's face—and Jehovah's sword turned against the stone.

He came back several times, but each time she met him on the porch. She stood on the top step and listened to him on the bottom. Hell-fire paled in the sunshine and on the bottom step. Eventually he ceased to come.

Brother Ansley had died six months later—enrolled with the immortals, Preacher Douglas said—and right afterward Preacher Douglas, who liked to be called Mr. Douglas, appeared at her well.

"Now I didn't stop by to preach, just to get a drink. I declare, my mouth is like cotton."

He talked like that, easy and smiling, and he was an easy, smiling young man, more brotherly than Brother-like. He did not scream like Billy Ansley or Billy Sunday or Billy-Be-Damned, though he could start the Hell-fires roaring when he wanted to.

Toy answered warily, "It's hot for October right enough."

He tipped the dipper back and drank. He set it down and stooped to slap his knees. They were caked with red clay, drying and dusty, and his old Ford was slick with it to the running board.

"Helped Brother Tate shoe a mule. I don't figure a preacher is put in this world to talk. He's put in to help out when need be. Jesus never minded raising his hand to turn a chair leg or catch a fish, and I reckon I'm no better than he was." He laughed a little.

Toy said uneasily, "Well, you can have all the water you want. Now you'll excuse me—"

He held out a hand. "Now don't rush off in the heat of the day. My old granddaddy used to say that the Devil likes idle hands, but I swear, I believe he likes busy ones better. Folks get so busy they can't think about Him, and you know, you want to or not, you got to think about Him. *He's* there."

Toy stood quite still and waited.

"Now I wasn't fibbing when I said I stopped by for water, not for preaching—I sure needed that water—but— Why don't we sit down on your porch?"

Toy said coldly, "I'm sorry. I got folks waiting."

"Now I come at a bad time. I can see that. But I sure would like to talk with you. Maybe some evening. Maybe tomorrow evening—"

"No use your talking to me."

"I want to, and I got to. I can't rest easy, knowing you're lost from the fold—"

"I ain't lost from the fold. The fold is lost from me."

"Now I heard about your troubles, but don't set yourself on the judgment seat. Only God belongs there. Don't judge others before you judge yourself."

"I judge myself."

"No, you don't, because no man can judge himself and find his brother guilty. Do you think you're different from anyone else, your troubles special? No, you're forked same as Job and Joseph and Jim-Next-Door."

"I'm forked the same, so I can walk different if I want," she said.

He said sternly, "You're forked the same, so you can walk one way, God's."

"If God's way is the way that flock of yours is walking," she told him, "why, I'll take my chances in the rocks." She had walked away and left him, her shadow leading the way.

Lovick Jones complained, "Toy—I swear, Toy, I've spoke to you two-three times. I said, you ought to keep cold drinks here to the mill."

"Too much trouble."

"Now it wouldn't be neither. The Nehi folks would give you a cooler, keep it filled. All you'd have to do is get the ice—"

But she shook her head and moved away. It was an old argument, renewed every time the thermometer got past seventy. Not even the thought of the cash-money she could make changed Toy's mind about installing a cooler; a cooler was like saying that she had changed, even in a small way, and she would not let people think she had changed anything but her inches.

She sacked up Wick Bloodworth's meal, her hands moving quickly. It was hot through the cloth of the sack. She took her toll and moved to dump the last of Wick Bloodworth's corn into the hopper. She coughed, clearing the dust from her throat, and brushed an arm across her wet forehead.

Alvin's voice came in a deep, unexpected growl. "Truck coming. Got dogs." He turned fiery red at his temerity.

Everyone turned to watch with interest. Now a man might bring one or two dogs to the mill, casually, showing them off, or for trading purposes, or just because a dog naturally clung to a man's heel, but half a dozen dogs meant something more than tarry or trade.

The truck stopped, and four men swung down long legs. They were carrying guns and smoking cigars. Toy wondered where they got the money for cigars. Neither the Frazee boys nor Tim Martin had a nickel to cheat charity.

Lovick Jones threw up a palm. "Hi, boys. Set down." He was bursting with curiosity, but courtesy dictated that the first revelation come from them.

"Ain't got time. We're helping the sheriff."

"Why for?"

"He's looking for a killer, that's why for." They threw out their chests to give importance more place to light.

Lovick Jones yelped in pleasurable fear. "Killer—Lord God, who's been killed and who's killing?"

"Some of them tramp scutters. Way it happened was over to Happy Valley t'other evening. Tracy Turner heard a noise in his chicken yard and flung a shot. Someone yelled and run off, and Tracy started after him. Only he tripped over a root, and the old gun went off and pure blew Tracy's chest apart."

Wick Bloodworth's pleasant face shaded. "Turner had a wife and three young'uns. We'll have to do something for them."

Old Man Willing squealed, "How that make anyone a killer? He shot hisself."

"Wouldn't have if he hadn't been protecting his property."

Jim Frazee growled, "We got to gang up and drive these scum from the hills. It's gitting so ain't nothing safe, mules nor chickens nor women. We got to hunt 'em down."

Tim Martin declared, "It's them Russians' fault. They got folks all dissatisfied."

Bob Frazee said scornfully, "You don't know nothing about nothing. It's this depression. It's drawing them Yankees down here, 'cause they ain't got the guts to stay where they are." He thought. "They never had the guts."

Depression. It had become a familiar word in four years. It had touched Plum Gap in small ways, but in deep ways.

There was the Mimosa Hotel's bread pan. It stood by the kitchen door, a long iron pan which the cook heaped three times daily with the leftovers from the dining room, half-eaten biscuits, spareribs, pieces of baked potato, anything but the slops saved for the hogs. Those who wanted food, tramps or Negroes, could lift the cheesecloth which kept out the flies and help themselves. In 1931 Clay Murphree complained that there was more business at his kitchen door than in his dining room. In 1932 the bread pan vanished.

There were the road-walkers. Plum Valley had seen road-walkers before, mostly its own people who had gone off to work in other places, Negroes who had gone to Savannah or Brunswick to roll the resin on the wharves, and now returned home, heel back and walking.

They said, "Man, I sho is glad to git back. Dem city folks doan know how to treat a feller. Walk like dey got crowns in de seat of dey britches, and so mean-hearted."

They said this to farm kin whom they had left five or ten years ago, scoffing at them for "handkerchief-head niggers" and "kissingfoots." They had spread around big talk about the times they would have in the cities, Diddy-Wah-Diddy with dime stores instead of pearly gates.

Now they returned to shacks of tar paper and scantlings in the middle of cotton fields or behind "big houses," vowing love and saying cities were hard. "Nigger in de city live on de south side de house, draws all de heat." But most of them yearned to go back. Cities suited their sociability.

There were whites, too, who had gone from the valley to the cotton towns. They had worked in the mills as spindle doffers and perchers, draw-in hands and slasher tenders. Suddenly they found their wages cut to near-nothing or the mill gates chained against them. They returned, bitterly talking of "family rings" and "the stretch-out."

They said, "Chandlers owned the mill where I worked to, four-five of them. One was this J. Andrew, Junior, didn't do nothing but play golf and set on his toadstool, but they paid him twenty-five thousand a year. Then there was this old maid, Lucy, they couldn't marry off. 'Efficiency expert,' they called her, but the onliest time you seen her was her car tracks on the road going past. They give her twenty thousand a year, and the only finger she lifted was her elbow. 'Twasn't banana extract she drunk, like you and me; 'twas champagne. You know what they was giving me to the end? Three to eight dollars for a week's work—if I got it."

They said, "They laid off half the floor and made you take care two-three more machines than you belonged to. A bastard was all the time standing over you with a stop-watch whilst you went to the toilet, and they painted the corners white, so's you was ashamed to chew or spit—might slow you down. Then," they burst out in the final grievance, "if you done something they didn't like, why, they cussed you out in front of everybody just like you was a damn nigger!"

These new walkers were a different breed from Gristle's people, or the occasional tramp or gypsy. The tramps and gypsies were an accepted part of the valley, for often they gave as much as they got, a funny or exciting tale in exchange for a heel of bread and ham to go on it, a fortune read in a palm, or a fine bird-dog in exchange for an old blanket and no questions asked.

The new walkers, men and women both—and it was a shocking thing to Gristle that women were walking the road; gypsy women, of course, did not count; they were "foreigners"—were sullen and defensive. They did not ask for food; they demanded it and barely thanked you when they got it. And if you did not give them something, often they stole. The gypsies and tramps had stolen too, but it was a game with them, it was expected. These people stole awkwardly and angrily, and when they were caught they made you feel guilty. Now how was that?

Toy knew about the depression, because of the people returning to Gristle with tales of jobs lost and mills closed. She knew because of the strange new phrases the men around the mill used, like Legge's Farm Board, Hoovervilles, CCC, RFC, and relief.

She knew all this, but when she saw the silent, sullen walkers on the road, she thought, City folks. No more guts than a goose. And she got a fierce satisfaction that the alien mighty had fallen.

The men in the truck were getting ready to leave. Cigars were down to nubs. The dogs were restless; they leaned their flews into the breeze, snuffling.

Ben Frazee paused with his foot on the running board. "Toy, what you do if one of them road-runners give you trouble?"

She said, "Why, kill him."

Three

I T WAS three years since she had been in Cardiff, and the clay road was worse. Rounding the last curve before town, Toy braced her feet against the floor of the truck, but not because of the road.

She thought, People. People and no mill to stand behind her. She wanted to vomit again. She had vomited twice before leaving home, going away behind bushes so that no one could see her; and now the familiar bile surged up. She clenched her teeth against it.

John Goforth said cheerfully, straightening from the wheel of the truck, "Well, there it is."

Cardiff came into view around the curve, a scattering of houses and buildings under oaks and dogwood and sourgum. It was tethered to the world by two electric lines running above the road, singing and shining in the light. The singing was audible, a high-pitched hum as the wind brushed the wires. Swallows, clinging in rows, were ecstatic. Two fluttered from line to pole. The next moment one tumbled dead to the base, electrocuted by this new and wonderful twig.

Toy averted her eyes and asked, "Swapping won't take long, will it?"

"Take as long as it has to."

He had a truckful of things to trade, and for the life of her Toy did not know who would want the head of an old brass bed or five yards of roach-chewed percale. But John Goforth said that on Swap Tuesday in Cardiff you could find a fool for anything.

The town was a rectangle of stores two blocks deep around the courthouse square. The stores facing the courthouse were roofed by a long continuous marquee supported by gas-pipe stanchions set in the cement curb, useful for children to grip one-handed and swing around and around until they were dizzy.

Today no one swung. No one was on the streets but an old cat salving its breast in the doorway, and a Negro wearing a flowered apron and carrying a tray of Cokes. A few merchants stood behind show-windows, but for the most part Cardiff looked as if someone had taken it by the heels and shaken it loose of people.

Tessie cried from the back, voice shrill with disappointment, "But I don't see nobody!"

John Goforth grinned over his shoulder. "Listen. You hear?"

Toy heard a muted sound from beyond the trees bordering the town, out where the quail thickets began. It was made up of dogs howling, livestock carrying on, and trucks and wagons clattering around. Mostly it was voices, women and children shouting and laughing, men swapping anything that could be laid down, except their wives.

Toy gripped the roll of bills pinned to the pocket of her dress. In the back of the truck, Harl Junior's pup howled.

John Goforth had said, coming to pick her up and seeing her empty hands, "Now money's all right; times you got to give it to boot. But Swap Tuesday you got to have something to *swap*."

The pup had crawled out from under the house, a brown and white pied hound, stretching its gawky legs and clicking its jaws in a yawn.

Dolly cried from the truck, "You got you a new dog."

She said, "And wouldn't mind getting shut of it."

Harl Junior had yelled, "No, he's mine!"

"First I heard it."

Ammi Watts had pressed it on her in return for grinding, swearing it was a good rabbit dog. "See the way the hair sort of lays against the grain along his spine?"

The boy cried, "No, you can't have him!" His skin, which never tanned even in the hottest summer, was pinched-looking around his mouth. He jumped for the dog.

Tessie was quicker. She snatched it up and cried, "Lemme go, Toy?"

It was plea and threat both. Toy had told her that she could not go with them. Now she held the pup away from her brother's grasp, twisting and turning, but ready to let it go any minute. Her hair was a burning bush, her eyes reckless of consequences.

"Lemme go, Toy!"

John Goforth chuckled. "She's got you, Toy. Just as good let her come."

Cardiff ahead, the pup yelped again.

Dolly called, "I hear swapping! Wish we were there this very minute."

Tessie cried, "Toy, let's stay all day?"

"No, we going when Mr. John finishes."

John Goforth said easily, "Aw now, Toy, ain't no harm letting the young'uns enjoy theirselves some. Why"—he twinkled a little —"you might too, you let loose."

"I don't want nothing but to get my mule and get gone."

She did not owe him anything, neither time nor money. She had paid him in meal for the trip. He had not wanted to take it, but she made him.

The truck turned east and rattled past a block of frowzy Negro stores. A butcher-shop window held trays of pig ears and tails; a dry-goods store showed a dress of "nigger pink." They crossed railroad tracks and cut around a cotton gin, a vast corrugated-iron shed. Mule Lot was across the road from it.

Toy thought, I can't do it, no.

There were hundreds of people, men with overalls that had been through the briars hunting, women with crimped hair dusted with gray—sure sign that they had used flaxseed slime to "set" it—and old people spreading their brittle bones in the sun. There were young'uns playing Fox-and-Goose and Stiff-Starch, entertainers who would pick a piece for you on their guitars—any piece you named—for a nickel, and trucks and wagons parked every which-way on the dish-shaped lot, people and all the things they had come to swap.

Horses and mules, of course, tethered to every tree and bumper; dogs enough to make a panther pack its fur and move off; plows and traces; homemade hickory chairs and quilts and clay jugs; firkins of butter to make the biscuits fly, and jam and jelly; eggs and old clothes, knives and guns, kerosene lanterns with bull's-eye globes, and one-wheeled walking planters; settings of "guaranteed" tomato plants and Never Fail scuppernong grapevines, a roll of used chicken wire, a cup and saucer gilded inside, boxes of doodads and jinglebobs.

Things to swap and things to eat, parched corn and warm boiled peanuts, hot dogs and homemade candy, fried chicken and fish, Nehis and coffee strong enough to float a wedge edgewise.

John Goforth parked at the far end of the lot. The near places had been taken at dawn.

Dolly tumbled off, shrieking, "I'm gonna get me some of that candy."

Toy watched her and Tessie start off and thought, What's it like to be like them? What was it like to be a woman who had nothing to do but live around her skin?

She called, "Tessie."

The red-haired girl halted reluctantly. She wore a faded blue dress that had belonged to her mother. Some trick of shade made her face like Rose Crawford's, a Rose young and untouched.

Toy said, "You—you better take this." She held out a dollar.

Tessie took it almost tentatively, face blank, and then she exploded with joy. She went racing after Dolly, shouting, "Wait, wait!"

John Goforth, hauling the bed head out of the truck, said, panting, "Glad you done that."

Toy said nothing; she was already angry at herself. She reached for the liver-and-white pup roughly. It came, limp and without hope, tail curled tightly around a leg.

John Goforth said cheerfully, "Now you watch out swapping. You know, that's how come the Twelve Apostles only had twenty-three eyeballs, Swap Tuesday."

He moved off, raising a hand in greeting to someone. Toy followed hesitantly, the pup a shield across her breast. It was panting heavily, though the morning was cool; its eyes were wet with fright. She thought, You and me both.

No one bothered her. People brushed against her elbows; some looked at her, their mouths ready with a smile or a word, but her face stopped them.

People went on. A brief rain came up, a wetter not a soaker. It only increased the laughter and excitement. When it was over, the sun shone brighter, the leaves of the trees at the far end of the lot had a new patina, dust washed away. Dogs shook themselves; mules and horses steamed sulphur.

They were at the far end of the lot under the branching trees, most of them, and Toy walked faster. Her eyes, fixed on them, left her ears open.

". . . told my young'un he could help birth the calf, he didn't ask no question. Well, he done so, eyes getting bigger and bigger. At the end he busts out, 'Daddy, I just got to ask you one question.' I says, 'All right, one.' And he says, 'Daddy, how fast was that calf running?' "

". . . this little old dog's got a mouth like a bell."

"Yeah? More like a clapper, way I hear it."

". . . fish popping anything hits the water. I got me some strips of rubber from the recap place, and Lord, if them bass didn't hit them for eels."

". . . a meat-gun for sure. Point it at a squirrel and tell the old woman to get the frying pan ready."

There were strings of horses and mules tied in "the boneyard," a few ponies thrown in. The mules had a certain smugness of expression. One white Joe-mule had his teeth laid over the neck of a little roan horse.

A gangling youth on a brown mule called, "You wanting a mule?" Both his legs hung over one side of the mule; an old cigar-box guitar was laid over his knees. "How about Wreck here?"

Toy asked, despite herself, "Why you call her Wreck?"

"Well," he drawled, "that's what she is, ain't she? An accident."

It was evidently an old sally; men around laughed.

One called to her, "Joe-Jim don't want to swap the mule. He just brings it so's he can meet pretty gals." He faltered, cleared his throat, and said loudly, "Joe-Jim, grab that eucalyptus of yourn and give the lady a song."

The boy said briefly, "It's broke." Her question had ended her usefulness to him. Already his gaze was over her shoulder, looking for another girl.

Toy walked on. A minute later she stopped and let the pup down. She tied her belt around its neck and went on.

Dolly and Tessie ran up. Each wore a string of borax beads, multicolored as linoleum.

Dolly shouted, "Pa sold that old piecy bed. Feller bought it for a pasture gate. Pa got us these."

They had gotten rouge somewhere and painted feverish flushes on their cheeks. There was chocolate around Tessie's mouth.

"Feller bought me candy. I still got my dollar." They ran off again.

A rotund man with a city hat but shoes colored by the country roads was selling Pink's Preventative. He cried, "It builds your blood." It was made of creek water, blackberry root, and the ground-up membranes of chicken gizzards.

Peepers chirped in the trees, gladdened by the rain, and were gulped by crows. A dog raged at a pet coon chained to a branch of a tree; the coon sat on its hind legs and looked down like a surprised child. A gigantic Negro strode by dangling flapping chickens. Women folded their arms and told how many fingers of dill to put in a gallon of green-tomato pickle. Men squatted on their heels and flipped knives and talked swap and politics, swap and crops, swap and mules. They talked about Mule Pete who lived down in Greene County.

"You hear about when Mule Pete was riding to Penfield, ready for a high-heeled good time? The mule he was riding stopped in the middle of the road and tried to scratch his side with his hind leg, knocked Pete's foot out of the stirrup, got its own foot caught in it. 'Now looka here, mule,' says Mule Pete, 'if you gon ride, I gon get off and walk.' "

Knives flipped faster. One slipped and fell on the ground. A man said, "Asa, if you'd been holding your tongue right, why, that knife wouldn't have slipped." He picked it up. "Now that sure is a hell of a knife, so dull my youngest boy could ride it to the mill and never scratch his britches. Still and all, I might take it off your hands, seeing we're friends."

The first man retrieved the knife and made as though to snap it shut. "Uh-huh, I seen what you got to swap. That knife of yourn ain't got a blade, just an excuse."

John Goforth staggered past with a load of copper worms from a moonshine still.

Someone yelled, "Hey, John, you gonna get Cyclone Mary after you." Everyone snickered at the reference to Mary Armour, Georgia's Carry Nation.

The storekeeper called, "Well, she can quarrel with the sheriff. That's who I got them from." The boiler and the rest of the set-up were on the truck. He loaded the worms and turned to Toy. "Found you a mule yet?" She shook her head.

"Well, a feller just brought in a white mule yonder."

She went, tugging the pup after her. It had regained a foolish confidence and barked at a blue-ticked hound. The hound turned its head, and the pup ducked between Toy's legs.

A man chanted, "Give boot, take boot. I'll swap, sell, or buy. Prettiest mule I put in my eye. I reckon I might take the cow, but she better have a calf to go with her. If you got no calf, why, money'll do."

Toy was just in time to see the halter of the white mule change hands, a dealer handing it over to a tall young farmer.

The mule was pale gray with white tail and mane. It stood some fifteen and a half hands high; its eyes were extra wide-set and full, its ears straight and pricked forward.

Toy wanted it. She wanted it so badly that the weakness of death went over her. She hated the young farmer who laid a hand on its neck.

He was dirt-dog poor; his knee patches had patches. He wasn't more than twenty-three, the girl with him a few years younger, and the child he lifted to the mule's back perhaps five years old.

"How you like him, sugarpie? How you like our pretty new mule?"

The child had two little skinny black braids and wore a too-small dress. She wailed. "I can't see my foots."

"Why, honey, they up there with you." He turned to his wife apologetically. "I reckon I oughtn't to have held out for a white mule. We could have got one of them others cheaper. Only—I had to have it."

The girl's eyes were tender. "I'm proud you got it, Joe. You ain't had nothing in the longest. And you treat me and the young'un so good."

He smiled. "Well, I figured if I got to look at a mule's tail the rest of my born days, I want it white."

Toy walked away, jerking the pup along. There was more than disappointment choking her; everything choked her. Everywhere she looked people pleasured themselves. They got what they wanted, and they wanted what they got. Suddenly, for no good reason, she began to notice the young bucks and the girls. The girls switched by, tongues going like clatterbones, never seeing the boys, of course; and the boys, gathered in groups, sniggered and called boldly after them.

They never paired off—or only the boldest did—but they looked, and they marked, and a few days or a few weeks later a girl would go by a boy's house on some errand, or a boy would drift by a girl's front porch, rifle under arm. Now they only looked at one another, sheeps' eyes in lambs' heads.

Toy noticed one boy and did not know why. He was small and dark and skinny, but there was something about him that was lacking in the others, the bite of barbed wire or bamboo vines. The boys surrounding him deferred to him. It was "Bud this" and "Bud that" and "Bud, what you think?" Girls, passing, threw him three glances when two would have done.

Toy walked by scornfully. Why, he didn't look like he could hold out to plow a rod, much less plant an acre, and preening himself so. His eyes came round and caught the flint in hers. A spark jumped. He was a man who loved a No, and the world was so full of Yeses.

He called, "What'll you swap for the pup, tall gal?"

She did not reply.

He called after her, "Now I sure like a woman walks high-heeled no matter what she's got on her feet."

Her mind derided the remark but could not forget it. She began noticing how other girls walked, some splatter-footed as ducks, others nervous-kneed as grasshoppers, a few casting their hips around. Toy saw her shadow. It set down its feet crisply, and left tracks without little scuffles at the heel.

The second time she passed him, he came a step or two forward and spoke softly.

"Tall gal, I never seen you to Swap Tuesday before. Where you from?"

Her tongue answered over her inclination. "Gristle."

"I'm coming over there some day soon. You be around."

It was a command and a promise. Then a boy called, "Hey, Bud," and Toy hurried on, furious that she had answered. "Gristle" was one word, but one word too many.

She thought, What got into you anyways? Joking is all it was.

Half a dozen children played Squat Tag around a wagon. One squatted and bit her nails. Another yelled, "You better quit that. Your ma'll sop 'em in bitter-berry." The squatting one retorted, "I can if I want, but I won't." She paused and sought a hit-back. "My ma says your uncle ain't got nothing in his pockets but his hands." The other retorted, "My uncle's got more money than God, Jesus, and witches."

A man scraped his fiddle and raised a song full of two-for-a-penny rhymes: "I'm so blue, 'cause you ain't true . . ."

John Goforth, passing by, tossed a dime in the hat beside him. "Now, I figured you'd have you a mule."

The pup was sprawled on the ground, scratching behind an ear with a hind foot. Toy wished she was shut of it; it was a pain dragging it around.

She said, "Reckon I'll tie him to the truck."

The storekeeper let down the tailgate so she could hoist the dog in.

"You see the white mule I told you about?"

"Another feller got him. You—you got much more to swap?"

"One-two things. If you're in a hurry—"

"I ain't in no hurry."

She walked on, and now she noticed people as faces, not as bodies. One or two smiled at her and nodded, and she nodded back stiffly. She looked over the mules with an eye that didn't hold out for white, and marked several that might do.

She felt thirsty. There were coffee pots on half a dozen fires, soft drinks in half a dozen washtubs of ice. Some venders had brought benches or hand-cut branch chairs for their customers, and people sat eating and drinking and gossiping until they had to drink more.

She found a bench and bought a bottle of Nehi from a small boy and girl. They were preternaturally grave, the little girl packing the sawdust back around the ice to keep it from melting too fast, the little boy carefully stowing the nickel away in a tobacco sack.

Toy offered awkwardly, "Got you a heap of money there."

The boy looked up opaquely. "Yes'm."

The girl burst out, "We got us three-seventy. We gonna get us—"

The boy said warningly, "Lissie." The girl cupped both hands over her nose and mouth, eyes horrified.

The boy told Toy gravely, "I told Lissie and told her, 'We in business. We got to keep 'rangements in our own hands.'" It was both explanation and apology.

Toy nodded. "That's how I do."

She found a piece of ice stuck to the bottle and pulled it off and sucked it. When she was a young'un, she'd been crazy for ice chips. She and Dolly used to tease Elijah Clarke Johnson for pieces, and the one who got the "milk" piece was smug for the rest of the day. Milk ice meant early marriage. She had gotten a heap of milk ice.

I'm coming over there some day soon. You be around. When Bud had talked, others listened, and when he listened, others' words took on a shine because he lent them his attention. He was five feet five, but her hope drew him to fit her desires.

A fat middle-aged woman came up, shepherding an old man. He was lath-thin, suspenders hoisting his pants to his armpits. He was saying in monotonous tones, "I want me a grape soda, Mary, I want me a grape soda." His eyes were blue and vacant.

The woman said wearily, "I'll git you grape soda, Pa. Now you just set down here."

"I want me a grape soda."

The woman bought one and gave it to him. She got one for herself and sank down tiredly beyond him. Toy set her eyes to the front, uneasy, wishing they had not picked this bench. She sipped the Nehi, and then felt something on her arm. She looked down. It was the old man's hand.

It was cold and raspy like grasshoppers' legs. The nails were horny and veins and tendons left no room for flesh. His eyes, oddly dehumanized, met hers. Before she could move, the woman leaned past his shoulder and spoke.

"Leave him, honey. He won't hurt you none. You know, small minds is pleased by small things, and fools by less."

Toy sat taut. She saw, as though for the first time, the brownness of her skin, the sun glinting on the light hairs, the prickle of sweat in her elbow. The old man dropped his hand. His expression had not changed, but something around his mouth had plumped out.

The woman whispered, "See? He don't mean no harm, but he do love young flesh. Only time he fills up in the face is when he gets to touch it."

Toy ventured, "He always been so?"

"No, honey, no. Why, ten-fifteen years ago he was just as sensible as you and me. Then Ma died, and seemed like he didn't care none to live." She shook her head, an old wonder returning. "Thing was, him and Ma pure despised each other." She paused. "You don't watch him, he all the time tries to swallow lightning bugs."

Children said, "Swallow a lightning bug, you die." Toy gulped the rest of her Nehi and got up. As she started off, the woman added, "Swallowed eight already, and he ain't dead." Her voice was querulous.

It was eleven o'clock. Dolly swung by, elbows linked with another girl, six Nehi caps stuck on her blouse.

She laughed at Toy. "I swear, them boys. Think 'cause they buy you a nickel drink—"

Toy interrupted, "You seen Tessie?"

"Not for the longest." She giggled. "Guess she's got her ten caps."

A few feet beyond, a man was trying to back a mule into a space between two wagons. The mule was resisting, stiff-legged and rigid-necked.

"Now c'm on, Bud," the man begged. "Get that kink out your legs. Come on, Bud."

The mule was smaller than the white one, a cherry-red bay with shapely legs and extra full eyes. Right now the eyes held a monumental indifference. The man at the bridle might have been a fly.

Toy asked, "You swapping that mule?"

The man stopped tugging. "Might." He was fleshy, with a sugar-bowl haircut and teeth like a child's or an ear of corn, small and all of a size. "Got something to swap?"

"Got a good squirrel dog. Got some boot money."

"Well, I love to have something in my pocket, and I love to have something in my hand."

"The pup is yonder. I'll fetch him." She turned away, turned back. "That his name, Bud?"

"Why," he said amiably, "Bud, Red, Muley. Call him what you want."

She hurried off. Four little Negro boys played mouth organs and cakewalked for pennies, and the song they sang was "Uncle Bud": "He were a man in full, back as strong as a Jersey bull . . ."

She untied the pup from the truck, and it came, wriggling with excitement, nose going everywhere.

Halfway back she saw the white mule. The young farmer was showing it off, and now Toy saw him clearly, a sandtrap farm and gullied fields, chicken-foot soup on Monday nights, and the mule shed a heap of brush piled over two low-hanging branches.

He looked up and smiled at her.

She called suddenly, "White."

He laid a hand on the mule's flank. "White."

Red was brighter. The cherry bay mule's hide shone as though it had rolled in new straw. It looked corn-fed, not grass-gutted.

She said disparagingly, "Second thought, he don't look like he could hold out to do no heavy work, he's so squatty."

"Why, he can jerk any stump. He can pull a freight car."

"I wouldn't give no more than thirty dollars and this pup for him."

"Throw out the pup and throw in your pocket kerchief, it'll be the same difference."

"This pup can run squirrels all night."

"And chickens all day."

She said, "Well, I like red. Might make it forty."

"Feller over there said sixty and a gold watch."

"Fifty, that's all." She half turned away.

"He *said* it was gold, but his belly was green as yonder grass where it rubbed. Fifty and the pup."

She turned back. "Give you a note for the other twenty." When the man poked out a lip, she added, "You don't like paper, you can take it out in meal or grinding, one. You know Gristle mill?"

"Now I heard a woman run it. You her?" She nodded. He said briskly, "Take him. He's yours."

Would it follow her? She laid a hand on the red mule's bridle. It was faintly greasy. The mane had not been clipped. It was long and she would leave it so, blowing free and pretty.

She said, "Come on, Bud."

It followed without hesitation, nose at her shoulder, and she went, feeling everyone's eyes on her and no longer minding. Clusters of wild flowers took shape at the corners of the lot, tansy with yellow buttony blooms, orange coneflowers with bulging brown centers. She led the mule to the truck, and John Goforth looked up.

"Well, look now."

She turned her head so he could not see the pleasure in her eyes. She rubbed the mule's soft nose and scratched the long jaws.

"Got me a mule."

"No arguing that." He nudged the animal to make it show its points, and peered at its teeth. "What you give for him?"

She would have said of the white mule, proudly, "Fifty." But more than a mule was involved here.

"Enough."

The storekeeper stiffened. "Wasn't meaning to pry." He got very busy at the back of the truck. It was loaded—rose bushes wrapped in damp moss, and bales of burlap bags to be used for hooked rugs or mule collars, rolls of chicken wire and canvas, a box of knives and another of vanilla, a setting of Warhackle eggs in a pine-needle basket.

He tightened a rope and squinted at the sun. "Noon. Reckon we can make it home and do some business, we go now. You thu?"

"I reckon."

"We'll take off, then. Now wonder where them gals is at."

She volunteered, "I'll go look for them."

They might be anywhere. They might be over near the big oak tree where the boys had stood. They might be, but it did not matter, for that was where she was going. Maybe he would be gone by now—likely he would be—but that did not matter either. His heel mark in the dirt, his shirt thread on a twig, his very space would do.

And he was gone. All that remained was a heap of discarded

bottles where he had lounged and drunk soft drinks while the hard, hard girls walked by.

Toy looked at the place. She looked at the soft-drink bottles and the althea twigs frayed by chewing, and a blue button, and turned away just as Tessie hurried up, eyes searching.

"There it is." She snatched up the button and straightened in alarm. "We ain't going?"

"Got to." Toy's eyes focused on her sister's blouse. She said dryly, "Unless you still thirsty?"

The redheaded girl followed her gaze and giggled. She brushed a complacent hand over the dozen bottle caps fastened on her blouse.

"Them fool boys." She held out her hand defiantly. "I still got my money. I'm gonna get me that piece of goods to Goforth's and make me a blouse for the dance."

Toy started off without answering. Tessie hesitated and trotted after.

She called, "I figured you'd say something, boys buying me all them soft drinks."

Toy went on, eager to see the red mule again.

"Anyways, it wasn't a heap of boys. One mostly. He bought me six-eight drinks all by hisself."

She would buy a new bridle for the mule, Toy thought, a shiny one with silver on it.

"This feller thought he was a dog, but he was just a tail right on."

The bridle would shine, and the mule would shine for all Gristle to see.

"He said, 'Hand me a hair, Firetop. My cigar's gone out.' I says, 'I'll hand you one. Don't look like you're man enough to take it!' He says, 'Sugar, I'm bull high and cock low.'"

They were nearing the truck. John Goforth was craning his neck, looking for them. Dolly sat on the tailgate, leaning a heavy head against a roll of wire. The mule was flinching flies from its hide.

Tessie drew level with Toy. The day had given her a shine. Her eyes sparkled, her upper lip was beaded with sweat, and when she put her tongue out to lick it, her tongue was the color of cherry Nehi.

"That's when he started buying me drinks." She giggled. "That ole Bud."

Silence held the name. Two men passed. One said, "Ole Gene Talmadge says, 'You farmers don't have but three friends, Jesus Christ, Sears Roebuck, and me.'"

Toy said, "Bud?"

"Uh-huh. See, I got it spelled out with caps." She turned body and blouse toward Toy, stepping backward and skipping a little. "Got the B and the U, part of the D. Wish I could of got all the D, but Bud run out of nickels."

She turned back and saw the mule. "A mule—we got us a mule!" She ran toward it and laid a hand on its withers.

John Goforth asked, "You ready?" He took off his old hat and wiped his brow. "You got everything?"

Toy climbed up into the front seat for answer. She looked into the rear-view mirror. Tessie met her eyes and called, "Toy, what we going to name the mule?"

John Goforth called, "You two ready?"

Dolly sang out, "Ready, but not willing."

"Let's go, then." He put the car in gear. "I mean, we had us a day. I'm glad to get shut of it." They moved out of the lot past the slow straggling crowd. It had thinned, but after dinner it would thicken again. Trading would continue until dusk-dark.

Tessie called, "I know what let's call him. Let's call him Trumpet after that vine grows around the sweet gum in the side yard, you know, has the red flowers."

There were a few perished-by-dust blooms in the undergrowth along the road, jasmine, wild verbena, Grancy Graybeard. In another month the thickets would be massed with flowers, and children lagging to school, rebellious and aching for summer, would point to the yellow tansy and the orange cone-flowers with their bulging brown centers.

"Pee weed," they would shrill. "Shit weed!"

Four

EVERYONE was asleep, shadows of night blurring their out-lines. Tessie slept on her back, legs spraddled and a hand flung up in invitation. Harl Junior slept on his face, a dead man floating on a sea of crumpled sheets. Her mother and the old dog, Joe, slept curled in knots, noses to knees.

It was the time Toy had awaited. She had gone to bed with the others, Joe the last. The dog had turned around and around on the hearth, snugging night out. Now secure behind closed eyes, he continued the rabbit-chases of the day.

As Toy rose and stepped softly over him to pick up her clothes, his hind legs jerked. His front paws scrabbled, going down an endless warren, down and down to where all rabbits were graveyard rabbits with four hind legs.

She said softly, "Sick 'em, boy." The words were an offering, a penny crossing the palm of night. She picked up an old pair of her father's pants and put them on.

"Whip. Whip!" a poorwill sighed.

She stepped to the door and squinted her eyes into the dark. A whippoorwill calling at your door meant a death in the family. She picked up a stone and slung it. "Scat!" The bird tumbled away. "Whip, whip!"

The clouds were piled high, light edging them. They were like clotted sheep. The moon hid like a little billygoat; every now and then it would butt its way into view, scattering the flock, small white horns dripping. All the peepers in trees and ditches would taste the moisture in their throats and set up an ecstatic chirping.

Trees bent and straightened in a gust of wind. Half-light lay in patches across the ground. A spotted skunk moved across one. It was heavy with the young which would be born next month. If Aunt Baptist were around, she would catch the animal and remove the gland. She kept a bottle of the liquid buried in the loose earth under a rosebush, declaring, "Nothing better for cutting mucous."

The skunk, nose down for buds and berries, did not see the fox that trotted into the yard. If it had, it would not have paused. The fox, a handsome male cross, gave way grudgingly. It turned and trotted over to the well, sniffed, and lifted a leg. Pride salved, it moved on toward the chicken yard.

Toy thought, So you're the critter.

She took a step back to where the shotgun leaned in the corner. She threw it to her shoulder, the night filled with thunder, and the fox vanished.

She turned to replace the gun. Harl Junior was standing in the bedroom doorway, shivering in his drawers.

"What you shoot at, Toy?"

"Fox. Go on back to bed."

He turned obediently, but she saw him go and squat on the night crow, face blank. He would go to bed, and in the morning he would remember nothing of getting up.

Neither Tessie nor her mother had awakened. Toy listened for a moment and moved out into the yard. The hens were fluttering back to sleep under the scuppernong vine. Beyond was the garden plot and the bull-shouldered swell of the furrows. Toy thought, I'll tell Tom 'twas a fox took off the chickens—and frowned. A fox or a weasel, one, would explain the three hens which had disappeared over the last few nights; it didn't explain the other things.

Yellow Tom had told her of the first theft three days ago, the day that she had brought home the red mule.

"Whoo-eee." He had sucked in breath at the sight of it. "Georgia Red for sure."

"Things all right to the mill?"

"Goes any better, they pass theirselves. Only we gots to do something 'bout them stones."

"Going slow?"

"Been going slow."

"We'll pick them out tomorrow."

It was a job that had to be done two-three times a year. The furrows on the stones got so worn that it took three times around to get twice the meal. She and Tom had to pulley up the top stone—they used steel tongs controlled by a wooden screw set beside the rocks—and, using steel picks, chip out new furrows.

She asked, "Anything else happen?"

"Pot of grits gots gone from the cupboard."

He had taken to sleeping and cooking occasionally in a lean-to off the mill. If it had not been made of corrugated iron, she would not have let him; corn dust drew sparks like gas or gunpowder. As it was he had a cornshuck mattress in a corner, a piece of stove made from an oil drum, and a wooden box nailed to the wall for a cupboard.

"Mice?"

He rubbed a slow paw over his skull. "Biggest mouse Noah snatched out the flood, must be. Took the pot, left the soot."

"Some of that walking trash. I tell you, if I catch one of them around—"

Wednesday, Thursday, Friday, and now with the new moon on the increase. Three days, and every one something missing— hens, a jar of crabapple jelly from Tom's cupboard, a pan of skim milk set out for the new calf and, when the calf was fetched, gone. Missing something until yesterday, when they had found the hat.

It had come swirling down Mumbling Creek, turning round and round on the current, an old felt with a red feather stuck in the band. Tom had reached an arm and a bamboo pole and snaked it out. They had examined it together.

He decided, "Don't b'long to nobody round abouts."

"No." She hung it on a branch and looked up the race to the broad-breasted pond dotted with tree snags and coontail moss, the edge selvaged with willow and sand myrtle and hickory. A man could hide in those thickets.

The Negro followed her gaze. "You reckon?"

"He could if he don't mind getting killed."

There were copperheads and moccasins in the thickets, and that morning she had seen a rattler swimming among the bonnets, buttons up.

She had been talking to a big farmer when the hat swirled into sight. She turned back to him.

"How about it? You can use my mule, and the plow's by the shed. Wouldn't take but an hour-two."

He squinted at the sky, "Why, I don't mind none. Free grinding is clear money. But might be better to wait a spell. Looks like rain seeds." It was midmorning, and the sky was stippled with cloud flakes.

"Can't wait too long. The moon's on the increase."

"Lord God. I 'most forgot. I got to get my 'taters in, too. I'll get it done this afternoon sure."

The plot was plowed and furrowed. Now she picked up a sack of seed corn and stepped off the porch. The moon rushed out, butting clouds aside. She hardly needed a lantern, but she took one anyway.

She could have waited until tomorrow morning. She could have waited two days or three. All that was necessary was that the corn be planted on the increase of the moon. The waxing moon burst the tense kernel. Leaf reached up, root reached down, and each kept pace with the swelling moon. Three moons, three months, and the corn would touch its tallest leaf, and the moon could go back to moving the seas.

She could have waited, but night was all that day had left her.

Day was a great eye, rayed and watching her, and she had to be what the eye said she was. Only when the eye was out could she be what she knew she was, soft and waiting.

Earth swelled beneath her toes; her heels broke clods. She walked between the rows, and the moon and lantern showed her the furrow where the seeds must go. "One for you, one for I, one for the hole, one for the fly." June, and tassels would tickle the wind, and baby skunks would chew a thinner milk.

The lamp flickered, the moon ducked in and out, the sack lightened. Crazy work for a crazy woman, people would say if they could see her.

Lovick Jones planted by lantern-light many a spring, and people said nothing. It was all right for him. It was natural.

She hung the empty sack on a post and set down the lantern. Stars disappeared, leaving luminous patches behind. Buttony white feverfew shone in a corner of the garden; the juice of feverfew was good for clearing eyes. The night was full of odors, fruity and scorched, resinous and spicy. She sat on the chopping block and turned her face.

What was "natural"? Who was "Toy Crawford"?

Once Coke Williams, finding some little Negro children swimming in a wash hole on the branch, made a skull of white clay and put great dog teeth in it. He had set it on a pole in the middle of the creek, and when the children saw it, they fled, screaming. They knew it was clay, but they had fled anyway. Why? What had made the clay bone to them? What made a rack of bones Toy Crawford with hard bones in her face and this soft and treacherous marrow within?

Sweetness blew across the world. Toy raised her head sharply. Why, it was sweet shrub—bubby blossoms, the old folks called them, from their sweet reddish-brown puckers like a woman's nipples. Yet it was before-times for such to bloom; they came along in April, when the wild azalea flowered and little girls lifted their skirts in innocent exhibition.

Sweet shrub. Memory assailed her. It turned her soft and astonished. It set her fingers tracing the hard grain of the chopping block while her mind went back to the time when she was twelve, and had met a thin black-haired boy.

Jim Jay his name had been, but it was not his real name. People only called him that because he was like the boy in the nursery rhyme, "caught in the middle of yesterday." He was "a natural," and that June he had come to stay with a family on Atkins' Ridge. He was a cousin or a nephew or some such.

It had started out a bad summer. Dolly was off visiting, and the boys who had been friends all year or inactive enemies took to whispering in thickets and looking at her. The bolder asked if she knew what "switching tails" meant.

She did not, not in so many words, but in dark and terrifying images. It was enough to make her throw rocks furiously, not so much at them as at the images, and run off and jump in the rain barrel. Her mother whipped her for spoiling the water, but she did not care.

After one of these flights she met Jim Jay. He was standing in a patch of poison ivy down near the pond, pulling at the trefoiled leaves. First off she thought that he was one of the boys, and then he turned, and she saw he was a stranger. He had lank black hair and eyes quick and beady as a squirrel's. He had a squirrel's way, too, of cocking his head to one side and listening. Distantly there were shouts and splashings, boys swinging on grape vines over the wash hole on the branch and dropping in.

He complained, "They won't let me play with them."

"Me neither."

They stared at each other, the boy with his high peaked shoulders and eyes that never stopped very long anywhere, and the thin tangle-haired girl in the too short dress.

Finally she offered, "You're standing in poison ivy."

He jerked a leaf. "I don't care none."

She jerked one too. "Me neither."

So they drew together, casuals of the summer. They did not

get poison ivy, but they got crab-apple colic. They were dosed with blackberry wine, which made them drunk and giggly, the cure worth the condition. The remedies for red bugs and sin were not so pleasant, kerosene baths and a week-long revival at a tent in the woods. The first two nights of the revival were fine with people falling down in fits and testifying. But after sin was reamed out, what remained was a vast clean tedium. They longed to get out and fill it with new sins, but had to wait until the preacher raised the final amen. It made sin less worth while than crab-apple colic.

They passed the long green-gold days in ways that most twelve-year-old girls and fourteen-year-old boys had put behind them. They found and tried to tame a crippled catbird. They got catawba worms and caught fish with safety-pin hooks. They slid down the shuck pile at the mill. They said, "Rabbit, rabbit; bunny, bunny," when they had to separate going around a tree.

One morning he told her he had found a bush of bubby blossoms. She started to run, shrieking, for the buds were better than any perfume, squeezed on your collar or the hem of your dress. He ran after her, and his long legs and slat body got him first to the shrub. He stood against it, grinning and cocking his head as she panted up.

"No use running," he said, and then she saw that he had stripped the bush. He had all the buds in his pockets.

She begged, "Aw, give me some."

"Nope."

"Come on."

"Well, what you give me for them?"

She offered, "My yellow taw?" He shook his head. "The ole catalogue?" For he loved to look at the toy pictures. Yet he shook his head again. "Well, what?"

He said, "Well—switch tails, Toy?"

She could not move, taken unawares; and before she could, he stepped forward and put his nose to hers. Gently he rubbed it back and forth, clicking his tongue softly with pleasure.

A week later he went back to wherever he came from, down around Thomson. She never saw him again, but years later someone told her that he had gotten bit by a blind worm and died.

Joe wandered by, nose to new earth. He had aroused from dreams of rabbits to present scents. He made a business of snuffling the chopping block, never looking at her, yet his neck was ready at her hand; for he was not a penny-feist or slinker-pup, loll-tongued and belly-up. He had affairs afoot.

She stroked the bony dome and hard neck. She brushed a tat of mud from his ear. The hound was quiet at her knee, standing pressed against it, eyes like moonstones staring across the night. Only hogs' and men's eyes did not shine at night, Aunt Baptist said. Now why was that? Two of a kind?

The hound's body tautened against her knee. She felt the flinch. His tail came ruler stiff and straight; his nose was like a needle. He broke away, bounding in great lopes across the ground and baying in near-hysteria.

Her hand closed on an ax, and her first thought was, Fox again. Yet the hound's voice said, More than fox. He flickered through patches of moonlight and shadows and disappeared around the side of the house. She snatched up the lantern and ran after.

The hound was growling, head lowered, spraddle-legged, at the potato shed.

It was a tumbly thing. She had thrown it up last fall when the sweet potatoes came in scant and poor, and she found children and grown-ups too raiding the straw-lined beds dug in the ground for storage. Free feast was early famine, so she had built the shed and locked the door. Now nothing remained of the potatoes but a few nubs half gone with brown rot, and the lock hung open in the hasp.

Something moved within the shed, larger than a fox, large as a bear. Joe's growls rose. He advanced, leg over stiff leg.

The ax had a hickory haft and a bright cutting edge. She gripped it, breath shallow in her lungs, and lifted the lantern.

"Come out of there."

Night and whatever crouched in the shed hung on the words. She could feel the wary, waiting silence.

"You hear? Come out."

Shadow gathered in the doorway. A man hitched himself out, hanging to the jamb. A white shirt glimmered. Whiteness that was a face moved back and forth. A voice complained.

"Now you ever seen a feller unlucky as me?"

She did not know what she had expected. She did not know if she had expected this. She swung the lantern high. The man threw up a palm.

"Now you caught me. Don't blind me, too."

He was her height, and she was not a tall woman. He was crippled, his left dungaree leg cut away at the knee, bloody rag showing. There was nothing to fear here. She could hit him with an ax before he got started. She could grapple and ride him to the ground.

"Who you? What you doing here?"

His voice went on behind the palm hiding his face. "It do look like the Lord would show a feller some mercy, don't it? Half-starved, shot up, now caught with a rotten potato in my hand— looks like you had you a sorry crop—"

"Move and I'll ruin you twice. I asked, who you?"

"Why"—he dropped his palm—"Peanuts Stonecypher. And you know, I'd be money ahead if I'd never been born?"

His mouth said the words, but his eyes, blinking a little in the light, denied them; they were black and bright. He had thick dark hair combed straight back in little bobcat ridges, and sideburns fringed his long jaws.

He continued. "Know why I'm so short? Got caught in a snowstorm when I was twelve and stunted my growth. First snowstorm they had in Limus, Alabama, in fifteen years, and I had to be out coon-logging. It took my ma four hours to thaw me out, but 'twas too late. Next year she died. Pa, too. They was getting well from typhoid, but pure famished—you know how them old doctors starved fever?—and here was this pot of potatoes. They et them right down to boil water—"

"You the reason things has got gone, the grits and milk and chickens." Suddenly she remembered the men in the truck and accused, "It was you in Old Man Turner's chicken yard. It's how you got shot."

"Now I won't lie; it was. I went in that yard to steal anything I could eat and I don't blame that feller for taking shot at me—"

"You know he's dead? You know he tripped chasing you and shot hisself? You know they looking for you?"

He drew a breath. He said, "It's the Lord's will. It's the Lord's way of punishing me like he's been punishing me all my life, stunting me and taking my folks, stoppering every way—"

She interrupted. "Who you think you fooling?"

His head snapped up.

She said, "You're little, but you're rough."

His mouth had been down-curved in sorrow. Now the corners twitched, and suddenly he laughed long and ringing to shock the night. Joe growled and backed away.

He hitched himself erect by the doorjamb. "Why, hell, you're right," he said cheerfully. "But when you can't stand, you got to lie." The weak piety was gone. "Well, now you know, what you gonna do about it? Turn me over to the sheriff, so's he can slap and snatch me around?"

"You figure you got less coming?"

"I figure, for I cherish my hide like Poor-Kitty-Popcorn. And there's something you ought to figure, too. It's gonna cost you to put me in jail." She stared. "Sure, don't you know there's nothing costs like doing right? It costs time, and it costs money. That's why there ain't hardly anybody cares to afford it."

The words meant nothing. They were a loop he threw around her attention. He was enjoying himself.

Her anger grew and hardened with his voice. She waited until he stopped, then leaned forward. "Mister," she said slowly and deliberately, "you got a smooth tongue. Lick this clean. I'm going to kill you."

She did not mean it the moment before she said it, but when she said it, she meant it. She would kill him and cut a blood-eagle on his back. She would chop ribs from spine and draw his lungs out to lie like red wings on the ground. She would laugh and say, "See can you fly."

The man stared at her and knew she meant it. His face closed. "By God, you would."

"I would."

A spicebush moth came swirling around the lantern and caromed off Toy's cheek. It was soft, but her face and Peanuts' were hard white bones.

He kept staring. He said slowly, almost curiously, "What kind of woman are you anyways?"

"No kind you're used to."

"Now I know that, we can get somewheres." He crossed his arms. "You got two choices, put me in jail or make money out of me. You tell."

"Two cents a pound," she said. "You worth about that, somebody like you."

"What you mean, somebody-like-me?"

"A ridge-runner if you wasn't a road-walker." A moonshiner, she meant, who ran his liquor over the back hills to town. "A somebody won't stay in one place when two worse places is beyond. I know a somebody-like-you."

"You know nothing. You don't know I'm the best guitar-player from Limus to Leon County, Florida, and I've played them, the both. You don't know I can take a piece of glass and out-chord a feller with a five-dollar pick. You don't know I can take a thorn and play a string tied between my thumb and finger."

She said incredulously, "Now I bet."

"I can." His voice overrode denial. "That's where I was headed when I got shot, the mountain fair to Hiawassee—"

"Taking short cuts thu chicken yards."

"The fiddling-and-picking contest. I figured to take first prize. I figured to head to Nashville where the dollars is—"

"You sure lacing your coat with gold."

"I'll get on the radio. They got this program called 'Ozark Jubilee'—"

It was as real to him as Diddy-Wah-Diddy was to a Negro child, Diddy-Wah-Diddy where the roofs were made of pancakes and roast ducks flew by with knives and forks in their backs, quacking, "Sweet, sweet, come eat." Real as Diddy-Wah-Diddy and as unreal, for such bounty had no reality for her. She was held in the hard cleft of the Lord's promise, bread and water: "In the sweat of thy face shalt thou eat bread."

She lowered the lantern. The man's eyes focused.

"What you fixing to do?"

"Glad you mentioned the guitar. I might get me a dollar-two out of it."

His chest rose convulsively; she saw it under the thin white shirt, too thin for the chill that lay across the night, the fog wrapping the hills in dampness. Muscles moved along his shoulders. She thought he would spring. She grasped the ax.

He said—and it was as near as he ever came to begging—"I can work."

"I wouldn't turn on my heel to have you."

He was dogged. "Give me a couple days till my leg heals, and I can work out what you figure I owe you. You wouldn't have to give me nothing but rations. And you need help to the mill; I been watching you from the plum thickets."

The white bloom had faded from the Catawba plums. Yet they held a faint perfume still, a strange incalculable fragrance. It seemed to cling about the man's clothes. Yet wildy perfume wore off soon; everyone said so.

He said, "That ole nigger you got, he's thu. You know it, and I know it."

It was true. Yellow Tom held out less and less to work. He sat and gave fire something to warm. He was dry and shrunk like an old brown twig. But yonder the plum switches were full of tiny green nibs turning to sweet red fruit in June.

He said, "You need me."

"You say."

"I say. But you think about it and you'll say so too." His voice had lowered. It was a soft, seeking thing; it sought out the cracks, the half-closed doors in her. "Now say."

Gristle would see signs and tell tales if she took him in. Gristle was like a horse in a boarded-in pasture; it watched the world through its legs.

He added, "Or you afraid?"

Fury was immediate. "Not of you, nor of horses!"

Stars swept the night in patches, black at the borders and unknown. A three-legged cat veered away from the lantern light, lurching.

She said harshly, "I'll give you a job. You'll feel the pinch and grow an inch, time I get thu with you."

Five

WHEN people learned that she had taken in a strange man, they thought the worst, as she had known they would; they thought she was a woman. Lovick Jones came to learn more, laying against the wind in his eagerness.

Peanuts asked him, "Now ain't I a mess? Bound for Nashville —got me a job promised there—and get stove up on a rock. Toy yonder figured I was one of them road-walkers. She came at me with an ax. I told her, I said, 'Lordy, you remind me of the time I dreamed widows all round my bed; woke Monday morning and found I was dead.' "

The plump postmaster came away wheezing with mirth. "That little feller to the Crawfords is a sight. Keeps an extra tongue to tell tales."

Everyone took to drifting by the mill to see and hear for themselves. The place took on the air of Goforth's store, and Peanuts' jokes were passed from tongue to tongue, swelling as they went.

"You hear what Peanuts called a friend? A good-looking enemy."

"Well, you hear what he said about the weather? 'Hotter'n a sinner who is in Hell, writing to a gal who's there as well.' "

Ammi Watts gasped. "Lordy, Peanuts, how come you so bright?"

"Why, my daddy was the sun, my mother the moon, and I'm a fallen star."

Aunt Baptist said grimly, "Fallen star is right. A star named Wormwood. Tastes good going down, but he'll give you affection of the brain, you mess with it long enough."

Alone of the valley, she and Wick Bloodworth distrusted Peanuts. The morning Toy had sent Tessie to fetch her to doctor Peanuts, she had been rough but amiable enough.

She surged into Yellow Tom's lean-to at the mill and declared, "Shooting's too good for these road-walkers. Ought to tromp 'em into the ruts. Be of some use then." She dropped heavily to her knees beside him and set down her basket. "Now, boy, where you hurt?"

Peanuts grinned. "If you can't see, somebody better finish the job."

"He ain't dead yet," she said approvingly, "whatever this one says." She jerked her head at Tessie, who was hanging around the doorway, hair standing out from hurry and excitement. "Let's see that leg."

She put a hand on it; and a change came over her.

Toy could sense it and see it, the stillness of jelly-like back, the stiffness of neck under the gray oriole nest of hair. The quiet, too, Aunt Baptist who was never quiet, who was a dragon with a tongue full of tatters.

Now silently she cleaned and bandaged the wound and, finished, got to her feet.

"You'll be all right in a week-two." Her words were short. "You can hit the grit then."

Peanuts grinned up at her. He was enjoying something, and it was more than the cornbread at his elbow or the pot of chicory-coffee Tessie had brought.

"Now who says I'm going?"

Aunt Baptist whirled on Toy. "He staying? That true?"

"He's staying."

Morning had cleared away night thoughts as sun cleared away the night mists lying in the knucks of the hills. Toy could see the last of them dissipating, rising into the sky in thin, light sheets over Atkins' Ridge. Peanuts was something to be watched, but only because he was a natural-born liar and thief. The menace that he had exuded was night-menace, soon gone.

Aunt Baptist said tersely, "Lord help you."

She gathered her basket together, her movements abrupt. Her big breasts quivered; the stays of her corset jutted like arrows. Her men's boots tromped the hard-packed earth as she stalked from the lean-to. Toy, knowing it was wanted, followed her. The big midwife swung to face her.

"Get shut of him fast as you can."

Beyond them the mill stood motionless, for Yellow Tom had not come. Yet the sun was high enough and bright enough. His millstone-tombstone was unfinished. Maybe it would always be.

"I got to have help to the mill."

"Get Ammi Watts. Get the Devil. Don't get him. For I've seen men like him before, varmints and wildy like raccoons or foxes. You can take them when they're pups. You can hand-raise them and think they're tame, they're pets. But the day will come when they will bite you or bite theirselves, one, to get loose. Either way it's hurting."

"I got to have help."

Aunt Baptist threw up her hands. "Small head, small wit. Big head, not a bit." Her wrath fell like the autumn leaves, sudden and careless.

Wick Bloodworth's wrath was a slower thing, but the more inexorable for that.

He came to the mill two weeks later, the same morning Yellow Tom returned. It was a high and sunny day, but the Negro wore a vest over a coat, and a sweater tied by the sleeves around his waist and draggling like an old gray tail. The layers of clothes gave him the flattened, bulky look of a turtle; his gait was as tedious.

Toy met him on the path. "You don't have to work, you don't want. I got a someone."

He nodded slowly and went on to the millstone. He lowered himself inch by inch to the ground and got out a hammer and chisel wrapped in the piece of old inner tube. He began his interminable tap-tapping.

Cardinals were sparks in the willows. A stray bitch who had dropped three pups in the shelter of an old pine root had them out and was nosing them tenderly into activity. Nearby Peanuts sat on a bench, leg propped up, keeping toll, a jug of buttermilk by him. Tessie had brought it; she or Harl was always bringing him something or hanging around him. Once Toy had blurted, in an unease that she would not recognize, "This here is a man —not one of them Bud-boys of yourn. Best stay away." Tessie had laughed. "Man? Why, he's nothing but a little old watch-fob —could hang him from my buttonhole."

Now he demanded of the men around him, "What's that nigger doing, tell me?"

"Cutting his gravestone. Now ain't that a sack of hell, cutting a millstone for a gravestone?"

"Just like a nigger." Sitting still, short and crippled, he was twice as alive as the lounging men. Life was packed in him so tightly that it constantly overflowed in motion, hands shaping his stories, black eyes skimming everywhere. "Reminds me of a nigger I had once. Asked him what he wanted on his grave should he died. He says, 'Why, Boss, just plant a watermelon on it, and let the juice soak thu.' "

A man straightened. "Here comes Wick." The tall fair man had parked his truck and walked over. He extended his hand, smiling.

"Now you must be Peanuts."

"And you're the preacher." Someone had told him that Wick took the pulpit when the preacher was sick. Peanuts flung up his other hand in a sudden warding-off gesture. "Now, Preacher, I'll repent! I'll leave liquor and wild women alone, if you will."

Everyone chortled. One man called, "What you say to that, Wick?"

"Why," Wick said, "I say, Thank you for promoting me to preacher. I thought it took the Lord to do that, but seems like His puppy can, too."

The listening men fell over themselves; they coughed and spat. "Now he's got you there, Peanuts. He sure has. The Lord's puppy—you got the size and the voice. I swear, Wick, you got it about right."

It came to Toy—Wick was angry, Wick, who was never angry. People said that you could stand Wick Bloodworth in the middle of the floor and throw coals at him, and he wouldn't get angry.

Peanuts had joined in the laughter against him, mouth stretched wide. "Now you know you right, Wick? The Lord's puppy. Now you know he's right, fellers? 'Twas pure jealousy made me talk like that, all the good I been hearing about Wick, here. And, well, you know the little dog wants what the big dog's got."

A man called approvingly, "Takes a big dog to say so."

Wick turned to Toy. "I brought you that basket you wanted. I'll carry it in."

It was a seed-catcher, deep and hamper-shaped. He took it into the mill and set it under the sheller. "Better get shut of this old one. It's got more holes than hold." He stretched and looked around. "Can I get up a trade with you?"

"What?"

"Gunpowder shell for half a bucket of honey—found me a bee-gum couple days back."

"Keep the honey." She wanted to say, Everything you've done for me, the ways you can be counted on . . . Only her lips were too stiff. She got a shell from where she kept a few extra in the toll-box and he nodded his thanks.

"Poison oak again?"

"Put my hand in a thicket before I knowed it." He showed a wrist covered with tiny watery blisters. "But gunpowder and sweet cream will dry it up every time."

"Looks like you'd keep you a gun and shells around for that if nothing else."

His big head moved. "My hand draws back from them."

He was an anomaly in a countryside where a rifle hung over the mantel or stood in the corner of every house, as much a piece of living as the bull-eyed lamp dangling by the back door. He trapped rabbits, and he fished, but a gun he hated. He said, "Killing by long-distance—an animal ought to be safe from that. A man ought to be safe from that."

Outside a guitar fretted. Peanuts' voice lifted. "Mhm, mhm. Think I got it, fellers."

A premonitory tingle went all over Toy's body as he began to sing.

> "Yella Tom was a nigger.
> Went to meet the Lord.
> Lord says, 'Tom, can't take you—
> Best go down the road.'

"Tom says, 'What I done, Lord?'
Lord says, 'Quite a load—
You ain't got a tombstone.
Best go down the road.'

"Tom took a millstone,
Cut, 'Heaven's My Abode.'
Lord says, 'Who wants that trash?
Best go down the road.'

"Tom took it to the Devil,
Squashed him like a toad.
Devil yells, 'I don't want you.
Best go down the road!' "

Peanuts was always making up songs, comical ones. Toy could not keep her mouth from moving up, though it was a mean song, too, and she knew it.

A man yelled, "Give up cutting, ole feller. The Lord don't want you, and the Devil won't take you."

Another said, "What's he cutting, anybody know?"

Two got up and lazied over. If Yellow Tom heard them coming, he gave no sign. If he heard the song, no one knew. He huddled into his coat and at his work, the hammer going tap-tap as interminably as the bees buzzing in the crab-apple clusters and red clover.

One man called back, disgusted, "Aw, it ain't nothing but his name and 'Jesus Made Up My Dying B-e-something.' What, you reckon?"

"Couldn't be nothing but 'bed,' " Peanuts told him. "You hear the one about the nigger had to go to the doctor? Doctor says, 'I can give you something for what's ailing you, but it'll cost you two dollars a bottle.' Nigger says, 'What's cheaper?' Doctor says, 'Stay away from women.' Nigger says, 'Gimme the bottle.' "

The men drifted back, laughing. Yellow Tom kept tapping. Toy muffled compunction with the thought, Niggers is used to such as that. They did not feel things like that any more than a fish, taking a hook, felt pain. It just swallowed air and died.

She looked up and found Wick watching her. Something in his face made her feel obscurely ashamed. She flashed out at random. "Peanuts is just funning."

"Mean fun. He mocks a man down to nothing, and he picks ones can't fight back, like Tom yonder, or ones he figures won't. He's little, not outside but inside, and he stretches himself up by pulling everyone down below him."

Toy repeated uncomfortably, "He's just funning."

Wick kept watching her, big hands tying shut a sack of meal. It was not his job to do, but if work lay at hand he did it.

"You're taking up some for a feller you've knowed only a week-two."

The air quivered around the statement. The words lay there; they had a nakedness. A wasp, gold and shining ebony, spiraled upward to its hole in the rafters, and beyond the door men's voices and the intermittent thump of the guitar held a meaning beyond sound.

Toy felt this along her spine where the hairs roach on an animal. She felt it and took a sudden involuntary step backward from Wick, Wick so large and alien-male, Wick watching her and hinting at something that she did not want to know.

The words blurted out of her. "I got to get to work." She strode to the door. "You!"

Peanuts looked around, mouth cat-curled from the song. He looked again, and cried in mock terror, "Stand back, boys, I'm about to get a knot jerked in my tail."

"Get busy and tot up what they owe, hear?"

He cried, mock-Negro, "Yas'm, yas'm!"

Toy turned back into the mill. This, at least, was known and constant. She touched a stone for remembrance.

Wick spoke at her shoulder. "Toy, send him away."

Chaff stirred in the chute. Her thoughts were like the chaff, but there was no wind to blow them away like the ungodly things they were. They swirled and tormented her. She shook her head.

He asked quietly, "Now why? You know he'll take off sooner or later. If you don't believe it—count the days when he's gone."

"Then what difference do it make, sooner than later?"

"It's what he'll do before he takes off that frets me."

"Nothing." She turned and threw the lever that raised the floodgate. Water spilled down the race, tumbling and carrying everything before it. It carried off her thoughts. It fixed her mind on the business of grinding. "He won't do nothing."

"I sure hope not. But he's bad, and there's a shine to badness like rotten things. The shine gets in your eyes and your nose, and after a while you can't see, you can't tell."

She was stubbornly silent.

He said, "I knew it wouldn't do no good, but I was obliged to speak."

He picked up a sack of meal and walked out, not looking at her again. Toy was glad and sorry too—how could a mind be so mixy-maxy?

Outside, voices and laughter died down. Wick was talking to the men around Peanuts, quiet words lost in the rush of the race. Toy saw their faces change like clay under a skilled potter's thumbs. One minute they were loose and without resolution, a slickness on them. The next they firmed and took on contour and steadiness. Wick raised his hand and went to his truck. He threw in the sack of meal and drove off.

Peanuts' laugh rose shrilly. "Now Wick sure thinks he's Jehovah's sword, don't he?"

The men looked at one another. One cleared his throat. "Wick's all right."

Another nodded. "Uh-huh. Like he says, we don't belong to make a fun-box of Tom."

"A millstone's good as a milestone on your grave, I reckon. Me, now I'll be lucky to get a shingle—if they don't need it to patch the roof."

Laughter, growing easier, went around.

Peanuts echoed it. "Me, now, I'm gonna have a shoe on mine."

"Boost you up, or 'tother way?" It was halfhearted. Already there was a general stirring of movement as men prepared to leave. A few spat, not looking at Peanuts. Others hitched up their belts as though taking a fresh grip on manhood.

"Neither one. To remind the Lord that a feller's foot is bound to slip now and again. He can't help it. I wish I had a nickel for every time I've made a fool of myself, like with Wick. If I did, I'd be the richest man with the sorest bottom in Georgia."

Laughter went around, but the men continued to move. They whistled up dogs. They spat final juice into the weeds. They pulled hats over their eyes against the sun, now high. They moved off toward trucks and wagons.

One called back, "Stay poor now."

"If you stay honest."

Small dust rose as the trucks moved out. Horses shook their harnesses and followed. The road to Gristle and the small trails turning off into the hills held little knots of dust for a while, but finally they smoothed out, and nothing was left but quiet.

Peanuts sat with boot-tracks to keep him company and a solitary eagle, riding an updraft over the rimrock. His face was flattened into empty planes, his body was taut and ready, only there was nothing to be ready for. He had never come to the eagle's peace with space.

His eyes came up and found Toy's watching him.

A sudden and curious empathy flowed between them. It drew his brows together; it shocked Toy.

He blurted, "Toy. That's a hell of a name."

She said nothing.

"Your daddy sure didn't know what he was about, naming you that."

"My ma named me."

It was something that she had forgotten or, when she remembered, she accepted as she accepted a bruise, as a misbegotten thing. Now a new thought came to her. Her mother had named her Toy, and once it had meant something, a play-pretty, a happiness made flesh. But time had been up to its old tricks; the toll that it took was tenderness.

Her shadow lay on the earth, and it was kind. It blunted the sharp bones of her hip and chest and concealed her high-cheeked, sharp-chinned face.

Peanuts said, "I saw her once."

There were questions in his voice, though she was certain-sure that he had heard all the tales that mouths could hold about the Crawfords, hard old Ard and Hug-Me-Tight Harl and Crazy Rosie. What did they call her, Toy? Hard or crazy or another word altogether? Certain-sure they did not call her Hug-Me-Tight. Yet there were areas of softness on her body.

She blurted, "She's sick."

The word "sick" surprised her. It was a long while since she had used it. The word had been worn off by the gibes of Gristle and finally lost in the inexorable turning of the millwheel. Her mother had been lost, too. She was an extra plate, a midnight trip, a giggling in a corner.

Harl Junior pelted into the mill yard and yelled, "Ma's in the baptistery again. Lovick Jones said tell you."

Six

EVERYTHING in Toy shrank.

She told the boy, "Tell Tessie hitch the mule."

"She's doing it. She's coming now."

Harl's thin face was white with excitement. Given an excuse, he got sick and vomited, and Tessie lost her temper, two reasons Toy never took them along to get their mother, times when Rose Crawford wouldn't leave a place. Sometimes it would be a parlor somewhere, and she would be giggling in the best chair; other times it was Goforth's store, where she was as persistent after tidbits as a cat in a smokehouse. Lately she had taken to the baptistery.

Tessie clattered up in the wagon, standing and urging the mule on with flicking reins. She called, "He's mean today."

The mule swiveled a measuring eye. It had been crazy lately. It would have no one but Tessie bridle it, and it must be done in a certain way, the bridle slipped over the right ear without bending the ear, then over the left, and cinched just so. Afterward it would chase Tessie across the pasture, heels flinging fire as it thundered down on her, swerving at the last possible moment. They were a fine and foolish sight. Toy wondered, If he ran at me, would he cut away?

Peanuts said, "Want me to go 'long?"

"No."

He rose and flexed his leg. "I know how she's sick—she's crazy as a coot. How you figuring on managing a crazy mule and a crazy woman both at the same time?"

The word "crazy" had a painful astringency, but it absolved her of pretense. It was true, she could not handle both, not with the mule's eye fixed for meanness.

"Come then."

Tessie said eagerly, "I'll come too."

Toy's eye swung in surprise and quick suspicion; never did the red-haired girl offer to help with her mother.

"No, one's aplenty."

Tessie sulked. "You never want me to have no fun." She told Peanuts saucily, "I'll keep your seat warm—the whole three inches."

The mule's hide flenched, questioning, under Peanuts' hands on the lines. He shouted, "You give me any trouble, mule, and I'll spring your staves."

The mule's ears laid back like a cat's, hesitated, and settled forward demurely. It leaned between the traces; the wagon made a circle and followed Toy's finger.

They forded the creek where it was shallow and turned up through oak and hickory laced with heart-leafed sarsaparilla vine and goldenseal. Haw bushes poked out staying thorns where the clay trail narrowed. The wagon wheels passed over rocks worn into view by recent rains. The jolting set Toy's teeth on edge; she hung to the seat.

Peanuts yelled, "This is purely the Rocky Road to Dublin like they got to carnivals."

She shouted, "It's good, times, but the rains has wore it down."

"It far, the baptistery?"

"Two miles maybe."

She wondered how Lovick Jones had known about her mother. A hunter or a spring-enchanted child must have told him. Only a child or a hunter would be around a church this time of day.

The trail broadened. It looped around a small pond sparred with old cypress trunks. The banks were thick with cherry-laurel and fig, the water with mule-footed lily pads and bonnets, a fine docking place for snails, as a wood-duck had discovered. She sat on a piece of oak branch half fallen into the pond, and her beak darted out and came back. She gulped, tail twirling in satisfaction.

Toy felt a lightness. It always pleasured her to see wild creatures feed. A deer muzzle-deep in blue chicory and a mockingbird balanced on an eight-foot sunflower, both of these were sights she had seen for a brief instant, yet they remained with her. When the mill was hot and choking, or her mother naughty in corners—the deer bent its neck, or the mockingbird lifted her heart into lighter spaces.

Peanuts whistled, toe tapping out an unsteady beat against the joggling floor of the wagon. It was a bouncy tune, one she did not recognize, though truth to say, she did not recognize many,

a few hymns and folk songs, one or two radio songs, the perish-
in-a-day kind that the men whistled around the mill.

"What's that?"

" 'Song of the Volga Boatmen.' Heard it in a show month-two
back. Now there was a picture. These two brothers, see, were
slaves—serfs, they called them—in Russia and had to tow this
boat up river. They had this rope around their chests and I mean,
they was scratching. Snow on the ground, half naked—"

"Don't sound like they had much to sing about."

"Hell, they wasn't singing. They was letting their guts hang
out their mouths. Thirty-forty of them and a patroller on horse-
back with a whip. And instead of killing him they was crawling
on their bellies."

"Maybe they couldn't help it."

"They could help it. You got the guts, you can help anything.
You got to make your own way. There ain't nobody gonna say,
'Lemme give you a hand.' You know that."

"Maybe so. Still—"

Still she hated to believe it. In spite of everything.

"Now they saying, 'Help the nigger. Don't call a Jew kike.'
But I say, 'The hell with that.' For if they was where I am, they'd
do the same and twice again."

"Yellow Tom's a good nigger—"

"If he was where you are, how'd he be?"

"I been fair to him—"

"A fool wants fairness. I don't. I want people to try and stamp
me, for then I can crawl up their bellies and down their backs."

She asked curiously, "How about me?"

He looked at her; he said softly, "I wouldn'ta crawled down
your back."

Her breath held.

The world was full of small winds. They stroked the trees, and
the trees arched their backs. They moved down and prowled the
shrubs. Ragged-robin stirred indigo and mauve and white, and

dusty miller bloomed in white patches. The winds moved the shrubs aside, and there was the Gold Mine Church.

Peanuts sat up. "Now that's a helluva looking place."

It had been built in the old mining days. A circuit rider had made people build it, though they protested, "Just as good build it in the southeast corner of Hell. Them miners been raised on the shorter catechism. They'll steal the pews off the seats." The circuit rider said, "They'll have to come inside to do it—then we got them." He caused wide iron bands to be sunk into the rocks at each corner. The church had no steeple, no vestibule, and, with the bands, it had the look of a little strapped trunk.

"Well, where's this baptistery at?"

"Down yonder."

They cut around the church, past the graveyard. The tombstones, abandoned in weeds, leaned this way and that, lamb and dove and folded marble hands carved upon them. Beyond, long rows of wooden tables were set up under the trees for homecoming dinners and suppers-on-the-ground. The road, slick with pine needles, dipped down the hill.

A raccoon lumbered across the road, heavy hindquarters trying to outrun the front. His black domino turned over a shoulder to watch them.

Peanuts yelled, "Wish I had me a gun!"

They heard the voice at the same minute, clearly above the sound of running water.

The spring gushed through a pipe lying beside the road. It led from the woods to a rock pit some ten yards away. The baptistery was a hole four by six feet wide, three feet deep. Steps helped the repentant down into one end, a plug let sins wash away at the other. Now the pit was full and slopping over. The ground was muddy, the water full of trash; leaves and chinaberry sticks speckled Rose Crawford's body.

She was standing, fat and naked, in the baptistery, singing.

". . . tree by the river, sassafras tree, store had Cokes, no dime, no dime, no dime. But Jesus paid it all, Jesus paid it all. Wash sin, wash sin—lye and ashes and pork grease—"

A scream cut the song; a coffee-pot sawmill beyond the hill bucked a hardwood knot. A lesser noise had killed the shrew. Toy had found the tiny mouselike creature one day in a wild-bee nest. She had taken it home, nest and all, and set it on the kitchen table while she got supper. She had been fascinated by its orange teeth and implacable hate. But she had dropped an iron skillet on the stone hearth. The shrew had drawn up its tail, shut its eyes, and died.

She did not shut her eyes; noise would not release her as kindly as it had the shrew.

Her mother had found a catalpa leaf, large and heart-shaped. She put it on her head, giggling. Her hair was cropped short. It was easier to cut it than to catch her and comb it. A pone of fat lay on her neck. It was an obstinate pone, and the way she hunched her shoulders forward was obstinate. The way she cut her eyes at them, cutely, was obstinate.

"Washed away, washed away . . ."

Toy felt the wagon stop. She felt Peanuts jump down and heard the reins thrown around a bush. Twigs snapped, sand squeaked under foot.

He said disgustedly, "Looks like you could keep her to home."

Words loosened the knots that held her. She felt weak all over. She climbed down from the wagon and found her legs wavering. It angered her. She held to a wheel furiously.

"What you want me to do, smash her toes like a chicken?"

"They got places for such as her, Milledgeville."

"She's my mother."

Splat!

The water hit them with the sudden sting of cold bees. Rose Crawford had taken her cupped hand and splashed them. She giggled vacuously.

"Saved, saved, saved, saved, saved . . ."

Peanuts turned away, disgusted. "Where's her clothes, any-way?"

Toy drew breath into her throat. A danger, unknown, had been averted. She pointed to the change-house.

"Maybe there."

It was a hut of gray scantlings just beyond the baptistery. Cow ivy veiled the roof; hickory limbs hung over each door. People, prior to immersion, changed in it to old clothes. Now owls made it their home; there were neat pellets of fur on the floor. Roaches and beetles rustled.

There were no clothes.

Peanuts said, "Throw a croaker sack round her, then. There's one in the wagon."

She shook her head stubbornly. "No, she had new shoes. They cost three dollars."

"You looking for these?" Ora Watts appeared out of the bushes. She held clothes on a thin arm.

"I took them, 'cause I was afeared she'd th'ow them in the water or some such. And I could see"—her voice was wistful—"them was new shoes."

Few new shoes came Ora Watts's way. Few new anything. She had been born into a large poor family and married Ammi to repeat the tale. They had eight children, but not a rooster to crow good morning. How she made out to feed the family, no one knew, or how she clothed them—maybe she plucked fur from her breast as rabbits did.

Toy said, "I thank you." She took the clothes awkwardly. She felt the reluctance with which Ora Watts let them go. "How you come to find Ma?"

"Jenny and me come to clean my granddaddy's grave. I heard her splashing and singing, and sent Jenny to Lovick Jones right off."

It was right, it was natural, that Ora Watts should be clean-ing an old grave on a high and sunny morning. She was as dogged in her duties as a bantam hen.

Peanuts said, "Cleaning a grave?" His face and voice were innocent and interested. "Now that's a fine and Christian thing to do. Which grave would that be now?"

Mrs. Watts flushed up to her thin, blue-veined temples.

"Now I just bet you're Peanuts Stonecypher. Ammi's been telling me about you, how you play the guitar and such. Wish I could get to the mill and hear you." She pointed a finger proudly. "It's that grave yonder, the tallest one. My granddaddy was a man of substance. He had him three-four farms, only the war come and the Yankees burned him out. But Grandma made out to get the stone cut. It's got a poem on it wrote by a real poet."

"How do it go?"

Unconsciously Ora Watts's work-swollen hands rose to her breast and clasped as though in prayer. She wore an old blue sunbonnet and men's shoes run over at the heels. But she had a tall tombstone and a poem written by a real poet.   .

> "Farewell, my wife and children all,
> From you a father Christ doth call.
> Mourn not for me, it is in vain
> To call me to your arms again."

She opened her eyes, breathing a little more quickly. "Ain't that beautiful?"

"Sure is. Now my daddy drowned a few years back and my ma had a stone cut. It had a poem on it, too."

Ora Watts's face was bright with pleasure. "I'd be proud to hear it."

Peanuts recited solemnly, " 'Ma loved Pa. Pa loved women. Ma caught Pa with one in swimming. Here lies Pa.' "

The little woman's smile faded. She looked at him, confused. "That's—that's right sad."

"Ain't it just?"

Toy moved forward sharply. "This ain't getting Ma home." She looked at Peanuts. "I can manage; you watch the mule."

He grinned. "Why, sure."

He limped over to an oak tree and sat down on one of the sprawling, contorted roots, stretching his leg before him. Mrs. Watts moved closer to Toy's elbow. She had not taken her eyes from Peanuts.

She whispered, "You—you reckon his daddy really had that on his gravestone?"

"Yes." Toy wondered why she bothered to lie. She turned. "Now, Ma, you got to come out of there."

Her mother giggled.

The spring bubbled coldly up from an out-thrust of rocks; fiddlehead ferns clenched themselves against the chill. Rose Crawford took no more notice of the cold than one of the whirlybugs that skittered across the surface of the water, though her flabby skin looked gelid.

"You come and I'll take you to Goforth's. I'll buy you a Coke."

Rose Crawford's hand snaked out. She seized a whirlybug and threw it away. "Hateful ole things." She hummed again.

Mrs. Watts stepped forward. "Now, sugar, you gonna get a cold, you stay in there. You let Ora help you out."

Instantly Rose Crawford sank beneath the surface of the water, hiding.

Peanuts chortled.

Sourweed bloomed nearby. Bite the red stem, and bitterness filled your mouth. Yet it was less bitter than what Toy tasted now. Tears stung her eyes, and she fought them back as she would have fought the deadliest enemy.

The words jerked out of her. "Maybe when she comes up—maybe if you took one arm—"

A hoar of bubbles rose. Her mother followed, splashing and snorting. Water plastered her hair to her round skull. She was flabby and round with no handle to grab her by. Toy tried. She seized an arm, and Ora Watts got a piece of shoulder.

Rose Crawford yelled happily. She thrust out wet and heavy

arms against them. They staggered and nearly pitched into the water before letting go. She vanished, a strand of hair floating upward like a troll-token.

Peanuts was doubled over, trying to hold mirth in his body, but it was too big; it came out in whoops.

"She—she don't—want to come—looks like."

Toy said dully, "I'll go in, take out the plug."

She kicked off the old tennis shoes and bunched her skirt in one hand. The fieldstone steps were cold and slimy underfoot. Water bit her ankles and crawled inexorably up her legs. She could not see what her mother had used to plug the drainage hole —some piece of trash, likely, for the water was wallowing-dirty. She took a deep breath to pull her shivering flesh close against her bones and went under, hand groping.

Her mother's flailed out and struck her. Dimly her mother floated beside her, squatty and white as a monstrous frog, her mouth open with glee like a frog's. The hand came out again and caught her across the bridge of the nose. She cried out involuntarily and came up in runnels of cold, eyes skimmed and bitter.

Ora Watts's voice came dimly. "You get it?"

She shook her head, choking. Her eyes cleared a little. She saw Peanuts standing on the edge of the baptistery. His bare ankles were on a level with Rose Crawford's eyes as she bobbed up. A fat hand shot out. He pitched around, arms flailing, and sat down with a thud on the muddy ground, one leg hip-deep in the baptistery.

He was up, yelling. He danced around, shaking his leg, trying to shake cold and wet off. There was a heart-shaped patch of wet on his seat.

Toy choked. She thought it was water in her throat, but it was laughter or tears, she did not know which. She was afraid to speak, but Mrs. Watts spoke. She called helpfully, "You sure got you a little ole wet bottom!"

He stopped dancing and shaking. He knelt by the side of the baptistery.

Toy thought, He's trying to get Ma out. Then she yelled, "What you doing? What you doing?"

Water dogged her steps as she stumbled toward him. The wind, warm earlier, seized her in terrier teeth and shook her. She grabbed his arm.

"Quit that! Quit that, you hear?"

Peanuts had an arm thrust into the water. It held down something which had been quiescent for a moment in astonishment, but which now bucked and thrust and tried to break free, break the surface for air, Rose Crawford's head. But he would not let it. Face merciless, arm hard as cordwood, he held her under the surface. Mrs. Watts wailed, swollen hands knotting helplessly, "Dear Jesus, he's adrowning her!"

Words rasped in his throat. "She likes water so much . . ."

Toy could not budge him. His muscles were quilted solid against her hands. He was rooted in fury. He held her mother under the water until an ominous hoar of bubbles burst up.

Toy had no strength. Her fingers were little white sticks. They could pick, but they could not pull. Her eyes found a stone, wedge-shaped and fitting to the palm. She hardly knew that she picked it up and hit him. He fell back.

Her mother floated to the surface of the water, eyes turned back in her skull, fingers scratching weakly at the side of the pit. Mrs. Watts wavered up and began tugging at her mother, tugging and begging, "Sugar—sugar—" until Toy put out a hand and helped pull and tug the heavy body up on land. It lay like a beached and nameless water animal, retching.

Ora Watts repeated breathlessly, "He tried to drown her, you seen? He tried to drown her."

Blood throbbed in Toy's ears. She thought, He'll be waking up any minute now. I didn't hit him so hard. She thought, smoothing wet strings of hair from her face, He'll be mad.

Ora Watts, faced with silence, became uncertain. "I mean— you reckon?"

She said, "No."

Maybe he had been trying to drown her mother. Maybe he hadn't. Maybe he had been washing his hands, and her mother's head had gotten in the way. What difference did it make? Her mother was out. Now she wished Ora Watts would go; this was no affair of hers any more.

"Well, what was he trying to do then, he wasn't trying to drown her, tell me?"

"Make her come out."

Maybe he had been. Likely he'd tell her when he woke up. Now he lay limp as any bundle of rags a child drew a string around and called "doll." His jaw, thrust up, had an oddly scraped and vulnerable look. Two buttons were popped from his blue shirt. Yet one knee, the wet one, was drawn up, as though he was ready, even unconscious, to spring up and fight.

Toy bent and put the knee flat, and wondered why she did it. Even flat he surged away from the earth, neck and back and knee. He would hate it when he woke and found his neck where his foot should be.

Toy thought, He'll go to raring. Sudden excitement stirred through her. It drew her muscles, weak and quivering from re-action, into taut attention. She thought, He'll tear up the patch.

Ora Watts said, "Well, all I can say is, it sure looked like he was trying to drown her."

Rose Crawford stirred nearby and whimpered. It was the whimper of a child in a nightmare. Her gross body moved con-vulsively, drawing away from the dream, or maybe only draw-ing in on itself for warmth.

Toy walked over. Her clothes clung wetly against her mo-tions. She said, "Ma, get up."

Rose Crawford rolled her head in the sand, retched weakly. A trickle of water came from her mouth. She moved her head away from it like a child, still whimpering, eyes half open but not seeing anything. Gooseflesh sprang up and raced along her body.

Toy bent and shook her roughly. "Ma, get up. Go to the wagon. You hear me, Ma?"

Her mother lurched to her knees obediently. She hung there like a sick dog, pendant all over, flesh hanging down in rolls. Her ankles were swollen, blood puddling in them.

Ora Watts sprang forward. "Sugar, let me help. Come on, come with Ora. Ora's got your clothes, your nice new shoes. See now?"

Rose Crawford lurched up, eyes on wagon. She staggered, hardly seeing Ora Watts fussing and clucking at her side. She got to the back of it and half fell in. She sighed and, as Toy had known she would, curled up and went to sleep.

Mrs. Watts whispered, "I swear, you see that? And a minute-two ago—"

The trouble was over, and now she wanted to talk about it. Speech was her way of extracting the meaning from life; she did not know what she thought until she said it. She was ready to put the episode between her teeth, and tug and shake and gnaw it free of meaning.

Toy shrank. She said quickly, "I'm obliged, Mrs. Watts."

"Why, it wasn't nothing, honey. I was proud to help, you know that. I only got two hands, but I love to leave one free for the other feller, though a lot of folks can't spare a finger, looks like. It's me-and-Bob-and-four's-enough." She took a deep breath. "I declare, I'm all to pieces after that tussle. Your ma's a load, ain't she?"

Toy said clearly, "I know you got to get on. I'm obliged."

"Why, no, sugar, I got nothing can't wait—"

She stopped. She had started to turn around and search for a seat, a rock or a stump. She turned back, and her eyes went from Toy to the man prone and recalcitrant on the ground.

"Why," she said slowly, "I reckon— Yes, I reckon I got to get on."

Hesitantly she started off toward the graveyard. Once she

paused to look over her shoulder. Toy stood silent, face without encouragement. Her mother snored from the wagon. The mule, reaching for a limb to browse on, tinkled its chains. A stick cracked as Peanuts stirred.

Mrs. Watts shrilled suddenly, "I don't care, I still think he was trying to drown her! And you don't look out, Toy Crawford, he's gonna do for you!"

She disappeared, skirt switching her heels. Toy turned to find Peanuts propped on an elbow, fingers probing his scalp, watching her.

She said directly, "You want to know—I hit you."

He said nothing. His fingers continued to probe. His black hair, combed straight back from his forehead, had little tomcat spikes. He had the silent bunchiness of a tomcat about to jump.

She said quickly, warning him, "No use having a hissy. You know—you were about to drown Ma."

"Where's she at?"

"In the wagon. Sleeping."

"I'll be damned." His fingers found something. He winced. "What you hit me with, Stone Mountain?"

"Piece of it."

"Feels like." He added casually, "Gimme a hand."

Maybe she had hit him harder than she thought. Maybe the wound in his leg had broken open. She put out a hand. His own clenched it, and she knew that he needed it no more than the wind.

She twisted back, but he wouldn't let her go. He rose. "Now two-three men have hit me, but no woman at all."

Her voice was not hers. "First time for everything."

He did not reply. Instead he began twisting her arm one way with one hand, the other way with the other, Indian-burning. She cried out and flung herself against him. His chest was hard as a weaver's beam. They went off balance and toppled into the sand, tumbling about like cats. The scuffles of childhood came back to her; they had had an ephemeral cruelty, but this was different. This was deadly. No part of the body was immune. She had a brief glimpse through stinging eyes of the sky, and then they were up and apart and panting.

"You think you're hard," he said softly. His cat-ridged hair was over his black eyes watching her. "You think you're hard, but you're soft. Now how soft are you?" They stood breast to breast. "Soft as cotton," he whispered. "White as cotton."

White as bay flowers that bloomed behind the change-house. Bay flowers and bubby-blossoms sweet, and water going by somewhere—where? Dewberries shining through the cracks in the change-house, honeysuckle putting green fingers through the cracks.

He kissed and bit her, one as necessary as the other. He whispered, "Poor little ole Toy. Poor little Spook."

The pond was high, and the river was in spate. The floodgate lifted.

Seven

THE soft-drink cooler came the next week. It was white and it drew the eyes of Gristle and the tongues of Gristle.

A man flipped his plow over to start another furrow and called to a neighbor, "Hey, you seen the new drink box to the mill? White as sin before Satan, Satan before sin."

The neighbor told his brother, "And when I went to look-see, there was Peanuts, feet cocked up on it."

The brother told his wife, arm-measuring cloth at Goforth's, "And Peanuts says he's thinking of putting in coffee, sugar, and smokes."

John Goforth complained to his wife, "Told Bob, 'Goforth's meat's rotten. Throw it against the wall, and it'll stick.'"

Annie Goforth's pleasant face was thoughtful. "Toy letting that little feller do like that—you reckon—?"

Wick Bloodworth stopped by the mill one day. He tipped his head back and scanned the sky. "Looks like it's fairing off some."

She said stiffly, "Looks like." She thought, He come like the others to talk about the box, how come I let Peanuts get it.

She was unsure herself. Peanuts had talked about it when they were driving home from the baptistery. Even now the scratch of brambles along the sides of the wagon, and her mother's sucking snores were in her ears.

"Spook, I been thinking, rations ain't enough."

A black snake whipped across the road, a mockingbird fierce upon it.

"I mean, a man needs more in his pocket than his hand."

The bird swooped, and the snake writhed on with a broken tail. The bird would attack until it broke every vertebra in the snake's body.

"I figure, five dollars a week."

She only paid Yellow Tom $1.50 a day when he worked, and grinding was slacking off. The time of light biscuits had come. The only corn was ripening on the stalk.

"How 'bout it, Spook?"

"All right."

He grinned and laid his hand on her knee. "I'll buy you a two-dollar diamond ring."

Her knee jerked back from his touch and longed for it again. She was bewildered. Was this love, drawing to and pulling away, living between the chip and the bark? Aunt Baptist said, "Love is hoggery." Wick said, "Love caused us first to be; Love died upon a tree." Tessie said, "So-and-So's got a rose bush. It has a red rose, a red and white rose, and a white rose on the same stem. It's called Careless Love."

What, beyond the onset of blood, was love?

He went on briskly, "You know, I been thinking. You missing a bet not having a little store to the mill. If you sold soft drinks, smokes and coffee and such, you could make you a heap of money."

She roused herself. "I don't want a store."

"You wouldn't have to mess round with it. I'd do it for you." He grinned. "I'll even make you two promises: I'll be there payday."

She shook her head. "I had a store, there'd be people. They'd talk to me. They'd figure I owed them something. They'd figure they'd won."

She broke off. Words had been too long away from her lips. She could not explain that her only victory over the people of Gristle lay in removing herself from them. The only thing they couldn't stand was being let alone.

"You too touchy. You got to get over that. Stay around me long enough, you will."

After a minute he started whistling absently, eyes narrowed against the sun or his thoughts. After a while he cupped her knee again. And this time, shivering, she let him. . . .

Wick went on, "Well, hope the weather holds up. We got the Green Pastures Quartet coming to the sing next Saturday."

The sky was a cool milky blue; the ground was spongy. Silver trickles slid down the hills. It had rained a storm for three days, rained enough to drive the snakes to high ground. A copperhead had slid past her foot that morning and hardly noticed her.

Peanuts unlaced his fingers from his chest and dropped his heels to the ground.

"Now I been hearing about this sing. It going to be an all-nighter?"

"No. Afternoon."

Wick was not going to mention the cooler; a weakness went over Toy as she realized it. Wick would not mention the cooler or look at her as the others did, a look that made more out of less, a look that said, I knowed it all along; you no better than me.

"What's it costing, bringing the quartet over? I hear tell they pretty good."

"Nothing. We take up an offering."

"I'd want a guarantee, it was me." Peanuts rose and opened the cooler. It stood just inside the door of the mill. Already it was coated with meal-dust. "How about a drink, Preacher?"

Wick shook his head. "I thank you."

Peanuts grinned. "Oh, I was figuring on making you pay for it. How about you, Spook?"

She shook her head and moved away; she put space between herself and the nickname. She took a scoop and began to fill a five-pound sack with meal.

Wick said, "Spook. Now that's a curious name."

"I call her that because spooks is so white."

His voice was too innocent. Toy burned; heat mounted her brown arms and throat and flowed to the edge of the brown U on her breast.

Peanuts went on, "Hear tell all you singing to the sing is spirituals."

"Most people think spirituals is a sufficiency."

"Oh, don't figure I'm throwing off on them. Can't afford to, though General Sherman has already invited me down—'Come help me strike matches; Hell's too cold.' No. Only I hear there's other songs, say—love songs."

"Love songs?" Wick's voice was meditative. "Now I like a good love song myself, though it goes so far and no further. You ever been in love?"

The question was sudden. Toy saw Peanuts' mouth jump to answer. He stopped. "Why—sure. Ain't everybody?" He added deliberately, "Hear you was once yourself."

The hill-hidden trickles of water slid down; it was a lonesome sound even when birds interrupted.

Wick nodded. "Her name was Flonnie, and I never felt so close to God as when I loved her. Everything had a shine. Everything I touched, I felt twice, finger and heart." He asked quietly, "You ever felt so?"

The small man dropped his bottle into a crate. It made a harsh clatter. His face was set in lines as harsh.

"No." His face might have been handsome then; it came closest to honesty. "You think I'm trash, don't you, Preacher? You think I be-nasty folks' minds with my jokes and songs and such. But you know and I know that you can't be-nasty something ain't nasty already. I give the monkeys an extra tail to play with is all. And you know and I know another thing, that what people call love is nothing but a drop of pus. They squeeze it out a core of hate and lying-to-theirselves and torn bed-sheets, and it makes them feel better a minute or two. But the core is there right on!"

Wick's face was taut. "I'd be sorry for you, I wasn't sorrier for others. You're right, you're trash, and you be-nasty everything you touch. But you're worse than that—you're a fool."

"You—"

"Fool. For all the time you think people is laughing with you, they laughing at you. For one thing I know and you don't is, people want to believe. Or why we got the word 'love'—why we got the word 'hope'?"

Peanuts laughed shrilly. His eyes went here and there like an animal's seeking a hole. Toy stood with a fist clenched to her breast. He seized it. His small, hard arm went around her waist. His fingers pleated the skin under her breast.

"I believe, Preacher. I believe what I can touch. Like this." His hand hardened. "I live under my hand, Preacher."

Wick's big hand went out and closed around Peanuts' throat. The small man's arms flew wide against it. He fumbled and strained against the iron fingers.

"If I lived under my hand, Peanuts, where would you be? Now tell me." His hand dropped. He walked away without looking back; they heard his truck start and pull off.

Peanuts turned. He tried a laugh through gasping breath. "Now—a minute there I thought he'd do it."

"Wick wouldn't do nothing."

"He's so good, why didn't he help you when you needed it, say? You remember, you made it alone." He reached a hand. "Poor little ole Spook."

Flesh to flesh then, and faces to the floor.

After a while he murmured, "A little store, Spook, a few counters, smokes—"

"No!" She was on her feet, alien to her flesh. Mi-Maw Mary, she thought confusedly. You're worse as Mi-Maw Mary.

She had been an old woman, crazy and half forgotten, who had lived in a shack in the woods. Folks thought her a witch because she had painted names on her porch plants—Grace, Soul, Ruth, Psalm, Star. By her front door had stood a cracked churn planted with elephants' ears, and it had two names: Love, Hate.

Now why two names, Toy had wondered, and those so opposite? Why "Hate" when so many others suited "Love" better —"Beauty" or "Hope" or "Honesty"?

Now she thought, She was right.

Love and hate were entangled. Wiser women than Mi-Maw Mary had tried to sort the one from the other and failed. Love and hate were entangled—and a cracked churn held them.

A few days later she drove in to Gristle to deliver meal to Goforth's—Tessie's job when she and Harl were not hanging around Peanuts, but she had taken off as usual.

Peanuts went along, but dropped off before town. "Got to see Coke Williams about something."

She rattled on to the store, thankful to be alone and wondering why. The store had changed hardly at all. There was the colored walk of Nehi caps, a black cat licking its thumb by the stove. Only the tray of Trot was gone, victim of hard times.

Dolly called listlessly, "What Pa owe you this time, Toy?"

She was folded across the counter, cutting a fly trap. She wore a pink dress, a brown spit curl on one temple, and her lower lip poked out.

"Four-fifty."

"Here 'tis."

She slid the money across and went back to the fly trap, a circle of cardboard with a hole poked in the middle. She began smearing one side with syrup. Her lip was still out, but she said nothing. Toy was surprised.

Once Lovick Jones said, "Dolly swallowed a rabbit tail when she was two, and she's been trying to spit it out ever since." It was true. Every time Dolly saw Toy she took up a tale in the middle: ". . . and there's this man . . ." It was always a man Dolly talked about, and that was natural. Dolly was curved for men, and where she was not curved for men, she was curved for babies. She would have married at thirteen, but her father had shaken his head.

"You too young. It ain't gonna hurt you to wait, be sure."

Dolly had wept. "Sure? What difference do sure make?"

For any man would do Dolly. All she needed of him was the initial act. Babies were her end-all. The four-year-old child, the three-, the two-, and the lap baby who had never been born to Dolly were the unluckiest children in the valley.

Toy asked, "Something wrong?"

"Ever'thing!" Dolly slapped the circle of cardboard into the top of a jar filled with water. It fitted in tightly, syrup side down.

"Ever'thing, you want to know. Pa said I could marry Jack!"

Flies hummed around the jar on high notes of surprise.

"Thought you was so crazy 'bout him."

She had heard of Jack Nimmons, a boy with grin that never knew a stranger, redheaded and a good shot; pace off ninety steps, and he could pop the head off a turkey. The rest of the time he was shot with hard luck. He saw-milled, and the contracts ran out. He farmed on shares, and drought burned the cabbage to nubs. He turned to driving, but his brakes failed on a grade, and the truck clammed over on him. He rubbed the scars and grinned. "Now ain't it rough to be poor and hired out?"

Aunt Baptist declared, "Jack'll have ten-fifteen children. Stands to reason. He won't never have a dime, so the Lord'll even it up other ways."

Dolly and Jack suited each other. Everyone said so, and everyone thought it was a sin and a shame. Children might be Heaven's blessing and earth's comfort, but after the first eight or ten they were rabbits right on.

John Goforth moaned. "I'm gonna end up supporting a dozen young'uns, you marry Jack!"

Dolly had opened liquid, uncomprehending eyes. "But they're young'uns." It was the final justification.

Now she wailed, "I am crazy 'bout Jack, and he's crazy 'bout me, but Pa says we can't get married till I'm seventeen. Two whole months off!"

"It won't hurt you none to wait."

"It will too. It hurts me right now. It hurts me here." Dolly's hand pressed her breast, and with more honesty moved to her stomach. She said defiantly, "It hurts here, Toy Crawford, you want to know. You just don't feel such as that."

"Maybe not."

Dolly made an inarticulate sound. She flew around the counter and threw her arms around Toy. No one but Dolly had ever circled her with their arms. Even Peanuts' whatever-it-was took a shorter time and a straighter line.

"Aw, sugar, you know I didn't mean that. Now you know I love you like a sister. I been watching you and Peanuts. He's—" Even honest, man-loving Dolly faltered. "He's strange-like, ain't he? But"—Dolly's creed returned strongly to the fore—"anyways he's a man."

The screen door creaked. Four men came in, passing conversation around.

". . . 'bout your wife?"

"Bo'cat don't worry about his wife, do you, Bo'cat? Heard him in the dime store over to Cardiff last week. He was talking to this little gal to the candy counter. She says, 'No, you're married.'

Bo'cat says, 'No, I ain't.' She says, 'I heard.' Bo'cat says, 'I ain't married. I ain't married 'till I get home.' "

Bo'cat said equitably through the guffaws, "Anyways, I always come back to taw."

A tall man who had followed Bo'cat in turned. His eyes found Toy's; he came toward her, hand outstretched. "Now you done a good thing. I want to thank you."

Automatically she put out her hand. His was big and warm and brisk. It suited his face, but the face was a stranger's.

She said uncertainly, "You got the wrong party, I reckon."

"You Toy Crawford?"

Peanuts bounced in, the center of a group. "Hey, Spook, what you doing holding hands with Sam?" He cocked his fists and danced forward on his toes. "Now let go my gal, Sam, or I'll bash your brains in, I sure will!" He made a pass, hit the tall man hard on the hip, and danced back in broad consternation. "Now I'd bash his brains in—I could reach them! Lordy, look at the reach on that feller, will you?"

Sam was red-faced and mad, but he made his mouth turn up in a wry grin. He rubbed his hip. "Now maybe it's a good thing you can't reach my brains. That sure was a wallop."

"Have Toy kiss it, make it well."

In the yelp that followed, Peanuts acted a vast contrition. He sidled forward and slid an arm around Toy's shoulders. He smelled of smoke and sweat and stump-rum. "Aw, now, Spook, you know I'm just funning. You know I'll joke when I'm jerked to Jesus."

He would joke, and she would listen. Her mind would say, A tinhorn man and don't know how to blow. And her flesh would reply, Live in hope if you die in despair.

She blurted to Sam, "What was you thanking me for?"

"Why, lending the clubhouse for the sing." His face cleared. He had the deep chest and wide mouth of a man who loved to line out hymns. "Thought first we'd use the church, but like Peanuts said, it'd do more honor to the Lord if we sung His songs from a place beside the church. And he said, did we use the church, he couldn't sell Nehis outside; it'd be sacrilegious. But did we use the clubhouse, he said, he'd give us a per cent of what he cleared."

"He said a lot, didn't he?"

The blood was thick in her throat and wrist. She turned and walked out. She let the voices break around her. She let Peanuts call and run and finally catch up with her as she switched the mule. He heaved and fell spraddling on the front seat.

"By God," he said, panting, "you'da gone and done it. You'da gone off without me, let me walk back." The wagon jolted his words; dust clouded them. "You was gonna leave me squatting on my tongue."

She flashed, "Squatting on your tongue, telling folks why they ain't going to use the clubhouse for the sing."

He said, "Stop the wagon."

She drew on the reins; the mule halted, jingling. The road was empty before and behind. The only sound was the rustle of beetles and lizards in the dry grass.

"You know what I am? A damn li'l' monkey on a stick." He swung around, eyes bitter as tannin, and repeated, "A damn li'l' monkey on a stick. You've seen them to the fairs? Jerk a string, and I been running up and down and shaking my tail, I wanted to or not. Well, I got a bait of it."

This outburst was different from his others; here was something from the bone.

He repeated, "I got a bait of it."

"What's that got to do with the clubhouse?"

"I figured to make money to the sing. I figured to sell drinks and smokes and candy. There'll be a heap of people; I could make me something. Later I figured to buy into the jook Coke is fixing to open on the Cardiff road. He says can I put up a little cash, I'll be half-partner. I figured to quit being a monkey on a stick."

She said, "Hiawassee. Nashville."

"Light talk on a black night."

She said flatly, "You're lying."

"You say so, so it's so."

The mule stamped; greenbottle flies were pestering the life out of it. After a while she took a breath.

"All right."

"The clubhouse?"

"Take it."

The mule flinched flies off. They were bad at the house too. Maybe a trap? The flies knew there was something wrong with that sweet little hole. Yet they were obliged to crawl through.

Eight

THE days before the sing, Harl Junior and Tessie were back and forth between house and clubhouse like fools. They told Toy everything that happened, not because she wanted them to, but because it was the finest thing that had ever happened to them and their skins could not contain it.

"Everyone buys me Cokes, Toy," Tessie gloated. "They say it's a Christian thing you doing. Everyone says, come to the sing."

She said, "Tell them, next time."

"Will you go next time?"

"Maybe."

Another time Harl reported, "Tuck Tate is fixing to set up front with the quartet, and he's been eating ramp."

Homebrew and rampion, the little wild onions, were a fine spring dish; every man in the valley was alien of breath. Harl wailed, "He'll blow the quartet clean out of the place."

Sunday noon, an hour before the sing was due to start, he burst in, shouting, "Peanuts and Wick is fighting 'bout you."

Toy felt the strength drain out of her wrists. She had been doing the dishes, Tessie's chore, but Tessie was off hanging around the clubhouse and taunting Peanuts. "Hi, Mr. Watch-Fob," she'd say. "What you doing, Mr. Watch-Fob?"

"Sure are." He amended reluctantly, "Well, they ain't, to say, hitting each other, but they sure talking right up to." He took a breath. "Way it started, the candy man asked Peanuts for some money and Peanuts says, 'You bad as the horseleach's daughters, crying, "Give, give," all the time.' Wick come by and says, 'You know the Bible good.' Peanuts says, 'You surprised, Preacher? Why, every time I done something wrong when I was a young'un, Pa made me learn a Bible piece. Time I was ten, I knowed pretty near the whole Book, I was so wicked-mean.' Wick says, 'And I misdoubt you've changed. I been meaning to talk to you; now's as good a time. You know, I been Toy's friend, though lately I've seen how much I failed her. Now, though, I'm telling you, she's had a sufficiency of sorrow. You do anything to hurt her—' Peanuts says, 'You your sister's keeper, Preacher?' Wick says, 'Laugh all you want, but remember what I say.' "

Toy let her breath out. "That wasn't no fight."

"You'd seen their faces, it was a fight."

"Never mind. Come help me with these dishes."

"I can't. I got—I got—"

The words trailed after him as he ran off. He had nothing to do, and that was the hardest job of all; he had to spread himself so thin to do it.

She closed her teeth and finished the dishes. She spread a cloth over them to dry, and went out on the side porch. A gourd vine had started up by the kitchen steps. It was no more than a few little spadelike leaves, a reaching tendril; by midsummer it would take over the dooryard.

She thought, I belong to jerk it out.

Instead she sat down on the top step, hands loose between her knees. Heaviness seemed to press her all around. It was more than the heat, more than sleeplessness. She lay awake these nights, and her thoughts went around and around, seven times seven, but no Jerichos tumbled.

She did not know if she believed Peanuts or no; and she did not know if she wanted to believe him or no.

The hope of spring was everywhere, green healing the browns and irons of winter. Milk and wine lilies bloomed by the fence; dogwood ascended Atkins' ridge; stones were hidden by leaping grass.

She thought, If a person could start over so.

Yet a person was trapped two ways, by what he thought about himself, and by what others thought about him.

Now if she could go to Wick and ask, What to do? If she could go to Wick and lay her troubles on his strong knees, lay her head on his strong knees— Her mind jumped before the thought, startled and abashed as a wild thing caught where it had no business to be. No, she had not meant such as that; it was the kind of thought that came these nights to plague her.

Far off a rifle cracked, someone hunting rabbits in the folds of the hills. Nearer a woman called a cow, "Coop! Cush, cush!" A car rattled by on the clay road; the first people were coming to the sing.

Soon people went by on whatever moved, trucks and carts and jolt-wagons, with rows of chairs set up in the wagon-bed and people joggling and laughing. Tuck Tate went by on muleback, a dozen dogs trotting beside.

Eventually the flow slowed. It became a trickle. A last man approached. He came from the direction of Gristle. He was thin and dressed in preacher-black and a dog tugged him along, a feist the no-color of tobacco-spit. It strained the rope tied to its neck, nose fixed on distance. As the man neared, Toy saw that he had a canvas pack on his back and a heavy staff in his free hand. He poked and prodded the earth.

She thought, A road-walker, and blind. What business did a blind man have on the road?

He came abreast of the trail leading off to the clubhouse and stopped, head lifting this way and that like an animal's, listening. Distant voices hummed like insects; a shout or laugh raised above the hum. He started again.

Toy thought, Now what's he want yonder?

Again she wished that she could see the clubhouse, but the trees were too bushy; green interleaved with gold blotted it from sight. She could see a corner of the mill, a piece of the creek, but none of the pond.

Restlessly she got up and walked across to the pasture. Gourds were coming up along the rails. Well, she would let them stay, for there was nothing better to poison moles than gourd seeds. In the fall, too, children cut the largest and straightest-necked gourds for banjos. They would shave off one side, paste brown paper over the opening, and string them with cat-gut. They were better than cornstalk fiddles and shoestring bows.

She thought, If I walked a piece up the trail, wouldn't nobody know.

Yet some latecomer might see her and tell fairy tales. Then Wick would come as he had come twice, and beg, "Come go." And she would have to say, as she had before, "Another time, maybe."

She thought, The road-runner is getting to the clubhouse. Any minute now he would pull out a cup and claim charity. She thought, Tuck Tate's dogs'll tear him to pieces.

She slipped between the pasture bars and ran. She slipped under the farther bars and across the road to the trail. It had been little used in the last six-eight years, but today's traffic had torn it open. Grass was trampled until it was grass no longer; bushes and young saplings were leaf-stripped and twig-broken.

She yelled, "Hey," into the leafy tunnel.

The blind man halted, ears prehensile. The leash jumped and jerked; the dog wanted to go on. It lunged, front paws dangling from the earth. Then it sat down and began licking its belly, nose inquisitive in crevices.

The blind man's voice was thin and reedy. "Someone?"

She said loudly, so everyone could hear and know why she had come, "You got no more sense than to go where you don't know where you going? You don't know there's a dozen dogs ahead'll tear yourn to pieces?"

"I been in fifteen states and Mexico; never been set on but once. A billygoat butt me."

"Well, Georgia dogs is mean dogs."

He thrust out his staff. "Hickory'll bring 'em to grace."

He had no teeth, and his eyes were like marbles, the whites and blues run together. Sun-red skin was stretched tight over cheeks and chin.

"Woman told me 'twould be a sing here today. Lived over the ridge she did, a Christian soul, give me coffee and bread for my breakfast. There's some won't give hay to a billygoat. Now, seems I can hear the sing yonder." He cocked an ear and extended a sleeve. "If you'd lend a poor blind man a hand . . ."

The sleeve was sun-warm and greasy; it smelled of dirt and small animals. She hated the odor and the confidence.

"No need. Straight ahead." She added shortly, "I'll go with you a piece."

Her feet sloughed in the loose white sand; his echoed hers. The dog's nose forged even with her ankles and stayed there.

It was queer about the earth, she thought; it seemed to take its color, like men, from where it lay and what passed over it. Yonder was the red-Indian clay gullies, gashed and bleeding, little used for farming. Behind her was the rich black soil that grew cotton so finely but must be watched and coaxed. Finally there was the sand, edging in everywhere, blinding your eyes with its whiteness.

The white ran off into a grassy clearing. The pond was on her right, the clubhouse set back from the water. Cars and horses and wagons were parked catch as can everywhere under elms and oaks and chinaberry.

Most people were in the clubhouse, but a dozen or so stood

around Peanuts' cooler, farmers with an instinct for the out-of-doors. Some tilted bottles, some smoked. Peanuts was urging them on while Tessie mocked from the steps.

"Drink up, fellers."

Tessie echoed, " 'Drink up, fellers.' "

"Remember, I'm giving part what I make to the quartet."

" '. . . part what I make to the quartet.' "

" 'Cause I got no more sense than a fat gal setting on the steps, dress to neck."

" '. . . sense than a fat girl setting on the steps—' " The dress jerked down. Tessie flew up and snatched and threw a pine-burr. It bounced off Peanuts' turned shoulder. She yelled incoherently and ran off while everyone laughed.

Toy thought, She don't learn. If a woman couldn't stand up to Peanuts—how could a child?

The blind man nudged her. "We there, sister?"

"We there."

He called cheerfully, "Hi-dee, friends. Blind Eldon, the Bible man is here."

He slung off his pack. His dog barked. A dozen or so dogs appeared around the corner of the clubhouse. Some stopped and stared intently across the pond. Others sniffed the ground, on the trail of great foxes or giant rabbits, and drew closer, paw by paw.

The blind man called, "Dogs? Someone call 'em off."

A man made a swipe at them with his hat. "Go on, now. Git!" The dogs stopped and looked reproachful.

Peanuts picked up a cigar box and rattled it. "How it sound, Spook? That's a dime chorus and a dollar refrain."

She said quickly, "I just come to bring him." She jerked a hand at the blind man.

A man said, "Blind Eldon? Know your name if I don't know your face. From up round Gatlinburg, ain't you?"

The blind man beamed. "Sure am, brother. I can see I'm amongst friends." He rubbed his shoulder. "I swear, I'm proud to get shut of that pack a spell. It's sweet joy to carry the Good Book, but them corners poke like a billygoat's horns." He fumbled a buckle loose. Small cheap Bibles spilled out on oak tassels and chinaberry boom. "Wonderful words of life, friends. You can't afford to be 'thout them. You got one, why, git another, and you'll be double-strapped against the Devil."

Peanuts slid from the cooler. "Well, I'm going in." He tucked the cigar box under his arm.

She called quickly, "Hear you going to give some of the money to the quartet"—and wondered why she stood and talked to him, why they faced each other and talked, two bodies jounced together by accident, a tasteless mischief.

"Uh-huh. But I'll make it back. Well, see you later, tell you straighter—maybe."

He mounted the two shallow steps to the long porch and disappeared inside.

The last of the loiterers went by, two women leading Blind Eldon, and a man who paused to spit brownly against the steps. A dog trotted in and slunk out with its tail coiled around a leg, ears dropped against shouts. Benches scraped. Voices raised. Someone ran a scale on Annie Goforth's piano, borrowed for the occasion.

"Folks!" John Goforth's voice boomed out. "Folks, if you'll bow your heads, Wick'll lead us in a word of prayer."

Wick's voice rose, deep and resonant, making you believe the words, "O Lord Who is our blessed assurance . . ."

Peanuts could have asked her, even knowing what she would say. He could have asked her, "Come go in?"

". . . for we are lost in Thy love, and so should we ever be. For this is Thy blessed assurance, that when we lose ourselves in Thee, we are not alone. . . ."

She was alone. The horizon, even the part that she could not see, encompassed her, clubhouse and mill, house on hill and all around the ridges. She was alone, the horizon surrounding her; she could never outrun the horizon.

John Goforth shouted, "It's my piano. I get to name the first song. So we gonna sing 'Nothing but the Blood.' Bob, you got enough books in the corner there? Sim, throw a couple yonder."

> "What can wash away my sin?
> Nothing but the blood of Jesus. . . ."

She thought, They always got to have blood.

She turned and walked off. Birds were coming back; a heron waded in the shallows and stabbed snails. A water-thrush teetered along, toes longer than heels. Steps hurried behind her.

Wick said, "Someone told me you were here." His face was bright with pleasure. "Come go in."

She could not resist him any more than a freezing man could a fire. His touch held a warmth that went beyond the skin; it touched the cloven muscle in her breast. Still, she held back.

He said, "They're singing," and meant, They won't pay you any mind. He said, "You don't have to stay, but come."

She went in with him and sat down.

> "No other fount I know, the blood of Jesus."

John Goforth waved a hand on the platform. Three men sprang to take his place. They jostled with a good nature that was half serious.

"Now Jim can't carry a tune in a gourd."

"Rufe led to camp meeting all summer."

None gave way. The spirit moved them, and the innocent passion of "me first." Finally a dime was tossed; the winner clapped his hands.

"Now I got the floor, I tell you, I'm a tiger on the leap. So we gonna sing 'There's a Great Day Coming.' "

Wick sang deeply and strongly beside her. Toy sat mute, wondering, How did I get in here? Thinking, I got to get out. Wick's eyes turned and touched her, and she remained.

The hymn concluded, and another leader stepped forward.

"Maybe I can't carry no tune in a gourd, but I reckon I can hold to the vine." His mouth stayed mock-solemn in the laughter that followed. Women laughed the hardest, for none of them ever led. " 'At the Cross,' folks."

His arm descended. It described a straight line and crossed it in a looping T.

"Alas, and did my Savior bleed, and did my Sovereign die?
Would He devote that sacred head for such a worm as I? . . ."

Toy dared to look around; she dared to let her eyes meet another's. She examined the clubhouse almost curiously. Wasp and birds' nests were gone; dogwood brooms had swept the puncheon floors clean, and the raised stone hearth of the big fireplace had been scoured. Funeral parlor and church had been stripped of benches, but still people stood along the walls by the deep windows.

The leader sat down. Peanuts clapped loudly. A black spider sat nearby; it had been driven out by the dogwood brooms but returned. It sat cleaning a narrow tooth.

John Goforth jumped up. "Now, folks, it's time to introduce the real reason all of us is here today, the Green Pastures Quartet." He paused for the applause. "They come from Sopchoppy, Florida, and their voices is as golden as the oranges down yonder. I know 'cause I heard them sing to Gainesville last year. I went in figuring to drop a quarter in the plate, but time they got thu, I put in— Well, that ain't none of your business nor Annie's yonder. Tell you this, though—I had me a five-dollar smile when I come out." He beamed at the applause and threw out his hand. "Folks, the Green Pastures Quartet."

Two women and a man rose; a second man sat down at the piano. Nobody looked past the first woman. She wore a blue silk dress with a blue plush vestee. She had thick brown hair, a face as heavy and handsome as her legs, and a space the size of a kitchen match between her two front teeth. She smiled lazily.

A man whispered to another, "Hot damn."

The women in the audience looked at her pink silk stockings and orange lipstick, noses sharp and wistful. "Blue Waltz perfume," they identified. "Mell-O-Glo powder."

John Goforth stepped forward and stuck out a palm. "Willard, sure glad to see you again."

The leader of the quartet pumped it. "Now I'm proud to be here, John. This is our first time to Gristle, I believe, but I trust and pray 'twon't be our last."

He resembled a bob-back, one of those toys mounted on a round base which, hands folded over tummies and wide smile under plaster of black hair, bob back no matter how hard they are pushed.

He added doubtfully, "But thought we was to sing to the school."

Someone called out, "It burned down."

He folded meek hands. "Well, all places are God's places. Now you don't want us standing round talking, so we'll get to the singing. 'Cept I do want to make one little announcement. Wednesday night we going to be over in Enocee, South Carolina, just 'crost the line. It's going to be an all-night sing, and we sure would be proud any of you could join us." He retreated a pace and looked at the heavy, handsome woman.

She thrust her big head forward. "Mmmm." Her voice was deep and rich. " 'O Jesus, Lord and Savior, I give myself to Thee. . . .' "

The piano picked it up; Willard and the other woman raised their voices. The first woman sang richly, her whole body yearning forward, heavy shoulders cupped.

" 'For Thou didst give thyself for me. . . .' "

Toy knew the curve of body, the thrust toward a lover. She had the sudden thought, She wouldn't let no man worry her. If he tried, Toy could see the big laughing mouth and the spaced teeth gleaming. "Honey," she would say, "I *been*."

" '. . . for thee alone.' "

People smacked their hands, standing. The people by the windows stamped their feet. Someone whistled. The quartet nodded here and there. A woman cried out, "Lord bless you sweet singers!"

The big brown-haired woman called back, teeth gleaming, "Lord bless you sweet givers."

John Goforth threw up a hand. "Folks, folks, the quartet's gonna come back in a minute and sing. They say they'll keep singing as long as your ears hold out; they just proud they don't have to spread fertilizer to raise a tune." Everyone laughed. "Now, though, how about Wick coming up and leading us in 'Blessed Assurance'?"

Wick rose. "I got to go. Will you stay?"

"No."

"Wish you would." He seemed to hesitate, then went up the aisle.

Warmness went with him; the farther he went, the more chill gripped her, until by the time he stood on the platform, she was bunched upon herself.

He called, "Not 'Blessed Assurance.' How about singing 'Stand Up for Jesus' and stand while we singing it?"

Toy thought with a swift upsurge, I can leave now; won't nobody notice. For everyone was rising; her getting up and going out would be lost in movement.

" 'Stand up, stand up for Jesus, ye soldiers of the Cross. . . .' "

She slid quietly toward the door, stepping over a pair of feet. She gained the open air and thought, Lucky he picked "Stand Up."

Wind was shaping the trees; it bent them and let them go again. The wind was a clement thing.

Suddenly she thought, Why—Wick picked it so's I could leave. The truth swept her. She did not even question it: Wick had wanted her to stay at the sing, but, like the wind with the trees, he had let her go when he sensed that she was bent farther than she could bear.

The hymn came strongly through the windows: " 'Put on the gospel armor . . .' "

She thought, Armor's got nothing to do with it.

Armor, iron or gospel, had not won the true victories; it was the little saving chink in the armor, the flash of flesh that said, "The foe yonder is flesh, too," that had won them.

Pine needles were slick underfoot; cherry and elm leaves crackled. Bushes held out prongs and thorns as she cut through the woods and came out by the mill. Two kittens had found a dead heron by the creek, and prowled the green breastbone. Yellow Tom's grindstone lay in the springing grass.

She thought, I ain't seen him in a time.

Two weeks or three? She counted back; compunction gripped her. Closer to four. She had not seen him since that morning Peanuts had sat outside the mill and mocked him: "Best go down the road."

She thought, Suppose he's dead.

For the solitary died in their solitary cabins and were not found, times, for weeks. There had been the old man who had run the last ferry on Mumbling Creek. He had passed on in his house near Teaspoon Hill and not been found for three weeks. Luckily it had been winter.

She began hurrying.

Yellow Tom's cabin was on the creek, up around the bend toward town. It was his fourth house. The other three had burned down, leaving only their fieldstone chimneys.

A fire, she thought and hurried more. She rounded a crab-apple thicket and drew breath. The cabin stood.

It stood, anyways, if sagging roof and sagging porch and sprung sides could be called "standing." They seemed, rather, to cling to the stone chimney. She picked her way past a washpot and a garden patch and stepped onto the swaying porch.

"Tom? Tom? It's me, Toy."

There seemed a stirring in the dark interior; there were two windows on either side, but they were shuttered.

"Sho' now." The voice was like thorns crackling under a pot.
"Miss Toy—"

She took the words for invitation and stepped in. The odor hit
her first, the rank, fetid odor of a cave, more, the odor of age, the
odor of old skins sloughed off eleven times seven, but not ever
again. The odor of death approaching.

It caught at her throat. She burst out, "I oughta come sooner."

"Poke up the fire."

Obediently she found a stick of wood on the floor and poked at
the ashes in the fireplace. Smoldering brands caught, and little
flames rose. Now she saw with her eyes what her nose had told
her: Yellow Tom was dying. His skin was pinched back against
his skull, his lips pleated from his teeth, and his eyes held reflec-
tions of what he would see next week or next month.

She cried out, "Let me warm you some grits." Food was a
bulwark against death.

"Nuh, thank you. But you kin reach me the water."

She found the gourd and dipped it in a bucket. He drank
slowly, in little sucks.

"Feller kin makes out without food. Can't hardly without water. What day it?"

"Saturday."

He nodded as if satisfied. "Friday. That the day. Friday Tom
gon stand on the high bank. He gon listen for the Voice out the
wind. Voice say, 'Tom, walk on the water,' and Tom gon skate
'crost Jordan like a twirly-bug on the pond." He sucked. "Friday next, 'bout noon."

"A doctor—"

" 'Twouldn't do no good." The lids raised. "Glad you come,
though. Bent my mind you come today."

"Let me move you to the lean-to—"

"Bo Squatty there, you 'member."

Now she knew for sure that he meant to die, speaking so about
a white man.

"Don't talk no more—"

"Bo Squatty. He squatty in the body, he squatty in the soul. You put that soul his'n in a sack, it wouldn't peck the corner." His voice wandered. "Been remembering. Remembering ole woman used come thu the quarters. Carried two sacks trash—ole brokity cups and dishes, rags, sticks. One day I ask her how come, and she say, 'I gots to; dey mights get stole.' They was trash, they was weigh her down, but she obliged to hold on to them."

Her eyes were getting used to the dark, or the fire had freshened, one. Now she could see around the shack. It was poor past bareness. There was nothing in it but the fireplace, a box with a little food, the cot in the corner. A year ago, she remembered, she had given him an old armchair taken in trade on some grinding.

"Where at's the chair?"

He pointed to the fireplace. Suddenly he seemed to shrink in upon himself. His lids fell. There was a single ragged old quilt about him; he barely bulged it.

"Trash," he mumbled, "trash. What a man gots, what the other feller 'spects a man to be, it trash, it all trash. Jesus—"

She thought his head sagged. She waited and called, "Tom." She stepped nearer. "Tom."

On one shrunken temple was a vein like a knotted rope; it seemed to pulse. He was not dead, only sleeping. How long? Until next Friday?

The need for haste possessed her; she must run back to the mill; she must move Peanuts from the lean-to and move Tom in; she must call Aunt Baptist.

She ran. Once she had to stop and pull thorns from her leg where she brushed against a prickly-pear cactus. They were tormentingly beautiful with their yellow squash blooms, but they were tormentingly hurtful. Her leg still smarted when she reached the lean-to.

She thought, But where's everything?

The little room was swept clean. There was not a shirt or a sock in careless sight, not a comb or a card or a coffeepot. She saw the familiar roll in the corner, Peanuts' blanket strapped around his possessions.

He was leaving.

She climbed to the loft and sat down by the front window on a pile of sacks.

Maybe she dozed, maybe she thought; later she did not remember doing either. She remembered how her leg hurt; she had not gotten out all the fine thorns. A few remained to irritate her skin. She wet the patch with her finger, and rubbed it.

It was dusk-dark when she heard Wick's truck. She rose to look. Evening was not far off. Little shadows stained the ridges, the last steepings of day. The car stopped, and not Wick, but Peanuts jumped out, carrying a cigar box, and ran into the lean-to. She padded down the stairs, her shoes making no sound on the mealy floor.

He came out of the lean-to, the roll under his arm, whistling: "Ida red, Ida red, I never cared for Ida red—"

She thought, He's got the quartet money.

Nine

SHE did not know how she knew, perhaps it was the way he handled the cigar box, as if it was heavier than it should be. He had stolen the quartet offering sure enough, some way, and was pulling out.

Far off, acquiescing, a train hooted like a hunting owl.

He threw the roll in the car.

She stepped out of the mill. She called, "Hey, Bo Squatty."

He whirled, "What you doing— *What you call me?*"

"You heard." She walked toward him. "Bo Squatty. I got a right to give you a name, ain't I? You give me one, Spook. I

don't know where it come from, but you got the right one.
That's what I been, a spook. I been a shadow when I oughta been
me, Toy Crawford." She repeated, "Bo Squatty."

He could never jump in the car and leave those words behind.
"Big talk from someone who's a woman no place but one."

It shocked and pained bitterly; her breath drew, easing it.

"Big talk from someone who's a man no place at all. Bo
Squatty—Tom said it true. You're bo-squatty in body, bo-
squatty in mind." Every word was a release. "You're reprobate
silver. You're all wind and no weather. You got no guts to buckle
down to nothing, so you always up to something. Like stealing
from the quartet."

He jumped back, hand clasping the box. He was no longer angry; he was wary as a fox hearing dogs behind.

"How you know? Not that it matters none." His lips lifted;
his tomcat hair lay in spikes. "Yeah, I got it, and you know what
you're left with? People pointing their fingers and saying, 'There
goes Toy Crawford give yard-room to the one run off with the
quartet money.'"

She was not aware of moving, but she must have; his fist caught
her on the cheek, small and hard. It knocked a blur into her eyes.
It knocked her off balance. She staggered back and twisted to
fall, hands spraddled out, ground coming up, breath jolted out of
her.

His voice came. ". . . thinking you so big with that ax. You
was a fool and free. For you believed what I said, but only half
I said, *the half you wanted*. You like everybody, hear 'You'll die
and go to Heaven,' and you run round shouting, 'I'm going to
Heaven,' never mind die."

He was moving to the car; she could hear him. She tried to
draw up her knees and rise, yet knew she could not catch him.
He would be gone, hidden in the ridges, in the night, before anyone could be warned. Every dog and device might be used, but
he would slip through.

Bushes moved before her blurred gaze.

Coke Williams was there, complaining, "Now you sure a hard man to catch, boy!"

"Why—why got places to go. Bits and places, you know what I mean. Well—see you Saturday, like the nigger said."

"Wait a spell." Coke's hand was on the car door; his spade chin was sunk on his chest; his eyes were needle-bright. "You can't take off. First I got a bone to pick."

"Let go, Coke." Peanuts' voice was testy. "You talking about that dollar I owe you, I give it back, remember, last time you come out for a Coke. We square."

"We square." The other nodded. "Only you threw off on Tick."

Peanuts was fidgeting. He twitched tentatively at the car door, but did not try to snatch it open. He knew, well as any man in Gristle, Coke's temper when aroused; it would try any flesh it found.

"Tick?" He stopped and stared. "You mean that blue hound of yourn." He laughed incredulously. "Now, Coke, this is pure crazy. I got to go."

"You said he was a rabbit dog, but he ain't. He's a bear dog. I paid bear-dog money for him. You was throwing off on me. You was making out I was a fool."

"Coke, you know better'n that. Why, we *friends*. I wouldn't throw off on you. Didn't I show it, paying you the dollar? Hell, we *square*."

Coke nodded placidly. "We square. So now I'm gonna beat hell out of you."

"Coke, you crazy!"

"Nope. If you hadn't give me back that dollar, I'd be obliged to leave you go. You can't beat on a man owes you money— folks'd look down on you. But you paid me back. We square." He took a shuffling step forward, hands dangling. "So now I can kill you."

Peanuts panted. "A big feller like you—a little feller like me—"

Coke said placidly, "Why, I never did measure what was on the other end of my fist."

It caught Peanuts high on the skull; he spun back, hands flailing, while methodically Coke beat him to the ground. He finished with a kick laid along the ribs.

A stray feist wandered near. Its nose jumped from spot to spot; it couldn't stick to a single scent.

Coke's lip lifted. "Yonder's a *rabbit* dog." And he stalked off without looking back.

Toy got to her feet and picked up the cigar box. Far off, but coming nearer, the train hooted.

Peanuts clambered up. His face was bruised past humanity. He stared at her, when a shout came from the road.

"Toy!" Wick was hurrying toward them.

Peanuts backed away and jumped into the car. It wrenched around and sped toward Gristle—not that he would go there, Toy thought, not with all the side roads, not with more ways out of the county than in.

Wick came up, big chest heaving. "He's sure played Hell now. Toy, I got something to tell you— *What you got there?*"

She held out the cigar box. "What you looking for."

He took it; he raised his head wonderingly. "You got it back. Now how in Lord's name? Look like he got beat up."

She thought, Peanuts lied and cheated and got by with it. He mocked and tormented and nothing happened.

"Why, he done one honest thing, so naturally he got the living Hell beat out him."

People were coming up the road; she saw them distantly. They sent their cries before them, thin and angry in the dusk.

She told him, "I'm going home."

The house remained as she had left it when Blind Eldon came along. She lit a lamp against the dark, opened the food safe, and got out a dish of cold grits. She put water in the stained pot and threw in coffee. When the water boiled, she poured sorghum syrup on the grits and ate and drank quickly. The syrup was thin and sour-sweet, some that a Negro had traded for grinding, but she ate without tasting, stoking her lean body.

Harl Junior burst in. He had been running through the woods, for his pants legs were covered with sticker-bugs.

"They got Peanuts cornered on Teaspoon Hill! You know where they're sawmilling? Way they found him, they found Wick's truck wrecked by the railroad tracks."

Her mind jumped to Teaspoon Hill. It was over beyond Atkins' Ridge, a little bluff covered with first-growth pine and cypress. The trees were coming down at a sickening rate, for a coffeepot mill nibbled away inexorably. She herself had gone over a few weeks ago to get a heart-plank of cypress for the millwheel. Truck roads were gashed out of the undergrowth; small trees were crushed; birds and little animals had been driven out.

She saw Peanuts trying to hide in the thin, sour undergrowth. He would have no more cover than a marauding fox; the hunters would find and poke him forth.

She thought grimly, Wonder how he'll like being on the other end of the stick?

Her brother cried, "Hope they kill him dead! You know what he's done?"

She turned to the window; she thought she saw something in the dark, something sliding around the pump. Maybe it was Peanuts returning, or Tessie, maybe only her mother. Rose Crawford liked to slide in slyly; she seemed to get more pleasure from what she could steal—whether food or warmth—than from what was given her. But it was only Joe, the dog, following some elusive trail of his own.

"He's got everyone turned on us again, that's what he's done. They all saying it's your fault, taking him in."

"But they got their money back."

"That don't make no difference with them." His thin, pale face screwed up; the easy tears came. "Some is even saying you all was gonna divide it!"

She heard the words, but they held no meaning. Outside the

dark flickered; it was full of things with sharp teeth creeping toward the chicken yard and the calf stall. She grabbed the rifle from beside the door.

Creeping things—she could hear their rustle in the dark, all around the yard, possum and coon and skunks with little human hands after the jelly-boned biddies.

She threw up her rifle and fired.

When the echo died away, she leaned the rifle against the door. It had killed a lot of meat in its days, some tough. Her mother could not eat the tough, for she was losing her teeth. Tessie and Harl would not eat it, for they were tender-mouthed. But she ate it; she had strong teeth.

She told Harl, "Go on to bed."

He protested, "It's early."

She said harshly, "What you got to stay up for?"

So he went, moaning and sniffling, and she followed, leaving the door unlocked. Night had never harmed her, only day, approving evil under the sun.

And the sun came early, searching through the sweet-potato vine on her window sill. The vine was in a glass jar, tendrils climbing up the pane. She opened her eyes on it, astonished that she had slept.

She got up and dressed, running a hand over her hair for a brush. Tessie's bed was still unslept in, though Harl Junior had slept hard enough for two. His sheets were roiled, his blankets tumbled to the floor, and his pillow clasped to his chest, not for comfort, but for a shield.

Sparrows cheeped, sounds busy and frayed. A skunk went by and left its anger on the air. She went to the front door and looked toward Teaspoon Hill.

She thought, He's crawling on nobody's belly now but his own.

Harl cried behind her, "Tessie's gone."

He was in the bedroom doorway, knobby chest bare, knobby hands holding a piece of paper. "She's run off with Peanuts."

The note read: "I have gone to help Peanuts. Am going with him if we get loose. Took the mule—you don't like him none anyway."

Tessie must have moved lightly as a firefly in the night, briefly as one. She had come for a few of her clothes, dropped the note beside Harl's bed, and gone off.

Harl cried, "What you gonna do?"

"Nothing."

"But who's gonna do the cooking?"

"Looks like you, don't it?"

The words came automatically. She was looking down the road to where a car was coming, Lovick Jones's car. It turned off the road and stopped.

Wick swung out. "Peanuts got away."

She said, "You better have you some coffee."

He followed her in. She poked up the fire and shoved the coffeepot closer. There was bacon in the food safe; she went to get it.

He said to her back, "You don't act surprised none."

She sliced bacon, words jerking. "No need—seeing he had my own sister helping him." She dropped the bacon in the pan of cold water to freshen and stooped to get meal for dodgers.

He was silent, then he said, "We wondered how he got free." He told her, "Glad you taking it this way."

She whirled, knife in hand. "I'm taking it no way. I'm taking it! What they saying about me and the money?"

His chin was freckled with beard; she could see the hairs glint gold in the light. He rubbed it, watching her. "Harl tell you?"

"Never mind how I know. I know, that's enough. I know they saying, 'Toy Crawford give houseroom to the thief. Maybe she was gonna get some of the money.' Ain't that so?"

"Maybe at first—"

"First, last, and then the middle! If they quit, it was because you made them. Well, I don't need nobody to clean me with their tongue like a cat. I don't need no help—"

Her mother streaked across the floor and snatched the bacon from the pan. She was through the door, bare feet making no sound. A giggle floated back.

Harl, snatching up his pants, burst into the kitchen. "Now I knowed she was gonna do that. She done it every morning if Tessie didn't watch. If you think I'm gonna get breakfast—"

Wick rose swiftly. "It just come to me—why you getting breakfast? Where at's Tessie?"

"Gone."

Gone—ended, past, dead.

She had started after her mother. Now she kept walking, out to the side porch. Pines held the sun between them like an orange ball. The well winch swung and creaked. She sat down on the steps, her bones letting her down, fluid and empty. The boards pressed coldly on her buttocks; the knife she carried hung between her knees.

Wick said, "Likely they gone to Nashville. We could—"

She shook her head. "They gone. Let them."

Gone. Escaped. Free.

Yet one man or woman free meant another bound; for the free leap from the shoulders of those kept. The jump is a selfish thing, yet it must be. So Tessie was gone, and she was tied to Gristle, and where was the shoulder for her—not to jump from—to catch at?

Her forehead sank to her knees.

Wick sighed deeply above her. He sat down beside her, shadow beyond her. "You got a right to cry, but I'm worse off."

Her face lifted in brief astonishment. She saw his tormented eyes and his lips that strove with thoughts.

"I'm worse off, for you got hurt, and I done nothing. I'm worse off, for I got to weep twice, seeing you and seeing myself."

She stumbled. "You done nothing. You not—"

"I done nothing—you're right. I've put off when I belonged to *do now*." He turned and looked at her gently. He said, "You need me, and I need you."

She could say nothing.

"I need you more than you need me, for you got too much to bear, and I got nothing. A man's got to bear something, or where's his strength to come from at the end?"

Something grew and stretched within her. She hardly recognized joy or hope; they were unfamiliar things.

He said, "I mean, marry me."

She shook her head back and forth, back and forth, denying the quickening within her.

He repeated, "I need you, and you need me."

She blurted, "You reckon need—" She stopped. She said stiffly, "Might be—need's enough to go on."

PART
III

One

A WILD storm rose that night. It rained and blew with a fury that tamped men's flesh against their bones when they ventured forth, and drove them back into dryness, mourning, "It'll pure rot the seed in the ground. It's unpeeling the world."

When it cleared on the morning of the third day, they drew breath. "Well, we been overlooked this time. But I tell you, another day and you just as good have shot me dead with a butcher knife."

Even as they spoke a wind stirred up from the south. The west turned green, and great thunderclouds with crazy billowing bulges towered into heaven. There was a constant play of little lacy lightning, and birds beat north as if they swam through yellowish-green paste.

Suddenly, at evening, a black ribbon wove out of the clouds. It spun itself round and round like a bobbin winding thread, until it was funnel-shaped. Then it drove forward on its point. It struck Gristle, exploding a brick house outward, ripping roofs and palings. It tore the core out of a forest and scooped a river dry to leave spawning shad gasping in the mud and turtles plunging at the mottled bellies.

After it was over, men tried to dry things with curses and shirt-tails. They met to talk the affair over, repeating wryly what a Negro had said: "Meanness met Rain outside Chattanooga, and they et breakfast together. Then Meanness said to Rain, 'Let's breeze on down to Gristle and shake that thing.'" They raised their heads only briefly to gossip— "Wick and Toy? What you know. She can't get on with no one till daybreak, but it's Wick's doings"—and lowered them again to look at the ruined land.

Nature, above compassion, saved Toy. She knew it and was grateful. She had feared, with a real fear, the things that might be said, not about herself but about Wick: "Now Wick's carrying charity too far. You suppose—her and that Peanuts—" "No. But you know you can't sit with black without getting up gray. Not even Wick."

She thought, Maybe it'll be all right. Maybe I got— She would not say "a chance," or think it.

Still unreality possessed her. The last few months seemed like the siege of cat fever she had had when she was eight. She had ducked in and out of a red tide for a day and a night, only later they told her it was three days. She had said things in the fever that had made her father's face go pi-jawed, her mother shrill, "*What you been doing*, missy?"

She had done nothing; it was all the fever. Even getting well was not the end, for long afterward she was chill and nerveless. It was as if the fever had consumed more than her flesh; it had consumed the essence that was Toy Crawford. No more did she look at violets and think, Little rooster heads, or watch her father cavort without the sharp sweet pain of knowing people thought him a fool, or see a mother cat eat an unwanted kitten and cry, "Hateful."

It was the same now.

The following Saturday, Dolly drove by the mill in her father's old sedan. She leaned a plump arm out of the window.

"Now what you doing?" She saw the mound of raw yellow earth that means only one thing wherever it is found. "Aw, no— Yellow Tom?"

Toy nodded. "Died yesterday. Like he said he would."

That was unreal, too.

She had been to see him each day, taking soft grits and pot likker, but he would not eat. Living, he had already gone beyond.

It had been without surprise that she opened the door yesterday and found him turned on his left arm, knees drawn up. He seemed one with the earth, dark and dried up.

She had gone to Tuck Tate and asked the big man to make a coffin, help her bury the old man. The big mule-dealer had wiped a hand across his face.

"Now ain't that a thing to tell around, nigger buried under a grindstone?"

Feeling came then, a slowly mounting bitterness, a desolation so keen it nearly made her sick. Yellow Tom had lived long and loved long. She could not have done without him, nor could the mill. Yet now that he was dead, no one would remember him any more than a tat of dirt they kicked off their heel. If they did, it would be, "Yellow Tom? That's the crazy ole nigger got buried under the grindstone, ain't it?"

They would remember her longer, for the mill would remain when she was gone. The mill would remind them. "Toy Crawford? She run the mill. Mean as a horn." And Wick, how would they remember Wick? "Wick Bloodworth? Couldn't find a better man between Rabun Gap and Tybee Light. Till he played the fool."

Played the fool. Married her. Wick, she thought, deserved a better remembrance than that.

Dolly said, "Poor old creetur." She shook her head; the same motion might have dismissed a gnat. "Well, what I come to tell you is, Wick found you some niggers. He says come-see if they suit you."

She remembered; last week, talking, Wick had said, "Your mother and Harl would be suited better to your house. Maybe we can get a couple to do for them, woman to cook, man to help to the mill."

Dolly said, "Well, come if you going to come."

Tell Wick today, she thought; tell him, I don't need help, and you don't need hindrance. Tell him, Marry someone else. You'll get naught but trouble from me.

She got into the truck. Dolly hoisted her skirts and shifted gears. Her tongue started up like a clatter-bone, Jack and weddings, Jack and the store, Jack and Jack.

Toy knotted her hands in her lap. Sunshine washed the world, drawing ugly and fair together in a golden confluence.

She thought, He never said "love."

". . . ole black hootnanny." Dolly laughed. "Looks like she could wrestle your ma past Monday. And the little feller—well, I sure can't see him to the mill."

Toy asked sharply—only the mill would have aroused her from her thoughts—"Sorry?"

"Wait, see."

The woods, the occasional farmhouse tamped into its circle of trees, gave way to thicker dwellings. Goforth's store stood in a dust of traffic. Half a dozen people lounged around the gas pumps, eating soda crackers and drinking Nehis. A circle of children played a counting-out game, their voices raised clearly. "Monkey, monkey, bottle of beer. How many monkeys are there here?"

Wick was talking to a big black woman standing by an old Dodge touring car. It spilled over with children, and a small yellow man clung to the door handle.

"Now you understand about Miss Rose? You got to keep an eye on her?"

The black woman grunted. "I keeps it."

The little man moaned counterpoint, ". . . toting sacks. Boss, I jes can't hold out to do nothing like that."

"You can start Monday, Mary. And Fig, you and the boy come to the mill Tuesday."

The big woman wheeled on the tumbling children in the car. "Billie-Dove Newsome, min' you manners. Ramon-Novarro, quit mommicking de dog!" She turned back. "My cooking ain't fancy. It field. But we makes out."

Fig's voice wove in: ". . . constitution's wore away. Proclamation's give out . . ."

Wick straightened. "Got what you need from Mr. John?"

"Yassuh. Rice, sowbelly, lard, coffee, syrup—"

". . . puny. Can't tote guts to a bear."

"Fine. Well, you take this road out a mile, take the left fork—"

". . . stoop, my ole back say pop!"

The woman rounded like a black behemoth. "Shut you grizzle! We gon take dis job. I sick-tired goan from roof to wrastle to roof. Git in!"

The man, hopelessness bowing his back, crawled behind the wheel. The car crept off.

The crowd began to drift apart. One said, "Now I sure do love to see niggers carry on, don't you?"

"Uh-huh. You seen that big one's neck? Why, you could slip a collar off her without unbuttoning it."

Wick turned. He lifted a hand and came over to Toy.

"Well"—he smiled—"you reckon they'll do?"

"Woman's kind of nubby-headed, ain't she?"

"Maybe. But claims she's a good cook."

"And that Fig." She did not like light Negroes; any but Yellow Tom she believed treacherous. Yellow skin was too close to white bone. "Sort of sorry, wasn't he?"

He said gently, "If grasshoppers is sorry. If crickets is sorry. He'll work out. Fact is—I wasn't figuring on him being much help to the mill. I was figuring on the boy."

"What boy?"

John Goforth stepped out of the store. "Dolly, quit gawking. Here's your bill, Wick. You want to sign for what them niggers drawed?"

"No!" The word jumped from Toy's mouth. "I'll sign."

Wick's smile had a question about it. "You or me, same thing."

This was the time. She had only to open her lips and say, "No." She had only to tell him, "There's no reason for us to get married and no rhyme." For marriage should be a rhyme and a singing. She leaned forward. "Wick—"

A woman cried, "Wick!"

She was a widow and lived on the ridge. She had brown curly hair and plump ankles, and was a good cook. Now she was full of good works, waiting on marriage or the grave. She held out a basket.

"I was just going around to Grandpa Willing. Poor ole soul, he's failing fast, reckon you know. I thought maybe a saucer of soup." She lowered her voice and put a hand to her mouth, mock wicked. "I won't deny I put a dollop of something in it."

Wick smiled faintly. "Old sinner wouldn't eat it otherwise."

"That's what I thought. Oh, and Wick, you know that little spat Mattie Jones and Ruby Williams had over where to put flowers at in the chancel? Well, I got it straightened out."

"Don't know what the church would do without you, Willy-Kate."

Toy thought, Now that's a fish-nor-fowl name. Though it was more fowl than fish; the widow was a frizzled old hen, tolling whatever rooster she could into her nest of sweet grass.

"I try, Wick. I mean, it's up to us Christians to witness by deed as well as word, ain't it?"

Toy thought, And so mean that she wouldn't transgress. She leaned forward. "Wick, sign for the rations."

Monday they went to Cardiff and got married.

Wick picked her up in his truck, repaired except for a crumpled fender. He gave her a hand bouquet of lemon-colored roses which smelled like lemon too, a sour-sweetness that matched the morning.

He said, "A tussie-mussie. I don't know what you can do with them, riding and all. But I figured you belonged to have something, a day like this."

He had pared off the thorns; the flowers did not prick her palms. Yet they should have, she thought; there should have been a single sharpness, a difference in the day. Only it was the same as any day going to Cardiff, to get a millstone or to go to Swap Tuesday.

She thought, It belongs to be different.

Her thoughts should be different, new and green to match her frock. Only they were not. Dolly had made her get the dress, crying, "You can't rub along in rags forever." Dolly had offered to come to Cardiff and stand up with her, too, but she had shaken her head. Words were offenders.

She and Wick were married in the parlor of the Baptist parsonage. The windows were hung with time-thinned red draperies, and the walls with stiff-chinned portraits. The air was filled with the smell of cooking collard greens, greasy and bitter. A part of her mind thought, Someone ought to drop in a spoon of sugar.

The preacher's wife had flung her apron over a chair and stood with head cocked toward the kitchen. She was half the age of her husband, a fusty little man who stopped smiling only when he laughed, teeth shining with the milk of human kindness.

"Got your letter, Wick. So this your bride, Toy Crawford, going to be Toy Bloodworth."

He knew her name and beyond her name; Toy could tell from his gaze. Well, what difference did it make? None. Except give a dog a bad name, and you just as good shoot him.

The preacher spread his Bible and began intoning.

Once Aunt Baptist had said, "Brides got heavy eyes and light brains." It was not so; her eyes saw everything, the creases in her dress, the scratch under Wick's ear when he leaned to kiss her, the yellow circle on her finger.

How final was a circle; it surrounded and locked itself at every point; it bent not only itself, but whatever was within it. Instead of a ring for a marriage seal, why not—a gold toothpick like the drummer for White Rose salve carried on his watchchain? A straight line was a freer and more honest thing.

The preacher waved them good-by. "Well, Wick, proud you picked me to marry you. Hope you find you a preacher soon for that church of yours. Good-by, Mrs. Bloodworth."

Mrs. Bloodworth. The name struck her with almost physical impact.

Wick backed the truck. A thin patina of sweat lay on his face. It was hot enough at that. Dust motes danced on the radiator. The road ahead looked like a rippling river. Only when they got to it, it was road right on. She sat rigid, senses tensile and extended.

After a while Wick straightened. "You hungry?"

It was eleven o'clock, and she had had only coffee for breakfast. "No."

She had meant to pack a lap-lunch. Mary, the Negro woman, who had come to the house before day, had asked, "You wants me to pack you a li'l' something take along?" But before she could answer, her mother had run out, yelling, "Git on, you ole nigger, won't cook nothing but rice and beans—"

The black woman said stolidly, "I cooks fried chicken and butts meat. I cooks turnip greens and sweet-potato pone. I cooks what you wants, and you wants what I cooks."

Her mother howled obliviously. They had had to wrestle her around. Then Wick had come, and she had not thought of the lap-lunch again.

She asked stiffly, "You?"

Wick admitted, "Some. We could have eat to Cardiff, but I forgot. Well, we can stop somewheres."

Only there was nothing but fields and woods and scattered farmhouses. The houses had an unkept, desperate air, shingles gone, paint flaking. Pastures had gone to seed; fields were unplanted and ragged with last year's cotton stalks and corn shocks. Negro shacks were worse off; they seemed held up by cockroach courage and bedbug spite and nothing else.

Wick said, "Now I remember something. There's a place up around the bend, a barbecue pit. We can stop there."

It was called The Rainbow, four oak stanchions supporting a tin roof, oak coals growing in a pit. Several cars were drawn up to it, a group of men were gathered around, nibbling cracklings and watching a Negro tend a spitted carcass.

One called out, "Hi-dee, folks, you just in time. I got me a special something going today. Just about done, you wait a minute-two."

He was a short man and low-down, wide as he was tall, with two missing front teeth. He came forward, exuding an odor of sweat and smoke and roasting meat. "It's calf barbecuing, folks. Ain't often you git that, I bet. Wouldn't had it today—generally got me a hog or goat or rabbits or whatever—but last evening the young'uns was frolicking in the barn. My two youngest was holding the calf, and Ruel—he's my oldest—was making out to jump on its back from the loft. Done it two-three times and rode the critter, steering its tail. Last time, plunk! You know, he broke its back clean in two? Dory come told me, and I went out and drawed a knife 'crost its throat. Then I told Hinky here"—He jerked his head at the Negro tending the spit—" 'Fire up the pit. We gonna have us veal tomorrow.' Whilst you wait, have you a crackling." He added, "Billidad's my name."

"Wick Bloodworth, and this is my wife. We're from down Gristle-way." Wick held out a hand. "Now we'll take a crackling, since you got it."

She accepted a piece of the curled, crisped fat, and the men went back to talking.

"Now I just wish I'd been there when Lex showed the sheriff the shotgun. By God, I wouldn't justa showed it; I'd used it."

"Uh-huh. When he come out to my place with the eviction, I says, 'Sheriff, you can maybe make you two dollars tacking up that paper, but 'twon't feed your widder long.' "

"Hear tell bunch farmers to Iowy took out this here judge was writing foreclosure orders and nigh-about hanged him."

"Nigh? Why didn't they *do* it?"

"More gizzle than guts, I reckon. "You 'member Phonnie, my brother, went out to St. Louis? He writes how they got a Hooverville 'long the river, three mile of shacks built of spit and spite. Leastways we got nothing like that here 'bouts."

"I don't know, Hank. I hear tell to Atlanta that men is standing 'long the streets clapping their hands to give theirselves something to do. Just clapping their hands like they was keeping time to a nigger doing 'Shine.' "

"Sho' now!" Everyone contemplated this.

The first man shook his head. "Well, Roosevelt will get us out of it, that's one thing sure. Roosevelt will get us out of it."

A small boy galloped up. His head was shaved clean as a chinaberry, and with his fat face he had the look of a little pig. "Pa, it ready? Pa!"

"Nigh about, Ruel."

He grabbed a piece of crackling and turned away, chewing it.

The words were forced out of Toy. "Now you must be the one rode the calf."

"Uh-huh."

"Kinda rough on the calf, wasn't it, breaking its back?"

He stared. "Don't matter none. It wasn't nothing but a little ole bull."

By and by the veal was done. Thick sauce-tanged slices were cut off and slid on bread and garnished with cole slaw. Soft drinks were brought up. They ate, and afterward Wick paid. When they left, Billidad waved after them. "Now don't stay 'way so long next time."

Toy waited until they had turned off on the highway before bursting forth, "A young'un of mine done such as that, breaking a calf's back, I'd wear him out."

Wick asked, "Toy, why you so easy on animals and so hard on people?"

"Why, animals can't help theirselves none; people can. You know that."

"I don't know as I do. Now when I hear a woman say, 'I don't know what I'd do without that ole cat of mine; she's company'; or a man say, 'People is mean; I'll stick to my dog; leastways he don't bite,' I think to myself, There's someone taking the easy way out."

"Easy!"

"Sure; for one reason people is kind to animals is because it's easy; it don't take no work. Call a pig, 'Shug, shug,' a rabbit, 'Map,' whistle up a dog or horse, and that's all you need. An animal's simple; he's one word. People, now, people is a book. They're hard to read and hard to understand. People can't help theirselves times, but it's a lazy man says, 'People ain't worth a damn; I'll stick to my dog.' "

She panted. "You—you—" The accumulation of a week burst open. "We had no more business getting married. We had no more business in this world! We're too different—I don't know why we done it."

"I know—"

She overrode him. "And don't think you going to change me, Wick Bloodworth. I won't change for no man. I won't go to church. I won't set foot in a place says Glory to God, Devil with men. People making out they so good, when they're just snake-eggs inside—"

He said quietly, "Toy. Poor crowded-in Toy." He asked, "You don't remember the morning your daddy was killed? I give you a lift. Booger got you, and I asked why. You said things was crowding in. They been crowding in ever since, ain't they, crowding in more than you got room for?"

"Quit—quit—" She thought wildly, He says any more— She would jump out with the car going and never mind what was underfoot, rock or ditch. She would jump out and die. Only he did not speak again, and soon they were near Gristle; there was the mill, solid and safe and known.

She blurted, "Stop."

Wick stopped without a word. He leaned an arm across her to open the door. She snatched it from him and jumped out.

His voice held her. "Toy."

She paused, face set away from him.

"You want I should come for you?"

"No."

There was a moment, then she heard gears shift, and he drove off.

Honeysuckle looped the path to the mill door. Quail found refuge under the tangles. A mother quail led her babies forth to seek for dropped corn. Fish popped the surface of the pond. The breeze carried the smell of honeysuckle to her, the splashing of the fish, the sound of voices under the mill.

She went around past the motionless wheel to look. There was a great cave under the pilings, a damp spot where pale things bloomed and debris accumulated. Four boys clad only in britches were digging away, fishing poles beside them. Their chests were white, but with the incipient pink that would be brown in June, near-black in August. Toy knew they had been warned away from the mill: "Don't you go 'round there; she'll run that wheel over you." Maybe they thought marriage made changes.

She called harshly, "Get out from there, hear?"

When they disappeared, she went into the mill, but it seemed that she could not get shut of boys; one was standing by the grindstones, a Negro. He had a hand on them.

She called, "What you doing here? Who you?"

He jumped, arms and legs jerking like a golliwog.

"N-Nuthin. I jes going."

"Just a minute." The shape of his face assumed familiarity, the tar-colored skin, the squat body. She guessed, "You one of them Newsomes."

"Yas'm."

"Well, what you doing here?"

"Nuthin, honest. I jes looking. Never seed mill before." His eyes returned to the stone. "Dis the grindstone, enty, ma'm?"

"Grindstone? Yes."

She could hardly make out his speech. It was clotted with unfinished words and words turned edgewise. She wondered if he was a Geechee, a Gullah-talker. Yellow Tom had told her once, "A Geechee be's a cross 'tween the Devil and a rattlesnake. One bites you, it sure death. When an ordinary bad nigger die, he turn to a mule, gots to keep on working thu eternity. But when a blue-gum die, he turn to maggot, gots to eat dead corpses."

"You Geechee?"

"Nuh'm. How de corn get 'tween dem stones?"

"Drops thu the chute into hole in the middle." She stopped, considering him. "Times it comes out hot enough to burn your hand."

"Nah!"

She moved, on impulse, and shoved the lever raising the flood-gate. "Look out the window."

He looked and a cry burst from his lips. "Water coming!"

She thought, I'll run a pound or two, show him.

Sometime later, how late she did not know, she caught her dress on a nail. She started to jerk loose, as she always did, and stopped. Green cloth, wedding dress. Why, the sun had climbed its way up one side of the pines and was sliding redly down the other. It was evening.

She drew a breath. She threw the gear that stopped the wheel, the rod that stopped the stones. She turned to the black boy. "I got to go."

He had been working furiously, skin shiny with sweat. Now stillness came over him. He ducked his head and watched her from under the boss of his brow. "Gwine wuk fo' you?"

She stopped, rolling down her sleeves. This boy suited the mill, and the mill suited him. "Why—sure."

He insisted, "I your nigger?"

"If you got a name."

"Hart. It Bill-Hart Newsome."

"Then I reckon you hired. Now go 'long and come back to-morrow. I'll be here—"

Only maybe she wouldn't; she had nearly forgotten. She was married. Wick would have a say in where she was and what she was.

She ended abruptly, "If I can."

She went on without looking back, or she would stay. Sooner done, sooner past. A second thing impelled her, honesty, the same impulse that made her give full measure of meal for bushel of corn. She would not let a kernel remain on the floor of the bin, or tie the mouth of the sack too soon.

She thought, It's another measuring.

Measuring herself and giving a man what was due him, not by the cup, but by the ring.

Only first, she would go by the house and see if Wick had picked up her suitcase, as had been planned. She was not delaying the moment when she must go down the road and turn in a strange gate, she told herself; she was only saving a trip.

She ducked under the pasture rails. Grass was warmly tickling against her ankles. The blackjack oak by the farther rails was yellow. Maude had loved scratching her bristly chin on it. Mule and tree had grown old and swinneyed together. Now it was dying.

She crawled through the farther rails and crossed the yard. Chips lay around the chopping block, yellow and resinous; the ax hung in it like a handle. Three chickens were pecking in the garden patch. She snatched up gravel. "Scat!"

They fluttered, squawking, among the rows of hand-high corn and beanpoles and settled back a few yards along.

"That nigger!"

The Negro woman, Mary, ought to have kept an eye out the window; she ought to have seen the chickens and shooed them away. Toy went up the steps and snatched open the kitchen door.

"Now—"

Wick sat at the table, smoking a cigar. Aunt Baptist was slamming around the stove.

". . . church with nothing but women like them city ones. I tell you, they no better than the split dog who run across a scythe and got cut in half, nose to tail. Doctor sewed him back, but wrong-to, nose to tail, tail to nose. He could run coming and going and bark at both ends, but he wasn't worth a damn. That's a church with nothing but women—"

She turned with an earthen bowl held between two dishrags and saw Toy.

She boomed, "Well, she's come!"

Two

WICK got up. He had changed from Sunday serge to work pants. They were black-muddied and grass-stained, a tear in one leg. There was a ragged cut on his arm daubed with a black tarry substance, Aunt Baptist's doings. He held the cigar beween thumb and first finger.

"Now nothing to get worried about—"

"What you doing here?" Questions popped to her mind so thick and fast she could not select the first one. "Why you smoking a cigar?"

Aunt Baptist snorted. "He wouldn't take a drink, though I begged him. I said, 'You got a right to a drink, such happening!'" She slammed the earthen dish on the table; the steam of rabbit stew arose.

Wick grinned. "I need to hold up, not fall down."

Harl blurted, "'Twas Ma." He came out of Rose Crawford's bedroom. He told Aunt Baptist, "She's sleeping, that stuff you give her." He told Toy, "She fell, broke her arm. We was to the infare at Wick's—"

"Infare?" She had not thought of such as that. She had not thought of people coming to Wick's house with presents, food and quilts and crockery, just as they did for other newlyweds.

"Uh-huh. There we was, setting round waiting for you, when here comes this feller . . ."

A man had found Rose Crawford at the bottom of a gulch near Atkins' Ridge, but he had had no way to get her up; so he had gone for help.

"I mean, Wick had him a tussle. Ma fought like a bobcat, one-armed."

Aunt Baptist snorted. "Crazy folks don't need but one arm. They got no arms, they'll bite. No teeth, they'll quarrel with their toes. That's why you got to keep her quiet if you don't want her arm setting jibber-jawed."

She flung herself heavily into a chair and reached a hand into the stew bowl, pulling out a bone thick with meat and dripping with gravy. Her other hand reached out and poured coffee.

Toy came to the table and set a hand flat on it, unable to take things in. "Ma broke her arm—"

Wick set a chair behind her; automatically she sat down. He stretched a long arm across the back of her chair. Bristles had sprung out on his jaws since morning; the smell of cigar smoke was rank and unfamiliar.

"Nothing to worry about, if we keep an eye on her two-three weeks. Aunt Baptist set it, used cardboard and poured boiling water on it. When it dries and shapes—"

"Mary. The nigger woman, Mary—"

"Gone. Took off this morning, kit and cat and sowbelly. It was my fault. I knowed I oughtn't to have trusted that Fig—"

She said slowly, "Not all of them. There's one to the mill."

"No. Now which one?"

"Boy, 'bout fourteen."

"You reckon they forgot him?"

"No. He just stayed on."

"Well, that's one good thing." He ladled stew into a dish and shoved it toward her. "Best eat. It's kind of early, but we got things to do."

The "we" tightened her body and weakened it, both at once.

Aunt Baptist tore a final shred from her bone. "Now I can eat meat any time." She stuck a finger in the waistband of her old brown skirt. Seams strained perilously. "It ain't that this skirt is too tight on me. It's just got too much in it." She boomed laughter and dropped the bone on her plate. A broad thumb reached across her mouth, wiping grease free.

Wick turned to Harl, who was standing by on one leg, eyes worshipful. "Get some bread out the safe, would you, Harl? And fill up the wood box?"

The pale boy went without a word. Toy nearly gaped. He always whined when she told him to do anything. What he had needed all along was a man to ask him, instead of a woman to tell him and pop his jaws if he didn't.

Aunt Baptist swatted the table. She was holding up the rabbit's shoulder-blades, wing-shaped and greasy, white and tan.

"That all the cradles you gonna fill, one?"

Toy's fork faltered. She had forgotten that you could tell fortunes by the shoulder-bones of a rabbit.

Wick took the cigar from his mouth and said equitably, "You going to tell our fortune, go ahead. We got no way to stop you."

The big midwife said smugly, "No." She twirled the bone and pointed to a socket. "This the house. Deep or shallow tells if you'll be rich or poor. This'uns deep. You'll have your share of this world's wealth." Her finger moved on to a little hole. "Cradle—you gonna have one young'un." Briefly she touched a nick. "Maybe two, though looks like this one'll be stillborn or early dead." Her finger continued to opaque white spots. "Sicknesses, and the biggest is death, the pale horse without a tail and a mane made of little-finger bones."

Wick said pointedly, "It's good you don't call yourself a churchwoman."

She nodded complacently. "Ain't it?" She heaved herself up. "Now I'll just take one more look-see at your ma, Toy, and go on, though I know you all would love for me to stay!" Her guffaws trailed her into the next room and back. "She's sleeping." Her bulk heaved; she picked up her satchel and stuffed things in it. "Now I sure wish I could set on your keyhole—this is one marriage is got to grow in grace for it's sure starting in ruin—

but I'm too big and it's too breezy." She billowed to the door. "Call me when you got something to drop in that cradle."

Final laughter went down the path. Once she stopped and gathered sage—good for steeping and combing through your hair to bring back the black—and went on.

Wick said, "Now there's a good woman, but she calls you a liar if you say so." He passed a hesitant finger along his jaw. "Looks like we gonna have to make out here for a while, your ma sick. We can take turns keeping an eye on her, see she don't pull off the splints, until we get someone. Harl." The boy had come in with his arms loaded with wood. "I count on you to help us."

"Sure, Wick, sure." His voice was eager. He dumped the wood in the fire box and dusted his hands. "I can carry my share."

A week before he had wailed when she told him to fix supper; now manhood filled his shoulders. "We'll make out, Wick."

Briefly Wick's hand touched him. "You helping, we'll make out." He turned to Toy. "I'll go on down to the house, water the stock and milk. You want me to bring your suitcase back when I come? I took it a while ago."

She had left some clothes here, but no better than what you'd put on a mop handle and run over a dirty floor. She had one or two new things in the suitcase, a gown, for instance, white with a drawstring around the neck.

"Or—you want to make out without it?"

His cigar lay in his coffee-saucer. She wished that he would smoke it, and be a stranger again. A stranger was easier than a friend; a stranger required only what he could see and hear. A friend or a husband went beyond that. He knocked at the very gates of your being, the ones that said, "This far and no more."

She thought, A full measure. She said, "Bring it."

She watched him disappear around a clump of red spruce. The trees grew in Canada, here, and nowhere else. They were as tykish a thing as this marriage.

Harl dropped wood into the stove. Coals must be kept up. May was a windshee month, the weather blew as the wind blew, hot and cold. The days were hot, but the wind came up with the dark. The voices of frogs and cicadas were thinly chill.

Voices and horses' hoofs lifted on the road, a group of men going by, coon-hunting. There was a big bear coon who hung out around the pond. When anyone tried to catch it, the coon would jump in and swim toward the other side. If they split up and were on the other side waiting, why, it did not come. Somewhere between sky and water, it disappeared.

Harl called, " 'Tater pie." He had taken a tea-towel from a plate on the stove.

She asked, "Who brought it?" thinking of all that she must do, sweeping and straightening the house, taking a bath, washing dishes.

"Aunt Baptist, I reckon." He got a knife and cut himself a wedge. "Piece?"

She picked up a broom. "No."

When she finished sweeping, she started on the dishes. She came to the shoulder-blade from Aunt Baptist's plate and held it a moment between thumb and forefinger, cradle to grave. She went to the door.

"Joe!"

The shambling old hound came and closed his jaws on it and took it off to lick in a secret place.

She finished the dishes and moved on to her room to make the bed. It was hers alone now Tessie was gone. Harl had slept in the plunder-room for months, his bed between a pile of traps and an old sideboard. She stripped the bed and put on clean sheets, pulling them so taut that a nickel would have bounced high, a dime higher. She could do nothing for the room. Time had been there before her.

"Eggs." Harl came in with half a dozen clutched to his breast. "Wick always eats two for breakfast. He told me." His words

were only words until the meaning came to him, then red
patched his temples.

She said quickly, "Grits, too."

He agreed with relief, "Grits."

He was near a man—she had found the signs in his bed—but
not to the point yet. It did not hurt to ease him past the point.

The thoughts that she had tried to quell in a fever of activity
calmed. Well, she could do nothing until the time came to do it.

She put on water to heat and took a bath. She put on a clean
old dress and afterward went to the door and looked down the
road, letting a dusky wind blow against her. Wick was long in
coming, but May was a three-milking month; most days you
had to milk three times to empty the bag. Above the door the
Paul's Scarlet rose shook its first petals. Next month it would be
covered with blooms.

"Aah, aah, aah!"

The sound brought her whirling. Her mother stood in the
doorway of the bedroom, wavering on puffy bare feet, puffy
face hidden in tangles of hair, broken arm stiff and brown as a
turkey wing before her.

"Aah, aah, aah!"

"Ma!" Toy jumped forward. "Get back in bed!"

Aunt Baptist had said the sleeping medicine would last four-
five hours, but her mother had ever been beyond normal things.

"Aaah, aah, aah!" Suddenly her mother threw back her head
and shrieked. "Eeeeah!"

It brought Harl on a tumble from the other room.

"Help me!" Together, some way, they stumbled and wrestled
her back toward the bed, their voices doing more than their
muscles; she seemed to hear their voices, even when her eyes
were rolled back under their ridges. She was momentarily quiescent as her spine touched the sheets. But the minute they took
their hands from her she surged upward away from pain or toward their flesh, and the bleating recommenced.

"Aah, aah, aah!"

It was down, take their hands away, and upsurge. It was that way until, miraculously, strong hands reached past and Wick's voice soothed.

"It's all right, old lady. It's all right." So he might have spoken to any ailing creature, to mare or man or mouse in a trap, his voice as healing as the balm of Gilead buds that Aunt Baptist gathered for salve. His hand gripped the puffy one. His shoulders shut out the dark things whirling and licking in the corners.

"It's all right, old lady. It's all right."

Toy breathed. "You come." She straightened. "We couldn't have held out no longer."

Already her brother had fled, his momentary manhood disappearing in choking gulps. She heard his feet thud out of the house and knew that he would take refuge in a leafy nook like a rabbit. He would pass the long hours watching squirrels whisk up tree boles, and spiders planted on their spokes of webs. He would draw himself in to be as small as they. Only she could not hide, she could not shrink, she must stretch beyond her normal stand.

Wick said, "Now she was due to sleep four-five hours." His free hand went out and jerked at the quilt. Automatically Toy moved to help him. Together they drew it smooth and listened to her mother's harsh hasseling slack off.

"I know, but—" She flung out a helpless hand. "You got to hold her every minute."

Rose Crawford seemed asleep, inert as dough. Wick drew his hand from her arm. Instantly her eyes flew open. She flung upward, smoothness destroyed in thrashing legs. "Aah, aah, aah!"

They wrestled her back to quiet. Toy panted. "See?"

Wick groped behind him and dragged forward the stump-toed rocking chair. "No need us both setting up. You go on."

She hesitated. "If we take turns."

"You want."

She went to her room and lit the lamp. Her suitcase was set where Wick had returned and placed it by the door. She got out the new gown and put it on, wondering how long she and Wick would be here. Her mind did not go further than that; it slid around corners and edges like a cat.

She slipped between the taut sheets and lay in geometric straightness, quilt folded across her breastbone, hands along her sides, like a child at graduation. Dark held sounds that she knew, a cricket tuning wing on leg, the squeak of the well winch, and another sound she always listened for, asleep or half asleep, the sound of Someone or Something coming, to do what, she did not know.

A new sound intruded, a rhythmic *creak-creak*, the chair in her mother's room.

Wick was rocking.

Creak-creak. It girded her around. It was barely audible, yet it filled the old house and shut out the other sounds. It shut out the sound of Someone, or Something, coming.

She was safe in the center of the sound, safe for the first time since she stumbled down a clay road and saw her father's foot sticking out from under a bush. The sound was a ring encompassing her. Perhaps a ring was not a prison after all; perhaps it was a world stretching indefinitely, herself and another at the center, and the center always holding true.

She slept.

And after a long while she awoke.

She knew that it was long, for the shadows on the walls were different. They were not bruised and tired like the first shades of night, but a fleecy clear black spotted with gray. It was perhaps four or five o'clock in the morning. Why, she had slept all night, a sleep so deep that nothing had disturbed her, Harl's night-moaning, her mother's prowlings—

Her mother—she came upright in bed—Wick. She sprang out, lighting the lamp, and reached for whatever came to hand to cover herself. She found an old frock that buttoned down the front, faded but clean and starched. She drew it on and, taking the lamp, went to the next room.

Wick said from the dark, before the light touched his face, "You slept some."

"Some."

She stood by the bed and something was gone from her mind and limbs, fear, and the favoring of fear which is more deadly than fear itself. Somewhere in the night both had vanished.

She told him, "You were due to wake me."

"No need."

"Anyways, I'll stay now."

He rose, she took his place. The chair was warm from his big body. It held her in a second security. She put her hand on her mother's arm. Rose Crawford slept with little noises trickling from her jolted mouth like steam from a teakettle.

Wick told her, "She's quiet enough, you keep touching her."

She nodded and watched while he brought a chair from across the room and sat down beside her. She was not surprised, but waited while he leaned forward, hands clasped between his knees.

Harsh sounds rose, horses and men returning on the road to Gristle, the coon hunters. A voice was raised here and there, but the words were lost in a mufflement of liquor.

Wick cocked an ear. "Now they never caught old Ring-Tail. About now he's dragging himself up on shore and saying, 'Thanks, Lord, for wide ponds and hollow trees.'"

She remembered. "That old oak trunk halfway across." She guessed. "It's hollow, and he hides in it."

"Uh-huh. I figure he dives down and comes up thu a hole in the trunk. There's an air space above, and he just hangs there long as he's got to."

"You seen him do it?"

"No, but I don't have to see something to know something."

Now she could meet his eyes in the light of the lamp. They were clear and blue under the light brows, the whites luminous, hollows of sleeplessness under them. *Creak-creak* the chair had gone all night. It had covered her deep and warm with its quilt of sound.

She said, "I didn't mean all I said yesterday. You caught me wrong." She groped. "I try not to get caught wrong, but times wrong catches me."

His voice came quietly. "You think you alone? Wrong caught every one of us at the beginning of things. God told Adam and Eve, 'Cursed is the ground for thy sake; in sorrow shalt thou eat of it all the days of thy life.' He didn't destroy them for their sin; He drove them out together to till the earth. Man belongs to *live*, Toy. It don't matter if the living is easy or hard. All that matters is that he does it best he can."

"Marrying me—you made it harder on yourself."

"Marrying you—"

He put his hand on hers which covered her mother's wrist, that cold, flaccid wrist of a woman who had gone beyond feelings—pity or sorrow or love—a woman who was a dog except for the fur, a cat except for the purr, little that was human remaining. And Toy's hand rested on the animal, fearful and uncertain, feeling the cold, her own flesh taking chill from it, until Wick's hand closed on hers.

"Marrying you, I made it easier on myself. For how does a man warm hisself alone? The fire he builds with sticks is a lonely one; he's got to keep it company if he wants to stay warm. This one"—he touched her hand, warm flesh against warm flesh—"why, it's everywhere this world is hung, if he'll only reach out." He stopped. "I'm talking in parables. The natural truth is"—he spoke simply—"I'm lonely. I'm cold."

A thing quickened in her; it built and leaped up through her body and down along her fingers to her nails, pink-tan and knicked with little white islands.

"I need to love you; I need to have you with me."

Pride that she had never known moved her to humbleness that she had never felt. "A man like you—a woman like me—"

"You're everything, all you'll let yourself be—"

"Wick—"

"Wick." Harl stood in the doorway. He was grass-wrinkled, but he looked at them without excuse.

He said, "I'll watch Ma for a while, you want."

Toy rose and walked out to the kitchen. Wick followed. She rested her hands upon the sink. Outside, beyond the road, daylight was upon the trees.

> Day, oh, day.
> Yonder comes day.
> Day done break into my soul. . . .

The old song touched her thoughts even as Wick touched her arm. "Now I spoke too soon."

"No."

Suddenly she found tears in her throat and behind her lids, richly salt and ready to spend. No need to save them. No need to catch them in a tear-glass as the pages of old queens had done. She could use them any time she wished. She was richer than old queens.

"Wick."

"I'm here."

Over his shoulder she could see her room. It was as she had left it, clothes snatched around, the bed roiled and spoiled. But who wanted a tight bed? Tight beds were for timid souls.

She said, "Yonder comes day, but not for a while yet."

Three

ONE May morning, three years later, Toy labored to the top of Atkins' Ridge and rested on a windfall of logs. She looked down on her world below and thought, I'm an unnatural woman.

The farm—Wick's farm, her farm—lay between her feet, so

much in such a little space. The house was white clapboard with
a hipped roof of red tin. It stood on fieldstone posts, the space
beneath a fine place for children to play on hot summer days. A
porch, clustered with rail plants and chairs, ran across the front
and down the left; side steps led into the kitchen. The bathroom
was a box tacked on behind, its single window so small and high
that only birds and cats could be curious.

The house sat in the midst of corn and cotton, tobacco and
soybeans. Mimosa and elm, chinaberry and oak trees surrounded
it; outbuildings were scattered beyond, a crank-sided tobacco
barn and chicken house, a tractor shed of corrugated iron, and a
gray barn. In and among these were fodder and straw stacks,
cribs and pens, a well and a washhouse.

Over them all, lacing the farm together, were the electric lines.
Electricity had come in 1936, tall, raw poles breaking off from
the main lines and marching in regiments into remote farmyards,
each bearing its little REA tag.

One evening Toy pulled a cord and Wick switched on a radio.
Light bloomed and music welled up.

Toy drew a breath. "No more smutty ole lamps."

"And music any time you want it. Now radio must be what
the Lord was talking about: 'Sing many songs that thou mayest
be remembered.' "

The little hairs along Toy's spine no longer roached when the
Lord was brought into the conversation. She had come to terms
with Him. "I'll warm a pew for you," she told Him, "and raise a
tune for you, for it makes Wick happy. But don't figure I come
to spend the night and stay the day."

So she made her manners to the Lord, and Gristle began calling her "Sister" as they called Wick "Brother." Only she knew
all along that what she really was was "Wife."

Wick said, "You can have you a refrigerator now. I got thirteen cents a pound for the cotton I took to the gin this morning."

She marveled. "Double what we got two-three years back."

She added slowly, "I'd be proud not to tote no more ice, but maybe we'd best wait on the refrigerator."

"Now why?"

The radio murmured, "Blue Italian skies above . . . Isle of Capri . . ."

Italy, she thought, that old clay boot dug in blue ocean, Capri one of the specks that went for islands, maybe one that she had tried to scratch off the page when she was a child, taking it for dirt. She had wanted a wide unsullied earth, forgetting earth was dirt right on, black dirt buckling up behind a new tractor, yellow dirt heaping the base of a light pole, brown dirt calling a child, "Come make toad-houses."

She said, "I got so much now."

Things were coming too thick and rich, like cream rising to the top of milk, cream choking her because she was not used to it. She clamped a hand over her mouth.

Afterward she took the cold rag Wick held to her neck, and mopped her face.

He said, "Better get you a washwoman for a spell."

She whirled. "Now you knew! How'd you know?"

His broad face was luminous. "I been hoping for three years."

The towel was old and near napless, yet there was enough nap to catch her nails. A month before they had become long and horny, her breasts engorged. She had been incredulous, so long had women wondered slyly, "When are you and Wick—?" so long had the Negro girls who had come to cook for her mother and Harl asked at her every illness, earache to stone bruise, "You knocked up, Miss Toy?"

She said, "I figure June."

His hand rested on her shoulder. "Maybe the road will be finished by then. Maybe we can get a doctor instead of Aunt Baptist."

The road was another miracle. No longer would it take half a day to cross Atkins' Ridge on the old clay trail that the weather turned muddy or sandy. Now all a feller had to do was get on his stick and jump over. The road was a part of a scenic route starting in central Georgia and winding along the swell of the Blue Ridges.

"They gonna call it the Rhododendron Trail," a WPA-er told John Goforth. "I says to the foreman, 'Folks don't need rhododendron. They need rations.' He says, 'We gonna pay twelve dollars a week.' I says, 'Now I can learn to eat anything for that.' "

The road cut off just below the farm, and just above the old house and the mill. It crept along during the fall and winter and next spring, a blackberry winter with the air so clear that she could hear from a mile away.

". . . know yourself Sam Hicks never hit a lick he could duck. But he goes to the Commodities office, and they give him pants and dresses, eating 'taters and Irish 'taters, beans, apples, and two bed ticks."

". . . kudzu crowns. County agent says, 'Plant them along the gully, and you won't have to stand on the bridge and say, "Yonder flows Gristle county." ' "

As the weather waxed warmer and peach trees pinkened along Atkins' Ridge, men began coming up into the yard and asking for well-water. She put out gourd dippers and talked with them. They always asked when the baby would be born, and she would tell them, "June." They would recollect a friend or relative born in June, and, a tacit bond established, would go on.

"How you all making out?" Meaning, "You having it rough as me?"

She satisfied them. "Nothing braggable."

"Me, too." They would talk on leisurely, the gourd armoring them against the shouts of the distant foreman.

One discovered, "You got no outhouse."

"Got blowed down in the tornado last year. We got one indoors."

"Now ain't that fine? I tell you, I don't mind to plow and fight

flies, and eat and fight flies, but when I set and got to fight
flies—"

Noon would invariably bring a man or several to ask, "You
all sell anything to eat to the mill?"

She would tell them, "Cokes and cinnamon buns, canned beans
and peaches, sweetened condensed milk."

The store had happened this way. Harl had applied for CCC,
but it did not look as if they needed him to fence pastures or
build fireboxes, plant pine seedlings or clean and grade ceme-
teries. So he hung around home, chin lower and lower.

Bill-Hart told her one day, "Mr. Harl is hunting armydillos."

"Iron-plated possums? There's none around. They're just hear-
say."

His eyes slanted at her obliquely. "He gots to catch *nothing*,
he can't catch sumpin, enty?"

She thought about this while Bill-Hart worked. The Negro
boy was chest deep in the pond, mending a hole in the dam. Icy
water prickled his black hide, for it was March.

"You mean he's got to have something to do?"

Bill-Hart studied a nail with great attention. He hit it a whack.
"Was adding up de toll book yes'day. Couldn't. Mr. Harl run a
finger down de page and say, 'Four sixty-seven bushels.'"

Toy eased herself down on a rock and began rubbing her legs.
She was not sick, but her legs burned and stung. She was constantly rubbing them, trying to put the fire out. Wick urged her
to see a doctor—"More sorry women from being half-tended at
birthing"—but she would not.

She told Bill-Hart, "Harl always was good at figures."

The Negro heaved himself out of the water and shook himself like a bear. He had grown in the last three years; he was
quilted with muscle, and when he took a breath his chest was a
black barrel.

"Mens from WP and A stopped by again dis mawning, asked
did us have sto' to mill."

The baby sprang against her side. She pressed a hand to still it, dully. Why did she have small mean feelings instead of full, fine ones? Why did she fall short of life? Dolly was on her fourth child, and excited and happy as if it was her first or second— Zadie or the twins, Huel and Ruel. She and Jack would stop their old rusty car by the house, and Dolly would shout joyously, "Little bugger is pure kicking the chitlins out of me!"

She told Bill-Hart, "There used to be a store to the mill."

"Sho' nuf?"

"In the lean-to yonder."

She had not even begun a layette. Annie Goforth had told her last week, with scarcely concealed disapproval, "Now when I was expecting Dolly, I kept the quilting thread whistling."

She said to Bill-Hart, "Granddaddy run it, but my daddy didn't care to take the time."

She had seen a baby in Gristle day before yesterday, but she had not stopped to look at it as other women did.

She told Bill-Hart, "I reckon it could be opened again."

Harl turned red at the idea of running a store. "You—you reckon I could?" His voice firmed. "I could, Toy—sure I could. Why, every time I go to Goforth's, I think, if 'twas me, I'd put the lace by the cloth, or, Folks'd come in quicker if you put candy or beads by the front door 'stead of cotton hampers." He stopped. "But you never wanted no store before." His voice was accusation and question.

"No WPA money before."

He was satisfied. He went back to talking of what he would do and stock. "Put up some shelves and a counter. Sell them little nickel packs of cinnamon buns. Get me an oil drum and cut it down for a stove."

Wick listened and watched, turning through a book on tobacco-curing. He had taken to raising Burley and had two acres edging the woods, new land so that the soil would be "clean." At the last sale the "long red" had fetched fifteen cents a pound.

Harl finished and went out, and she rose to clear the table. Wick put down the book.

"Now that's a fine thing you're doing, leaving him to run a store."

"It don't disfurnish me none."

"Now no need of being ashamed of a good deed."

She wanted to ask him, "Tell me, how good is a deed born of an evil seed?" Samson drew honey from the carcass of the lion, yet the lion was corruption right on.

Three weeks later, on a day when crows dropped down like black leaves on the fields, the store was opened in the lean-to. The boards across the windows had been taken down. Fresh air swept in and paint lightened the place further. Shelves had been raised and stocked, and a counter laid across two barrels. An oil drum had been cut down for a stove and set on a brick apron, and Harl gave away free Cokes. Gristle came to drink and draw its own conclusions.

Ora Watts pointed to the new sifting machine in the mill, a mesh barrel turned by a crank. It separated the grist into extra fine meal, medium, and "shorts." "Babies is like a sifter," she declared. "They fine a woman's grain."

Toy heard and would have laughed at a lesser lie. Instead she was mute when women began to visit her, saying, "Hear you ain't had a chance to get you a 'let.' " They would produce gifts, half a dozen diapers, a gown or shirt, a paper of pins, or a crocheted bonnet.

She did not have to talk; her body spoke a general language.

One woman would say, "You carrying it high, ain't you? Now certain-sure it's a boy."

A second would deny. "No, boys lay low. I remember my Jimmy—"

One would say, "I had milk leg the worst."

A second would recall, "Abscesses—and the worst ole stretch marks—"

The men of Gristle took over the store, resting their heels on the stove and giving the spit-cup a tuning, *ping-ping*. They bought a dime's worth of rat cheese or a box of soda crackers or a bottle of chill remedy, but it was the WPA workers who made Harl's pencil jump: canned tomatoes and cocoa, plug tobacco and light bread, sardines and coffee and cinnamon buns. They averaged twelve dollars a week in wages, and that was high on the hog; for ten years most of them had been on the pig end, back by the tail.

Toy took to staying away from the mill as the store got busier, grinding slackened, and her time drew on. Increasingly she labored up Atkins' Ridge and rested on a fallen log.

Now she looked down at the world between her toes and thought, I'm an unnatural woman. And thought again, Maybe I'll feel different when it comes.

Burgeoning life within her tied her to burgeoning life without. The distant cotton would be thigh-high in September, shirting for her son. The new heifer, watched by Wick and Isaac, the Negro tenant, would give milk for him next spring. Everything moved and had a purpose to the new life except herself. She was dry and still as the husk that a cicada had left on a nearby pine.

Distantly Wick and Isaac parted. Wick paused on his way to the tractor shed and looked up toward the ridge, white with serviceberry. He knew she took walks, and he shook his head. "Now for your sake, if not the baby's, stay around the farm. You know the hills is full of snakes and deadfalls from the tornado."

She had not given up the walks.

She watched as he turned away and thought, If I was Dolly . . .

If she were Dolly, she would stay home and sew. She would clasp her stomach tenderly instead of catching her cold elbows with colder fingertips. She would give up ridge-roaming.

She thought, I hate sewing. And trees don't ask, "What you want, a boy or a girl?"

If she were Dolly, she would live in a lean gray house with broken fences held up by honeysuckle vines. There would be chickens wandering unpenned everywhere, witch weed and plantain choking the corn, and a swing between two pines where you could lie and touch a lazy toe to the earth, to and fro.

She lived yonder, tall chimneys, tight fences, green fields.

"Cotton in the shed, boys, sugar in the gourd," the old song went, and it was a gracious plenty for most women, cotton for her family's shirting, sugar to sweeten her days.

Not for her.

Cherokee roses looped a stump. Bay blossoms bloomed; the air was filled with their pungency. Dewberries outdid blackberries in size and sinful sweetness. Rose and bay and berry drew bees. They dipped and crawled from fruit to flower, then flew away. She traced one to a hole high in a black gum. Within the queen laid eggs, and the workers fed the young on bee bread. A bee became what it was fed. Royal bread made a royal princess, drone bread made males, common crusts made a thousand workers. A bee became what it was fed, but a man became more, or less.

"Sugar in the gourd, honey in the horn . . ."

Sugar and honey, but her marriage had been more than these. She could lie down like stone at night, and then Wick would touch her in a certain way, and her body was leavened. Sometimes she would laugh, a small sound in the dark. Wick would mutter, half asleep but always hearing, "Tell me?" And she would answer, "Nothing."

A bee became what it was fed. Man's love should be stronger than bee bread. She should be full with the love Wick gave her. Yet her child would be born in June, and she had not picked a name for it or claimed for it, "I'd rather have a girl; you can dress a girl"; or "I'd rather have a boy; they so manly."

Slowly, her world between her feet, she came to sense the nature of the beast, and it was this: she could not wholly believe in goodness, and at the same time she was jealous of it.

Two ways pulled her awry; she was left dangling with a self-inflicting impotence.

A night in early June she went to bed, and sometime later woke, hot and reluctant. She was lying on her side, her burden supported partly by the mattress, more by her own flesh and bones. Suddenly they seemed unable to bear it. They dilated agonizingly.

She woke Wick. "It's coming." And lay detached, watching him spring up, big and heavy-eyed, but eyes clearing to anxiety. He snapped on the light and snatched his clothes.

"Calla!"

Isaac's daughter, who had been sleeping on a pallet in the kitchen the last week or two, stumbled in, knuckling her face.

"I'm going." His face bent over Toy; lines pulled his mouth taut. "Take it easy, hear?"

She parted her lips, but suddenly the millstones started. They began grinding her bones to make bread, fee, fie, foe, fum. She was furious at the millstones for the mistake. They belong to grind grist.

"No!"

Later the stones slowed and stopped. She was surprised to find that she was panting as if she had pushed them herself, not the black waters. She turned her head and asked the Negro girl, "Where's Wick?"

"Went to phone de doctor." Calla was sixteen, with a bullet head and jaybird heels. "Mr. Wick sho ain't no hen-husband. Mostest mens flaps and squawks round—"

"Maybe it'll come before he gets here."

"Do, Lord!"

"Maybe it will." Maybe it will kill me, she thought. Maybe it'll be ashes-ashes-we-all-fall-down. And heard a voice somewhere cry, "No!"

"What you needs is a li'l' sumpin." Calla's throat was a long black snake moving; her eyes were elliptical with greed. "Gots 'tater pie in kitchen, ham ends wid greens—"

The millstones seized her again. She was sucked between the grooves, whirling and grinding, heat and grinding pain. And when finally they slowed and stopped, Calla was sitting nearby, pinching bits of ham from a bowl between her knees, voice running on like juice on her purple lips.

". . . Essie gots chil'yun on feather bed 'n straw bed 'n shuck bed 'n pallet 'n shakedowns. I tells her, 'I was you, gal, I puts dat Dick in jail till Jabo comes.'"

Toy gasped. "Jabo—Baby Jesus got nothing to do—" And broke off, for she did not know what she said or what she meant.

Later she asked, "Mr. Wick come back?"

Calla shook her nubby head.

By and by a millstone wears down. It grinds a final grist, a flat mat of meal or raw head and bloody heels, then slows. Its edges dull; it stops. "Bill-Hart!" Toy heard herself crying. She would wear that nigger out, letting the stones get so, letting the mill stop. "Bill-Hart!" She opened her eyes.

Wick was bending above her. Sweat shone on his temples; the wings of his nose were pinched white. But he was smiling, and she heard the word, "Girl."

So she did not need Bill-Hart. She closed her eyes, and her hand moved with an age-old instinct. "Flat," she discovered with relief; "flat"—and was ashamed that she thought only of her own body, not what it had brought forth. She opened her eyes to escape her thoughts, and saw day streaking the trees beyond the window. Thursday it was, a day that had far to go, and already it had started.

Wick asked, "What you want to name her?"

She looked at the streaked trees and said, "Mary Morning."

Five days later she got up, torn and tottery. She tried to nurse the baby, hand stiff on its damp back, but her milk seemed thin and sour. It displeased the baby, who mewled, mottle-faced, fists

knotted weakly. So Wylma, Calla's mother, who cooked for Rose
and Harl Junior, took it to her own breast. There it clenched itself greedily, light skull cupped in her dark, horny palm. Wylma
said tenderly, "Her de hungriest."

Now Bill-Hart smashed his hand. As he was winching up the
millstones so that he could clean them, the screw slipped. It was
a wonder that his whole arm was not crushed. As it was, Toy
had to go to the mill more often; and between times the garden
and crops swelled with summer. There were seven Negroes to
be worked and fed, and they had to be stayed behind every minute.

So the baby fell by necessity to Calla and Wylma, but the necessity was not all-absolving. Toy felt a guilt that she could not
quench; the mother-love that everyone told her was "natural"
had not come.

She thought, August.

Laying-by time came in August. There was a breathing spell
about the second week of the month. Corn and truck had been
laid by; cotton would not burst its bolls for another week or so.
Bill-Hart would be well. She would have time to sit down with
the baby. She would learn to say "her" instead of "it." Familiarity would breed love. Everything would come right in laying-by
time.

Relieved, she turned to the summer swarming in.

Corn tasseled up, and tobacco flung up suckers and blooms
that had to be pinched off. Onion, okra, cabbage, and chain-
gang peas ripened; tomatoes and peppers swelled. The canning
kettle danced on the stove. A mile away the WPA workers sang
at the bridge they were building over the creek.

> ". . . sure be a wreck,
>   When Grandpa gets his ole-age-pension check."

They still stopped by the well, but now they spoke with more
easiness. Warmth made them confident as cats or crickets.

"Roosevelt's gonna pull us out of this. I tell you, I say that man's name in my prayers."

"Still and all, telling a feller to plow under every third row of cotton—it's beyond nature. First time I tried it, my mule just looked over his shoulder and wouldn't budge. He knowed he didn't belong to do such as that."

"Uh-huh. And you know who's telling us to do it, don't you? Two little loafers and a trade-made cigarette setting up there in Washington."

"Still and all, if Roosevelt feels like it's gonna help us, I say, 'Plow it under, good God almighty, plow it under!'"

Later she heard their voices from the bridge again:

". . . That old-time religion,
It's good enough for Roosevelt,
It's good enough for me."

Afterward she remembered it as a summer of roses. "White December, rose June," people said, and it was true. Fall and winter had been hard. A calf had drowned in the pond and not been found for two days. A dozen chickens had died of sour craw. Two shoats had eaten lantana and, throats swollen, died of starvation. Hardly a day passed when the new highway did not take its toll, skunks and coons, possums, dogs and cats, an armadillo—so there were such as that, she thought. All the bodies had to be buried; Bill-Hart or Isaac dug them into the rose roots.

The roses swelled from the bones. Lady Banksia weighed the trellis outside her morning window, the trellis leaning under the weight and propped up. Rambling roses—Dorothy Perkins, Bob o' Gold, and Evergreen—covered the noonday fences, so that the weathered rails were hidden. French and Provence roses, Glory Dee and Paul Neyron, banked the veranda, their thorns and perfume reaching out indiscriminately at night.

One evening, passing a dogrose, she saw the hips outnumbering the blooms.

Why, she thought, laying-by time is gone.

How had September come without her noticing? What had happened to laying-by time? It had come and gone, gone with the tomatoes and beans she had canned, hands stained red and green; gone with the cypress cups she and Hart had put on the millwheel, climbing, drenched as otters, along the mossy wheel-rim. For already one or two people had come for grinding. Already biscuits were losing their flavor for cornbread.

Fall had come yellowing the persimmon in the tree. Golden-rod blew along the shoulders of the highway, and chinquapins were brown and tight-clenched. Flying spiders flung their final webs. Toy saw one hang twenty feet down from a pine-bough. A breeze came, and he rode it, swinging himself forty feet to a cedar limb.

Fall had come; laying-by time had gone. The baby had fine light hair and Wick's cut of cheek and chin. Calla said, "It eats good," and Wylma said, "Her de *goodest*."

She saw the child, but she could not feel the child, only her own guilt.

Four

ONE day in early October Aunt Baptist came by. The big midwife's flesh had fallen in upon her. Her iron-gray hair was white, and her teeth were gone except for a few stubs, but she would not let them be pulled, claiming, "I love to hang my tongue around them."

"Well, the baby don't look like you, and that's a blessing." She eyed Toy with disfavor. "I swear, gal, I seen new mothers look-ing poorly as snakes, but you looking poorly as a lizard—and won't even a cat touch a lizard. Don't Wick say nothing about how you look?"

Toy bent and jerked out a dried pea vine, cornshuck hat shading her face. "No."

Before, he had talked in the evening while she cleared away the supper things. "We," he would say, and when the baby came, "Us three." Lately he had talked less and looked more, looked at her and looked at the baby. He had taken to going out and sitting on the back steps, hands clasped between his knees, looking up at the stars. Once she had called tentatively, "Skeeters will eat you alive." After a while he answered, "It's cool." Suddenly, it had come to her: He's praying.

Anyone else but Wick, and she would have turned on him, a warm and busy enemy; for she knew anyone else would be praying, "Lord, help her," the meanest prayer in Christendom. For it plumes itself, "I don't need help"; it disclaims, "Her trouble's got nothing to do with me."

She could fight someone like that, take a gun and shoot him dead before eight o'clock Monday morning. But a man who prayed, "Help me help her"—well, what could you do with him?

"Wick hasn't said nothing? Then he's changed more than he's got a right to." Aunt Baptist's eyes pinned her. "It's the baby, ain't it? You got no more feeling for it than if 'twas a sack of meal, and Wick knows it."

Toy's breath jumped. "No."

"Don't lie to me, gal. I've dangled more babies by the heels than there is leaves in Vallambrosia. I've seen mothers holding their babies with one hand and saying, 'Ain't he cute?' while the other touched their bellies, and they was thinking, Thin-gutted as a wasp again, thank God. I've seen them start out the door, fine and free, and suddenly stop, realizing, I can't, I got the baby. I can't do nothing I want no more. I've seen them wake up to the yelling in the night and hide their faces, wishing, Why don't it die?"

"No!"

"Yes. For love ain't a lonely thing; it's got company like everything else in this world. It's got hate. Two is the nature of things.

The hill is obliged to have the hollow, and laughter cuts the lines that tears follow. Adam drew trouble from a rib and returned it through a belly. What I mean is, hate belongs as good as love."

She cried, "I got to get shut of it!"

"Praying is one way out. There's a better."

"What?"

An apron waved. Wylma was running across the yard, black arm signaling. "Miss Toy!"

She glared at the Negro, hardly seeing her.

"Miss Toy, dey was gone when I got back. I tawed Calla, I tawed de young'uns, but dey say dey ain't seen dem."

"What?"

"Mr. Harl's pants and de split-oak stool belong on de back porch. Dey gone like de rest."

Aunt Baptist said sharply, "Stealing? First I heard."

Toy told her, "Nothing much. A well-cover, dishes, a broom." She said, "Now—clothes."

Wylma said, "He go-to-meeting pants. Mr. Harl sho burning thunderwood. He say he find who—"

First she had thought it was Wylma's children taking things. She had lined them up and faced them down. Finally she had believed their trembling "*Nuh*, ma'm"'s. When the cups and saucers, three of each, disappeared, she suddenly wondered, Ma? —and asked, "Ma, you got those cups, saucers?"

Her mother's chin tucked down. Her eyes cut up cute as a lying child's. "No, *these* mine." She showed the ones on the table.

"Now, Ma, you know what I mean."

Her mother kept shaking her head. "No." Once, however, she added plaintively, "The rest is acorns."

"What?"

"Nothing—"

Aunt Baptist heaved herself up from the stump, shaking her head. "That ma of yourn is sure a stone of stumbling and a rock of offense, ain't she? Now I'm gonna send you some cohash. Brew you a tea; it'll make you loose as Saturday night, and twice as green." She started off.

Toy cried, "Praying—and what else?"

"Grace."

Wylma left, and Toy finished pulling the pea vines. They would be raked and piled for fodder. Hogs loved pea vines. Fall before last she had seen a curious sight, hogs toting pea vines in their mouths, loops over their shoulders like shawls. An old-timer had declared, "We'll be rabbit-hunting in the snow." And so they had.

She pulled the final vine and straightened. October browned the leaves along the edges. Wasps had ceased to dance in the sun; they crawled slowly, wings spread, along the baseboard in the house, seeking warm holes. Sneezeweed blew down the highway and clung to car radiators.

Toy looked down at the baby. It lay on a blanket on the grass, wavering and jerking like a stranded fish. Its chin was milk-clotted, and it needed changing again.

"Calla." The colored girl uncoiled herself from the side steps. She was chewing sweet-gum resin and wore a string of dried chinaberries around her neck. She took the baby. It clawed at the beads.

"Now ain't that like a gal?" She giggled. "Gots to have her a pretty."

Toy hung her hat on a peg. "What you make for supper?"

"Pot pie and chicken fixings."

She whirled. "You kill a chicken when we got ham, a pot of hash—"

"Mr. Wick told me. He say something soft."

She was puzzled. She went into the bathroom and bathed, seeing through the high window snatches of sky and pecan branches, the twig ends heavy with nuts. A jay lit on one end, bracing its tail like a woodpecker, drilled a hole, and ate. A few nuts rustled to the ground.

Voices approached.

". . . the mostest of cotton picked," Isaac said importantly. "The rain hold off day-two, we gets de rest. What you wants us to do 'bout dem pecans, Mr. Wick?"

"Gather as many as you can and take them over to Gainesville. You can have half of whatever you get."

"Thanky, Mr. Wick, sho will. I gets Calla, the boys—" There was a sudden sound of hat slapped against leg. "Git 'way from dem nuts, dog!" He complained, "Now looky yonder; that piece of stovepipe round de bottom keeps de squirrels from climbing, but it don't mean a thing to dem jays and crows."

Wick asked, "Now you got everything straight, the cotton, the stock? I'll be back Monday morning the latest."

"Don' you worry, Mr. Wick. You go to meeting and laugh de Jesus-laugh. I takes care things here."

Voices retreated. Toy lay stiff in the tub. "Be back Monday . . . meeting." Wick had not gone to a protracted meeting since they were married.

"Hello, Calla." Wick's voice lifted and lightened. "Well, look there. Hey, sugarpie."

"She sho know you, Mist' Wick. She don' take on like dat for nobody but her daddy."

Wick hummed, " 'Hush, li'l' baby, don't say a word. Daddy's gonna buy you a mockingbird.' Where's Miss Toy?"

"Taking her a bath."

She was discovered; she felt an intruder in her own house. She raised her voice. "I'm thu."

He called, "Take your time."

Quickly she slipped out of the tub and dried herself. Water or sweat trickled down her spine. She drew on clean clothes and, opening the door, stepped out on the back porch. Breeze touched her body, cooling her; planks were gritty under her bare feet.

" '. . . if that billygoat runs away, Daddy's gonna buy you—' " Wick came around the corner of the house. He had been bouncing the baby on his arm and laughing, but he stopped when he saw her.

"You waiting on me?"

"Not particular."

They ate supper, pot pie and chicken fixings. Wick fed the baby pieces of chicken, slipping them between the parted lips. He did not speak but smiled often, and the baby bloomed with warmth. Again and again it put out a hand to touch the smile. Sometimes he and Toy talked, mouth-talk, good enough in its own way, but its way was not between husband and wife.

"I hear Aunt Baptist come today."

"She come. Harl tell you, his Sunday pants come up missing?"

"Your mother, you reckon?"

"Maybe."

She waited for him to tell her about the protracted meeting. She waited for him to say, "The preacher asked me to help out." She wanted him to say, "The preacher asked me, so I couldn't say no." She wanted the preacher to blame.

He said, "Best turn on the light."

She rose and pulled the cord. The words came of their own accord. "Don't know why you wanted Calla to fix chicken."

"A baby can't chew ham."

"It can't chew nothing."

"She can chew chicken; she's got teeth. You didn't know that?"

She was helpless against the accusation—for it was an accusation—helpless and guilty. For she had not known about the teeth. It was a crime beyond nature that she had not known about the teeth.

"It's got none—I'd have seen!"

"You didn't look. She's had them two weeks, only you didn't care enough to look."

Her breath was like to choke her. It came out in a gasp that could be a laugh. "I hear tell most everybody's got teeth. I hear tell some folks is lucky—they get two sets!"

"You can joke." He rose and went into the bedroom and put down the baby. He came back and looked at her across the table. "You don't care nothing for her, do you?"

"No." She set her teeth in a truth as hard as any she could tell.

"You love me?"

A hard truth came easier than a tender one. She was mute, but he knew. He came and put his hands on her shoulders.

"Then where do it stop? She's part of me and you. Where do it stop for her?"

She said dully, "I don't know."

His face loosened. He dropped his hands and stepped back. "That's why I'm going to the meeting. You heard me tell Isaac? That's why I'm going, so I can pray and fill my eyes with people praying. I want to see people seeking God."

Briefly she flared. "I seen how they seek God to them protracted meetings."

The last protracted meeting she had attended—the summer she was twelve, the summer of Jim Jay and the sweet shrub—the meeting was opened with the "Holiness" song:

> When first I went to Holiness
> I thought it was a shame
> To see the people jump and shout
> In praising Jesus' name.

After that the preacher had gotten up and shouted, "Once our young folks used to sing songs like that. They wasn't ashamed of the Lord! Once they used to sing, 'Do, Lord, oh, do, Lord, do remember me.' Now they sing 'Do, do, do what you done, done, done before, baby'!"

Later he had cried out, "Let your feelings flow, folks. Get up and show the Lord you meaning it when you shout, 'Save me!'"

And they had done so. Toy remembered the gathering under the trees, the fireboxes flaring in the dark and warning how Hell looked, the people shouting and praying, dancing in the aisles and jerking. She remembered one girl clinging to a tree and jerking convulsively, long black hair cracking like a wagon whip and laughing the "Jesus laugh" deep from the chest, barking.

She said, "I seen how they seek God to them meetings, rearing and pitching and barking. Barking up the wrong tree!"

"Their way of finding God mayn't be mine, but it's theirs, and they're seeking. It's better to seek than to sit. It's better to have too much of something than nothing at all. And maybe some of what they got will return to me. For"—his voice was desperate, his face haggard—"I've lost God. Once He used to walk beside me, and my eye saw, my heart understood. Now He's gone, and the earth is past walking on. My heart knows bitterness. I've lost God."

The agony reached out to her. She felt it strike her breathless and go on, leaving a terror to match his.

She managed, "You just tired. You been working—"

"I'm tired. I'm tired in my heart."

He was gone Saturday morning when she woke. There was his pillow, and nothing on it; there was his cup empty; and outside in the dust his truck tracks went off past the cotton fields.

The doorjamb was chill with dew; the fields glistened. Soon the dew would be drawn up into the clouds in thin white sheets. Isaac and his children would move up and down the cotton rows with their long sacks. Monday Wick would take the cotton to the gin.

If he came back Monday.

Behind her the baby started to cry, a thin formless wail.

"Calla!"

"Unh?"

"Hush it."

If Wick came back Monday.

The truck would return, yes; Wick would put a long leg out. Jit, the new black feist, would bounce up to him, and Wick would bend, smiling, to push the importunate black muzzle this way and

that. "You a mess," he would say, "you a mess." Finally he would
raise his head and see her; then she would know if he had
returned, all of him.

The baby wailed and choked, a weak and sickly sound.

"Calla."

"Unh?"

"Take care of it."

"You goan somewheres, Miss Toy?"

"The mill."

The old security enfolded her when she entered. Bill-Hart was
swinging himself through the window. He carried a pulley-belt
in one hand, and a welt lay across one black cheek, the end touching his eyelid.

"Whupped loose and flung out de window." His hand raised,
exploring. "Like to put my ole eye out."

They had to scare up a ride into Gristle and buy a new belt.
They returned and put it on, but the gate wouldn't raise. Bill-
Hart, descending into the water, found it caught and pierced by
an oak root swept into the sluice someway. They had just
removed it when Harl came, complaining about his pants.

"Ma's took them off somewhere, I can tell. But she puts a finger in her mouth and cuts an eye around, you try to get her to
say where. I got to get me another pair, for tomorrow's church."

Tomorrow was church, and Wick would return Monday. Perhaps.

She offered—it was an offering to Wick as much as anyone—
"I'll watch the store."

There were few customers, for Saturday people went to town
or to Cardiff. A few WPA workers stopped in before noon; they
were complaining about the new rotation of jobs.

"You can't work but so many weeks, then they cut you off.
You just about making buckle and tongue meet, and the gov'-
ment says, 'Take a tuck in your belly.'"

When Harl returned with new pants, she left and climbed down
along the pond to check the water level. Here were the banks

where moccasins sunned themselves, and turtles slid off slowly. Here were the sluices where small fish played, the swaying grassy barriers over which shad and catfish ran. There was the club-house, a clump of mystery lilies blooming by the door. They appeared each October, tall leafless stems capped with red trumpet-shaped flowers. She picked one to put in a glass and walked home. Shadows were shortening on the grass.

Wylma had cooked supper. The baby lay in its crib, quietly chewing its fist. She told Wylma, "You know it's got two teeth?"

"Do, Lord."

The last thing she heard before going to sleep was the baby sucking its fist. The first thing she heard when she woke the next morning was silence.

The baby was gone.

Her heart died before it came to life again.

The mute sheets, the empty milk bottle accused her, the curtains belling at the open window, the dust motes dancing in the open door. They said, You thought it wouldn't matter. You thought space was better than company. Now you got space; what you going to do with it?

The room spread out on every side, the house, the yard, the world beyond. The baby was somewhere in the space, lost in the space, fist in its mouth. It thought its mouth was the world, and its fist the key to unlock it. Chew the fist and wail, and it would be fed. Beat the fist and howl, and it would be wiped. Reach the fist and whimper, and it would be given.

It could not conceive deaf ears and monkey-paws. It could not conceive Rose Crawford.

Toy knew that her mother had taken the baby.

She dressed. Her hands moved while her mind raced in circles of no more use than the ripples created by a stone cast in a pond. Only the stone was a solid; the baby was gone; her mother had taken it. And there was no one to help her find it.

She saw a wide and sunlit world, a Sunday world with everyone gone. She stood on the veranda with paths running off like spokes in a palm-leaf fan, and no one on the paths. WPA workers were gone, most of Gristle was at the protracted meeting or at the Methodist love-feast in Shiloh, beyond Atkins' Ridge. Nor were Isaac and his family home; their house beyond the trees was shuttered and smokeless. Bill-Hart had gone to Cardiff.

She was alone in a sunlit, Sunday world, and the baby was anywhere and somewhere, somewhere with three cups and a well-cover, a sedge broom and a pair of men's pants, somewhere with her mother, deaf-eared and monkey-handed.

She began running.

A sharp-shinned hawk rode a slope wind as she crossed the creek; it sought southing birds and found only wisps of fog among the trees. She struck off down a dog-leg between laurel and oaks. The smell of new earth came to her; someone had been grubbing with a mattock, Aunt Baptist likely, harvesting the fat roots of fall, sassafras and 'sang, wild yam and bloodroot, blue flag and green briar.

Up half a mile and over where the creek branched she went, past a wash-hole created by an old mountain man digging clay for his pottery. He had passed on years ago, but yonder was the ruins of his kiln, a shallow tumble of bricks and shards of pots, jugs, pitchers, churns, firkins.

There was no sign of her mother there.

Her heart beat in her ears, her heart or the heat. She could feel a pounding in her temples; sweat ran down her cheeks, little cold trickles along her jaw. She wiped them away and went on.

So many places, as many as the whims in a twisted brain, up hill or down hill. She turned down and cut off through smilax tangles and shale outcroppings until she slid down a side road. Yonder was the Negro church, a little gray box with a shuttered steeple, like lowered eyes. The graveyard behind was filled with violet glass. It was on the graves, pieces of pitchers and platters, goblets, glasses, and vases. They had been put there long ago, and time and sun and sand had turned them brilliant amethyst. Stones were few; many graves were topped with cement poured into board frames, the name and age scratched in. There were few eulogies beyond "A Good Wife," or "Worked for the Watsons 52 years," as if even in death the essential man or woman must be concealed.

Her mother was not there.

The sun blazed down, the violet glass gleamed, yet she perished before the sun because she was wicked. Her throat parched, her blood ran too quick and thick because the sun saw the stubbornness of her guilty heart. The sun was to see by and grow by. Yet all she had seen was herself, all she had grown could be measured by her shadow on the ground. Now the sun, punishing her, sought to quench her.

A lizard flicked by. He carried no shadow under his belly because he was the snake's kin. Her own shadow was scrouged down and trying to hide under her toes. She cried out and ran, trying to lose her shadow among the leaves. She tore through the woods, trees looming and leaving. Yet when she finally stopped, breathless, there was her shadow, black and burrowing under her toes like a little beast. "The spirit of man that goeth upward, and the spirit of the beast that goeth downward to the earth."

She sobbed out against her shadow, "No!"

Leaves quivered, birds tumbled away at the sound. Little rustlings stopped or started, freezing or fleeing according to their natures. She looked around and saw nothing she knew, woods and beyond them woods. Fumbling and flinging out her hands to hold aside vines, she made her way through the trees, going nowhere, careless where she stepped until she stepped in mire.

Mire. She stopped, feet steadying. Mire and swamp smell, noisome and miasmic. Bonnet Slough—she was at the edge of Bonnet Slough where Coke Williams ran his hogs, creatures lean and mean as the snakes they lived on. She turned and began to follow the irregular edge of the slough, jumping from hassock to hassock of solid grass.

A cinnamon dusk hung over the slough. Shadows were never clean there; everything was too thick and rank; water oak and cypress tangled with smilax.

Suddenly she cried out. She thought she saw two bears fighting, the one's teeth buried in the other's shoulder. But it was only two tree stumps covered with a bull-grape vine. Yet there were bears. A few years ago some of Coke Williams' hogs had turned up missing. So he had built a pen and "set" two hogs to catch the thief. A few nights later he had shot, not the man he had hoped for, but a black and clownish yearling.

The pen remained, a rectangle of rotten saplings. She began to run.

Muck squelched under her feet; mire filled her shoes; vines and branches clutched moistly at her. She thrust them aside, eyes straining, and finally saw it, the corner of the pen. Simultaneously she heard a thin wail. She parted haw bushes, thorns tearing her hands, and saw the house.

For it was a house. Rose Crawford had not kept house for a long time, but she had not forgotten how. A broom was needed, a pair of britches, and a baby. There was the sedge broom—its parallel scratches were on the moist dark earth—there were Harl's britches laid over an old chair—she had thought the chair long gone for kindling—and there was the baby.

Toy's fist went to her mouth.

The baby lay in an old dough trough. It was set near the table —Toy recognized the well-cover—and the baby lay in the boat-shaped bowl half swaddled, bare feet kicking convulsively. It cried endlessly, whey face screwed up, fist in mouth, hungry.

Rose Crawford was setting the table. She hummed high and tunelessly as she put three cups and saucers on the well-cover. There were already bits of broken plates on it, acorn cups, and an old iron kettle. Suddenly she swiveled an eye bright and reasonless as a monkey's.

"Honey, that you?" Her voice was mincy, a child playing a

woman but, frighteningly, using a woman's mouth. Monkey see, monkey do.

"Honey?" She minced forward, thumb tucking hair behind her ear. There were pones of fat on her neck and ankles.

"Aw." She flung a palm downward. "You just saying that." She switched back. "I got supper fixed, all the things you like." She cocked her head. "Her? Why, she's been just as good all day. Ain't made a sound." She dug rigid extended fingers into the baby's stomach. The baby howled. "She just Mama's precious sugarpie, now ain't she? Yes, she is."

Her voice turned petulant. "You ain't et a speck of your grape pie! I stood over that hot ole stove all morning fixing it, and you ain't et a speck." She reached over and picked up the piece of plate and pitched it into the bushes. "Now you et it. Ain't it good?"

Toy hung to the hawthorn and did not know that blood pricked her palms. Moisture seeped through the leaves on her head and shoulders, rain remembered after rain was gone, just as love is remembered when love is gone, she thought, even a pinching, picking, and pulling love.

"No!" Her mother flung up. "We ain't gonna set round the house. They having a dance to Cardiff and we going." Furiously she grabbed the pants and shook them. She pitched them after the plate and said peaceably, " 'By." She giggled. "Better men in Bugtown. Don't need a banty, I can get me a rooster." Her face contorted. "Honey, honey . . ." The word ran on and on, looking for someone, and she found it and seized the baby. "Honey— Mama's li'l' sugarpie, precious li'l' ole— She loves her mama, no one else do, don't she?"

Suddenly, carelessly, she dropped the baby on the ground and walked off. She walked off, bare feet sloughing on the earth. Branches crackled after her, and the baby was left on the black earth, staring and whining and kicking.

Toy went to the baby. She found herself trembling all over,

her very thighs weak, whether from anger or fear or relief she did not know.

She picked up the baby, but it reared away from her, stiff-spined with rage. It screamed. It had not been fed, it had not been changed, it had not been held. It had not gotten its due.

It kicked her in the ribs. It fought as it had fought from the womb and would fight to the windmill end of the world. It fought for its dues, but it would never get them, never in this world.

Toy said slowly, "No good taking on."

The baby screamed. A maple leaf or two drifted down, the color and shape of monkey paws. The world was full of monkeys today. She hated monkeys. They were nasty-minded, they forgot, they carried branches. Why, it was a monkey world right on. A human was obliged to fight unless he wanted to go down under the branches that the monkeys carried.

She said more slowly, "Take on, if you want."

The baby did not. Suddenly, abruptly, it stopped screaming. It gave up. Toy could feel a quiver along her arm, a sudden dead weight as the stiffness went out of the tiny spine, the baby settled limply against her. It had surrendered, and surrender is next door to death.

It nearly tore her heart to pieces.

The agony was palpable. Her heart squeezed as though caught between grindstones. The juice was being pressed out of her heart. She was dying.

"Gal." She groaned. "Aw, gal."

A chapped cheek was uppermost. She pressed her lips to it. Her hand cupped the thin light head, and her mouth moved up along the brow. A thin bleat came from the baby's lips.

"Aw—"

Her joy was as keen as her agony. She bent and bit her daughter on the neck.

PART
IV

One

MARY MORNING walked when she was eleven months old and talked when she was eighteen months. She stumbled through her first full prayer at three.

"Matthew, Mark, Luke, and John, Bless the bed that I lie on. Four corners to my bed. Four angels there spread. Two at foot, two at head, Four to carry me when I'm dead."

Toy did not teach Mary Morning the softer version: "One to watch, one to keep, Two to guard me when I sleep," nor tell the child when the old dog died, "Joe's gone to dog heaven; he's running rabbits in the goldenrod." No; she told her bluntly, "Joe is dead."

Dolly protested, "Now that's right cruel on the child, Toy. She'll learn about dying soon enough; you got to start her so early?"

She could not tell Dolly, she could not explain, "It's because I love her so bad." That would make Dolly's love a weak thing when it was not weak, only different.

She could not say, "I love her so much, I got to give her everything—even the truth." For deep in her there was the knowledge, hard as the stone that old Joe had died with under his jaw, that a man's soul could not be brave if it had nothing to be brave against.

She wanted everything for her child, beauty and bravery and strong bones.

The child was pitifully frail.

Often Wick lifted her from Toy's lap to his; he pretended to count the ribs jutting like knives against the skin stretched like white silk, too thin.

". . . five, six. Now you know this one here is called the floating rib? You reckon that's because old Noah tied his Ark there? You reckon?" His fingers tickled, and the child would stretch and contort and squeal with pleasure, face an unfamiliar pink. The ribs, the pink— Wick's eyes went to Toy.

She murmured, "I been getting an egg-nog down her morning and afternoon, but it's a pure fight."

The child heard. ". . . them ole specks of yellow."

Wick said cheerfully, "Why, honey, that's nothing but little chickens. You love fried chicken, don't you? Now you just believe it's fried chicken right on."

When the child ran off, he looked across at Toy. "I knowed it."

"What?"

"That you were like this."

She could meet his eyes, smiling, unabashed now before happiness. "Ma's old broke arm."

Meanwhile the war in Europe was swelling.

The Atlanta Constitution reached Gristle, and the Cardiff Weekly Progress, but they carried little news of the war. They carried "stories" about the war, tidbits that reduced men's fighting and dying to a thing read about on a chew of tobacco and spat out with the next.

Mussolini had conquered Ethiopia. His emblem was a bundle of rods enclosing an ax, and his aviator son said, "The bombs bloomed like roses."

Franco flew from exile in the Canary Islands and fell on Madrid, "responsible only to God and history"; and Japan devoured China. A New Jersey car stopped at Goforth's for gas. The woman in it wore diamonds and cotton stockings. She explained, "We're boycotting silk until Japan withdraws from China." Lovick Jones shook his head. "It might stop them Japs. I misdoubt it'll mean a thing to the worms."

Wick was increasingly angry and distressed. He said, "Folks is making blood a coloring for the Sunday comics."

September came in, hot-blue and dusty. Toy returned one morning from the henhouse and dropped the egg basket on the table. It was empty. She cried, "Listen to them."

Wick did not reply. His big fair head was cocked toward the radio.

". . . into Poland," it said. "The British cabinet met in extraordinary session—"

"Crowing, and not an egg. They hardly laying as it is, and what they laid last night—the three or four—they ate up!"

"—Chamberlain stated that England had no choice but to declare war—"

The word caught her attention. "War? They having another war?"

Wick turned his head. "Hush."

Puzzled, she listened. War made little difference. They were always having wars yonder. The same ones started them, Germany and Japan, Spain and Italy, roosters who thought they crowed the sun up. Everyone knew what happened to roosters; Sunday found them hung by their shiny spurs, and the preacher honing the knife and saying, "I like the breast and all the rest."

Anyway, those were other roosters, other barnyards. She was concerned with her own barnyard, the one beyond the grape arbor where hens crowed and ate her child's breakfast eggs.

She picked up Mary Morning from the floor. The child wore only pigtails and britches against the heat; still she had rash along the folds of her elbows and knees. She was prey to everything, croup and colic, earache and "risings."

Toy murmured, "You gonna have you an egg, don't worry none. If we got to go to Aunt Dolly's—"

". . . a state of war officially exists between England and Germany," the radio concluded.

She lifted her head. "War?"

"Looks like."

Wick switched off the radio. He wore khaki work shirt and pants, and his skin was dark from summer. There were new lines about his mouth; he had not grown heavier the last few years, only solid in content.

"Yonder is a wicked man, Hitler. He's got a bloody bone in his teeth. Now England's been drawed in, I'm afeared."

"Feared of what?" Already her thoughts had gone beyond him, back to the henhouse.

"Feared we'll get in."

Astonishment riveted her attention. "Get in the war? You crazy? It's got nothing to do with us. It's yonder. We here. It's their doings. Let them kill theirselves off. Mad dogs in a meat-house."

He rose and took Mary Morning from her. Their arms, touching, passed the light load from one to the other. His face did not lighten as it usually did when he held the child.

"Men, women, and children right on. And it's got something to do with us. It's got this to do with us, that a country *chooses* the sword is obliged to *use* the sword. They can't let it go. Sooner or later it'll get to us."

"Sooner or later is a fool's horse; runs in circles. No use talking about it until it comes."

She did not believe war would come. War far off raised dust at home, but nothing else. It would not touch this land. The wars that had done so were safely locked away in history books.

"What I want to know is, what we going to do with those egg-eating hens?"

Wick's mouth was wry. He let Mary Morning slip down, and she ran out into the sunshine. "Now you got a way of bringing me down to scratch."

She flashed, "Wouldn't have to, you'd stay in your own barn-yard."

It came quick as quick, there and gone. Wick chuckled, and she let her own mouth move up in acknowledgment. She did not know what had gotten into her lately; she was always coming out with things like that. She had studied on it and decided, "Second childhood." Happiness was a too tender word. Say it, tear it.

Wick said, "Well, you just as good kill them, I reckon. I'll get us some new ones from Aunt Baptist."

She offered, "I could can them. I got a lavish of jars left over from the cowcumbers, they come in so short."

"If you never put up but one cowcumber, it'd be one extra."

She said peacefully, "Well, they look so pretty in the jar."

Together they moved to the door and stood watching Mary Morning play among the late roses. Fall was around the corner with its burned and used-up sunshine. The cotton must be picked, the hogs butchered, the cane ground. When those things were done, the year was done, and the slow slip into winter would begin.

She drew a breath. "It's been a year."

Wick smiled, but not so widely as he might have done. "Well, we been luckier than some."

She knew that he thought again of the war.

September was a time of sickness. Mary Morning took a hard cold, and Toy stopped her eating watermelons. She accused herself to Wick. "I belonged to have remembered, there's a chill in every watermelon et in September." Harl got malaria, and neither infusions of fever-bush bark nor Black Draught helped him; he shook and shivered.

One morning she went by the home-place to see him. He had a quilt drawn around his shoulders, though heat baked the earth beyond the stone walls, and a Bible open on his knees.

She asked, "How you feeling?"

"I can't get warm, seems like. Then I'm so hot."

"Where at's Ma and Wylma?"

"Gone off." He turned. "Toy, you know who I been studying on, setting here? Tessie."

She had started twitching his bed to rights. She jerked up. "Tessie! Now what in Lord's name made you think of her?"

"I don't know. But, Toy, don't you never wonder about Tessie? Don't you never think how it was when we was young'uns together?"

"No."

Her denial was automatic, untrue. She had thought Tessie was a closed door, dust on the latch; yet lately the door had been stirring. She had seen Tessie in her own child, the way Mary Morning had of throwing out her left heel when she walked. Tessie had done that. They used to tease her about it: "Heel in, heel out, heel running all about." And there was Mary Morning's fear of thick trees. Tessie had felt the same, claiming, "I can't stand to walk under where trees is touching. I feel like I'm about to drown."

Toy wondered, Is she drowning in cities, tall buildings over her?

Harl said, "I think about her all the time." His voice dropped. "Toy, don't you never wonder—is she dead?"

She said loudly, "Someone would tell us, was she."

Yet would they? Perhaps Tessie had lost them as much as they had lost her. Perhaps they would never find one another, and she would die, some stranger bending over her and shaking his head: "Nobody I know."

Tessie lost, a stranger. It was a new and terrible thought.

Harl said, "Anyways I hope I feel some better next week. I plan on going to the revival to Whiteoak."

Four men were set aside for preachers at the revival, Harl was one. The way it happened, the preacher was preaching on dictators. The word was new and everyone was using it, one way or the other, just as all the young'uns were naming white cats with black noses "Hitler."

"You all heard of the Tater family?" the preacher asked. "Now I'm gonna tell you about the Tater family, and see if they *kin* to you or *skin* to you. First off there's Dick Tater. He's the head of the family, the big bull in the pasture, and you better git back or daisies won't tell, 'cause you'll be buried under them. He's always bellowing—don't know why—'cause he's the only one likes his own voice. Next there's his wife, Agee Tater. She's always foot back and walking, walking from 'You hear the latest 'bout?' to 'I'm telling you this for your own good, sugar.' Everyone's Sugar to her, and time she gets thu stirring them up, they're dissolved. Next off there's the daughter, Imma Tater. She's got to keep up with the Joneses, don't matter if the Joneses is going to the dogs—she's gonna get to that pup before they do. Right now she's talking about sex; she figures she freer than her mammy. Shoot, folks, she ain't free; she's just unbuttoned. Last off there's Speck Tater, the brother. He just sets and watches. Christ is crucified, he watches. The Commandments is broken, he watches. When the dead is raised on Judgment Day, there he'll be setting with his knee bones under his chin bones, and he'll be surprisest soul round when the Lord points. 'You there, boy.' "

Harl fainted.

Secretly Toy believed that it was from malaria and excitement, but from whatever cause it was, two women sprang to help him. Both began to yell, "Look, look!" for there was a sort of mist around his mouth. One minute it was there, the next it was gone. But everyone swore the Lord had touched him; it was the Lord's spirit entering into him.

Harl himself believed it. He came home talking less about the store and more about Seminary. He wanted to study to be a preacher.

First frost came in November. It sweetened the sorghum cane, and Wick cut and stripped the cornlike stalks. The best he saved for planting next March—they would be buried flat and each rhizome would produce a plant—and started in to grind the rest. A dozen stalks in, and one of the steel rollers in the old mill cracked.

A day or two later Dolly and Jack rattled up in their car. It was overrun with children. Dolly had a baby in her lap, an extra under her apron.

"Pa is having a grinding Tuesday. He heard your mill broke down, and he says come." This out of the way, she turned to the important things. "My, ain't Mary Morning growing? She's near about as tall as the twins. How you, sugar? Toy, when you gonna fetch this young'un a brother or sister?"

Toy shook her head. The thing closest to her heart was furtherest from her mouth always. She could not talk of her hopes, so she asked, "How's Chrissie?"

Chrissie was the lap baby, round and fat, with tiny hands and feet. "Born to die early," Aunt Baptist predicted grimly. "Never seen it to fail. Them kind's got neither feet to stand up to life, nor hands to hold on to it."

"You can see. Now ain't she fat?"

Dolly knew of Aunt Baptist's prediction and wept secretly. If the child died, she would grieve deeply and richly. Yet the same night she would turn to her husband and stretch out a white leg as instinctively as now, the baby whimpering, she drew out her breast in a quick rounding motion.

"And Zadie yonder is trying to get her big tooth."

Zadie clamped her lips over her teeth. Her words squeezed out. "The old one won't turn aloose."

Wick moved up, smiling. "Why, honey, get you a little red-headed boy to kiss you, it'll turn loose." He turned to Jack. "Tuesday, you say?"

"Uh-huh." Jack ran an eye over the stacked cane. "What you reckon it'll run?"

"I put in a third an acre. I figure thirty gallons maybe."

"Might have to trade you out of some. Hail got the most of mine." The years had not dampened the red of his hair nor his generosity. "Got you something." He reached down. "Now chain that to a platter with 'taters."

It was a fresh-killed possum, young and plump.

Dolly said cheerfully, "It ought to eat good; it et a lavish of our biddies. Sucker got hung up in a hole under the fowl house, is how we caught it." She waved to Mary Morning. "See you to the grinding, sugar. Aunt Dolly'll save you a big ole piece of taffy."

The week end was wet. It poured, drowning thundersnakes in their holes and driving a flock of mallards from the sky. They came low and swift, southing, but veered suddenly and dropped on the pond. They stayed the rest of the day and night, green heads tucked under brown wings, armor of feathers turning the slashing knives of storm. The morning fair, they flew away.

It rained again in the afternoon. The wet-weather ponds filled up, and trickles became branches. Fish fled deep into rock and mud caves; crimson toadstools branched on felled wood. Monday it slacked off, only spitting once or twice to show what it could do. Tuesday dawned cold and clear. The air had a peculiar high sparkle. Birds seemed pinned against it larger than life; axes rang from miles away.

Toy asked, "You reckon we can carry her to the grinding, we wrap her tight?" She wanted to keep the child home but would not let herself; she would not raise her in little nibbling fears.

"Sure we can." Wick jiggled Mary Morning on his arm. The kitchen was warm and smoky, the child's cheeks were pink. "She's fine as fine."

The child's thin arm clutched his neck. "Doggy?" Blue eyes focused on infinities of animals. "Muley?"

"Sure, sugar, you going to see doggies and muleys. Uncle John's got him two sugar mills and three mules—one's white."

The grinding took place on one of John Goforth's tenant farms, out on the Cardiff road. Two mules circled endlessly, a pole attached from their collars to steel rollers set in a wood frame. The rollers squeezed the juice from the cane and trickled it into a cloth-covered bucket. Occasionally the mucky cloth was scraped into a skimming hole, the pressed stalks thrown aside.

Lovick Jones drawled, "Now, John, why don't you let that pore ole creetur on the offside lay down and die? You're flogging Lazarus."

"Now, Lovick, you know white mules don't die—"

"Whoa, now. What you saying?"

"Don't die," the storekeeper repeated gravely. "You know they live to be fifty and turn into Methodist preachers."

Laughter rose. Recently the postmaster had switched churches, Baptist to Methodist. He claimed that it was because he did not believe in total immersion any more, but everyone knew that it was because Methodist services started an hour later than Baptist.

He said equitably, "Maybe so, but I'll tell you one thing about our preacher. He don't climb to damnation and sit on salvation."

Laughter ran the other way. A few weeks before the Baptist preacher, climbing a tree to pull scuppernongs for wine, had fallen and sprained his ankle. He had preached his next sermon sitting on a cushion. It was embroidered, gold on purple, "Rejoice in Salvation."

John Goforth admitted, "You right, boy, but still and all, a Baptist preacher kin out-think a Methodist any day. You know what ours done when he couldn't get them grapes? He went to Aunt Baptist and asked her to put him by a little wine. She says, 'I will, parson, and no pay—if you'll thank me from the pulpit come Sunday.' So come Sunday he gets to his feet and prays for this one and blesses that one, and then says, 'And I want to thank Aunt Baptist for the *fruit* she give me and the *spirit* in which it was given.'"

Lovick yelled, "You lie, you lie. You know you lying!"

Toy sat on a log, holding Mary Morning. The child wriggled to be free. Other children whooped and ran around.

"I can run faster'n you!"

"Well, I kin count to a hundred before you. Ninety-nine cows and a stubborn ole mule!"

Dolly sat down by her. She was holding Chrissie, and her face was flushed from the cookhouse. Steam billowed and sulled in the doorway, and occasionally Jack was visible skimming the boiling juice.

Dolly shook her head. "He'll be high-fevered and hurting tonight. I told him, 'Let the niggers do it; they got skins,' but he said he was obliged to help, all Pa's done for us. I told him, 'It ain't hurting Pa,' and he said, 'It's hurting me.'"

Mary Morning wriggled. Her long thin legs in black stockings reached for the ground. Her cap slid half off her hair. Toy could smell her sweet as a little house-cat, and her arms tightened. The child bleated.

Dolly's eyes softened. "She wants to git down."

"I know." She made her arms fall away; the child slid free. She watched her run off, thinking, A pear ripens wrapped in paper, nothing else.

Dolly went on, "Jack is so prideful. I told him, 'You got children, you can't be prideful.' He says, 'I can't be nothing else.'" She sighed and rocked gently, soothing Chrissie. The baby under her belt bucked. She giggled. "See him? He wouldn't be so quick to come did he know where he's got to sleep, under my elbow. There ain't an extry bed in the house." She raised the cane cup to Chrissie's lips.

Mary Morning tumbled around the corner of the shed. Children fled before her. She screamed out, face flushed with delight, "Tag—tag!"

Noon mounted, but shadows remained constant, pale and diffuse. The syrup jugs outside the cook-shed increased, two to twenty to fifty. The stacks of wood and cane dwindled. Cries came more hoarsely. "Wo-haw, mule," "Git up, bony!"

Wick went back and forth between pick-up truck and cook-shed, carrying jugs. It looked as if their patch would run to thirty gallons. Now and again he paused to talk to one or another. "We need a good tenor to the choir, Gip; when you coming to church? Tuck, you still wanting a partner in the stockyard? I been thinking—" Finally he came to her. "You give me out? We about thu."

"It run much?"

"Thirty-two gallons. I gave John the over for grinding."

He put the rest of the jugs in the truck, packed them in firmly with croaker sacks between. Toy rose to be ready. Cold wind plucked her legs, and she pinched the collar of her coat closer to her throat. She raised her voice. "Mary Morning?"

A whimpering answered. How long it had been going on, she did not know. It sounded like a crippled dog or bird, but she began running for the skimming hole. Mary Morning was in it, sliding and scratching weakly at the banks, able to get out, but panicked into inability.

She was pulled out, soaked and sour, a blanket was thrown around her, and they drove home, reckless of the jugs dancing in the back of the truck. By evening the child was coughing, thinly and occasionally; by night she had a fever, and the cough was a constant racking.

She was sick for two weeks. Helplessly they watched the hard-won flesh drop from her bones. It seemed as if she could be carried on a white silk handkerchief and never dent it. When finally, cautiously, she was let up, she crumpled in a heap.

Wick groaned and snatched her up, laughing to hide the groan. "Now, Sissy, you got to do better than that. What's Santy gonna say, he come and you so sick?"

One day he took Toy out to the barn and showed her something. "Tuck Tate carved it."

It was a brown wooden egg the size of a shoebox, and when he opened it wooden animals tumbled out, cows and mules, pigs and goats and chickens, even a peacock. They were carved of ivy wood and stained or painted, each according to its nature.

Wick set half the egg down. It rocked gently. "Noah's Ark after he docked on Ararat. These is the animals stayed with him."

"They nice." She touched the peacock. "It'll pleasure her."

He picked up a mule. Tuck Tate's knife must have slipped; it was a swinneyed-looking thing.

"Tuck wants me to come partners with him. He needs money for a new barn; and I been thinking I might."

She was astonished. "You got enough to see to now." He worked the farm and did carpentry; he repaired tractors and clocks.

"Maybe. Only I got an idea that beef is going to be the thing; it's gotten so in Florida. They've moved away from citrus. I got an idea that this county will go to grass. It'd be good for you to have a share in such as that."

"Me? What about you?"

"Why—me too."

When they left the barn, she looked at the sky; it was early December, most of the birds gone south, yet there seemed to be a drifting across the silver face of the moon. She shivered, not entirely from the cold which frosted the air before their mouths.

"It feels—queersome."

"We might get snow. I've seen the sky look so when it's about to snow."

"It's too early yet. Time it comes is January, February."

He broke a twig from a tree; it made a brittle sound. "Maybe so, but I look for it to snow."

It started in the night, an imperceptible sifting, a whiteness that seemed to dissolve before it touched anything, yet touching and clinging until every blade and twig and shingle was sheathed in white.

Toy, rising to look at Mary Morning, saw it on the window sill. She went to the door and looked out. The sky, which earlier had had the look of marble, black and streaked and hard, was obscured by the drifting. So were the stars; the flush of the Milky Way, which children called "The Cow Cup," was gone. Only a constant white drifted down, little animal tracks springing up on it and running off in all directions, mouse and rabbit cruelly revealed to their foes.

An owl swooped past Toy's face. She jumped and shut the door.

Wick's voice came instantly. "Sissy?"

"Sleeping." She went back to the bedroom, voice soft so as not to arouse the child. "It's snowing."

He said drowsily, "I looked for it to."

The next morning he stomped the white stuff from his boots

returning from the barn. "Snow sifted thu that crack near the cow-stall. Goldy was trying to lick it up. Thought it was a new kind of salt stuff."

Mary Morning whimpered to go out and taste the snow. White snowballs would be as fine as the pink or purple ones that Elijah Clarke Johnson sold summer Saturdays in Gristle, calling, "Git you cher-r-ry, strawber-r-ry. Grape, too. Nickel'll do."

Toy told her, "Now you can't go out, missy. Make up your mind."

The child's fingers clung to the window sill. She turned a peaked triangle over her shoulder, greenish eyes, like Toy's, blurred with tears and fury.

"I want to go out! I—want—to—go out!" The wail mounted and broke in a hiccup. She saw it break against her mother's adamant face and seized the weapon that weakness knows best. "I hate you—I hate you!"

Pain flooded Toy. She recoiled against it, gasped breath against it.

"You don't do no such thing! Talking so—" She grabbed the child's shoulder with one hand, and her other sought anything it could seize, a belt, a peach switch. "I'll learn you, missy—"

As suddenly as she had moved forward, she recoiled. Her hands fell from the child, horror mounting as she realized what she had been about to do—punish the child for her own pain. Already she saw the excitement reddening the white cheeks and pinching the breath. When the red burned out, it would leave the body weaker than before.

She seized the child and drew the hot face against her as though she would stifle the fire. She murmured thickly, "You don't hate no one, no—you just saying so 'cause you mad. You don't hate no one."

Sound came weakly. ". . . go out."

"No." She sought desperately. "You just lonely is all. You want company. How—how'd you like a puppy in?"

Drying tears answered.

So she flung a coat over her head and plunged out. Snow crust crackled against her shoes, her hands lost feeling on the way to the barn. A stray pointer bitch had taken refuge there a few weeks before and dropped six puppies. The bitch watched, head lifted and whining, as she fumbled around among the squirming brown and white bodies.

"Now," she told the child back at the house, "you got company."

Never before had she allowed animals in: "They belong outdoors, except maybe cats." Wick had upheld her when the child wanted to bring in everything small and alive. "Now you know little things, puppies and such, don't mind their manners. And it's your ma's got the cleaning up."

When he came in later, he stopped in wonder. "What in the world—"

She said defiantly, "I brung it in."

He looked at the damp spots dotting the floor. "You sure did." He asked, "You couldn'ta picked a better?"

For always in a litter there is a weak-natured pup, one afraid of every human being except the one who breathed first on its nose. This was such a one. If you touched it, it went immobile while damp spread around its tail. It was risking pants or apron to pick it up.

She said, "Well, I'm going to swap it, first chance I get."

Mary Morning would not let it be swapped. When she saw the new puppy, she let out a gust. "Sam—I want Sam!"

They could not think whom she meant. Wick raised his brows in surmise, lowered them in recognition.

"Now, honey, this here is—is Benny. See how big he is, and can do tricks—"

"Sam!"

Sam returned, and now Toy remembered who had breathed on its nose first: she had. For everywhere she went, Sam was there.

A cold blob, sudden against her ankle, made her jump and become furious at the jumping. Sam had eight paws and two tails, and she stepped on them all once a day.

The pup was a pain. He was fit to lick palms and nothing else, but she wouldn't have hurt him, no; she wouldn't have killed him.

She could not know that he was there, could she? She was not like the boo-wooger that Yellow Tom used to tell about, who carried a basket with a sliding lid reading "One Way Only," and had eyes in his heels. She had never counted herself a boo-wooger.

Yet Mary Morning did. She thought that her mother, stepping back from the stove with the heavy iron kettle, ought to have seen the pup at her heel. She ought not to have tripped and flung out hands to save herself, the boiling kettle spewing on the pup.

Wick tried to pick it up; he tried to help it. Skin and fur came away in his hand. All the while there was the screaming—Toy had never heard a dog scream before; she closed her eyes against it. There was a thud, and she opened them. Wick had laid a piece of cordwood across its skull.

His mouth was clamped and awry; she knew he held back bile. He dropped the ragged shirt that had served the puppy as a bed on the remains, and then Mary Morning screamed.

They had to put her to bed finally; they had to hold her down, their voices less to her than the tick of the old clock in the parlor, the *scritch-scritch* of the icy branch across the window pane. She accused them with her eyes and voice and body.

"Kilt my puppy!" She accused each. "Kilt my puppy."

Wick's big hands tried to seize her frantic ones. "Honey, honey—"

Toy cried, holding herself rigid against the pain. "You think—you believe your ma would—"

The child believed; she measured by an inch rule, love and hate the same size and equally believable.

"Kilt my puppy!"

Finally, gasping, she fell asleep; and finally they could sleep too. Toy drew icy feet up under icy sheets while through the door, by the kitchen stove, she could see Wick undressing. Coals laid a red glow around his body; the ineluctable snow drifted down beyond the window.

His voice came. "I mean, it's coming down cross-leggy."

She hugged her cold core and watched the snow.

"Well, year of snow, fruit will grow."

The flakes seemed to press heaven and earth close together; earth shrank from the parlous embrace.

"It'll set the fruit trees, and you belong to have a nice chance of flowers."

He loomed beside the bed and got in; there was a freezing opening, then springs sank, blankets closed down. Warmth bulked, living, beside her. Yet the cold core immobilized her.

"Flowers—queer how a man's mind will go, times. Know what I was remembering yonder by the fire? A day last summer when I passed the McMinns' old cornfield. There was pink and morning glories twined around the dead shocks, and a Nigra girl sitting on the bank wearing a guinea-blue dress and selling water lilies."

Somewhere a branch groaned and broke under its burden of snow; it crashed to earth with a soft thrashing. Her cold rigidity broke with the sound, the voice.

"Saying such—believing such! I know she ain't but a baby, still—yet—"

He said gently, "Killing her dog? Why, a young'un *sees* what it *knows*—it ain't learned to see beyond. We're all children that way, more or less; we see what we know. Now and again it's given a man to be lucky: he sees what he *don't* know."

She cried obliviously, "I let her have the puppy in. I done everything—"

He agreed, "You done everything."

Grief came in a great self-accusing flood. "No—no—I done nothing. For what I done, I done to make up for meanness. I let her have the puppy in the house because I went to hit her for nothing. Everything I do that's good, I do out of a meanness, looks like, and what kind of good is that, tell me? What kind?"

She flung over on her side, away from Wick, drawing her knees to her chest, burying her face in her crooked elbows. There, in the little area of her breast, grief rent her. She was isolated and alone on a sea of grief as the bundled house was alone in a snowy world, an Ark welled in.

She saw herself an Ark of sorts, her soul mounting up. Only her soul was not a single and shining thing; it went in pairs like the beasts on the gangplank, the beautiful and the ugliness from which it came, the good and its abominable mate.

She gasped. "Won't I never live up to you? Won't I?"

And that was the master grief, not that she had failed, but had company in the failure, Wick pulled down who could not pull her up.

A familiar thing touched her neck, warm and slightly raspy on the flesh, Wick's thumb in the old caress.

"Now this is Wick talking, not God. This is flesh you feeling, not spirit." His breath was on her shoulder, a man's breath. "Look now."

She turned between snubbing gasps. She could see the hard round of his head, dim in the firelight.

"Flesh here." His thumb stroked her neck. "Flesh there." His breast touched hers. "And the heart is flesh." He asked, "You don't think I've failed? You don't think I fail every day of my life? And they all here inside me, the times I've failed, the oldest and the newest. You know one of the oldest? You know one I carry with me now this evening, a little one, but it's there? How I left my stock when Flonnie died. I went off and left them without food or water, cow unmilked, depending on my neighbors. When I come back I put a roof on the church, making up. Only *you don't never make up*, and that's the heaviest burden man bears."

His voice deepened. "Oh, God, I'm sorry for every man alive, wanting the good and knowing in his heart that he's got to have the good for happiness, trying and pulled back by his flesh at

every twist and turn. Pulled back and down until times he's like
a rut in the road, touched but don't feel, hard and dry and growing nothing green."

She was on his arm. He pulled her close.

"And then he cries—she cries—and the green grows."

Two

P EARL HARBOR was a thing for people to brag about.
        "Now you know I got no more memory than a cat. But I
recollect just as good as yesterday what I was doing when Pearl
Harbor come. I was . . ."

They were getting ready for church, most of them, and they
went and heard the preacher call the beadroll of sons and brothers
abroad: "Moses and Isaac Levitt in the Philippines, Sim Boyette
in Iceland, Jimmy Hobbs on the Atlantic deep . . ." Afterward
they joined in prayer.

"Protect them, O Lord. Put our boys under Thy special care,
God, and keep our country safe. Guide our forces by Thy hand,
O Lord."

They were close to God, they knew, closer than the Germans,
whose God dwelled far away, or the Japanese, whose God was
not.

Afterward they gathered under the elms in the churchyard.
It was a mild December, the weather aloof from cat and rat wars.
They folded arms and spoke of what they had been doing. They
measured the gigantic and incredible against the small and eluc-
table as if, by so doing, they could comprehend what had happened.

"I was tying a dead hen round Bill's neck—that dog chases
chickens every chance he gets. . . ."

". . . Li'l' Ed says, 'My ball is on the roof,' so I gets the ladder
and goes up, and that's when . . ."

". . . driving back from Adams' Woods, deer hair all over me, and passed this bunch of niggers on the road. One yells . . ."

"Well, you know what ole Wheat asked me? Says, 'Boss, where at's London-town?' I says, 'Yonder 'crost the ocean. Why, Wheat, you've heard "London Bridge is falling down." ' He says, 'Heerd "Build it up wid spit again." Didn't bee-lieve one no more'n de other.' "

Yet London must be believed, and Pearl Harbor and all the places in the ragged geography books dragged out from under the Bible, the seed and Sears catalogues, geography books made tall and thin so that maps could reach across two pages. Even then they did not reach far enough.

"Says here, says in Ab's letter, 'I'm to a place called Mariveles, across the bay from Corregidor.' Can't find no place *here* called Mariveles. Can't find no place here called Corregidor."

Soon the seas were crowded with exiles, the beaches with bloody deeds, and Wick said, "There's too much hate."

Toy asked, "What you expect?"

"Hate breeds hate. It's a running sore won't heal."

It was the following spring. Honeysuckle bent down the vine. Children broke off the brown blossoms and sipped the sweetness like bigger bees. Thin boys and plumper girls wandered through the fields and bent tall stalks of mullein. The boys, glancing around, muttered, "Mary" (or Sue-Ann, Pearl, or Belle), and girls bent the stalks and whispered, "Al" (or Bob-Lee, Cass, or Jim). If the stalks grew bent in the circle, why, they would marry, and the war would never touch them.

Yet the war was already among them.

Negroes moved among the row-crops, but their hoes were slow, and they lolled their heads back and watched the planes crossing the sky. White women called sharply, "You, Cully, Ruby, get along there. If Mr. Lou was home, you'd move!" Only Mr. Lou (and Mr. Connie, Mr. Ed, and Mr. Ammi) were off doing war work, making more in a week than they had in a month before.

Mary and Al married, as the mullein said they would. Nights were filled with sweet fern and moaning doves. Mary's belly swelled. One night Al blurted, "Sugar, I can't stand to leave you, but I can't stand to stay."

One June morning, Toy returned home past the depot—she had been looking for a cow up the ridge; no telling where it had strayed—and saw a group of draftees entraining. Some clung from the doors, yelling and waving. Others leaned pale noses against windows and stared.

A woman on the platform cried out, "God bless you, boys. I'll pray for you every night!" She told Toy, "My Buck went off last month. He's gonna be a soldier-boy. I told him, 'It's better'n being in a plane or on a ship. You got a chance on the ground.'"

The train spat steam and jerked. The men on the steps waved more slowly, faces flickering with sudden realization. The men at the windows raised to life. They waved hands and smiled; some smiles meant more than others.

"I told him, I said, 'Planes ain't nat'ral. Who sows the wind, says Scripture, will reap a bitter grain. You got a chance on the ground.'"

The train gathered wheels and speed, the ground shuddering.

"Buck and me prayed together the night before he left. We prayed, 'Lord, let this war be soon over. Let the tyrant be ground beneath Thy heel, and justice triumph, O Lord.'"

The last car of the train sped by. Black faces peered forth from a coach with barred windows, an old mail carrier that had been converted into a Jim Crow car.

"Why," said the woman, "we even prayed for the niggers."

The station master came up, a dry little man whose conductor's cap had been put out of joint by the flood of new uniforms.

"Well," he asked, "how you reckon the war's going?"

Everyone asked this—it had taken the place of "How you doing?"—even of her.

She told him, "Near about nowhere."

Even of her, because she was not involved. Harl was 4-F, and

Wick was over age. The draft board had not gotten around to Bill-Hart yet.

Truth to say, she was the luckiest woman in Gristle; others said it, and she knew it. Often she found herself saying silently, Keep it this way. Don't let it end. For the men necessary to her were home, and Mary Morning was her precious heart's blood.

Rose Crawford was gone to Milledgeville. The sheriff and his wife had taken her to the state mental hospital. They went on a bleak, raw day in February, and a few weeks later Toy and Wick had gone to see her. Toy bore it, seeing her mother junk with the other human junk, but on the drive home, she broke down. "It ain't fair, it ain't fair." It was unfair that nurses and patients looked the same, except for the uniforms that the nurses wore. She had the crazy feeling that if she could put a uniform on her mother, Rose would be cured. . . .

The station master asked, "Now how's Harl making out with his studies?"

"All right, I reckon."

Harl was making up school time over in Decatur. He was boarding with a preacher and studying to get a high-school diploma, working part-time as a short-order cook in a jook joint, a "just left" place. Soldiers treated for venereal disease said, "I just left Miss Mally's." People arrested for drunkenness said, "I had two beers to Miss Mally's. I just left."

He could have gotten other jobs, and Wick offered to help him, but Harl shook his head.

"No." The skin stretched white and tight across his forehead and around his jaw. "I got to grasp sin. I got to feel the slimy slide of it, so I'll know it when a man comes to me and says, 'Preacher, I drink—can't help it,' or a woman says, 'Preacher, I been with a man ain't my husband.' I can help them, but I got to endure sin, so's I can cure sin."

He endured sin, but it was only with his eyes; he still could not understand why men drank and cursed, or women accepted "dates" in parked cars behind Miss Mally's. His cure came down to "They belong to close up places like that."

Toy settled the straw hat on her head; the sun was rising hot. She told the station master, "Well, I got to get on. Anyone finds my cow, why, I'd be obliged."

The sun burned her neck as she walked. It came up early these days and set late, the Carolina wrens heralding it. Three o'clock in the afternoon, and even the Negroes got sunstroke. Isaac, riding the hay-raker last week, had pitched off, wall-eyed. Pond and creek were always edged with people fishing; there was generally a breeze across the water, and jacks whistled when they were caught. That was a cool sound, too, jackfish whistling.

The war was a friendly thing. People drew close together. A man from the north side of the county—"them city politicians" —could be friendly with a man from the south side of the county —"us farmers"—because both had sons in England. "Says, Jim says, he's caught him a Piccadilly quail. Now what you reckon?" A woman who hung her wash out early was tolerant of one who hung her heels on the porch rail. "Poor creetur, she's got three boys yonder, and her youngest fixing to go any day."

Ora Watts blurted, "I declare, I love a war. Long as nobody I know gets killed."

The children's Bible class learned a new song:

> I may never march in the infantry,
> Ride in the cavalry,
> Shoot in the artillery.
> I may never ride o'er the enemy,
> But I'm in the Lord's army.

Wick said, "Now I wish they'd found another song."

She said, "Children don't know what they singing half the time."

"More fault us."

Pearl Harbor found him calm where everyone else was angry or weeping. "It was due to come, and now it's here."

He grew quieter; it was as if something within him was re-
solved. He listened to the radio, hand over his eyes, but said less
about what he heard. He did not talk of everyday things as before. Still and all, it was queer that he had gone off that morning
without a word.

She thought, Maybe he went to Tuck's for a new cow.
We need one bad enough.

A thundering aroused her. An Army convoy, swapping gears,
mounted the rise behind. She jumped from the road and watched
the command jeep run by, pinfeather flag flying, pinfeather lieu-
tenant, knee cocked, beside the driver. The big trucks followed,
soldiers leaning out to yell and wave at her. Soldiers waved at
everyone, even the old and juiceless.

She waved back and thought with a sudden pang, They so
young to look at in the face.

She went on, remembering the untried eyes and voices shrill
against inner uncertainty. She thought of them until she reached
the house and saw the pasture empty.

"Fool cow." She had hoped that someone had found it. Last
week someone had; they had milked it and sent it home, bucket
splashing around its neck, and foundered. She had hoped that
would teach it a thing or two, but no.

The driveway was empty; Wick had not returned. Wylma was
with Dolly, who was expecting another child. Calla had left six
months ago to work as a maid in Augusta; Wylma had shaken her
head. "Sho sorry for de woman gots her; she doan want to work,
and Calla doan neither."

She went to the mill.

Children were playing in the shallows of the pond, some jumping from the millstone diving board, some grabbling for minnows
and shrieking with near-catches. Three boys dug worms under
the dark pilings; their voices came clearly, nascent on the air.

". . . cares? Any fool can catch a lightning bug, that ole light
they tote makes them go so slow."

"I ain't gonna catch 'em just to catch 'em. Gonna catch 'em

and mash 'em and smear 'em on my feet, so's rattlers won't bite me."

Mary Morning and Zadie, Dolly's oldest, were playing in the grass. They had their heads together over something, dark hair and light mingled. Mary Morning jumped up and bounced forward, peaked chin and laughter at the corner of her eyes like a squirrel.

"We found heartsease. Zadie give me the jugs to eat."

She held out a thin palm—she was still too thin for her bones. Great heart-shaped leaves lay there, and one of two tiny brown "jugs" that were the flower of the plant, sweet and gingery to the taste.

Toy felt the lightness, the ever-recurring joy that sight of her child gave her. She put out a hand and brushed the tan locks from Mary Morning's eyes, not to clear her sight, but for the pleasure of feeling the little brow-bone, warm and faintly sweaty, under her fingers. She spoke brusquely against the joy.

"Now I bet 'twas Zadie found them."

Zadie said shyly, "Well—we found them the same time."

Mary Morning stopped bouncing. She put a finger in her mouth and bit it. "Zadie found the heartsease, but I et it."

"Then reckon we better return the compliment." She turned to Zadie. "You want to stay to supper, spend the night?"

Mary Morning shrieked with delight. She veered away toward the pond, shouting, "Zadie's gonna spend the night, we gonna have fried chicken, and Daddy's gonna make us cherry-stone ear-bobs. We ain't going to bed!"

She built blocks of clouds, towering up; reality did not tumble her to earth. If something did not come true, why, it was true anyway. It was true because it had been in her mind.

Times like that, and times when she ran throwing out her heel, she reminded Toy of Tessie. The recognition was an ambivalent thing; it hurt and warmed her.

Zadie, three years older, watched with gentle tolerance. She looked down, twirling the heartsease between her fingers. "Aunt

Toy, you reckon it's true what Aunt Baptist says, you can tell what a plant is good for by how it looks? Like liver-leaf for liver trouble, squaw root for female complaint, this here for bad hearts and such?"

Toy hesitated. "Well, you know, old Mrs. Kitchens smoked life-everlasting."

The child's brow cleared. "It's true, then."

Toy reminded her, "Mrs. Kitchens is dead."

"Her body, maybe. Not her soul. She believed on Jesus, so her soul got eternal life. Preacher said so."

Once Toy would have denied it. Once, when she was too young for her own good, she would have cried, "What soul? What's eternal?" Now she saw the child's head, and it reached no higher than her breastbone, and her shoulder was thin as a new twig. She was too small and thin to bear the burden of space alone. Even the soldiers, khaki-clad and carrying rifles, had feared space. They had waved, and what was a wave but a reaching out across space, a grasp for assurance: "I got you, don't I? And you got me."

"Well," she said, "well—come when you ready tonight."

She went into the mill, into the old vibration. Bill-Hart was dumping corn into the elevator; the hopper was near-empty. Toy could see it without climbing halfway up the stairs and peering down, for the Negro had tacked a dime-store mirror over the hopper. It was one of the changes that had come lately.

He called, "Dis de last."

She nodded. "You can go when you want."

He would drive a load of meal to Cardiff. The mill was averaging seventy-five bushels a day, and they were selling all they ground, not only to John Goforth and to stores along the highway, but to the A and P in Cardiff.

She picked up the toll book. "You seen Mr. Wick today?"

"Seen him dis mawning. Doan know where he headed." He picked up a knobbed stick from beside the door and started out.

Toy remembered something. She called, "Now how's that baby of yourn?"

"Ain't wuth a shoot. Dat boy is Peter right on, walk de water day 'n night."

She locked the mill. It seemed queer, going home midday Friday, yet with Bill-Hart gone and the store closed, there was no reason to stay. When Harl first left, she had tried to keep the store open, but it was not worth while, no candy but Cuban stuff which tasted like dog rations, no cigarettes but Rameses and few of them, deliveries mixy-maxy.

She wiped her face, walking. It was hotter than a ginger mill. She was glad to turn in at her own road.

Wick was still gone. The pasture was empty.

She said aloud, "Fool cow." She hid her unease with sound. "Now if you went and broke into the milk-sick pen . . ."

Good riddance, though the pen was not a thing she cared for any creature to come on. It was a plot of land on Atkins' Ridge, a rocky outcrop covered with crustose lichen, huckleberry and sparkleberry bushes, and Johnson grass. Grass and berries were fine and green, but let a cow crop there, a possum pull the berries, and they would surely die. There was something evil in the earth, and there was nothing you could do about it, soda or lime, nothing but fence it off and put up a sign: "Beware. Milk-sick."

Zadie came at dusk. She carried a tote sack and covered dish. Her dress was clean, but it had run up on her; her waistline was under her armpits. Her hair looked as if it had been parted with a rough word.

Mary Morning greeted her, hopping on one leg, her face bright red with effort. "Mama says we can hunt banty eggs."

Toy snapped, "Well, stop that hopping then, and go on."

Fool creatures, banties. She didn't know why she kept them. They scratched up the flower seeds and were good for nothing but to look at and for boys to fight the little cocks.

The children ran out. Zadie's voice trailed back. "Once I found a hummingbird's nest. There was three eggs in it, pure white and no bigger'n beads."

She wished that she had not flown out at them so, but it was near dark and Wick yet gone. She tried to move the worry nearer: the dinner would be ruined if he didn't come. Already the juice was dried up in the smothered chicken, the corn dodgers were cold.

She looked up the road. Fireflies glimmered, bushes moved faintly in the breeze, but there was nothing else astir.

The children returned with a clutch of banty eggs; they dropped them in the basket on the food safe. She cast about for another way to get them out of the house.

"You know there's a king snake in the woodpile? He comes out around now for mice."

Instantly they started out. Zadie stopped and looked around. She said in a sudden burst, "Wish our house was like yourn."

"Now why?"

"Well—you drop a penny on the floor at our house, it scoots clear out the door, house leans so. And the shingles is pure frazzled. Last month Pa tacked a piece tin over the leak in his and Ma's room and left the ladder up. Our goat's took to climbing it. He stands on the tin and spills his pills. Ma claims she can't sleep a wink, Billy spilling his pills."

Toy's concern narrowed to the child before her; she smiled. "Why don't your pa take down the ladder or get rid of the goat, one?"

"Pa says if Billy gets on the well and spills his pills, he will." She went out. Her voice flew back joyfully. "Aunt Toy, you got a lizard on your back steps—good luck."

Toy had seen it earlier, a five-lined skink with a turquoise tail. Yet she needed no more good luck than Wick stamping his feet clean on the crocus sack and calling, "Anyone to home?"

Mary Morning discovered the stray puppy that had taken to hanging around the yard, hound-looking and no-colored. She ran toward it, but it slunk away.

"It's running off!" Never could she bear to be parted from an animal.

Toy told her, "Well, much it, see won't it come."

Both children squatted and extended puckered fingers in the age-old wooing. "Come on, puppy. Come on." The puppy, tail disillusioned, listened from a safe distance. The children "muched" it. "Aw, you the prettiest li'l' ole dog. You so pretty and cute. Come on now, come on, pretty li'l' ole thing."

The puppy crept nearer and nearer. It extended its neck to twice its length to sniff their fingers, and was caught.

Mary Morning cried, "Look here." Her fingertip traced the tender buttons on the puppy's belly.

Zadie said practically, "He's dirty."

Toy said, "Then you best rench your hands." She looked down the road once more. "We just as good eat."

Afterward she washed dishes while the two children played with the puppy on the back steps. Night swooped down. One moment the yard was visible; the next it was smudged out. The dark became canorous with the voices of those to whom it really belonged, the spring peepers and bullbats, toads and mosquitoes.

Toy called, "You'll be eat up. Come on in."

They came, Mary Morning holding the puppy belly up. Toy switched on the radio as Wick did at this time every night. There was stuttering, then a voice sprang out, English and young.

". . . ten thousand feet up and below was Vienna. I could see Saint Stephen's spire and the Danube, silver in the moonlight—"

She snapped it off, she did not want to hear such as that. She wanted to hear that ten German cities had been bombed, and ten thousand Germans were dead. She did not want to hear of rivers and churches. War was dead people. You piled the bodies like loaves of bread, and the side got the most, why, it won. It could call itself Bethlehem, House of Bread.

A fear that she could not define made her ruthless. She blurted, "I've run my last road after that cow. It can stay gone!"

The puppy slept, belly puffed with plenty. The light bulb

hung like a raw peach from the ceiling. The children were playing with an old stereoscope that had found its way into the house,
and a box of pictures, Venus de Milo, the leaning tower of Pisa,
Hoot Gibson kissing his horse, and such.

Zadie looked up seriously. "You reckon it's got snakebit or poisoned?"

"Maybe."

The words conjured up a picture of the heifer lying stiff-
legged and loll-tongued. If it had been poisoned, you could tell
that easily enough; grab a handful of hide and hair, and if it
stood in a peak when you let go, why it had eaten apple-of-Peru
or gotten in the milk-sick pen. Snakebite, now, the part bitten
would be swollen to twice its size, the flesh mortified.

And then her heart banged against her throat, for a car was
turning into the driveway. She jumped up. It was the pick-up
truck, Wick returning.

She went to meet him, watching as he wiped sand from his
feet. He took long at the task, as if it were an important thing.
His good black suit was creased across the knees and elbows; his
face was cut with weariness.

She asked stiffly, "You had anything to eat?"

"Coffee a while back."

"You want something? There's chicken."

"If it's handy."

He sat down heavily, and she put food before him and heated
coffee. Finally there was nothing more to fill her hands with or
carry her feet away from what he had to tell her. She sat down.
He chewed, eyes on his plate, and she knew that his thoughts
were cold and hard to the lips; they must be warmed in his mind
before he could speak them.

He pushed away a chicken thigh; he had taken one bite.

"I went to Cardiff. I ought to have told you—but I didn't."

She waited.

"I'm going in. I know I got no right—but I'm going in."

In. She heard the word almost curiously, so small a word for the territory it covered. Her mind could not encompass the territory. It went and hung on one small part.

She said, "The cow got gone again."

"You didn't hear? I'm leaving in ten days; I'm going to Camp Custer."

"I heard." The desolation would come later.

"I couldn't help it. I'm obliged to."

Obliged—how thick and round each letter was, how fat the word, a fat word to fill thin days and thin reasons.

She blurted the old Job-question.

"Why?" Wick repeated. He was tired, his body sagging. His anger flared. He cried out, "You got to have a reason for right?"

Three

LONELINESS was like the hole Calla had charred in the kitchen floor, carelessly and not watching like the larkspur-heel that she was. The hole caught Toy's toe as loneliness caught her body, bringing her up with a plunge, breath jerking, hands flung out.

There was nothing to be done about the hole or the loneliness except step around them, the one with her foot, the other with her thoughts. And that was the fine thing about the body, Toy thought; after a while her foot hardly ever tripped on the hole.

Loneliness loved to laugh. It loved to pleasure itself. Walk along the fence where dishrag gourds hung with heavy fruit, and loneliness jumped out: "Boo." Lift a coffeepot or hang an empty pillow out to air or watch the wilderness come to Wick's fields, and loneliness said, "Hey, Rufus Rastus Johnson Brown, what you gonna do when the rent comes round?"

For loneliness is a diminishing thing. It takes something away from the soul. It makes a woman less a woman, as war makes a man less a man. War shrinks a man to the size of the bullet that will pinch his heart; loneliness draws a woman in upon her piddling little affairs, piddle here, piddle there, and stop suddenly in the middle of a room, hands hanging, and wonder why.

Oh, loneliness is a diminishing thing—even the coffeepot said so. Yonder was her image reflected in the curved side, distorted and diminished to the size and hardness of a hickory nut. It had always done so, but before this she had looked up and met Wick's eyes, and a living liquid had filled her to the top.

Mary Morning chirruped, "Bet you glad you ain't got all them dishes to wash, Daddy gone."

"There's more things than dishes." She asked heavily, "Don't you miss your Daddy none?"

"Uh-huh." The word was dutiful. Already the child's thoughts had gone beyond. "Can I sleep in the bed with you now Daddy's off?"

She hesitated. "Now why?"

The child sensed the hesitation. She sprang up and down in front of her, jerkily, hands reaching. "Yes, yes, yes, yes, yes" —as if the word would weigh her mother down by sheer force and repetition. She was six and no bigger than four or five; her hair was lightly tangled about her thin temples, her legs scratched by briars; one wore a beading of blood.

Toy said brusquely, "Keep on like that, and you'll sleep in your bed, missy."

So the child slept with her, arms and legs afloat, and times she talked in her sleep. Toy would wake with a start to a voice, Wick's, she would think with a surge, and war was all a dream— then Mary Morning would say clearly, ". . . I come, and if you going to do like that"—threatening a daytime playmate. Or, ". . . ole humpy back. Go along"—shooing a booger that did not bother her any more.

Toy would ask, "Now what was you dreaming about so hard last night, talking in your sleep?"

The child would screw her eyes up importantly. "Let's see—let's see—"

Toy's world had diminished to the size of a child's dreams, small and self-centered, yet better them than none at all.

It was a strange summer and a stranger fall.

Rain fell the whole month of July. Swallows and bee-martins swooped and twittered through it, but other birds buried heads beneath feathered muscles and endured. Mold fuzzed mule traces and old shoes, and toadstools edged every rotten log with orange and red and cream.

The rains were a blessing that became a nuisance. The soaking wetness, coupled with the previous hard winter and late spring, killed a great many pests. Fewer pines wore arthritic yellow limbs from borers, corn had fewer rotten ears from billbugs. Garden patches flourished, but the cotton did not. Rain washed off the poison, and bollweevils settled in, singing, "I got a home, I got a home."

Wylma came in one morning holding a giant snail on her palm. "Now ain't he a rock-mama?"

"You crazy?" Toy struck the thing to the ground and set her heel on it. "Now you know I got cabbage leaves and bait around to kill them." She straightened and looked at the garden, high and green. "I mean, we got us a victory garden." She had read the term in the *Atlanta Journal*.

"Sho. Sho. And we git any more vict'ous, we gon be dead 'stead of ole Hitler. I 'bout give out on de canning. Things is no good noways. De tomatoes and peaches is pure mushy from de wet."

Toy repeated, "Anyways, we got us a victory garden."

If victory was measured by the flood of green crops, Hitler would be drowned in a quicker sea than the one beyond Tybee Light. She wished that this might be, for she hated the man Hitler and his little dance-step at Compiègne. She listened to the children chanting their new counting-out song.

Eeenie, meenie, minie, moe.
Catch ole Hitler by the toe.
If he hollers, make him say,
"I surrender, U.S.A."

She thought, If I caught him by the toe, I'd nail him to an iron board and set him in the noonday sun. I'd wait until he drawed up on himself like the snake he is, skin and poison and all. And then—

And then she would take a hoe and chop off his head. She would tack his skin to the side of the barn and invite people, "Come see."

There were half a dozen snakeskins on the barn, none under four feet in length. Isaac said that he had never seen such a summer for meanness: "Meanness yonder, meanness here." One day, harrowing, he saw a mother rattler playing with a dozen babies. Folks said snakes did not fool with their young, but the old mother rattler lay in a loose coil, and the babies were sliding back and forth over her like lace or shadowed water. Isaac ran off to get something to kill them with, but when he got back they were gone.

Toy, listening to the tale, thought, Snakes is the least.

A snake could be killed, and that was the end of it. A snake den could be burned out. But what did you do against the whole wilderness? The worst thing in the world was watching Wick's field go back to woods, a cluster of blackjack oak creeping in here, a strand of leatherweed there, and everywhere love-entangling vine killing all it twined.

Worse than the vine, though, was the briar. It had waited all this while, as sly as the cat-claw that it was sometimes called, and now that the man was gone, now there was a woman and a child and a Negro couple alone, it crept in. It massed at the corners and edges of fences and looped its thorny tendrils. It dug down fleshy roots that could turn a grubbing hoe. It invited rabbits.

They came, pale brown ranging to black, and dug burrows

under the roots. They ate tomatoes and iris rhizomes and peach bark, and bred in warrens among the thorns.

Toy cried out, "How the government expect you to raise a victory garden when they won't give you no shells to shoot the varmints?" For shells were rationed, like gas and meat.

Aunt Baptist suggested, "Now maybe Wick can get you some when he comes." She pinched a dry lip. "Now I forgot how he feels about guns. You know, I can't get over yet him going in, a Sunday sort of man like him."

Toy thought, Sunday the week long. The old question came: how did Wick face Saturday night—knives and guns and o.d.s dyed for killing from ambush—and Monday noon—business as usual, "I can get a tank for you wholesale"—a Sunday man like him?

Aunt Baptist pursued, "When's he coming, say?"

"Last letter said maybe November."

The world had been stopped and cut from its core and spread out flat like a scalloped orange peel, so that men could play soldiers across the surface. But on a day in November it would revolve again, if only briefly, if only for a few weeks.

Rain, gone in July, returned in October.

It started one evening, driving to earth with the hiss and thud of a loom batten beating up a web; only the pattern it chose was monotony. Gold of elm and bronze of oak were lost; scarlet of maple and purple of sumac ran. The rain reduced gaiety to pilgrim tones.

It fell for eight days and wrecked the mill.

Wick gone, she had clung the closer to what was left, Mary Morning and the mill. Almost she had forgotten the mill; it did not mean to her what it had meant when she was younger and alone, a security beyond the living that it gave. Even then, though, she had known it only a half-security, like that of the tramp's dog or the widow's cat. Now, Wick gone, every security she could find was necessary.

She returned to the mill. She ran her hand along the sill and thought she felt the old warmth. She leaned out the window and believed she recognized a certain stone. It had not changed; it was immutable. Always she had told Mary Morning tales of the mill. "You know in the old days millers used to wear wide sleeves? That was so when they was taking toll, they could catch a little extry down their arms. Did I do such as that? Why, sure. I was mean—anyone'll tell you."

Careless tales they had been; they cared less for the truth because the mill and the old days were less important. Now her tales took a new turn.

"You know once I found a banty rattler upstairs, under some crocus sacks? Now I didn't see it nor hear it, but I knew just as good that it was there? Smell it? Why, no. But something told me. Something."

Her tales of the mill were minute and particular, because that was what was left for her with Wick gone, the minute and particular.

Now the mill was wrecked. Rivers and creeks swelling with rain, overflowed their banks. The millrace was smashed. A great tree root, tumbling with the torrent, struck a stone piling with battering-ram force. The mill groaned and canted. The great wheel snapped off and fell against the bank of the ravine; and rubbish, pushed and tossed by the flood, caught in its cups.

Silence came down.

She was unaware of it first off. She saw only the destruction, her thoughts as numb as her face. She had run through the storm on the sixth day, unable to bear not knowing, old coat thrown over her head. Yet the rain sought her out, stinging her cheeks and eyes and laying a faint alum on her lips.

"No—"

The word was louder than its wont. The rain had drawn off somewhat, but wind sent the treetops wallowing like green whales across gray seas; they made a high soughing. It was the only sound. Always before the mill had held a multitude of little

noises, the scratchings of mice and bats, the under-eave flutter-
ings of sparrows and swallows, the clicking of beetles and
roaches. Now only the water sucked around the pilings, and fish
splashed in an endlessly wet world.

Why, she thought, they gone.

Gone, left, deserted, every mouse and bird and death-watch
beetle. In life they had challenged her charity, yet now that they
were gone, terror touched her. Her numbness was fading; her
skin prickled, and a knuckle she had skinned on a shutter
throbbed. Still the cold was an endurable thing to the colder,
surer knowledge within her.

"They figure the mill is dead."

Animals knew. They were strung on a thinner wire than man,
one closer to the earth, and attuned to the minor chords. The
wire was infallible where survival was concerned.

She cried, "No!" even as the rains renewed themselves, and
water, denying her, sucked at the marrow of the mill.

Three days later the rain retreated. It drew back in thinning
gray curtains and let the sun through. Toy opened the door of
the house, and Mary Morning bounded out into a bright world.
Puddles glimmered, and trees and bushes, stripped and leaning
west after their week-long burden of wet, yet had a springtime
look.

The child pranced on long legs, wrapped to her chin against
the cool. She laughed and pranced because she was outdoors
after a week of staying in, and destruction gave everything a fine
new look.

"The chicken house is tore up!" She danced and ran before,
beside, behind Toy all the way to the mill. She stopped at sight
of it and cried excitedly, "It's pure wrecked."

The mill was a tale told in a tub to her. ". . . feller says, 'Give
me a turn of meal, for I'm perished for cornbread and peas, and
I don't mean none of these fetch-on kind comes in cans' "—while
her mother grasped an ankle and used pummy-stone on
grained-in dirt. Or, ". . . an old turtle living under the pilings,

and what do you reckon was cut on his shell? Why, Ard, and that was your great-granddaddy's name"—while the water cooled and the bubbles flattened, tales light and lost as quickly as the bubbles.

Yet the bubbles were as real to Toy as the ring she wore or the world that men had unscalloped to play soldiers; tales were a reminder to Someone. The only difference was in their solidness, and they had become as solid as ring or world, for they were her hopes that she would be left alone, hopes that she had paid her price, whatever it was, and could go on.

Hopes gone now.

She touched the mill door; it was cold and sodden and greenscummed. She had clung to hope; she had believed. It was raining too hard that day to see straight; things weren't so bad. Only they were. The wheel, which was the heart of the mill, was shattered—where would she get metal or millwright or twenty-inch planks to repair it?—and a beam had fallen across the top grindstone, cracking it from eye to bosom.

Mary Morning squalled. Prowling the canted floor, she had slipped and nearly pitched through a window into the swollen flood below. Toy grabbed her, rage and terror mounting and equal.

"Now you going to stay out of here without I'm with you!" she cried, twisting the shoulder. "I ever catch you sneaking off here—"

Mary Morning writhed away and got loose. She slipped and slid and scrambled halfway across the slanting floor and fell down on her hands and knees in the mucky trash. Suddenly she began to sob, face screwed up in a furious puzzlement. She beat the floor with her fist.

"Old storm—old storm!" She beat her fist against the imponderables. "Old stinky storm—"

After a while Toy set her down. Her sobs had died away to little sighing catches of breath. Her foot turned on a rotten branch; Toy threw it out the window. She sought a way to comfort her. She kicked two Nehi bottles into a corner and threw a rusty oil can after them. "Now I'll give you a penny, every five pieces of trash you th'ow yonder."

The child brightened. She picked up an orange peel and said slyly, "Here's one."

"Now it belongs to be bigger than an orange peel."

The world was an orange peel, and it was spread out so that men could play soldiers across it. The world had stopped turning until Wick came home, but that was next month. Three evenings later, coming from the mill and seeing a uniform standing in the yard, all she thought was, Soldier hitch-hiking and lost.

She came closer and saw his face was Wick's.

Later, after they had flung questions at each other and taken no notice of the answers, Wick stopped and pointed a finger at her. "Now, you didn't figure it was me, tell."

She protested, "You said November."

"Mercy after judgment; we finished basic quicker than we figured—they trying to speed training up—and they let us go. I didn't write, for I wasn't sure."

She thought of something. "Then you didn't get mine neither."

For he would have said something if he had known about the mill. He would have said, "Now I'm sorry, for I know what it meant to you." Now she told him; she said, "A storm come. It wrecked the mill"—and watched little lines break the light on his face.

"You sure it's bad as you think?"

"Worse."

"The wheel—"

"Broke off."

"The roof?"

She shook her head. "I don't remember none. Stove in, I reckon."

"The floor—the pilings—"

She moved her shoulders, increasingly uneasy. "I don't remember none."

"The stones?"

"Seems—seems like one got broke."

Increasingly she was surprised and terrified. There was something wrong with her, not remembering all that had happened to the mill, every little detail, beam broken or feather dropped.

She cried out, "I can't remember nothing but the wheel. I seen it all—every bit—but I can't remember nothing but the wheel."

Wick took her and held her. After a while he spoke. Pain did not print every little thing on your mind, he told her, not the way some people thought. Pain pitied you. It narrowed you down to a single note. It made you live from minute to minute, object to object.

She was safe. She drew breath. She said, "You home—it's medicine."

The next morning Wick was up at daybreak. The east was gray, the old rooster's claw locked on its perch when he broke clods with his heel and breathed deeply of the frosty air.

He called, "I knowed what I was missing. Now I know again."

She called back, venturing, "Were it—were it bad?"

His voice muted. "I despise it. I hate the every minute." He broke another clod. "This field is played out, looks like."

She called back, relieved, "That's the least."

He wore his old clothes, faded khaki work shirt and pants, hardly different in color from his uniform, yet all the difference in the world. The work clothes fell into easy horizontal folds fit for stooping and crumbling earth or driving a tractor. The uniform, removed last night, had retained its vertical lines, stiff and alien. She had felt him a stranger in her bed. Then he touched her, not on stomach or hip as some men did at first, but his arm under her shoulder lifting her to him, and he was Wick and welcome home.

She called, "See them briar patches. We been about run crazy with rabbits."

"I'll clean them out."

He sowed the worked-out field to lespedeza and planted kudzu crowns on a galled hillside. He burned out an elm stump—it was a breeding place for snails—and castrated a young boar which would be fattened for meat next fall. He laid in firewood and repaired fences and cut out briar. He cleared acreage for a new pasture.

Toy asked, puzzled, "Whatever for?"

"When I get back, I figure not to raise cotton. I'm going to turn to cattle. Beef is the coming thing, like cotton is getting to be in California."

Time has turned things around, she thought. Nigras is going north, Yankees is coming south, cattle is heading east, and cotton is going west.

Once they went to the mill, Mary Morning on the come-and-go with them. The child had been half wild since Wick's return; she was weepy and fanciful and spoke of herself in the third person; "Mary Morning want . . ." "Mary Morning don't . . ." until Toy was out-done with her, and Wick said, "She wants things to stay the same, but don't know what the same way is."

She darted through the mill door before Toy could stop her; and when she was hauled back, Toy demanding breathlessly, "What I tell you, missy? You begging a switch?" Mary Morning cried, "I seen something sliding."

"A rat. A scritch-owl."

"No. No, it was something—it was something—" Her tongue fumbled with wordless forms.

Toy told her, "Well, you stay right along with us, hear, or you'll get the switch."

She and Wick looked at the destruction silently. It was made worse by the weather. The sky was a high, dull gray like the moldboard of a plow. Rabbit bread dotted the pasture, little white lumps of ice forced up by the cold. Wick drew his chin into his jacket.

"What's folks doing for grinding?"

"Store-bought meal or gone back to the Slow John." The little hand-mills, put away in barns long ago, had been hauled out, and every spare child and Negro set to turning them.

He said, "War don't wait."

He leaned a considering palm against joists. He shook his head over the floor buckled and strutted by the root-impact.

She said like a prayer, "After the war—"

Jack it up and get a new master bolt and wheel cups, she thought. Build the race back.

Wick agreed. "It might be done, could you get you the materials." He seemed to watch her out of the corner of his eye.

She was instantly alert. "But what?"

He spoke slowly. "I don't aim to hurt you when you been hurt enough, but you know the times of the old mills like this one has about gone; they been going, and the war is like to finish them off. The old folks'll come back—they habited to it—but the young ones will get used to store-bought meal or bread, one. Five-ten years and these old water mills won't be but a cur'osity."

She felt like the drunk who had played the zither for the old orator, Henry Grady: "Got a home, but I don't know where." Her eye went, numb with disbelief, from hopper to mill-posts to pulleys.

"No." Yet she believed.

He nodded slowly.

His furlough was nearly over; he was to report to Fort Knox, Kentucky, in a day or two. The morning before he left, he went to a farm auction in the east of the county and brought back a near-new wagon and a Davis and Barber clock for her to set on the parlor mantel.

He said, "It'll pass the time behind its back."

"If I don't look at the face."

He brought Mary Morning a silver ring set with a curious coral and gray stone. "It was on a tray of doodads and jinglebobs. I didn't give but a quarter for it." He turned the stone to catch the shine. "Feller said it was abalone shell come from California. Ain't it a curious, pretty thing?"

He had to wind thread around it so the child could wear it. She pranced and plumed it in every little ray of sunshine she could find. "Abalone shoney-haw bark lonely kimony." She was lightheaded with delight and the wonder of words.

After Wick was gone, Toy got out the old geography and measured distances between a thumb and finger, first between Gristle and Camp Custer, Michigan, then between Gristle and Fort Knox, Kentucky. Wherever her finger moved, her thumb remained constant. She took an obscure comfort from the fact that her finger never went so far that the thumb could not draw it back.

Mary Morning was in school. Toy thought that with the child gone, the mill gone, she would have more time. Only there was never more time, just other things to spend it on, the farm maintained during fallow times as well as fair, the stockyard in which Wick had bought an interest.

Tuck Tate stammered, "Now you know, any t-time you get in a tight or need help—"

She told him, "I don't need nothing, but I thank you." The offer touched her. She asked awkwardly, "You making out all right?"

He nodded his head and searched for reassurance. "Well, you know, I always got my mules."

Never a day passed that Mary Morning did not come home with something new. "Mama, I can spell Chicago. Chicken-in-the-car-and-the-car-won't-go!"

Or another time: "Mama, you heard the song about ole Hitler and the Nigra?

> "Ole Hitler tried to fool him,
> Said, 'You don't belong to fight.
> You got no home nor country,
> Flag nor civil right.'
> But the Nigra knowed the best,
> His deeds did prove the test."

A December day Dolly and Zadie came to visit. Dolly's mouth chirked up in the old way, but the rest of her face was tired. Milk-leg made her move stiffly.

"Thought I'd come while the weather held off and I had the time. I mean, it's a spell since we set and visited, but that don't mean I ain't thought of you often and again. Only it's like old lady Odom says, 'War's ruined company. Folks don't get together no more except in the cemetery.' Now how you making it?"

They talked of Christmas, two weeks off—"The children is looking for Santy Claus, but my doormat nor my money don't spell Welcome"—and the weather—"The old cat begs to come in, then sets with her back to the fire, sure sign of snow"—and Wick and Jack.

Dolly said, "Well, Jack's going off." She smiled at Toy's face. "Not to the Army. Lordy, even the Army ain't that mean, seven children. No, he's got him a job at Camp Gordon to Augusta. Going to live in one of them Toonervilles by the railroad track and send home what he can." She hesitated. "It'll be hard having him off, but we been drawed thin so long, maybe now we'll get even."

They talked of the children. "Chrissie's ailing again."

Chrissie was the child with the plump body and too small hands and feet, the one Aunt Baptist had claimed would never live to grow up.

Dolly's face twisted. "I know she won't never get well, but I don't know why she's got to stay sick."

Toy said helplessly, "Well, it's a sick, cold time."

It was a time when the weak and the aged felt what they had

forgotten, the inabilities of the flesh. Winter reminded them; it drove them to fireplaces where they huddled around their marrow and conjured up distant summer days, walking down a corn middle with blades rustling dryly or sitting by a roadside with baskets of red peaches and calling, "Sweetest by far, sweetest by far." Only memory could not cut the cold that found them, and so they became full of prejudices and petulances, making up with their tongues what they had lost with their bodies.

Toy said, "When the weather turns . . ."

Only it had a long corner, three months until spring. Meanwhile she let Mary Morning go and play where she would—except for the mill—and when she would, well wrapped. She would not make her into a Lob-Lie-by-the-Fire, even if the child wanted to be, which she never did.

"Can I go out?"

"Pity sakes—it's snowing."

"That ain't snow."

"No, it's dandelion fluff, I suppose."

She set the edges of her teeth together and let the child play in the snow, run in the wind down the lanes where crape myrtle reached iron twigs and rocks turned the ankle, forced up by the cold.

"Whoo-ee, whoo-ee!"

"Quit that racket. A body'd think you ain't been let to run since last July."

"I ain't—I ain't! It's different like, wind and trees, from July."

And always she begged to go to the mill, making up excuses. "A family is camping out there, and they got a monkey. You don't want no ole monkey messing round the mill."

"Now you don't stretch the truth. You pure strut it. Stay 'way from the mill." For it was less a building than a deadfall. A few days ago she had found a stray shoat trapped under suddenly falling beams, back broken, starved.

It was the season of injury, of sickness. John Goforth, hurrying down his back steps, fell. A leg was caught and wrenched, bone forced from the socket and sinew hollowed, the old Jacob-injury that the Bible spoke about. Annie Goforth sent an appeal to Toy: "Can you tend the store an hour-two?"

She told Mary Morning, "Now stay in, hear, till Wylma comes."

The child twisted the abalone ring around and around. Her eyes were as round and guileless. "Uh-huh."

Toy charged, "You're thinking of the mill. I know you, missy. Now if I find you been there, I'll whip the fire out of you. You know and I know—that's a fair promise."

Walking, her feet numbed rapidly. The air held a raw urgency; everything was decisive, shapes and sounds. Snow lay in patches under bushes, white shadows instead of black, nature turned backward, for the snow melted from the outside in. Trees drip-dripped. A child shouted on cow-bone skates on a frozen puddle.

Annie Goforth greeted her, a smile lightening the worried pucker of her mouth. "Now I'm grateful." The years had left her briskness untouched, but had turned her brown hair pewter and broadened and flattened her thumbs. "I mean, betwixt the store and Jack and my daddy, I'm jaded out."

Toy shed her coat. "Mr. Simon worsened?"

"Well, he don't get no better." She drew on her own coat; she went to the door and cracked it. Cold sent in a premonitory chill. "I mean, if I owed a feller a cold day, and he wouldn't take this one—I wouldn't give him another."

She left, and Toy took her place behind the counter, familiar for how many years—twenty-six? The men gathered around the old wood stove were familiar, too—not all the faces but the company, the thighs outspread to catch the heat. The talk was familiar, things they knew about and things they did not know but guessed, full of "ought"s.

". . . sorry field, and I told him so. I says, 'What you ought to plant . . .'"

". . . the Allies in Africa. Now what we ought to do . . ."

Their "ought"s were like an old man's spit, come to nothing. Still Toy listened and took pleasure in the listening. Now that words had lost their power to hurt her, now that she was girded against words, Mary Morning on one side, Wick on the other, she could enjoy them, the slow building toward the climax of a story, the increasing dryness.

". . . says, 'Nope, I won't join your church, preacher, but here's a kitten.' So fourth time he comes, and she reaches for fur, Preacher bursts out, 'No! Already I got more cats than congregation.' "

Eventually Annie Goforth returned, and she left, walking into the early dark, an icy wind blowing. It wrung tears from her eyes, and she stumped along, head down, the earth ringing under her feet. Sodden windrows of leaves blew against her ankles. She turned in her drive with relief, raising her eyes.

The house windows were dark.

Her breathing skipped; it came in quick short gasps as if her lungs were too shallow. They pricked—she did not know it. Heaviness pressed on her. It weighed her hand on the door. It squeezed her voice out shrilly.

"Hon? Hon—"

The fire was embers; they winked dully in the dusk. Cold held the room, long come and staying. Cold held her; her voice was freighted with cold, a half-whisper.

"Wylma? Mary—"

Dusk in the room and dusk outside and a few far frosty stars. Cold outside and down the lengthening road to the mill, a road that she had run time and again in nightmares, breasting terror, a road that stayed under her feet and would not go or fall behind no matter how fast she ran, breath stripping lungs, eyes on the ends of icy needles.

Someway the mill looming, heeled over on the bias, the great wheel dumped on disuse, water having its way. It ran free and sucked with heavy satisfaction, gray as the dusk and cold as hell, Devil gone.

Someway roots under her heels, pitching and slipping her down a dark slope, something blundering across her face, bird or leaf, and if it had struck, it would have shattered into a thousand bits, for her skin was iron and stretched across iron.

Now the dark well of the mill was above her, the gully and the gulping water before. The water fastened a white tooth on a bundle of rags. Come play.

The child would not. She lay, one leg spraddled out, odd-angled and twisted on the bank. Above a mill window showed a sill gone, leaned on and given way.

The head was in the crook of Toy's arm—she was unaware of moving—scraped bone and shut eyes. Her finger went forth. She smoothed a water-turned brow. She drew the coat together, carefully, at the throat. She tugged down and evened the hem. Little warm acts against a cold without pity, a cold enduring.

Four

WICK got leave and came home for the funeral, forehead white and stretched, voice deeper. His hand was different too. When he touched her, it meant less than a leaf touching her, shaken loose from a limb and drifting past.

"Now you can't blame yourself. You can't blame Wylma."

Her arms lay inert on the table. There was a plate between them, empty, but whether before or after food she did not know. She lived in cracks of time, aware only momentarily of what went on around her.

Wick's voice insisted, "You can't blame Wylma."

For the Negro woman had come to the house and found Mary Morning gone, but believed Toy had taken her to the store. She started down to see when a car stopped her. "Lordy, gal, where you going in dis cold? Ma'y Morning? Why, she to the sto'. Shuah, seed her wid my own eyes." So Wylma had gone home.

Wick told her, "She's gone. We got to accept it. She's gone, but I try to believe—we've not lost her."

She roused. "You speaking of her soul?"

"Her soul, and what we remember of her."

She said, "Take her soul, if you got to, but leave her body."

She did not know to whom she spoke, Wick or Someone else. She only knew that the thing she could not see was cheap; it could be spared. But the tiny tendons of the wrist, the small and happy sins, the dear flesh—they could not be spared.

Wick asked, "You think the thought didn't come to me? You think I cared nothing for her body?" His voice deepened. "I loved the little one. I loved her till I would have tore the flesh from my bones to feed her, need be. I loved her. Nights I used to get up and go in and look at her sleeping. You know how the hair fell in her face like? I'd smooth it back, so I could see her brow-bone. I loved her little brow-bone."

He would kill her. Memory would kill her. "Stop!"

Three other deaths came that week, but they only deepened her anguish, for each one of them was due—two old men and a child born never to grow up anyway, Grandpa Willing and Jake Simon and Chrissie.

Clods of earth clattered like coals on the four coffins; the preacher's nose and hands stayed purple. Tears froze.

Dolly wept. "What I hate is, the graves look so skimpy."

Grandpa Willing's grave had a Confederate flag, and Jake Simon's a piece of tree trunk carved in marble, for he had been a Woodman of the World. Mary Morning's and Chrissie's graves had only their names on little white cards tacked to sticks.

Dolly mourned, "If it was June, we could have roses and such."

There were wreaths of holly and firethorn on the raw mounds, a few jars of pink camellia-sasanquas, and a basket of chrysanthemums sent Grandpa Willing by Governor Talmadge. His card read, "In Memory of a Boy in Gray. There's thirteen stars extra in Heaven tonight."

Dolly brightened. "Anyways, the preacher preached good, if it was so cold."

He had called the children "little roses budded on earth to bloom in heaven." He had told parents to tend their children like gardens, so they would bring forth a richer crop for the glory of God. He raised arms like trellises.

Dolly pursued, "Come down to it, we had right smart a turn-out, seeing how cold it was."

It always came back to the cold, the cold that clutched her, indwelling, the cold and the darkness that pursued her among people, people casting shadows, and darkness and shadows closing her around, voices coming through the darkness.

". . . feel for you. I know . . . two die at the breast. It wrings a mother's heart, gone before they get up . . . you'll get past it someways. . . . The Lord . . . the Lord . . ." And over and over again, "We know."

She cried out, the louder because it was silent, You know nothing!

Every man and woman in the world stood an inch to the left or right of her heart. Could they feel what she felt, an inch to the left or right?

Dolly told her, "Jack went to Cardiff and had them put a poem in the *Weekly*. You see it? The editor wrote it special."

She had seen it; it went:

> God gave us the strength to fight it,
> The courage to bear the blow.
> But what it meant to lose her,
> Only God will know.

Dolly's tears rolled like summer rain, soon come, soon gone. She sniffed and turned from the mounds. "Wick gone back yet?"

"No."

"How long's he got off?"

"Three days." Every word came like a rock rolled up an end-less hill, or a ball of mud that a tumblebug pushed, mounting and straining with its black legs.

Dolly began to move away. "Well, I got to get on; I got din-ner to get. You know, things goes along." She hesitated and re-peated slowly, "Things goes along. If you could stop on that, Toy, and not go beyond and torment yourself—what good do it do? I loved Chrissie like you loved Mary Morning. Maybe you don't think so, all my other young'uns. But love ain't a thing you count on your fingers, put in a shoe and don't know what to do. Love is countless. I've bled my eyelids with weeping. Now, for the others' sakes, I can't bleed my heart with wondering. I mean —things goes along."

Wick left the next night. Before going, he told her, "I'd give anything if I could stay on. Maybe New Year's—" He hesitated. "Now why don't you go spend Christmas with Dolly? She asked you, you remember."

Her eyes, reclusive, lifted. "Maybe."

His hand rose and fell helplessly. "Now I've said all I can say." He put on his uniform cap.

It broke something in her, the cap and the waste of Wick wear-ing it, the waste of everything, womb and windmill end of the world and all between. An intolerable swelling rose in the mus-cles of her jaw.

She said, "I was remembering—"

His eyes questioned her.

"I was remembering how I took my breast in my hand and held it so's she could feed." She said, "I could have tore it off and throwed it to the dogs as well."

Anguish is a bunched thing. Rage diffuses it. And movement, started, is a continuing thing. She had followed Wick to the edge of the porch, where he had turned without a word, head averted.

She had flung her words at his olive back as far as she could see it.

"Tell me the use, you hear? Tell me the use."

Now her feet carried her into the yard. She walked aimlessly, going toward the barn. The chinaberry tree dangled dead twigs against the sky; a few of the little sticks loosened and rustled down. She hated the dirty tree, dirty three times a year, berries and leaves and twigs.

Isaac crossed her path. He was tugging a hat around his ears and looking cheerful. "Gots to go to town, git new ax-bit."

Go and stay and giggle in a corner at the Cat's Inn, he meant; she wheeled from the chinaberry tree.

"First off you going to 'gots' in the stove-wood!"

Anger was analgesic; she discovered this and fed it. She stared around with sharpened eyes, and the broken, the awry, the belonged-to-be-dones stared back at her. She seized them as fuel, caring nothing that they contraried the words she had shouted at Wick.

"And when you get the wood in, fix the pasture rail yonder."

It was broken. The heifer within was scratching an ear, cat-like, with a hind hoof; she could jump the rail like a goat if she found it. And yonder in the chicken yard the nests were foul, the grapevine hung shaggy, and a stench of skunk smeared the corner posts.

It was cutting-cold. Breath hung around her lips in gray puffs; her chapped knuckles split and the blood crusted. But she was inexorable.

"After that, clean out the nests and cut back the grapevine—you want the hens should get rot-foot from the damp? Then put out a couple of poison eggs for the skunks. Shut the dog up first."

Anger, mounting, moved her. She went into the barn, plump with hay, tight-shingled and fragrant and warm. All she saw were the cowpeas hung from the rafters in sacks, unbeaten and unshelled. She cornered Wylma's second girl, a thirteen-year-old.

"Now you get you a stick and thrash them beans, you want hog-jowl and peas for New Year's. Or you relish hulls?"

The girl's lip came out, plum-purple and plump. "Gots the ironing."

"I know the kind of ironing you got, spit, slide, and sit. Now get that stick."

The Negroes betrayed her. Christmas day they were gone, Wylma and Isaac and the whole brood, leaving her nothing to hang anger on.

Dolly came by, bringing her a fruit cake and two handkerchiefs with crocheted edges. She begged, "Come go with me."

Toy excused herself. "I got things to do."

Dolly said, "Well—come if you can."

A sudden great swelling filled Toy's throat. She blurted, "You know—you know you always meant a heap to me, Dolly."

Two days later Wylma and Isaac returned warily; they had only gone for a Christmas visit. Toy listened to them and said, "The peach limb yonder is about to break. Prop it up."

She could move herself, and she could move others, but she could not move past the hands of the clock, starry, sorry time. Inevitably darkness came; movement blurred and vanished. She went to bed, feet still, hands empty, and remembrance returned. Thoughts made her screw her head into her shoulder and clench her fists against her empty breast, emptiness filled with a fist.

The year unwound to December 31, a day of casting up scores as children cast up firecrackers. They began cracking at dawn, high and intermittent. Occasionally guns were fired and bells rang, but over and through these sounds the firecrackers kept up. "Kill the witches, kill the witches!"

A wind came up. It rattled down the last of the pecans and acorns, and squirrels searched the windfalls of brittle mast. Toy took a rifle against them, and they fled to the boles of trees, peering around and shaking out tails like furious dust-rags. She killed four and would have killed more if she could have found them.

Firecrackers kept bursting; early dusk came down. Isaac's ax rang from the woodpile beyond the house, blows spaced by grunts, "Unh, unh!" Toy bent. A marble was half buried in the earth, lost on a summer day and forced up by the cold. It lay in her palm, azure as eloquence and her fist closed on it.

"Miss Toy." Isaac came around the corner of the house, hands held behind him. "You wants dat ole elm chop up?"

She stared at him, half seeing. "I said so."

"Wants it dis evening?"

"I said so."

"Den"—he brought out a broken ax handle, dolorous with triumph—"gots to go to sto', git new handle."

She said instantly, fiercely, "Fan-Foot Alley can miss you this trip. I'll get the handle."

She was on the way, horse's hoofs ringing, wheels clattering against the frozen ruts, when she remembered: she had not been to town, she had not seen people, since the funeral.

Tightness took all of her muscles.

Fireworks burst. A fireball rolled across the northern sky. It went low and round and swift as a cat with its tail tied in a bag and set on fire. It sank out of sight behind Atkins' Ridge. All along the road lower lights burned from houses tamped into the trees. From any one of those houses, knowing that she passed, people would run out and say, "I heard about . . ." or "I ain't got the words to say how sorry . . ."

Stubbornness drove her on, and beneath it an obscure desire for the words. She could not understand it, but she suddenly needed them and the pain accompanying them. Pain was a justification.

Smoke frayed from Goforth's chimney. Voices mumbled beyond the door, and her hand flinched back. Yet she drew a breath and pushed in and was greeted by shouts, "Shut it, for mercy's sake—it's pure perishing!"

Here was the source of her desired pain, the thigh-spread circle around the stove, the ones who had no better home on New

Year's Eve. Tobacco *pinged* in a tomato can, and breaths drew in and out.

". . . a fireball the week Granddaddy died. I figure it was the Devil handing him a coat and saying, 'Start a hell of your own,' and Granddaddy was the one could do it, you remember."

Heads nodded. "Mean as flax, all right. Filled up the judgment book and had to be wrote in sideways."

Now they would turn to her, now they would say—

A man turned to her and said, "John'll be back directly, Toy. He's gone out back."

A few of the circle had told her, "I feel for you," but the rest had not; it was the rest that she counted on. Yet the kind of words she wanted were hard come by; she knew that and waited.

One man slapped his knee suddenly. "Now I near forgot. You fellers heard? They catched the ghost was banging around the Emmitsville bridge."

Breaths were sucked in. "Nah, I ain't heard no give-out. Now tell."

"Cotton. That's all 'twas, cotton. You know how good the crop was last summer? Well, the wagons and trucks was so loaded going through the covered bridge, pieces pulled off on nails and splinters. Moonlit nights it waved, 'twas all."

"Shoot!"

"Talking of ghosts, got a letter from Jerry couple-three days back. Said he seen his first German Nigra. His troop come in this little African village, near Gapa, and here was this house stove in from bombs. Jerry was prowling thu, and under a piece of door, why, here's this yellow hair and black skin. Jerry thinks, Lordy God, how'd he get over here? and goes close. Then he sees it wasn't nothing but a German been dead a week and turned black from gas. Jerry said he wouldn't never get over how he figured it was a blond Nigra."

They did not mean to speak, Toy thought. *They did not mean to speak, because they had forgotten.*

"Death?" they would say if you asked them. "Why, yes it

come by a week-so ago. Who were taken? Old Granddaddy Willing and Jake Simon, two of the biggest old liars. Were any-one else? Why, now you mention it, seems like there might have been one-two others, young'uns—can't call their names."

They did not mention Mary Morning, because they scarcely remembered her. She was a child gone before her name was hardly known, an old story or no story at all beside a cotton ghost or a late fireball, and Jerry's letter come two-three days ago from Africa.

Cold air blew in. John Goforth slammed the door against the rising cries. He said cheerfully, "I mean, a feller can hear every-thing around here but money rattling and people praying." He discovered Toy. "Now what you doing out late and cold?"

He had forgotten too; his brow was bland with his own affairs. "Things goes on," Dolly had said—oh, God, the ever-enduring day, the live night long!

She said, "A—a—" and did not know what she was doing out late and cold. Beyond the window the sky lowered. It smothered the earth with a gray wing, yet it seemed less smothering than the store. She fought for breath while her hand sought the door handle.

John Goforth called, "Toy—"

Air pricked her lungs, chill and resinous with the smell of pine smoke. The horse cast his cheek around to look at her. Ice thrust up from the ruts in fringes like dragons' teeth, crackling under-wheel.

Toy's thoughts were smoke. They rose and wavered off, dis-pelling themselves in nothingness. Gone was the heat of anger and activity, gone the warmth of people who took account for two weeks and went on. Smoke was left, wavering up and going no-where.

She reached home, and there was a letter from Wick.

It was in a long white envelope and lay under the lighted lamp. Wylma had brought it up from the mailbox, lit the lamp, and left it, a sign for her to see. The lamp was two white glass bubbles painted with pink roses and balanced on a metal rod. It made a small June in the room.

The letter was warmer.

Under her fingertips she felt the warmth reach out. The stiff pages rustled it; and the greeting was another thing to turn to and hold to: "Dear Wife." Her eyes leaped along the lines. They stopped and went back, unbelieving.

"This is something I do not want to say," Wick wrote, "but I got to. We got nothing left.

"I been thinking when I was home. I been thinking what you said. Is that all it has meant to you, the years we had, Mary Morning—sorrow for yourself? For I watched you setting and licking grief to a Me-point. I felt sick. I thought, Why, we got no more than the locust-bug left hanging to the pine tree, a dry hull—"

The pages made a little whisper falling. They lay under the light, half folded, their ends seeking the old creases. Crease as they would or might, they could not blot out the words. "Nothing left."

The terror started below her ribs, a sick throbbing. It spread, lemming-like, up her chest, out along her limbs. It trembled her limbs. It trembled the lamp before her eyes. It set the room trembling, shifting and swaying and hollow before her eyes.

She ran. The front steps turned under her heel. She half pitched and regained her balance, ankle wrenched. She went dragging it like a stone, cold through her, cold beyond the cold that held the night on far frosty pins of lights. And yonder was Wylma's cabin, light leaking through some crack not glued over with newspaper and flour paste. Her palm beat against the door. It opened, light spilling out.

"Miss Toy! You—you wants something?" There was a sudden quick sigh at sight of her face. "Aw."

Then the smell of musky grease enfolded her, and of all the years that the other woman had sweated to starve decently, living on others' land, scouring other people's hearths with brick and sand. A thin arm and thinner breast were there; they drew her in. Six children had hollowed them, and bone lay against Toy's cheek. It was a finer pillow than fat.

"Aw." Wylma swayed back and forth, arms around her, rocking and holding her in the old cradle cadence. "I knows. I knows. —doan know why, doan know how. She gone, Lawd, Lawd." She rocked. "Kin cotch de cat's steps and rattle 'em in de gourd 'fore He tell you why. Kin count de roots of de rocks, suck de wind 'fore He tell you how. Doan know, doan know." Her eyes closed. "We heah, we heah, doan know why, doan know how. Hand on de whirlwind, heel on grease—no hold, seems like. Hold to de Lawd!"

Warmness seeped through Toy. It came gradually—blue fire or black bone? She crept into it deeper.

Later Wylma whispered, "Put you heels up, baby."

Heat smote her feet, suddenly shoeless, and prickled the soles. Prickles dissolved into a warm tide which rose to her knees, engulfed her thighs, and curled along the small of her back. . . .

It was night when she awoke. Three stars ranged the heavens, and a single burning one ran at heel. A branch clacked against the frosty window. Shadows wavered around the walls, playing in and out with one another.

Wylma appeared by her pallet—how had she gotten on a pallet?—and said briskly, "Isaac coming. I gots to go."

It meant nothing to Toy, no more than why she was here. She lay in fluid warmness, mindless and enclosed as a child in the umbilical fluid.

Beep. A horn commanded from the night beyond the walls. Wylma was galvanized. "He heah!"

She leaped to put on an old hat over a clean head-rag and pinned the collar of her ratty coat together.

"Sho despise to leave you, Miss Toy, but I 'bliged to go. Goan Walk Egypt tonight."

Her hand was on the latch, and the fluid around Toy ebbed. She felt herself abeach in a place she did not know, every stone of which was familiar, but none that had anything to do with her. Sound broke from her lips.

"N-n-n—"

It was less a sound than a wordless reaching-out. Wylma had opened the door, and now cold, thin-boned as a feist, ran in. The fire drew back, flickering. The cold edged upon her. She drew her legs away from it. A convulsion seized her. Her teeth clashed and clattered.

"Do, Lawd!" Wylma was in an agony. Her glance wavered between door and pallet. Her black feet edged back and forth. She made a dart and a dive. She threw and held a quilt in place with a lean black arm. Her other arm guided. Toy found her feet moving, unresisting, toward the door.

It was killing cold outside, killing all the stars but a few, piling black cloud on black cloud. Frost twinkled underfoot. The old sedan gasped and shook on its axles. Isaac, an anonymous shadow, hunched over the wheel. The children in the back seat did not yell or squirm around; they were silent with the cold and the time. Only the baby beside Isaac whimpered.

It was a short ride, hardly long enough for Toy to realize that her feet were bare, hardly long enough for cold to touch her ankles and wrists, slipping through the celluloid curtains of the old sedan. The church appeared in the dark, windows winking with light. It was a nameless church, like all Negro country churches, its faith folded in upon itself, different and so hidden.

Isaac said, "Y'll go 'head."

She followed Wylma into the church; children jostled her along. The front benches were filled. She found herself on a back seat next to Wylma and across the aisle from Elijah Clarke Johnson, alien in a white collar and false teeth studded with gold.

No one noticed her, or seemed to. Everyone was intent on a man standing on the platform, head back, eye closed, skin like coal tar.

"And seal us, Lawd, seal us wid de red seal of Your mercy. Set

de seal as frontlets 'tween our eyes, Lawd, so's us kin see to follow You. For de seal of de Lawd is de sweet blood of Christ. It
gwine bring us out Egypt. It gwine carry us 'crost de river. It
gwine set our foots on de far shore yonder."

Kerosene lamps strung from the rafters sent out smoky swirls.
The stove glowed and snapped. A brown man rose and dropped
in a stick of wood.

Toy's thoughts came from far away. Nigra church—never
been in one before. What am I doing? Why—

Some had been in them, whites who returned and reported
with a laugh that might or might not have hidden a half-unease,
"I mean, Nigras is a sight. You ought to aseen them. 'Sister, is
you sanctified? Nah, she ain't sanctified. Send her round again.'
They sure love big words—don't care what they mean, just so
they sounding brass and tinkling cymbals."

A yellow woman sprang up.

> "I feels de salt of de sea,
> I feels de salt of de sea,
> I feels de salt of de Red Sea,
> Oh, Lawd, on my cheek. . . ."

An old man, ash-cheeked, took it up.

> "I sees de big white cloud,
> I sees de big white cloud,
> I sees de pillar of cloud—
> Oh, Lawd, under my foots. . . ."

Hands raised, dark on the outside and impervious, pink on
the inside and vulnerable. Fingertips plucked at God. Children
huddled silent, eyes liquid and rolling. One woman nursed a
baby at a breast like a purple eggplant, tears streaming down her
rigid face.

"Oh, Lawd, you knows us lets down de nets—"

"Fished all night, caught nuthin, nuh!"

"Oh, Lawd, you knows us lets down de nets—"

"Fished all night, caught nuthin, nuh!"

"Oh, Lawd, shows us where to let de net down."

"De other side, de other side!"

The other side, the other side . . . Smoke stifled Toy, smoke and words and stench of sweat. It trickled in oily globules down the cheek of the man before her. He had a massive skull, and hands fit for swords and staves. Yet they cupped knees smeared with a thousand kinkings.

She thought, The other side—this side turned backward. Black sweat choked her, thick and musky; she closed her eyes against it and thought inarticulately, But—but black don't show the dirt, do it, like white?

Suddenly the man sprang up.

"I tries to find de other side, Lawd—can't. Drops de net to de right, catches suckers, uh! Drops de net to de left, catches can, boot, uh! Drops it to de front, drops it to de back, tear on root, uh! Ain't fished de sky, Lawd—must I fish de sky?"

A warm, heavy thing, a living thing, dropped in Toy's lap. Wylma was standing, empty-armed.

"Fish de sky!" Her arm, black and knotted, was out, rigid. "Th'ow up your hands, brethern, fish de sky!" Hands raised, quivering. Smoke reeled. "I counted de stars coming 'cross de field, twenty 'n thirty!"

"Jubilee!"

"I counted de stars coming 'cross de field, for'-nine and one!"

"Jubilee!"

"I counted de stars coming 'cross de field—ten mo' dan de years de chillun walked de wilderness!"

"Jubilee!"

"Now de fields will rest in de furrow, door will rest on de jar."

"Jubilee!"

"De dog will be chained, de slave free!"

"Year of Jubilee!"

The mourners' bench was T-shaped and shiny with tears; a sooty girl sprawled on it, mouth torn with sobs. Two sooty women bent over her, weeping. "Do, do, do."

Warmness and heaviness on her knees, against her stomach, touching her spine—Toy's eyes came back from somewhere and looked down. The Negro baby on her lap, Wylma's child, slept on, cradled in the crease of her legs. Dark and heavy it lay where another had lain so light, so light.

Her knees stiffened, her belly drew back. The movement disturbed the child. Its mouth whimpered; its nappy head burrowed for the old security.

A thin, dusky man cried, "I looked at de clock. What time it say?"

"Tell, brother!"

"I looks at de clock—thirteen o'clock!"

A groan arose. The ineluctable past pressed them, the old seebacks. Sweat and smoke and tears drew them together in a common grief; they moaned.

"Thirteen o'clock, brethern, and de clock ain't broke, nuh! We jes dwelling by a time ain't ourn. We dwelling by de white clock, and we de black hands. We dwelling by Egypt's clock, yeah!" His voice fell deeply. "Pharaoh say, 'Make brick widout straw.'"

"Can't, Lawd, can't."

"Pharaoh say, 'Same number as befo'.'"

"Can't, Lawd, can't."

"Pharaoh say, 'Nigger, why you so lazy?'"

"Cause I can't rise, Lawd, nuh."

"Pharaoh say, 'Nigger, why you so dumb?'"

"Cause I can't speak, Lawd, nuh."

A woman whirled into the middle aisle. She flung up coppery arms, face sheened with sweat and torn with anguish. Deathly silence fell.

"Oh, Lawd, deliver me out'n de Pharaoh's clock!"

Her fingertips quivered, yearning. She swayed. She took a single shuffling step forward. A moan rose.

"Lawd, Lawd—deliver her!"

She took another shuffling, swaying step, and another. She lifted one foot, then the other, in a stomp, took three more shuffling steps and stomped again.

"Lawd—Lawd—"

A man fell in behind her. His eyes were closed; his arms dangled to his knees. He moved from his pelvis, the upper part of his body rigid. He shuffled after her, two steps, three, stomp, stomp.

"Who on my side, Lawd? Who?"

The crowd moaned, "Who, Lawd, who?"

Shuffle, shuffle, shuffle, stomp-stomp. The woman and the man moved as one, yet his eyes were closed. His feet felt the boards that hers had touched. That was enough.

Two lean women fell in, their arms open, fingers reaching, singing.

> "Dey crucified my Lawd . . ."

Someone else took up the song:

> "And He never say a mumbaling word.
> Dey crucified my Lawd,
> And He never say a mumbaling word. . . ."

In twos and threes, others fell in behind the four. Voices prayed, voices sang, hands cupped to catch grace or dangled in abnegation or clenched in an agony of despair. One man grunted powerfully, "Unh, unh!" No one looked down, yet every foot caught the cadence.

Shuffle, shuffle, shuffle, stomp-stomp.

> "Not a word—not a word—not a word. . . ."

Wylma's baby whimpered, eyes closed. The baby and Toy and a few sleeping children were the only ones left sitting; everyone else was in the long dark coiling line which went up one aisle and down another, never stopping.

Shuffle, shuffle, shuffle, STOMP-STOMP.

The lamps trembled on their ten handles. The stove flickered red and black like a firefly, the stomping jarring the coals alight momentarily. The heat was almost gone, yet there was no cold. Sweat sheened every face.

They walked the old year and its sorrow out; they walked the new year and its hope in.

"Walking Egypt, leaving Egypt . . ."

The words trailed away, the sentence dangled. Now Toy, trembling and unknowing that she trembled, was aware of a new thing, the silence.

She did not know when it had started; had a finger been laid to a lip or a heart? The line of people coiled by, but there was no voice raised in prayer or tongue in song. Prayers and song were forgotten; the people danced.

Shuffle, shuffle, shuffle, stomp-stomp.

The cadence was the same. Only the commitment was different. Eyes were open or closed, and even when open, closed; for now the individual was lost, the self forgotten in the universal rhythm. Bodies found what the soul had been seeking, the bond between man and the universe.

Shuffle, shuffle, shuffle, stomp-stomp.

The rhythm moved into Toy's soles; she lifted her feet. The rhythm was adamant; it laid hold of her bench and her buttocks; it crept into the nerves that laced the marrow to her bones. It plucked the marrow with a long and twanging chord.

She sobbed gutturally.

She could not help the sob nor the second that followed, nor the third. It was a thing outside herself. Rhythm was a ham-

mer shaping her; she had been rough with rage and fluid with
self-pity: "Why me, Lord?" Rhythm was a hammer shaping her
to the dancers, to all man: "Why us, Lord?"

The baby kicked. Its knotted toes thrust off the light blanket,
weak feet bound to a borrowed earth that every fool would call
"mine."

Toy sobbed, drew the weak feet into her hands, and held them
against her breast.

Five

THE old stereoscope found its way to her bed during her
illness. Wylma put it there together with the box of pictures, a few ragged magazines, and a harmonica, things to amuse
a child.

One day Toy's hand wandered out and fixed on it. Memory
touched her briefly, a child sitting under a circle of light and
crying, "But she ain't got no arms." Pain pinched her breath
where once it had closed a vise on her. She picked up a picture
and fitted it in the holder. Two views sprang together, merging
as one, the leaning tower of Pisa, three-dimensional and ready to
tumble down. She slid in the rest of the slides, one after the other,
the Venus de Milo and Hoot Gibson kissing his horse, the Carls-
bad Caverns and Little Egypt with bead skirt and arms folded
provocatively behind her head, a buffalo cow and calf and the
Taj Mahal—photographs without relation, catch as catch can.

The stereoscope dropped to her lap; her chin dipped with realization. She had seen the pictures more times than she could tell,
and certain ones had moved her to marvel—"India, and carved
so"—and others to contempt—"Undressing for men. Trash!"
Now she saw them not three-dimensionally but rounded by the
peace that possessed her.

For—realization raised her eyes—people and places and animals had a kinship beyond the cardboard that bound them, or the hand of the man who assembled them, saying, "Got to satisfy all the customers." They had a kinship in the nameless and numberless eyes that looked at them, the same lens but picturing the world in various ways.

She thought, The same eye—

Wylma came in. She laid a chapped thumb on the buffalo cow and calf. "Seen one them new Angus bulls Mr. Tuck gots to de stockyard. Doan look no different, low and black and squatty." She sucked breath. "Whoo-ee, now you looking *live*. Swear de Lawd, doan know how I come to do like I done, quilt on you head, feets bare. Tell you, seen Sweet Jesus fixing to sew you to Hisself wid white thread."

"Well, He didn't."

Death had never occurred to her, not even when she plummeted down and down the great swirling cone of fever, down and down the narrowing rings of cone to the final point. There, for an instant, she had poised on the point, tiptoe, terror building a bubble in her breast. It burst in a shout of laughter, and she laughed joyously and floated up and up, to Wylma pressing a wet rag on her forehead.

She repeated, "Well, He didn't."

The final burden fell from her. She stretched her arms above her head, clasping her hands. She felt her ribs spring out sharply, her stomach sink to concavity. Breath gathered. She let it out in a great gust.

Wylma leaped. "Hur'cane!"

She put a shamed hand to her mouth and grinned over it. "Ain't done that since I was twelve, thirteen."

Wylma said, "Now you oughts write Mr. Wick, tell him you been sick."

Toy's arms fell. "Later, maybe."

She had things to tell Wick, but telling was not enough; she had things to show Wick, but did not know what they were yet.

Wylma added, "Too bad ain't everyone frisky as you is. Hear tell Aunt Baptist is down bad, give out and puny."

The old midwife was in Toy's mind increasingly as she mended. It was a week before she got up, the room unrelated to her at first and rocking. It was another week as she found her way from strength to strength.

One afternoon she dressed and started for Aunt Baptist's. It was a mild and sunny day. There would be frost again, perhaps even a freeze, before spring came finally. But now birds and animals sported in the unexpected warmth. Bluejays and catbirds teetered and shrilled in the young pines. A mole, coming up for its daily look at the world, had been caught by a cat who toyed gently with it. A sawmill cut boards with a high keening like the cry of a southing curlew.

Amazingly it was answered from a tree.

Toy searched and found the bird perched in an oak, brown plumage and curved bill near-invisible against bark and frost-touched leaves. The leaves clicked and rustled, and the curlew cried again and flew away in long sweeps toward the mill, an orphan parted from its fellows wintering in Venezuela, parted and looking for the moist places that were all it knew of living.

Toy said aloud, "Nothing there, ole feller."

Yet the desolation she spoke of was human, wrecked wheel and cracked stones and ruined race. The curlew saw the tiny brown snails that lived on the lily pads, the mud for reed nests, and the constant water.

She said slowly, "Reckon you'll make out," and started walking again.

Her first thought, seeing Aunt Baptist's house, was, She's gone off—or dead.

The gate hung half off its hinges, the path was edged with dead chrysanthemum stalks, and unraked leaves blew in windrows against her heels. But a plume of smoke hung around the side of the house, and there was a roll of fresh cherry bark on the porch.

When she knocked, a voice called, "Turn the knob is the way."

She stepped in. Aunt Baptist raised her head from a heap of great fleshy hellebore roots that she was sorting. She stared.

"Now you know hellebore'll kill you—or cure you, if you crazy?" she demanded. "You know it's called the Christmas rose?" She added, "It ain't much, that piece of chair behind you, but it's better'n standing."

Aunt Baptist had had three operations in two years. Her flesh hung on her in little purses. Her big behind was just an after-thought. The last of her teeth were gone; her lips fell in on her hard, horny old gums. Memory came to Toy, an afternoon when those teeth had torn flesh from a rabbit's shoulder blade, a birth-ing night distant beyond that when they had crunched coffee grounds powerfully. Aunt Baptist did little granny-wifing these days, just girls caught short, and Negroes.

Toy told her, "You belong to be in bed, not scamping around."

"No, for as long as a body can scamp, he best. Lay down, and you finished, for Death do love a back and a bed. If I took down, why, he'd come and cut my toenails."

The room held remains of the fall harvest, trays with one or two boneset flowers or turtlehead leaves, bundles of hazel bark or Adam and Eve roots. Deer's-tongue leaves hung from the rafters together with strings of pepper, onions, and thyme. Warmth drew memories from the walls; Toy searched back through them.

"Remember when I used to go yarbing with you?"

"I remember. All eyes and ears, but you never minded to use the mattock. Only young'un I knowed never dodged work."

"No, I never."

Toy could admit it, not with the old bitterness, not even with pride, but as she might admit a wart on the web of her thumb, neither work nor wart signifying.

"Remember once you told me everything was named out of the Old Testament, the Book of Wrath—Aaron's-rod, Jacob's-ladder, Job's-tears, apple of Sodom—nothing out of the New, the Book of Love?"

"I remember."

She said, "I done the same."

It came to her. Now she knew. Wrath was the easy road that got the tracks. Wrath was the lazy man's little love.

She said, "I've changed."

Aunt Baptist watched her, elbows laid on her chair arms. Her thumbs hung broad and thick. "Glad to hear it—glad you ain't jealous of Abraham."

She stared.

"He got sent a ram in a thicket, you remember. You got a dead child right on."

Pain cut her breath. She could not breathe from shock and pain. "Why—why, I never said— I'd not hate again before I'm thu. I only said I'd changed, I'm different, for I ain't a stranger in a strange land no more, nor alone." She broke off. She stared. "Why, you contrarying me. You trying to hurt me, and I thought we was friends. I thought, Aunt Baptist and Wick won't never go back on me—"

"Just Wick—" Aunt Baptist's gums bit down hard on the words like an old turtle. She was hunched forward like an old turtle. "You come here telling me how you been changed. You think I care? You come here shouting love down a dry well. You think water'll tremble the rock? What you come here for anyways? You belong to be telling a living river, telling Wick. I'm dry— I'm old—I'm thu—"

Her face broke apart. Her mean old chin worked against the tears, jutting and clamped and trembling.

Toy moved. "You—you ole Devil!"

Aunt Baptist mumbled, "Halloween punkin, candle in my mouth, can't scare no one—"

"Can scare me any ole night, any ole day. Come here," Toy said. "Come here and let me hug your neck."

Later she said, "Now I wouldn't go see Wick. No reason."

"Now I smell something. I smell you on fire and burning at both ends to go."

"You smell your upper lip."

Later, walking home, she heard the sound.

It came from beyond the crows cawing in a dry-stalked cotton field, pecking at a water jug emptied of its trickles long ago, beyond the ringing road or mumbling creek or whatever hid in a stand of maples, their red leaves hanging like monkey paws. It was beyond these, but taking its shape from each of them, as water takes its shape from the earth it covers.

> Monkey, monkey, bottle of beer,
> How many monkeys are there here?

The old counting-out song, the old eenie-meenie-minie-moe with monkeys instead of men. She was humming it. A second sound rose in her throat, laughter.

> Cinderella dressed in yella,
> Went down town with a silk umbrella,
> Met her beau, took her to the show,
> How many kisses did he give her?
> One, two, three, four—

Darting in and out of the swinging loop of a rope—memory came to her as though it were yesterday—breathless and exultant, knees together and bent, up and down, sand giving lightly under toe, sun in mouth.

> Lady bug, lady bug, turn around.
> Lady bug, lady bug, touch the ground.
> Lady bug, lady bug, show your shoe.
> Lady bug, lady bug, skid-doo!

Waiting and springing aside and out, rope slapping a heel and empty air. Someone shouting, "You stayed in too long. You was s'posed to git out on the Doo!" "Got out anyways, didn't I?" "Well, you was s'posed to git out on the Doo."

Suddenly she bent her knees and jumped, elbows akimbo. One, two, three—she slipped, numb feet betraying her, a root betraying her. Breath caught in a little frost—still couldn't make the Doo. She laughed again, a sound like the push of rope on the air, light and going.

She threw open the door of her house and called, "Wylma, I'm taking a trip."

". . . crazy!"

"I'm going to see Mr. Wick."

"Cr—" Wylma broke off. She laid a thumb on her lower lip. Her eyes narrowed like an image in cherrywood. "Den you needs you a new coat."

"You ain't asking why?"

"Ain't gots to, way you done traveled upstairs, downstairs, out de front door right to de gate."

"That ain't the reason." She groped, then laughed again breathlessly. "I'm going 'cause I want to—'cause it's time."

She bought a new coat, gray with a red velvet collar. Wylma wore the old one going with her to Cardiff to catch the bus. The colored woman was scandalized at the soldier-jammed station; her knotted head-rag quivered at the driver's cry, "Servicemen first."

"What kind manners *dat?*"

"Well, there's a war on."

Almost she had forgotten it in her private grief. Now soldiers jostled past with sharp young elbows, reminding her; and when she lifted her eyes to the gray sky outside the station, she saw a blue flag hanging from an office building, ten gold stars on it.

She discovered something else. "It's snowing."

"You never makes it, sick lak you been!"

Tuck Tate rubbed his bristles worriedly; he had driven them over in his truck. "S-s-she's right, Toy. Traveling these times is a hard-scrabble, and you ain't never been off before. What if some-

thing happens?" The world beyond his animals was cross-set with
traps.

"Won't nothing."

"If it do, W-W-Wick'll purely kill me." He took comfort in ex-
travagance. "You sent let him know you coming?"

"A card."

She had told him that she would get off the bus in Grape
Grove, a small town near Fort Knox. She would wait in the station until he came. It never occurred to her that he could not or
would not come.

The driver shouted, "Women second."

She had to stand from Cardiff to Cleveland, Tennessee. There
a soldier got off, and she sat down by another who grunted and
turned a shoulder on her, angry at her lean body and colorless
face. She would have spoken, she would have agreed, "I know
what you thinking." But perhaps anger was all he had to go on.

She leaned back and watched the spill and pelt of the snow
against the window.

She changed in Nashville and stood again. It was dusk; the
whole world was gray snow hissing against the bus, clusters of
lights bobbing out here and there. Her earlier strength and cer-
tainty were ebbing; she clung to the edge of the luggage rack
with cold fingers.

"Going far?"

She turned her face to the old man standing beside her.

"Grape Grove, Kentucky."

"Got someone there?"

"My husband."

"Ain't it always the way? Find me a pretty woman, and she's
obliged to have a husband." His hands were kidney-spotted and
work-swollen; his pants were out-of-knee.

She said, "Ain't as good-looking as you." It was Dolly's voice,
Tessie's voice—finally her voice.

"Now," he said approvingly, "I love a jolly woman."

Talk made time go past the window. Talk made a light beyond those glimmering briefly in the snow and gone; it made things clear that she had not known she knew.

Once she blurted, "Why, I been talking to you like I never talked to no one, what I told you about Mary Morning and Wick."

"It's 'cause it's dark. It's 'cause I'm a stranger."

A few miles from Grape Grove the driver pulled up and ran into a café. He returned with a greasy brown bag, but when he tried to pull out, there was a clattering whirr which mounted to a roar, an ominous snap—silence.

"Fan belt. Well, you folks might as well make yourself comfortable until they send us another bus. You can get coffee, sandwiches in the café."

The restaurant was smothering; a kerosene heater threw off waves of oil and heat, and the naked bulbs strung across the ceiling had a shiny film. The waitress had a flowered handkerchief pinned to her breast, like a monstrous flower, and she snuffled with a cold. She was listening to a woman slumped over the counter.

". . . went to a fortune-teller. Know what—what she told me? 'Knowledge is power,' she told me."

She might have been young, she might have been pretty, and she was covered with little bows. They were tied everywhere, two red ones in her yellow pompadour, two blue ones on the breast, and two red ones on the hips of her black dress. Narrow black velvet ones were knotted at her throat and wrists. Every bow was careful, while the rest of her was on the bias, dress and make-up and stare.

"Looking for a rich man—write me letters. Knowledge power." Two soldiers walked by. "Hi, shug," she called. They grinned and walked on.

The waitress said coldly, "Now, Dawn, you know what Ern said."

"I can be friendly now—can't I?" the woman begged Toy. "It don't hurt—friendly."

"No." Toy looked down at the greasy hamburger and wished she had brought a lap lunch as Wylma had wanted, fried chicken and pound cake.

The woman focused. "Bet—bet you going—Fort Knox."

"Grape Grove."

"Been there—myself. Louisville, I mean. Been everywhere—everywhere this neck of—woods. Fort Benning, towns around—Friendship, Box Springs. Story—my life. Friendship, box springs." She gazed earnestly at Toy, but her eyes kept slipping off and climbing back. "Trust people— Hi, shug." Two bus drivers, conferring as they walked past, did not hear her. She shrugged. "Where—from?"

"Georgia."

She leaned an elbow on the counter, considering. It slipped off, and she followed it, wandering vaguely away. She moved from group to group of men. She put a hand on a sailor's sleeve. She rested a hip against a pinball machine and watched two defense workers playing. She hung between a couple of soldiers, arms resting on their shoulders.

The waitress sniffed. "If 'twas me, I wouldn't let her in even. But Ern—"

Toy looked at the flowered handkerchief pinned on her chicken breast, the buttonhole of mouth which few men must have kissed with a careless love. She said, "Men is the devil all right."

The driver raised his voice from the doorway. "All right, folks, those going to Louisville and points between, board bus number three-twenty-one in the driveway."

Pinball machines gave a final whirr. Greasy bags were passed over the counter, hamburgers "to go." Girls and soldiers walked out arm in arm, careless of ice under foot and snow drifting like feathers from a teal sky. It was ten o'clock; she had been due at eight.

Quickly she buttoned the red velvet collar and drew a scarf over her head. She bent to pick up her suitcase, and the hasp came unsnapped. She tried to shut it, but it would not stay, old and worn out. She snatched it up anyway and hurried to the door, the last to leave.

She looked back.

The café was empty except for the counterman, head bent and anonymous, scraping his griddle behind the kitchen partition. It was empty except for the two women, brave bows and hopeful handkerchief, standing on either side of the room, lonely by more than the length of the room.

She threw up a sudden hand. " 'By."

The yellow-haired woman brightened. She wove forward, hand out, staying. "Wait—now, wait." She stopped and searched. She brought out triumphantly, "Where—you from?"

The final few were through the door. The first had boarded the bus, and their faces pressed against the windows, white blurs. The wind muttered; snow swirled in little sudden lifts. The café lights blinked blue and red.

"Georgia—little town name Gristle. You wouldn't know it." She turned away.

The woman said clearly, "Know it. Red come—from there."

She whirled. "Red who?"

"Who?" She screwed up her eyes. "Never—said. Lived down hall from me—Louisville. Borrowed nail polish—never said." She said brightly, "Crazy gal on a party—cried."

The driver shouted, "Lady!"

Toy hung to the door in an agony. "What she look like?" Red, she thought, Tessie—*Tessie.* "What hotel?"

"Crazy gal. Doing good and took off—off to Augusta, Army camp. Said was—was there a street name Green, she'd be on it—country gal."

The driver shouted, "Lady, I'm going—don't know about you!"

She ran then, eyes stinging, cold cracking her lips. She got on the bus. She stood by the driver, suitcase at her feet, hanging with one hand to the luggage rack, the other to his seat, body swaying and knees trembling. She rested her eyes on a wrist.

A voice called from down the aisle, "Hey, Mrs. Bloodworth—you making it?" It was the old man.

She raised her head. "I'm making it." Tessie, she thought, Tessie and her pranking bones. Tessie who had shocked the churchly sisters with their crocheted-doily souls. Tessie alive.

The old man called, "Well, you gonna see your man soon. Bet you all gonna have a lot to talk about."

Talk was not enough. She hung between her wrists and watched car lights sweep upon them down the snow-blurred highway. Words were not enough. Once they had started out like an extra club-head or coal of fire, a convenience, no more or less. Now the convenient thing was words.

Sometime later the old man called, "We coming in to Grape Grove. Whoa!"

The bus was nearly by the town before it stopped. The driver flipped on brakes; the tires hissed. The door swung open on the darkened gas pumps of a filling station. A man hurried forward.

She stumbled out onto Wick's arm.

". . . fool thing." His voice was blurred by the snow, only the snow had stopped. One arm held her, pressed along her back. His other arm had her suitcase. Neither saw nor heard the bus door clang, the bus bear away into the dark, red lights winking. "Fool thing. You didn't know I might not abeen able to meet you? You didn't know I mighta been in the field?"

She said, "You here."

Their steps merged as if they had never been apart, her long stride matching his longer. Street lights lay on the snow in puddles. A feist ran around a corner, tail pressed against a shivering flank.

"By the hardest. Had to hitch me a ride in—didn't get your card till this morning—and the whole enduring day I been on the street begging a room." His big chest moved. "Well, I got us a something."

He led the way down a side street to an old two-story house. A light burned at the top of an outside stairway. Snow-sheathed bushes brushed against them. He used a key to let them into an upper hall. It was rag-carpeted, holes here and there, and smelled of damp wood, cooking, and people.

"Here 'tis."

The door swung open on a child's nursery, ivory crib and bureau with pink lambs sporting across them, Mother Goose pictures on the wall. A fire burned in a grate, and a big brass bed stood in the middle of the room.

The fire, Wick setting down her suitcase and turning to her—they did what the bus had been unable to do for all its jolting. She gave way. She half fell on the bed and sat huddled in the gray coat with its red collar, head bent to stay the swirling, rag rug coming and going before her aching eyes.

". . . sick?" Wick was beside her.

Now she saw him plain for the first time, the face brown and puckered around the eyes with concern, fair hair grizzled at the temples. She put out a hand. "It ain't nothing. I been sick some—I laid off and laid off to write you—but I'm mountain top now." She stopped. She said, "It's what I come to tell you—I'm all right. I'm *happy*."

He sat down wordlessly. Damp wool rose in a little steam. His boots, buckled and laced to mid-leg, were black with snow.

She cried, "You been standing in the cold-wet, and I never realized. Them boots—"

"Directly. Right now I'm listening." His arm was around her; his voice held a resonance it had never held before. "Right now I'm hearing something I've waited on."

Fire danced on a picture on the wall, Georgie-Porgie-pudding-and-pie. Crib and bureau leg bore scuff marks; there was an odor of baby.

She said slowly, "I remember when I was a young'un, standing by Pa and looking up whilst he poured me tea. The glass always looked to be full before it got filled." She shook her head. "I got pity for young'uns, everything full before it gets filled, everything tall or tomorrow, one. I got a pity for young'uns." She stopped. She said fiercely, "I got a pity for myself."

She felt him move.

She repeated, "For myself. For if we don't pity ourselves, who's going to do it for us? The One yonder? Times He will. Times He'll open a window and hold us to the light. He'll hold us, and we'll hear the beating heart of the world. He done that to me. Times like that we'll turn our lips to him like a sucking child, call him Love and the Bread of Life—our Father."

Suddenly her teeth rang against each other. She clenched her jaws, but the cold reached into the muscles beyond them. They chattered uncontrollably. Wick leaned swiftly and slipped off her shoes. She had not even known them wet. He took her feet in his hands and held them and rubbed them.

"Hush now." His voice was a father's. "Hush, you cold, you tired. Time to talk tomorrow."

"No, now." She sighed as the chill melted away imperceptibly, as ice melts from the reeds in spring. "Oh, it's fine to be warm again. I been cold so long." She looked at him gently. "I can see the Lord you love, and He's your Father and my Father. Only I see more; I see our Father Who art in Heaven Who'll kill us if He can." She shook her head as Wick started to speak. "Jesus knew it. It wasn't for nothing He prayed, 'Lead us not into temptation,' for He knowed His Father. Knowed God made us weak and wanting and would test us right on, knowing we'd break—obliged to! Wouldn't forgive our breaking, neither. Got to have blood twinkling down a cross to forgive us. Got the whole world in His hand, and got to have that little drop of blood under His thumbnail."

Something crowded her throat. She put up her hands and wept. She wept from the cold and the trip, all that she had felt Walking

Egypt and before. She wept as she would never weep again, she
believed, for all she had lost and all she had found, the terrible
love of God—no finer thing than the found or the given, and always she had believed it the earned.

He held her and talked to her, his voice a murmur. She felt his
voice as she felt the stiff wool of his jacket, and by and by she
caught a word or two. She smeared wet hair from her eyes.

"'A soon start in the morning'—why—why, it just come to
me, you getting ready, you going over." She repeated the words
as though repetition might make them less strange. "You going
over."

"Not right off, but soon. I feared to tell you, all else has happened. Didn't know could you bear it. Now I know—you can."
He said slowly, "Your way of coming to God ain't mine—"

"Going over." The words struck her suddenly, the desolation
of long seas over and a shapeless land that no finger could reach,
however firmly the thumb was rooted. "I don't know—I don't
know can I bear it!"

After a while she drew away. She told him, "I'm going too.
I'm going to Augusta." Her tears were dry. She would cry again,
but not with pained surprise. "I met this woman down the road a
piece . . ."

Wick listened. He said slowly, "It's a miracle, true or not. Still
you don't know it's Tessie. Red hair comes from the bottom of a
bottle, times, you know and I know. And might be whisky saying,
'Gristle.' "

"I know. Still, I got to go and see." She repeated, "I got to go."

For it did not matter if it was Tessie yonder. It only mattered
that she moved, that she put out a hand or took a step. It only
mattered that she *got going*, past the leviathan that Widow Blankenship had warned a fatherless girl of long ago, selling the girl
two millstones for twice their worth, past the behemoth that
God had rattled under Job's nose too, Job stripped of all but life
and having to watch a two-ring circus: "See the leviathan! See
the behemoth! The two mightiest monsters in the world! Cap-

tured on the far reaches of the sunny Nile, and brought to you at enormous expense by the management!"

And that was the main thing that she held against God, His blind spot, His inability to see His own inconsistency, suffering evil Himself, yet telling man, "You're a sinner."

She cried, "You think I'm scared of Augusta? You think I'm scared?" She did not address Wick wholly. She spoke beyond him. "I heard tell—leviathan ain't nothing but a 'gator spreading a tooth for frogs!"

She began to laugh. Sitting cold and journey-tired on a brass bed in a child's room, Georgie-Porgie kissing the girls from the wall, a lost pink lamb on a crib-slat, she laughed and gasped and laughed.

"I'm going to spite Him. I'm going to do like Job done—I'm going to spite Him. I'm going to take His light of love and shine it back on Him. I'm going to walk forward in the light while He ain't looking. I'm going to jerk a knot in that old 'gator's tail!"